RED

NAPA

IS FOR

RED

BLOOD

KATE **KING** & JOE **TURNER**

NAPA RED

ISBN: 0615532837
ISBN-13: 9780615532837

*Red is for cabernet sauvignon,
merlot and all the other great red wines
of the Napa Valley.
Red is also for blood.*

ACKNOWLEDGEMENTS

We wrote this book, a novel of fiction, with lots of motivation, encouragement and outright help. So we have some thanking to do.

First we were motivated by the strong men and women who created the Napa Valley as we know it today. Sure, they are glamorous almost mythical people but we know they risked everything, all the time, start to finish. We recommend that readers come to Napa to see what we lived. Before you go, read about the wine makers, the grape growers and the people who started it all. Come to Napa to see the beauty and to learn more about wine and grape growing.

One person in the Valley, a wine sophisticator with a great reputation for saving and altering poor wines, told us to make sure we got the wine growing and making process exactly right. Why? This is a novel and writing a novel gives one license to stray from what is real and accurate.

We were encouraged by so many people including, publishers Norm and Joni Rosinski, Napa advocate Tony Kilgallin, Pam Kindig, the Castles as well as others who put up with us but mainly, this one is for...

Dave Perry
Oh, Dave we miss you so much.

THE AUTHORS' COMMENTS...

Just about everyone who reads this book will recognize the places and the times and they might even think they recognize themselves. This is a novel, a work of fiction. Some of the characters might resemble people who have lived or even some who are living. But those characters are just that, characters in a novel.

The FBI is the model investigative agency in the world. Just about every country in the free world comes to Washington and to Quantico, Virginia to learn and to study. The FBI has our sincere respect.

The California wine industry has long been a model of integrity and honesty. Wine grapes come from farmers and, as a group, farmers all over the world tend to be plain people who work hard and love the Earth. Wine growers produce the grapes from which wine is made and they produce grape juice. Winemakers, the vintners, combine science, art and a rare form of personal magic that turns grape juice into one to the world's most delightful beverages. Their real accomplishment is this: They make wine that is better and better every year. The soul of wine growing and wine making is the Napa Valley of California.

The first part of this story is known by a very few people. We are not certain if they will be pleased with our effort to fill in what we believe to be an important chapter of American history. We do not suggest any conspiracy to keep it secret. We prefer to believe that the reason for this is that when The Plan was put into effect, communications were not as thorough as they are today. And, world events, namely World War II, held the nation's attention so stories about The Plan got pushed aside. The part about Napa and its somewhat arcane activities, historical and modern, is known by a few more people but is not generally known by the people who live in the Napa Valley or the North Bay area. The final part of the story is being told for the first time. We are sure many people will not be pleased.

PROLOGUE

In the movies when people get shot in the head they turn and scowl at the shooter and then slowly fall to the ground. It does not happen that way.

Anapa Krasnodar, a brooding, hulking Russian, was in the act of killing Jonathan Beale, a blustering fellow who happened to be one of the worlds's leading wine critics when he saw movement to his right. A howling, barking eight pound white dog was headed straight for him. The Russian was almost on top of Beale, a smallish, professor type. His right fist was raised and had just started for Beale's throat when that dog barking distracted him. His fist held one of the world's most deadly knives, a claw-like Spyderco that was specifically designed to produce tearing, ripping bloody wounds. He would deal with Beale and then with that infernal dog.

My wife, Kathleen Royal and I, were just outside Beale's office and about ten feet from Krasnodar. I was on one knee and was bringing my Glock to bear on Krasnodar. I knew

I had no chance in the world of shooting the huge Russian before Beale's throat would be cut wide open. But I would try.

A half step behind me, Kathleen did not hesitate. She had drawn her pistol on the way up the stairs. She fired two closely spaced shots from her Glock .40 caliber, a double-tap, in military parlance. A double-tap is a learned technique that requires the shooter to fire one shot and release the trigger just enough to reset the gun's trigger mechanism then pull the trigger a second time. Skilled shooters can shoot two shots almost simultaneously. Kathleen Royal was a skilled shooter.

The first shot entered the Russian just below his arm pit and destroyed his lungs and heart. One half second later the second shot impacted a little higher mostly because of the recoil from the first shot. The second shot ruined Krasnodar's lower face and, because the Russian had turned his head slightly to the right when he saw the movement, the bullet exited through the upper part of the back of his head. The window in Beale's office was painted with Krasnodar's blood and brain tissue. The window looked curiously like a store window just after a holiday painter had begun to create a scene.

The Russian dropped like a tree when a lumberjack yells, "Timber!" There was no scowl, no understanding and no attempt to break his fall. He was dead on the way down and dead on the floor. Solid dead.

Kathleen maintained her grip on her Glock and in the classic 'clear the room' posture moved into the room where the Russian lay and made sure there were no more threats. I did the same for the other rooms and spaces. I wondered how in hell we knew how to do this kind of thing. The building was an old residence that had been converted to a business office. The rooms were somewhat chopped up so I took some time to clear the upper floor. I took a position at the top of the stairs to prevent anyone from coming up to the second floor.

Kathleen turned her attention to Jonathan Beale. The blustering and posturing had given way to sobbing and trembling. She saw that he was not hurt. He had slumped into his chair and he held his head in his hands. She comforted him then stood and took one more look around the room. She placed her pistol in her belt so it would be hidden by her jacket.

She took a step back and leaned against the door threshold and put her hand to her head and with knife edged anger that anyone could see thought, "This can't be me. I didn't just kill a man, my second in a week. I did not agree to do this. I did not agree to become a killer but here I am with dead men piling up around me. I thought Clark and I were simply supposed to look around and make contacts within the community. I thought it was like playing cops and robbers. How in the hell did I end up like this?"

Crouton bounded over to her. Head held high, tail wagging. Kathleen bent and picked up her dog.

"I can't believe it. For the first time in my life I am glad my mother and dad are gone. I don't want to them to know what I have become."

She went to an empty office and slumped in a desk chair. She looked and saw that her slacks and her jacket were spotted with a dead man's blood. She took her hand from her head and saw blood on the back of her hand. A long ago story that her original FBI contact had told her flooded her thoughts...

THE PLAN

CHAPTER ONE

The horses were rounding the last quarter mile of the oval track, hooves pounding and dirt flying up as the beautiful horses dug down for the last ounce of energy in an effort to win the race. The cigar smoking man paid little attention to the fight to the line. Instead, he was imagining a whole new way to achieve his goal. His thoughts turned inward as he played over in his mind how his organization, the most trusted in the nation, was changing.

The man was short and husky. His perfectly tailored suit hid the extra pounds that came from living well. His hair was shiny and slicked back in the style of the day. In this box seat at the Del Mar Thoroughbred Track or in any room in the world, the man had taken charge. He had an aura of power that few men or women ever achieved. He was J. Edgar Hoover, America's top cop.

In the beginning, the organization that would soon be known as the FBI focused on crimes such as bank robbery and crimes that had their root in federal law and federal property.

These were primarily crimes that took place in the cities. Big cities meant big crimes; crimes that were much easier to solve in some ways. In those days crooks did their thing then went home. They were much easier to find. Sometimes the cops got to the crooks' homes before the crooks arrived.

Information was easy to get. The man had plenty of agents to keep him informed in the populated areas. But he knew that that the FBI's effectiveness was limited by the shear size of the United States. Criminal activities didn't just happen in the city, they also happened out in the vast open country sides of this nation. Those were much harder to solve for the FBI. A lack of information, in addition to poor communications made rural crimes nearly impossible to detect, much less solve. He knew that sending any of his existing agents into the rural areas of the nation was a waste of time. His agents would stand out like buffalos in a ballet. Add to the problem of getting information and poor communications was the difficulty in getting around the huge nation. Travel was difficult and even impossible in wet or cold weather. Storms and blizzards shut everything down.

The man's thoughts would come back to him over and over in the next 40 years. The fact was, much to his and his successors' chagrin, the FBI seemed to defy conventional descriptions. In the years to come the FBI's missions would morph from bank robbery, to spies in World War II to white collar criminals to immigration to post-9/11 terrorism. Countless lesser assignments would intrude almost constantly into the FBI's ability to be effective. He tried to play up the FBI's victories as they occurred. He endured the long stretches when nothing was happening that had any possibility of making his organization look good.

The man was all too aware of this problem and discussed it often. The country was still coming out of the depression and could not afford a true national police force. Some people in Washington doubted that the American people would take to national cops. But the man was, if anything, practical. He knew he had a problem and he continued to look for a solution. Could it be that he might have found the solution here - in a private box at the Del Mar Racetrack?

Hoover turned his attentions back to his companion, a tall, lanky rancher from Montana by the name of Daniel Magnus. Magnus was a raw-boned man in western clothing. He seemed to have a perpetual sun burn. His clear blue eyes took in everything in his immediate area. Magnus sat beside the man at the rail of the private box. Magnus never simply took a seat. He seemed to coil down into the chair. He leaned his long arms, stylishly contained in a fringed leather coat, on the rail and eyed the horses as they headed for the stating gate.

He said, "Yep, in our county we must lose 3,000 head of cattle a year," he said. "The local fellas try to track down the thieving bastards, but the place is too big and there are too many places to hide. They must head 'em down to Denver, maybe by way of a few other ranches in neighboring states that they steal from along the way," he added. He took a long drink from a frosted bottle of beer and shook his head in a defeated manner.

Hoover was stunned at the possible magnitude of a crime that he had never even heard of. Control, his control, motivated him. He felt that any crime that seemed to be organized was intolerable. He reached over to give Magnus a pat on the shoulder and said, "Enjoy the races. I have to attend to something." Hoover left the box.

After his meeting with Magnus, the man began to see a link between his desire to grow the FBI and what he saw as an epidemic of loosely organized rural crime. Fifteen minutes earlier he had never heard of cattle rustling. Now he was thinking of it as organized crime. He knew that anytime he could put the word "organized" in front of "crime", he had the attention of the US Congress and everyone else that mattered.

The man had heard enough. He cut his Del Mar visit short and returned to Washington by train that night. He enlisted the California Highway Patrol to escort him at high speed, lights and sirens going, to Los Angeles where he could just meet an eastbound train.

During the train ride he worked on ways to exploit this newly discovered "epidemic" of organized crime in the Western states. He made a note to ask his field agents for other "hidden crimes" that might be organized.

Back in Washington, Hoover made telephone calls to key political figures. The message was clear: He needed funding to prevent the "wholesale abuse of America's farmers and ranchers." The farmers were included because there were more farmers in those days than ranchers and it is likely that Hoover really did not know the difference.

He characterized his trip west as a "fact finding expedition" to look into rural organized crime. He presented himself as a jeans clad crime fighter complete with a western holster and gun and a cowboy hat and boots. The press bought every detail and expanded every bit of Hoover's fabrication. Actually, he had ordered the train to be stopped and held for thirty minutes so the agents could deliver his order of western apparel to the train. He had telegraphed the orders ahead from Denver.

From that day on, J. Edgar Hoover referred to his poorly defined new idea as The Plan.

Soon after he returned to Washington, Hoover finally got the support from Congress to change the name of his organization from the Bureau of Investigation to the Federal Bureau of Investigation. In a move that had been in the works for several months, Hoover wanted to strengthen his organization and knew that even symbolism and innuendo could work on his behalf. For example Hoover chaffed at the Constitutional restriction which limited the federal government from acting as police. He knew that was the responsibility of the states but he vowed to knock it aside and form an effective, not to mention intimidating, federal police force. He could not have known it at the time but in the decades to come federal police actions would be common and would in many ways compete with state and local policing efforts. The average American was poorly educated on states rights and federal rights. Confused people are easy to fool. Hoover was a master of confusing people, especially people in Congress.

CHAPTER TWO

In the early 1930's Washington was a more compact and closely knit community than in later years. The day when a television network could get wind of a story and have the story on television an hour later had not yet arrived. Newspaper coverage of Washington and the Capital certainly did exist but by nature it generally leaned toward the big picture stories. Plus, the media were easily manipulated. During World War II Franklin Roosevelt and Henry Luce of Time and Life, did not hesitate to tell the American people what Roosevelt and Luce wanted them to know.

Hoover's comings and goings usually did not rise to the level of national news. Of course, if Hoover's agents found some bank robbers and shot them in a pitched battle, real or staged, the papers did respond. But day by day, like most Washington bureaucrats, Hoover was isolated from the press so most people had no idea what he was up to aside from shooting crooks somewhere out in the middle of the country.

The bureaucrats and elected people in Washington were dimly aware of Hoover and his FBI. They liked the idea that a federal operation could fight crime and usually win. Some worried about Hoover's expansion and his obsession with power. Observers saw that Hoover moved his men around so his "stars" were always on hand to make arrests.

When a person can combine reasonable effectiveness on the job with a mastery of the media, that person can accomplish almost anything. Across the Atlantic a person with precisely those talents was about to plunge the entire world into the most destructive war the world had ever known.

In October of 1932 Hoover called a meeting of his most trusted aides and agents. In addition of Hoover and Graham, three men attended the meeting, including Jack Graham, Hoover's right hand man and confidant, Charles Ross, Robert Greenlease and Roger Touhy, agents who were in charge of the FBI in New York, Chicago and Philadelphia respectively.

Jack Graham was a tall patrician man with a graceful and courteous manner. His moves were fluid and easy, almost relaxed. He dressed in impeccable suits that surely were tailored for him and must have cost more than most family lived on in those days. It was clear that Jack Graham must have had family money. No one could dress like that on an FBI salary. He had white, perfectly trimmed hair and seemed to have a light tan in spite of the time of year. Jack Graham and Hoover were inseparable. They maintained separate homes but FBI drivers spoke quietly about picking up Graham and Hoover together at Hoover's home most of the time. They traveled together, went to events together and did just about everything together. Graham had little experience in law enforcement. He had a lot of experience with his pal, J. Edgar Hoover.

Rumors that Hoover and Graham were lovers were just that, rumors. No one ever produced real proof, the kind of proof that works with judges and jurors, of such a relationship. Those on the real inside of the FBI tended to think Hoover and Graham liked to play cards way into the night. And, after all, they had to be together to play cards. The world will never know the truth.

Roger Touhy must have been the prototype for the tough, red-faced Chicago tough guy. He acted tough and he was tough. Five feet four and 210 pounds, Touhy sported a shock of bright red hair and a sunburned complexion. His nose was marked with the veins of a heavy drinker. His suits either hung on him or seemed ready to burst depending on where he was in his annual 40 pound weight gain and loss cycle. Every other agent, if asked who he wanted at his back in a fight, named Touhy without hesitation. Touhy had been in plenty of fights, with his fists and with his guns. He was always the one who walked away. Western legends claim so many kills for this bad guy or that good guy. Billy the Kid was supposed to have filed twenty-one notches into the grip of his revolver. If Touhy had been into filing notches, there would have been little left of the grip on his old fashioned Colt revolver. FBI agents were required to use Bureau issued weapons. Touhy's colt was anything but. Still, his record spoke for itself and no one ever challenged his preference for the ancient Colt.

Robert Greenlease was an example of the Midwest's country boy gone to college and on to the big city. He was five feet eight inches tall and somewhat rangy. His suits were 3-piece dark wool that gave him the look of authority. He had an athlete's hesitant yet fluid movement. His big hands belied any doubt that one might have about his ability to take care of himself. Like the other three agents who would eventually set The Plan into motion, Greenlease was 100% dedicated to J. Edgar Hoover and the FBI.

Charles Ross, Charlie to those who were close to him, was the tallest of the men in the room. He was almost six feet four inches tall, athletic and fluid at 195 pounds. His suits were inexpensive but fit him perfectly. Pre-mature baldness was wiping away blond hair that set off his dark complexion. Ross had played basketball for North Texas State Teachers College where he earned All American honors. He was among the tallest basketball players in the nation the year North Texas won the national championship. Ross' father had been severely wounded in World War I. When he returned home he told his son to go to college and become a lawyer. "They don't send lawyers to battle," he said, "Lawyers are too important to fight and they don't get shot up." Ross's father spent his last dollar making sure Charles finished his schooling. The man died two days after Charles came home with his diploma from The University of Texas School of Law.

Charlie Ross became a lawyer for the Texas Department of Public Safety in Austin. Among other roles, the Texas Department of Public Safety controlled the Texas Highway Patrol and the Texas Rangers. The Rangers were one of the best law enforcement agencies in the nation. Its success has rested on its strong policies of delegating power and decision making to the diverse areas of the vast State of Texas. A tactic that works in El Paso might be totally wrong in Texarkana. The Rangers understood this and worked hard to dial in exactly the right tactics in every part of the state. After five Ross years he moved on to the FBI.

Ross would say in later years that the FBI seemed to be where the action was in those days. His son wrote in Ross' biography, "Dad told me that he felt like Texans were interested in ranching and oil. All the cases dealt with those two. But Hoover's organization and its attending excitement and energy were attractive to him."

Ross' biography also included the man's thoughts on the Hoover organization as compared to the Texas Department of Public Safety. He was particularly concerned that the FBI might never reach its potential with its control centered in one man's smothering, intrusive, central control.

Hoover ran any meeting where he was present. He took a place at the head of the table with Jack Graham on his left. No one sat in the chair on Hoover's right. A small, compact man, Hoover sometimes had a four inch platform installed at the head of his conference room tables. This elevated him above the others and enhanced his already commanding presence.

Hoover is sometimes compared to General Curtis E. LeMay, the legendary Air Force general of World War II in the Pacific and the creator of the Strategic Air Command. Both men were short in stature and huge in presence. Both smoked and chewed on cigars almost constantly. They had very similar management styles and very similar cigar habits. LeMay got his Strategic Air Command because he preached the ever present possibility that the USSR might suddenly launch nuclear strikes at the United States. Hoover preached that wholesale, out of control crime was an ever present possibility and a clear danger to the American Way.

Hoover laid it on the line. He wanted broader powers for the FBI but knew that meant more agents and better sources of information. He told his men that he wanted to know about crime before it happened. Then he held the nation's attention with stories of rampant, wholesale crime throughout rural American and in America's small towns and countryside.

Hoover talked about cattle rustling as if he was a ranch hand at heart. His inner staff knew he had never been near a working ranch. He ordered his staff to come up with a list of "ranch terms" that he could drop into conversations and use at press conferences and to Congressmen.

He told of schemes which were bankrupting the ordinary folks out in the heartland of America. Then he said he wanted that crime, that crime against truly innocent people, stopped right now. He emphasized that only the FBI could stop all that crime. The implication was that gangland crime was mostly crime by and against gangsters. But what was happening "out there in America" was intolerable.

He looked around the room and, in his style of challenge and veiled threat, said, "You are top guys. Tell me what you think and how to get this job done."

After a moment's silence, Greenlease leaned forward, took a deep breath and offered, "We need more offices, more agents, more equipment and more money, sir. Find a way to give us those things and we can get it done."

Hoover glared at Greenlease and continued to look around the room. Touhy looked at his shoes. Hoover's neck veins bulged. Graham leaned back so Hoover could not see his face and gave a questioning look to each of the three men in the room.

Finally, Charles Ross began cautiously to suggest something different. "Director, I've been thinking maybe there is a way to have what Bob Greenlease is talking about and not break the bank. What about this idea?"

He proceeded to lay out his idea for a "two-tiered" FBI in which citizens in small towns across the country would serve as the unarmed, unpaid and totally unknown "eyes and ears" of the FBI. Ross was aware that caution was a good idea anytime he or anyone spoke with Hoover. Hoover's violent reactions had made more than a few men think twice before offering a suggestion. Some of the men at the table visibly cringed when Ross began to talk. They were afraid that Hoover would see Ross' idea as a dilution of the FBI's solid, monolithic structure.

Hoover glared at Ross then turned to Jack Graham for a private head of the table conference. The others could see Hoover's demeanor softened a bit while Graham quietly talked. Finally, Hoover pushed back his chair and stood.

He said, "Gentleman, I have a meeting down the hall. Mr. Graham will sit in for me." A collective sigh was suppressed at the table. This was pure J. Edgar Hoover. Anytime a major change was to be made he let an aide take charge. That way, he reasoned, if the charge failed he could say his staff did it and publicly hand out the discipline. Everyone in the room knew what was happening.

When Hoover left the room, Jack Graham fixed his eyes on Charles Ross. After a minute, he said, "Charlie, tell us more of what you have in mind." Graham touched an ash tray to signal that it was OK to smoke.

Ross had never been a part of core decision making at this level. His background was in law in Texas. All agents in those days were lawyers, a curious rule that was rescinded only after Hoover's death, many years later.

He began slowly at first, "OK, I know it sounds crazy, but let's face it guys, we don't even begin to have the money to field enough agents to do what the Director wants the FBI to do. But make no mistake about it. We have to accomplish this. It is why we exist. We protect the United States of America."

For years anytime someone wanted to get support for whatever he had in mind, using the full name, United States of America, generally got everyone lined up on his side. Charlie knew this and used it like a knife cutting into the awareness and thoughts of the others at the table.

"I know this needs some more thought, but here it is. My notion is to recruit, very privately, small town lawyers and maybe others who will agree to volunteer to keep an eye on things for us. They won't technically be agents and they won't have titles or anything else associated with the FBI. In fact, if they decide to tell who they are, we might deny it if it suits us at the time. We can say they are confused.

"Call them America's domestic spies if you will. The moment they see something cockeyed, something just not right, they contact the nearest FBI office and then go back to whatever it was they were doing. They wouldn't participate in the FBI missions or raids, of course. They won't be armed and they wouldn't have any investigative, police or arrest authority. I suppose we could deny we even know them, if it comes to that. We can say they are well-intended folks who like to hang around with law enforcement. Best of all, we don't have to pay them, we just appeal to their patriotic side – tell 'em it's their role in protecting their country."

Ross sat back and tried to appear unconcerned. In fact, he knew that either his idea would be accepted or he would find himself looking for a new way to pay the bills. Graham studied the faces of the others at the table and after several minutes said, "Any idea how we would do the recruiting? How many do you suppose we might need?"

Robert Greenlease spoke up before Ross could answer, "I suggest we start with small towns and areas where something big might happen. Places like oilfields, harbors and other key locations. We need to identify the kind of places where crime might pay if we are not on the job. We can test out Charlie's idea, starting small to see if it's workable." he finished.

Roger Touhy jumped in, "Well, we could assign them to local offices in Dallas and Houston for the oilfield areas. The Chicago office might get people to watch the mid-west farms and food production." Graham took control of the meeting and said with force, "OK. That sounds good. Charlie, you and Roger and Bob work out the details and get back to me in, say, six hours. Let's meet at seven this evening." He rose and left the room.

The three agents waited while the others followed Graham out the door. Touhy said, "Charlie, you might have set off the most spectacular career bomb in history. Who knows? But this also might be the best idea to come down the pike in years. What the hell, let's give it a try." He put out his hand and said, "Top or bottom, wherever you end up I'll be there with you."

The three left the room headed for a smaller conference room filled with plenty of coffee and three large blackboards. They had less than six hours to reorganize the information resources of the FBI. No one in the organization had ever held such staggering responsibility. No one, that is, except J. Edgar Hoover.

CHAPTER THREE

Early the next morning Special Agent Ross, Greenlease and Touhy boarded special airplanes for special destinations: Denver, Dallas and Chicago. Each would be greeted by local FBI agents who knew nothing of their assignments but would do as they were told without question.

Air travel was emerging in 1932 but had not yet reached the maturity level where one could depend on schedules, especially on long distance trips. The highly reliable airplanes such as the DC-3 that made air travel dependable were still on the drawing boards.

Charles Ross' FBI Lockheed Vega 5 made the trip to Dallas in nine hours with one stop in Memphis for fuel. Vegas that were used by the FBI had extended range made possible by the addition two fuel tanks. The weight of the extra fuel limited the capacity of the airplane but enabled it to fly longer distances. Thunder storms between Memphis and Dallas prompted the crew to make the stop in Memphis. They were on the ground for about two hours.

The pilot invited Ross to stretch his legs while the ground crew topped off the fuel tanks. "I'm Tom Clevenger," said the pilot, extending his hand to Ross.

"Charlie Ross. Pleasure to meet you. How much longer do we have?"

"Well, assuming we don't have to go 'round any more of these damn storms, an hour and a half, maybe two, maybe more."

Clevenger was about 50 years old. He was spare and compact, about 5 feet 8 inches tall. His leather jacket had seen the back of plenty of airplane pilot seats. Like many pilots he had inquisitive eyes that surveyed the area and the sky from time to time. Ross noticed that Clevenger was mostly deaf in his left ear. He remembered reading that pilots lose their hearing in that ear because of the engine noise just a few feet away.

Ross bent down, picked up a small twig, and threw it towards the fence that surrounded the small airfield. He was searching for a way to pry a conversation out of the pilot. Ross said, "How did you get into flying? I always thought about it myself."

"I trained during the war but never got sent overseas. When the war ended I went to work flying. Mostly mail. Five years ago I was flying for the government when I got transferred over to the FBI. I like it."

"So you go all over, right?"

"You bet. When I drop you off, I'll head on over to Houston, and then back to D.C. I get to see a lot of this great country, I surely do."

"Sounds good to me, a good way to make a living."

Clevenger glanced at the Vega and said, "Keeps me outta trouble, I guess."

He scanned the sky briefly. "Looks like we're 'bout ready to get going. This part might be a little rough so if ya need to use the john, ya might want to do it before we take off. And once you get in your seat, be sure to keep your harness on," he finished.

Ross made a quick stop in the terminal and returned to the Vega. By the time he entered the cabin, the engines were running. The airplane began to roll the second the door was closed by the ground crew.

The Vega was as comfortable as flying could be in those days. It was not pressurized so lower cruising altitudes were mandated. This made the ride bumpy. Sometimes even reading was impossible. But the Vega was reliable, enough so that it was the airplane of choice for adventurers including Amelia Earhart and Wiley Post. Post's airplane, the Winnie Mae, was a Vega.

During the flight Ross had time to work out his plan for Dallas and his assigned area. Jack Graham had told him to work the area from Athens, Texas to Palestine in the west and over to Tyler and Kilgore in the east. Graham thought that area was a good starting point because Kilgore and Palestine formed an axis that ran through the huge oilfield that was being developed in East Texas. Athens was a practical limit in the west because it was an important agriculture hub and the county seat of Henderson County. A small lake club provided rural relaxation for some of Dallas' wealthiest families. Hoover knew about the club, Koon Kreek Klub, and sometimes wondered why wealthy people would go all way to Athens for fun. Sometimes he thought there just must be something about Koon Kreek Klub that he needed to know.

The Vega touched down in Dallas late in the day. As he stepped down out of the Vega, he was met by a young FBI agent named Arthur Bryant. Ross walked toward Bryant and heard Tom Clevenger yell, "Y'all be careful in whatever you are up to." He grinned and revved the engines to begin the short hop down to Houston.

Bryant was a string bean who looked very much like Charles Lindbergh. He wore a two-piece black suit that tapered down to brown wing tips, the kind with little holes in the leather of the toe. His tie was scrunched up to his collar and hung to the right like it was trying to make a getaway. Bryant's brownish red hair was just that, hair. It pointed in every direction. Ross thought Bryant would be perfect if he had a hay straw in his mouth. He stuck out his hand and greeted Ross as if he was a relative, a beloved relative.

Ross didn't waste time. "I want to drive as far as we can towards Athens tonight," said Ross.

"You ever been in these parts, Mr. Ross?" asked Bryant with a slight smile. "Not a lot of choices for rooms and comforts," he added.

"This car will be comfort enough, if it comes to that," retorted Ross. He was anxious to get underway and wasn't in the mood for complications or for resistance.

Experts say that one makes about seven to ten impressions on a person who is met for the first time. Charlie Ross had basically told Arthur Bryant that Ross was a no nonsense hard-assed kind of guy.

Bryant got the message and started the car. "It's going to be a long way to Athens," he thought.

Time and miles passed. Dallas and its mid-rise buildings quickly gave was to a two-lane highway. They drove past rich black soil farms and ranches. In the light of a full moon, cattle grazed right up to the road. Ross enjoyed seeing the white face cattle, the Brahma bulls and an occasional white tail deer.

Ross could see that his earlier comments had made Bryant tense and he regretted his curtness. Since they had to work together, that would not do, Ross thought. He tried to start fresh. "I understand you're from Texas." He said, "Me, too. What was it like growing up around here?"

"As you well know, Texas is special to Texans, Mr. Ross. I think those of us who were born here feel more pride about where we're from than non-Texans do. I guess we think Texas is special and that makes us special, too." He glanced over to his passenger to see if he'd hit another sour note with him.

"Really? I had not thought about that," said Ross with a smile. "Can't anyone become a Texan by moving to Texas?" This was a little gambit that Ross used to see if Bryant had a sense of humor.

Bryant thought for a couple of seconds and replied, "No sir. Moving to Texas does not make a person a Texan any more than moving to Japan makes a person Japanese. You have to be born here."

Ross saw Bryant beginning to relax and show what he was made of. He laughed, "Good point, kid. Now get us to a hotel somewhere out here in our 'Special Texas'."

Bryant pulled into Athens just after ten o'clock in the evening. The first business that he saw was a brick and clay products plant on the western edge of the small city. He pulled the car into the dusty lot and killed the engine. The night was suddenly quiet after the steady drone of the car's engine. Getting out of the car he stretched, did a little foot shaking to get the circulation back in his legs and ambled into the night shift office. Once inside, he displayed his FBI credentials and asked the plump, middle-aged man behind the desk if he could make a telephone call. The night manager seemed all too willing to point to the telephone and left Bryant alone in the office. On the way out of the office he got his coat and hat from the rack in the office. He stepped outside and immediately lit a cigarette.

Athens was the County seat of Henderson County, Texas. The small city was built around a courthouse square that was ringed with small shops, a couple of movie theaters and a coffee shop. The people in Henderson County were involved in cattle, farming and manufacturing. The brick plant dominated the western edge of Athens. A furniture plant was on the eastern edge. Every year people came to the courthouse square from miles around to enjoy the Old Fiddler's Contest, a day long celebration of music and food.

Bryant learned that a rooming house in Athens had two rooms for the night. Going back to the car, Bryant shared the good news with Ross and they headed for the Bookout Hotel. The Bookout was a square frame, two-story structure with eight rooms and a dormitory-like room where several men slept and snored the night away. The place was two blocks off the city square, the location of the Henderson County offices and the County Courthouse.

At five the next morning, Ross knocked loudly on Bryant's door and told him they were leaving in five minutes. Bryant, looking sleepy and confused, stumbled to the car and asked, "Where to, boss?"

Ross replied, "Kilgore and cut the 'boss' crap. You and I are going to work together for a long time so let's just treat each other like the partners we are. I checked the map. Go two blocks north and take a right on the north side of the square on Highway 31. Kilgore will be at the other end. Let's get going – but keep an eye out for a café so we can get some coffee."

The first town on the way to Kilgore was Murchison. In 1932 it was a busy little place with a school, nearby rail tracks and, Bryant was pleased to see a rooming house with a 'Café' sign above the door. A couple of cars and a mule drawn wagon were waiting in front of the building. The two men went inside. Ross's stern demeanor seemed to melt away. He took a seat at a four stool counter and motioned for Bryant join him. A pleasant enough looking middle-aged waitress immediately turned over the coffee cups that sat in front of them and filled their cups. The tired looking woman raised her eyebrows to ask if they wanted breakfast.

Ross said, "Bring us fried eggs over easy, sausage and toast. I like strawberry preserves if you have them."

The waitress, eying their business suits said, "Eggs, sausage and toast we got. This ain't the city. You'll have to settle for homemade muscadine jelly."

Neither Bryant nor Ross had any idea what a muscadine might be, but they nodded in meek acceptance.

Ross took a sip of coffee, sighed like his life was improving and turned to Bryant, "So, Arthur, tell me more about you. How long have you been with us and how did you get this god awful assignment?" Answering his own question he said, "I bet it was because you know every bad stretch of road and cheap hotel in the state."

Bryant replied, "It'll be a year in February, sir." Noticing the slight smile on Ross' face, he continued, "I guess I got this assignment because I am the newest and youngest agent in the office."

Ross, nodding, said, "I thought so. Let me give you some advice, son. Next time you get a crappy assignment, find something and break it. In this case, you might have driven the car into the building." Bryant looked at him with wide eyes, mouth forming a surprised O.

"Legend has it that one his first day in the FBI Melvin Purvis was ordered by Mr. Hoover to make coffee," Ross continued, clearly enjoying himself. "Purvis managed to set a newspaper on fire, caught the curtains on fire, too, and dropped the coffeepot while trying to put them out. The room was such a disaster that they had to renovate it by the time Purvis got done. Purvis never got another crappy job." Melvin Purvis was a legendary FBI crime buster.

Their breakfast food arrived and both men dug in. The muscadine jelly was terrific. It had a sweet/tart taste and a translucence that had to be one of God's little blessings. The eggs were fresh and the yolks stood up proud and firm. The toast was made from fresh homemade bread. It was a perfect country breakfast.

Bryant leaned over to Ross and asked in a low voice, "Sir, can you tell me what we are doing?"

Bryant's good mood turned very negative. He glared at Bryant and said nothing. He took another sip of coffee, stood up, fished a couple of bills from his pockets, threw them on the counter and said, "Let's go."

In the car, Charles Ross gave Arthur Bryant the lecture of his young life. "Don't ever let the public know who we are.

When you're in public keep a smile on your face and do not ever talk about what we might be doing. If they make us as FBI we want them to know we're in charge and do not doubt or question what we are doing. In fact, it is none of their business what we are doing. If it were not for us and 'what we're doing' the whole lot of them would be in constant trouble. There are open eyes and ears everywhere. Unless you want a new job, say, cleaning restrooms, keep your trap shut in public."

Bryant was confused. Why was it OK for Ross to talk about the assignment, but he had to shut up?

They drove in silence for more than thirty minutes. They drove through Brownsboro, a slightly different version of Murchison, through Chandler, a farming community with sweet potato fields and pecan trees. They drove through Tyler, the biggest small city in East Texas. Tyler was proud of being the "Rose Capital of Texas."

Finally, Ross said, "So you want to know what we're up to."

Bryant, still scared nearly to death, replied, "Oh, no, Sir. You do not have to tell me anything."

Ross, teased a little and said, "Which is it? Back at the café you wanted to know and now you don't."

Bryant squirmed in his seat, hesitated and said, "Well, Sir, I do wonder about it and maybe I could help more if knew. That's all. I am sorry about what happened, Sir."

Ross quickly said, "Son, never explain and never complain. Take what happens to you, learn something from it and get along with whatever it is you are doing. If there ever comes a day when you can't stand it, walk away."

Ross assumed a crime fighter no nonsense attitude and started to explain their assignment, "Crime is growing all over the country. We can help control the big stuff in the big cities but we are stretched too thin to get anything done out in places like Athens and Kilgore. Most small towns don't have much crime but some seem to attract it. The places where crime happens are places like Kilgore. Maybe it's all the oilfield workers and the easy money.

"For example, I noticed a lady of the evening was doing a business down the hall from us last night. Now the FBI does not police prostitution but I plan to call the local sheriff when I get some time.

"We need a way to take the pulse of Kilgore and other smaller towns, to tell where we need to have a presence and where we can stop crime before it gets started. If we can get wind of something that is about to happen, we can turn it over to the local police or to state outfits like the Texas Rangers. Like that prostitute last night. Or we can show up ourselves. We are looking for options and for sources of information."

Ross turned in his seat and said, "Son, you and I need to find someone in Kilgore who can be our eyes and ears."

He paused for a long minute and continued, "We have a week or so to get this done. After we learn how to do it, we can teach others how it's done and spread this idea all over the nation."

Bryant was brimming with questions, "Do these people become FBI agents? Are they paid? How do they stay in touch with us? How do we know we can trust them? People in small towns tend to more loyal to their town than to the federal government."

Ross relaxed in his seat and replied, "One question at a time, kid. No, these people will not be FBI agents and they will not be paid. Their pay is the privilege of taking part in the greatest crime prevention outfit in the world and in having roles, maybe, in the defense of honest people and the United States of America.

"They can call a number in the Dallas office or even send a letter if there's no urgency. All the calls will be collect. Trust is what it is. If we never hear from one of these folks it will be because they have nothing to say or, and I hope this isn't the case, they are part of the problem. Maybe we'll check on these folks every once in a while. And, we can never make these people think they're rats who are telling on their neighbors. They must think they are patriots maybe even like Paul Revere or one of those guys. Make sense?"

"I think I know now why this assignment is right for me," Bryant said with a grin, "And, I know that this will work, in Kilgore, at least. You see, my uncle is exactly the kind of person you have in mind. He's patriotic, smart and well placed in town. He knows what's happening everywhere. His name's Mark Larkin. He practices law with his mother, Esther Larkin. Uncle Mark is close to 50 so he knows his way around. He steered me toward law school and wrote my letter of recommendation to the Dean. He'd do this in a second and he sure doesn't need the money."

Charles Ross felt a huge weight lift off him. The idea of accomplishing his goal and returning to Washington in only a couple of days would please Hoover very much. As he was basking in the thoughts of being in Hoover's favor, they entered Kilgore.

CHAPTER FOUR

In 1932 Kilgore, Texas was the essential boom town. Oil had been discovered and the discovery coincided with America's growing need for oil products, especially gasoline. Dirt farmers became millionaires overnight. Life in the small town would never be the same after December 28, 1930, when the Lou Della Crim #1 oil well sprayed the area with a gusher that would later be measured at 20,000 barrels of crude oil per day. The call letters of the local radio station was KOCA – Kilgore Oil Capital of America.

Kilgore grew from 800 people, mostly farmers, to 15,000 in a few months. The place teemed with oilfield workers, "roughnecks", shysters, conmen and worse. Ninety-foot tall oil derricks gave the small town a skyline that was the envy of the nation. The neighborhoods sported huge mansions and even one that was personally designed by Frank Lloyd Wright. Kilgore's leaders realized that the oil discovery could make their dreams come true. In one of the most progressive decisions that had been made in any small town, they decided to create a junior college. That decision would have a profound impact on the future of Kilgore and, indeed, the future of much of Texas.

But in the fall of 1932, Kilgore was a rough place. Schemes and scams were everywhere as people tried to make a fast dollar without actually working for it.

A combination of automobiles, horse drawn skids and mule team pulling freight wagons created poor or nonexistent streets that made simply getting across town difficult. Retail stores and warehouses sprang up along the better maintained streets and the railroad. There was no rhyme or reason to development in Kilgore. Most people had never heard of zoning and when zoning became an issue, many hard boiled men considered it an infringement of their rights. That is why mansions and gas stations were side by side in some parts of the town.

To complicate matters huge oil storage and pumping stations were plopped down in the middle of working class neighborhoods. The odor of raw petroleum products filled the air night and day. All too often sparks or lightning ignited concentrations of oil vapors. Sometimes the fires consumed nearby homes.

The sun was out when Ross and Bryant got to Kilgore so the streets and roads were dry. They quickly found the offices of Larkin and Larkin. The office was located in the front of a small home on a tree lined residential street a couple of blocks from the center of Kilgore. The Larkins, mother and son, lived in the rear half of the house. Mark Larkin was a hard working local lawyer who took just about every case that came his way. His mother, Esther, was also a lawyer and one of the town's leading socialites and community workers.

CHAPTER FIVE

The Larkins lived in an early twentieth century frame house that was in good condition. A bright green shingle roof gave the place a friendly look. A waist high white picket fence mounted a small sign on dark wood with gold lettering, Larkin & Larkin, Attorneys At Law.

The twin status symbols of the era in East Texas grew proudly in the lawn. A Chinaberry tree and a Mimosa, each tree dominated one half the small yard.

A small two car garage, more of a carport, really, had been added in recent years. One car, a 1929 Plymouth sat in the right side of the garage. The other parking place was vacant.

A 50-ish male in dress pants and an open-collared white shirt with rolled up sleeves stood in the front yard holding a garden hose. The man seemed to be fit and was trim nearly to the point of being skinny.

Ross studied the man. He was amused that the man was wearing a white shirt and dress pants while he worked in his yard. He knew that some men simply did not own casual clothing. Their entire wardrobe ranged from a full suit with vest and tie down to pants from an old suit and a dress white shirt.

The man did not hear the car pull up because of the splash of the water from his hose. As they opened the doors he turned and smiled at Bryant and said, "Art, how good to see you. Come on over. Let me turn off this water." He traced the hose to the brass hose bibb and shut off the water and carefully coiled the garden hose.

He turned and said, "Well, Art, are going to introduce me to your friend? Come on in." The man opened the door to the house and motioned for them to follow him in.

"So, to what do I owe the honor of this visit, Art?"

Bryant, glanced at Ross and said, "Uncle Mark, this is Charles Ross. He's from Washington."

Ross knew that Mark Larkin was aware of Bryant's FBI job. Ross extended his hand said, "Mr. Larkin, Arthur has told me a lot about you. It's a pleasure to meet you."

Larkin took a seat behind a small desk and pointed to two straight backed wooden chairs. He asked if they wanted coffee or a soft drink. Both declined.

Ross took charge and said, "Mr. Larkin, we're here on official business." He saw a frown crease Larkin's face and continued, "No, no, there are no problems but we do need to speak with you. But before I say more I need to ask, are we alone?"

Ross looked around. He imagined that the home had two offices, two bedrooms, one bath and a kitchen dining room area. The lack of pictures or decorations of any kind gave the home a spare, brooding look. It was clear that the Larkins lived and worked in the home.

Larkin said. "We are. My mother and I share this home and office. She's driven over to Longview to the County Courthouse for most of the day. I assure you we're quite alone."

"Fine," said Ross. "Now let me get down to business. This will take a few minutes and I hope that's OK with you. If you're busy we can come back later." Ross tried to create an easy, conversational mood with Larkin.

Larkin said, "Please. Please. I'm at your service so take all the time you need. Are you sure you wouldn't like a cup of coffee or a Coca-Cola?" Folks from east Texas always pronounced the name of that beverage, "Cocola".

Ross replied, "Well, a cup of coffee would be nice."

Larkin stood and said, "Art, you, too?"

"Well, a Cocola sounds good."

Larkin left the room and returned several minutes later with two cups of coffee and a cold bottle of Coca-Cola. Water was condensing on the cold bottle so Larkin also offered a napkin to his nephew. "Take anything in your coffee, Mr. Ross?"

"No. Thank you." Ross took the coffee cup and began, "Mr. Larkin, the Director of the FBI, Mr. Hoover, is very concerned about crime in the vast reaches of the United States of America." Ross knew that the mention of Hoover always got people's attention.

"We know that cattle rustling, scams in farm country and elsewhere and, well, so many other crimes that I could take all day talking about them are all on the increase. Local police agencies try their best but they're usually out manned, out gunned and out thought. They do their best work with local crimes and the misbehavior of people they know, local people. The FBI wants to help those agencies and prevent crimes before they happen, if possible.

Larkin interrupted and said, "Why, Mr. Ross, that will take thousands of FBI agents. Frankly, I don't know if our local boys will look kindly to the FBI or anyone else walking in on their territory." Ross regretted the slight to the local law enforcement organization.

"Exactly, Mr. Larkin. You are thinking just like Mr. Hoover," said Charles Ross. Any comparison of any outsider to Hoover automatically flattered that person and moved him closer to the FBI's position. This always worked and it always helped Ross maintain control. He leaned back in his chair and took a sip of his coffee. So far the meeting was going just as Ross had hoped it would. Arthur Bryant was letting Ross do the talking. His sipped his drink and observed the two men.

"We cannot afford thousands of new agents and the organization that it will take to keep it going. People only approve increases in law enforcement when they, personally, have been victims. We need help from the folks who are close to the local issues."

Larkin leaned forward and said, "So, you want me to help you find some, well, unpaid volunteers. Is that it?"

Ross smiled and replied, "No, Mr. Larkin, Mr. Hoover and I want you to be our volunteer in Kilgore and the oilfield area. This is a very serious proposal. One that we have considered carefully. We have considered you carefully, too, Mr. Larkin and you are our man.

Ross glanced at Bryant and caught him stifling a smile at the notion that the FBI and considered his uncle carefully. The fact was two hours ago Ross had never heard of Mark

Larkin or anyone else in Kilgore. But due to the skills of Charles Ross, the deal was nearing the close.

Ross continued, "Mr. Larkin we want you to consider our proposal seriously. You will not be paid and you cannot tell anyone, with the exception of your mother, and you can only tell her if you can guarantee she will be discrete. If you tell her and she disagrees we would prefer that you step aside so we can find another volunteer. This must be totally confidential, Mr. Larkin. We don't anticipate that your duties would tax your day-to-day activities.

"We only ask that you keep you eyes and ears open and, if something should look a little hinky, call the Dallas office and report your observations. You cannot be armed. You cannot become involved. The minute you call the Dallas office you will step away and forget about what happened. I repeat, you must not become involved in any business of law enforcement or the FBI. You will not be sworn and you will not be an FBI agent in any way, shape or form. Is that clear?"

Larkin was a formal man who never used jargon. He had puzzled look on his face. He asked, "Mr. Ross, you said 'hinky'. I am not familiar with that word. Should I be?"

Ross laughed and replied, "I am sorry Mr. Larkin. 'Hinky' is a police word. It means 'odd' or 'unusual'. If you see something that you think should be brought to our attention, something 'hinky', just give the Dallas office a call. And, call collect."

Larkin was calmer than Ross thought he would be. He thought for a long minute and said in an easy and almost humble voice, "Mr. Ross, I consider it an honor that you came to me today. I consider it an honor to say "Yes" to your proposal. You have my sincere promise that I will take the role that you propose seriously and you have my word that my mother and I will be totally discrete. And, may I add, thank you very much.

"But there is one thing. My mother is a strict constitutionalist and a strong state's rights advocate. I cannot predict her reaction to your offer and I feel I must consult her. So, I may be calling you in a day or two to change my mind and maybe even back out. I hope that is alright with you and Arthur."

Inwardly, Charles Ross was ecstatic. He had pulled off Hoover's assignment in one day. He could hardly wait to get back to Washington.

Ross said, "Mr. Larkin, I understand and while I hope you do not make that call, I will, nevertheless, appreciate your consideration."

Ross continued, "Mr. Larkin, your contact will be Special Agent Wesley Barton in Dallas. He's from this part of Texas so I think you will be comfortable with him. Mr. Barton will contact you within a few days. This is his card and one of mine.

"Now, I will not take any more of your time today, Mr. Larkin. Thank you for seeing us. And, thank you for your patriotism. The cup of coffee is appreciated very much." Ross tried hard to conceal his emotions and turned to leave the office.

So, it was done, the first person for The Plan had been recruited. Ross felt better than he had in years. The two men returned to their car and headed back to Dallas. They stopped outside Kilgore at a gas station where Ross told Bryant to call Dallas and arrange for a flight back to Washington. He said he thought they could depart tonight around seven or eight. A tall, skinny yet attractive young woman ran the gas station. She had a polished, highly developed way of speaking. She said, "The two of you must be from out of town. I bet you have something to do with the oil business." Ross smiled nodded his head to acknowledge the young woman's curiosity. They bought Cokes, filled the gas tank and headed west to Dallas.

CHAPTER SIX

The Volunteer Plan slowly evolved with new volunteers coming on board slowly but steadily. Within a few months almost all the "hot spots" that Hoover and Graham had identified had volunteers in place.

But progress was slow. The volunteers had little to report. Some of their observations turned out to be the products of vivid imaginations. Charles Ross wondered if this was such a good idea after all.

The FBI has always been a crime d'jour agency. Due to limited resources and a cautious Congress, the FBI focuses on the crimes that mean the most at the time. The outbreak of war in Europe turned the FBI's attention to espionage, defense industry fraud and military matters within the United States. By the time Japan kicked off a second front for the war, the FBI's mission had changed. Crimes by citizens of the United States dropped into the background while war-related crimes moved forward.

The war put The Plan on hold for, as the terminology of the day described, the Duration. In the case of World War II, the Duration was until near the end of 1945 when the Army Air Force incinerated two cities in Japan and forced a total surrender.

As Assistant Director for National Security, Charles Ross threw himself into preventing crimes against war materiel factories, official secrets and deep cover projects. These were the areas that the Director considered to be essential to the war effort and, therefore, it was essential that the FBI protect them. Ross did his work from a desk in the FBI building. He formulated a basic standard that read, "Any secret process or product; any key element of national defense; anything that directly contributes to the war effort is, by definition a target of the enemy to destroy, steal or delay."

Ross and his volunteers had huge successes in protecting petroleum pipelines that ran from Texas to East Coast factories. Volunteers kept close watches on the men who worked on the pipelines and strangers in the area of the work. Most of the calls from the volunteers turned out to be harmless cases of misidentification. There were minor success and one really big payoff for all the work that Ross and his volunteers were doing. Acting on a tip from a volunteer, Ross and his agents interrupted an attempt to dynamite one of the pipelines that passed through Pennsylvania. The bombers were literally caught in the acting of planting the dynamite.

World War II drew to a close and Ross went back to domestic crimes such as cattle rustling and illegal schemes. Ross supervised recruiting more volunteers and replacing ones who got too old or lost interest or passed away.

CHAPTER SEVEN

Charles Ross retired from the FBI in 1975, about a year after he was promoted to Assistant Director, the second highest job in the FBI. Before he retired, Ross and his volunteers uncovered countless crimes in progress throughout America. He perfected the recruiting and training of volunteers. Almost every key area in the nation was under the watchful eye of the volunteers.

One of the last recruits that Ross supervised was made necessary because a long time volunteer, Bud Reese, retired and moved down to the Lake of the Ozarks. Ross asked an FBI agent in Kansas City, Ken Stremming, to recruit volunteers.

Things were relatively quiet in the Midwest during that time. Stremming recruited several volunteers but rarely heard from them.

In the late 1990's an opening for a new volunteer opened in Kansas City. The opening required someone with good access to all levels of the community.

Stremming went through his files and came up with several possibilities. One, however, stood out. The man had grown up in Texas, gotten a degree from the University of Texas and then moved to New York to work in management in the pharmaceutical industry. He and his wife had been in Kansas City about a year when Stremming called and asked when they could meet.

NAPA

CHAPTER EIGHT

One of the things Americans have in common is that a call from the FBI can ruin just about anyone's day if only their peace of mind. I was no exception. I was tense, but the caller, Ken Stremming, had a casual and friendly air about him. I told him we could meet just about anytime. I was surprised when Stremming asked if my wife, Kathleen Royal, could also take part in the meeting.

The meeting was confirmed for that evening in our home in Leawood, Kansas. My name is Clark Davis. I've lived in this town a couple of years. I work in the pharmaceutical industry.

Ken Stremming arrived right on time. Stremming was compact man about six feet tall. His suit fit like it was custom tailored. He had an alertness about him that suggested years of investigative work.

My wife, Kathleen, came in the door from the garage just as I welcomed Stremming at the front door. She was surprised to see a strange man in her home. I took a moment to put her at ease. I explained that because she was out all afternoon I hadn't had an opportunity to give her a heads up. I said, "Mr. Stremming, this is Kathleen Royal, my wife. Please have a seat." I motioned to our living room chairs and the sofa.

Leaning forward in my chair, I asked, "How can we help you?" I had decided to be assertive and maybe even demanding

The three of us took seats.

Stremming paused for half a minute and said, "I can set your mind at ease. There isn't any kind of a problem. Sometimes we just come by to ask for help. Before I continue though, I have to ask each of you to agree to keep this meeting, and our discussion, totally to yourselves. If what I say doesn't interest you, we can drop it and I'll move on. If you are interested, I'll share some things that, for national security reasons, must be kept secret. I know it sounds odd, but do you agree?"

I responded, "Fine with me."

Kathleen was more hesitant, "I'm not sure I know what 'national security' means and how it applies to us. Are you saying we can get into trouble if we don't go along with you?"

Stremming said, "Mrs. Royal, if you don't want to accept what I've said so far, I'll go. The offer means that if we do continue to talk, you agree to hold all that's said – by you, as well as by me, – in confidence. I can't see anyone getting into trouble. In fact, you are not in trouble and this meeting will not lead to you being in trouble. Certainly not either of you. The fact that I am in your home should tell you that we have a high regard for you and Clark as good citizens and patriots."

Kathleen paused then said, "OK. I agree, too. But I might decide to stop this – depending on what you tell us. The plain implication is that you have investigated us. Is that so?"

Stremming had the look of a man who would prefer working on a farm to the formalities of the FBI. His close cropped hair looked sun-bleached. His hands were large and calloused. He smiled and said, "Thank you both. Now, as I said, we need your help. And, yes, we have considered you carefully for the roles that I am about to present."

Kathleen and I looked at each other and then back to Stremming. Kathleen, who was still cautious asked, "How on Earth can we help you? The FBI? I guess I'm still a little confused."

Stremming smiled and said, "Mrs. Royal, why not sit back and let me try to explain why I'm here. Again, if what I say is not for you, just say so and I will go away."

Stremming's soft blue eyes and casual manner put me at ease and I could see that was beginning to help Kathleen work though her initial shock.

Kathleen and I began to relax. I remembered a time when I was seven years old and living with my parents in a tiny town in Texas. The FBI stopped by our home out in the country and commandeered our front room. They wanted to observe a home about a quarter of a mile down a nearby country road to see if a fugitive bank robber would appear. They told my dad the bank robber was the son of the man who lived in that home. The agents slept and ate and worked in that front room. My mother supplied food and coffee. The men were courteous but avoided casual talk and other any effort to make us feel at ease. I guess I assumed this visit was something like that.

Stremming told us a story of the FBI's corps of field volunteers, or stringers, and how the program worked. It was a fascinating story but it did little to tell me why there was an FBI agent sitting in our living room.

I said, "That is an interesting story. I never heard of that. It makes sense but what does it have to do with us?"

Stremming said, "Mr. Davis, I'm sure you have lots of questions, but please wait 'til I get a little further along.

"The FBI wants the two of you to become field volunteers for us. Actually, we want you to go through a training course and then become a little more than volunteers. I'll explain that later.

"Why do we want you? Well, Clark, you work for a major corporation in a critical field, pharmaceuticals. You travel and you have access throughout this area. Your boss owns the local American League baseball franchise and that gives you access to a lot of different people and places. You can show up just about anywhere and you will not attract interest.

"Kathleen, you work in the non-profit sector where you raise money and come in contact with people all over the greater Kansas City area. Together, there are very few places where you can't go and few people you don't know.

"Let me stop now and assure both of you that your work for the FBI will never compromise your integrity, your careers, or your places in the community. We are not looking for you to report on your employers. As far as I know, you both work for very reputable organizations.

"Based on what I've said so far, do you want to hear more or do you want me to leave?"

I asked, "You sure know a lot about us. How did you pick us? I know you said we have jobs that give us access, but there must be more to it than that. Lots of people have jobs like we do."

Stremming continued, "You're right, Clark. Of course, there is more. Kathleen, we initially focused on you because you fit the profile we have – your job, your education, as well as your contacts. As we looked into both of your backgrounds, it became clear to us that if both of you agree, you can help the FBI take our program to a new level, one that we've considered for a number of years.

"I should let you know that we have completed a top secret clearance investigation on both of you. You passed, so we're at ease sharing information with you."

I interrupted, "Mr. Stremming how does what you want us to do differ from what the FBI has done in the past? And are you saying that there would just be two of us?"

"That's part of it, Clark, but there's more to it. In the past, all the way back to the 1930's, FBI field volunteers were passive. That is, they really didn't do anything until they saw something that looked a little hinky."

Kathleen said, "Hinky? What the heck is hinky?"

"Cop talk. It just means something odd or unusual or something the field volunteers thought we should know about. After they called us, they went back to their private lives and we did any work that was done. They never got involved at all."

I said, "Are you saying that you want us to somehow 'get involved'? How?"

"Clark, let me continue with what I have to say. I think all your questions will be answered by the time I'm done.

"The new level of field volunteers calls for more active participation. Not only will the volunteers contact us when something seems to be amiss, they'll sometimes take part in the investigations and maybe even be directed to look into something we, or others, notice. Plus, the volunteers will be given instructions in how to do the job, applicable federal laws that control their activities and other important information. And, I guess we'll need a new term because "volunteers" isn't really a very good term for people who get paid.

"If you agree, we'll ask you to come down to the local FBI office to complete some forms. The forms are very much like those you would sign if you took a new job. Right or wrong, we insist on 100% confidentiality. The Bureau was built on this principle and we enforce it to this day. Most of the forms you will sign deal with just that.

"When that's been completed we'll ask you to stop by for the instructions and educational classes. There might be two to four others in your classes, or, it might just be the two of you.

"As for your compensation, the FBI will give you a retainer, tax free and off any record, that will more than cover your expenses, if any, plus an amount paid monthly for your time."

"Can you tell us exactly what we'll be doing?" asked Kathleen. She was obviously getting a little more interested in Ken Stremming's story.

Stremming said, "Tell you what. I am low on my daily coffee requirement. Would it be too much trouble to ask for a cup of coffee?"

I held my breath that Kathleen would take Stremming's simple request as chauvinistic. Hurriedly, I said, "No problem. I'll get the coffee started."

Kathleen saw right through me and said, "Clark you couldn't make a good cup of coffee if we threatened to shoot you. Sit back. I will do the coffee."

Stremming observed this little scene. He sat back and smiled. I think he knew he had made a good choice. He had a habit of looking over the room every few minutes as if he expected to find something. His gaze would alternate between the layout of the room then back to me. Then he would do it all over again.

My mind was reeling. Stremming had just asked us to become some sort of pseudo-FBI agents. A zillion questions popped up. My strongest impulse was to ask Stremming to leave our home. I knew, somehow I knew that if I let him stay our lives would change forever.

Small talk did not come to us. I fidgeted and Stremming carried out his constant surveillance of our living room. We waiting until Kathleen brought in steaming mugs of coffee and a little tray of Milano cookies.

Stremming took up where he left off, "Actually, at this time, we don't have anything specific. However, a couple of years ago we were interested in a young man who made weekly round trips from Kansas City to Las Vegas. He always took an aluminum briefcase, one of those Halliburton cases, with him and always returned to Kansas City without his briefcase. All the trips began with him picking up the briefcase at a bar in the River Key district. We wanted to have someone inside the bar when the pickup took place. We tried, but found that the people in the bar were on to us almost instantly. It was as if they knew every FBI agent in town. If you'd been available, we would have asked you to begin gcing into the bar and set up a story that one of you worked nearby. Your role would have been somewhat passive, just observing.

"Another time, in a city out west, a couple showed up and created marketing and management agency that they promised would take business and groups to an entirely different level of success and profitability. One of our volunteers took a look at the couple and asked us to check their backgrounds. We found that they had been involved in a series of scams where they took up-front money and never produced any work product. By the time the locals caught on, the couple had already scammed a lot of money from clients, mostly non-profit charities. We were able to shut them down along with a local lawyer, who had brought them in. It seems that they operated a 'Dial S for Scam" fraud in which someone would invite them to a small city, help them get credibility and then split the take. Not only were they criminals they were scamming hard won donations from non-profits. We shut them down. We have wondered why any group or, especially a city, would welcome such people without vetting them thoroughly."

I joined in, "How can we find out a little more about this? I mean, we need to know how much time it'll take and, well, whatever risks are involved."

Kathleen sat up a little straighter and asked, "Wait, this isn't dangerous, is it?"

Stremming sat back and smiled before he began to talk, "No, we'll not place you in danger. Never. We review our investigations carefully and we always make sure we control risks."

Turning to me, Stremming said, "Clark, I assure you that you and Kathleen can continue to work on your careers. Our time pressure will be relatively minor."

He stood and said, "Kathleen, Clark, I want you to think about this for a day or two. I'll call you in a couple of days to see what you think about all this. I will remind you that service to your country is important and that most people never get that chance."

He hesitated and then said, "For full disclosure, what I have just told you is in the very early stages. But it represents a major change in our long time volunteer program. Things could change. When and if they do you will be told all the details and you will have an opportunity to continue or to walk away, no questions asked."

With that final word, he took a last sip of coffee, sat the cup on an end table, said 'good-bye', turned and walked out the front door. We sat quietly for a few minutes. Finally, I said, "Well, let's get something for dinner. Want to go out?"

"I think I'd rather find something here to eat. After all, we need to talk about this. I think there's some of the left over rib roast in the 'fridge. Oh, we have some of those McGonigles Italian sausages that you like so much in the freezer. Light the grill and I will bring them out. We can make sandwiches. OK?"

I said, "Great. And I'll choose a bottle of Napa's finest as soon as I get the grill going."

We discussed Stremming's offer off and on for the next two days. By the time Stremming called we were ready to accept his offer or at least to go to the next step.

CHAPTER NINE

Kathleen and I accepted the offer to become field volunteers or stringers for the FBI. We signed the papers and completed the training courses in about a month. All the courses were done in the evening so our day to day jobs didn't suffer. We never met others in the program.

Years later I would write that my wife and I became FBI stringers because we were becoming bored with our routines and, more than either of us would admit, a little bored with each other.

The FBI program promised excitement and challenges that simply weren't available in ordinary lives. We had no illusions about solving big cases and bringing master criminals to their knees. Kathleen and I held the very popular, if somewhat flawed, view that the FBI was the most elite law enforcement agency in the world. It excited us to be a part of all that and to take a "secret" role in protecting the United States of America.

After the completion of the training, we were more than ready to assume our new professional roles. However, months passed with no word from Ken Stremming or any else at the FBI. The check that arrived in the mail once a month reminded us of their acceptance and of our commitment, whatever it turned out to be. Kathleen and I had decided to bank the FBI money. It would add to our savings and maybe even let us buy a new home some day.

From time to time we talked about things that seemed, to Kathleen, a little "hinky". That word had become one of her favorites and she used it freely. She thought the escalating salaries in baseball were hinky. The explosive growth of the population of Johnson County Kansas was hinky to Kathleen. She wondered where all those people were coming from and how they paid the prices for all those new homes. She even decided our neighbor was hinky because he painted his home turquoise. She decided there must be something hinky about McGonigles Market. After all, their Italian sausage was so superior to any other sausage in her world that something must be going on there and that something was hinky.

One evening, during one of our "catch up and connect with each other" talks, she was reading the local paper and half paying attention to me. She put the paper down and said, "I tell you this, Clark, this business of selling people liquor in Missouri and arresting them when they drive back home to Kansas really is hinky."

In those days Missouri had privately owned liquor stores that sold wine and beer as well as liquor. Across the line in Johnson County, Kansas, the area was dry. So Johnson county residents would take a short drive to Missouri to stock up on booze. From time to time the local papers carried stories of

someone arrested for transporting, say, forty-eight containers of illegal alcohol into Kansas. The forty-eight containers
turned out to be two cases of beer to lubricate a city or company league softball game.

Half interested, I replied, "What are you smoking? How
did you come up with that? It's legal to sell booze in Missouri
and it's illegal to transport it into Kansas. What's hinky about
that?"

"You don't find it odd that only the cars carrying liquor
when they cross the state line get stopped? I've been kinda
keeping track of the stories in the paper, and it's always folks
who just made liquor purchases in Missouri and nearly always
those who bought their booze at that big store on 103rd in
Kansas City, Big Billy's. It's a huge store so it makes sense
that they would have what people want. But too many of 'em
are getting busted as soon as they cross that state line. Which,
by the way, is only about a block away from Big Billy's?"

Big Billy's was located near an interstate freeway and
adjacent to one of the on and off ramp complexes. It was a big
store with a glass front facing the freeway. The parking lot
and most of the inside of the store were clearly visible from
the freeway and from the adjacent streets. I thought that only
my wife could see something sinister about a modern liquor
store.

Missouri had liquor stores as well as bars and taverns in
those days. Kansas was dry; no liquor stores and a few tightly
controlled bars, mostly in hotels and restaurants. In any wet-
dry situation, the cops on the dry side do prey on the people
who make purchase on the wet side and then reenter the dry
area. That kind of cat and mouse game has been going on for
decades.

But, to humor her, I pretended to be getting interested in her fantasy. I said, "Do you think some Kansas cop is secretly watching the parking lot at the store and tipping off his fellow Kansas officers?"

"That would do it and it might even be legal. Shitty but legal. But I think there might be more to it. Here's what I'm thinking. I think it might be someone in the store who is doing the tipping for the Kansas cops. That'd be even easier. I'm wondering if the Kansas cops are providing just the right incentive to set up something like that. What if they're returning the liquor so the store can sell it over again? The owners of the store could make some real money in a deal like that. For all we know that might even be legal. I bet the Kansas authorities get the fines, a hell of a lot of fines."

I was used to Kathleen's sometimes nutty ideas. I thought for a minute then said, "Wouldn't the Kansas cops need the booze for evidence?"

Kathleen said, "I thought about that but I bet most people who are caught don't even go to court. After all, they were caught with contraband booze. If they admit it and pay the fine, they don't have to go to a court date and life goes on. If someone opts for court, the case is thrown out because the evidence is missing.

"I read about one man who was caught with forty-eight containers of illegal alcohol. That brings to mind a real bootlegger, doesn't? But, you know, it turned out to be two cases of beer for his neighborhood softball game. The reality is not nearly as sinister as the cops' fantasy.

"Clark, you know how cops will bust a drug ring and claim they seized a million bucks worth of smack or coke or whatever? But you know what really happens; the cops divide the amount of the seized drug by the minimum possible dose and then multiply that by the maximum possible street price. The "million" was, in reality, $3,000 or so. Street mutts never have anything like a million bucks. If they did they'd do what we would do. They would get the hell out of the frozen town, buy a place in Florida and live forever in the sunshine. The cops have done this all my life. I think they do it because if the public caught on that a huge drug sweep actually amounted to a few hundred dollars and not a million dollars, they would stop the nonsense and tell the cops to focus on something productive like reducing real crime. You know, Clark, if cops told the truth about the real value of the drug use in this country, I bet people would be a lot less concerned. They have to exaggerate because, well, it would be hard to justify spending more on cops to stop drugs than the drugs were generating.

"I know this, if I was caught coming into Kansas with booze, I would do what I could to go quietly, pay the fine and keep it out of the papers."

Kathleen had always shown this level of skepticism about news reports, government information and just about anything. Her favorite quote was, "Follow the money". I went along with her logic and said, "Right. That's why I always get our booze on the way to work in Missouri and not on the way home. I've never heard of someone getting busted for buying booze in Missouri who stayed in Missouri."

"Smart man, Clark. So, what do you think of my idea? What can we do about it?"

"I'm not sure this is the kind of thing that would interest the FBI."

"Who knows? If I'm right, it's an interstate issue. And, remember that Ken Stremming said that in some cases they would simply hand it over to local law enforcement."

I liked the checks from the feds but had just about decided that we did not actually have to anything to get the money. I said, "Maybe. Why not give it a try? Call Stremming and see."

"I will."

The next day Kathleen passed the information about the liquor busts to Ken Stremming. He was non-committal but thanked her for the call. Kathleen wondered if he thought she was the one who was hinky. She even wondered if she had blown the entire arrangement with the FBI. She fretted all night that Stremming would think she was a ditz.

Stremming called the next day and asked Kathleen to go down to Big Billy's and pretend to shop. He asked me to also go to the store but in a different car. The idea for me to buy a couple of cases of beer, put them in my car and drive away. Kathleen was to wait to see if someone in the store placed a telephone call. I was to drive toward the state line but was not to go into Kansas. Kathleen and I would meet in a few minutes and transfer the beer to her car. She was to drive several blocks north and cross the state line in a neighborhood. I was to drive into Kansas.

I was less than a quarter mile into Kansas when a Kansas State Trooper pulled me over. The Trooper searched the car top to bottom. Of course he found no beer or anything else. He was pretty reluctant when he told me I was free to go. He was very clearly confused. He kept glancing back toward the state line.

Before starting the engine I said "I think you must be looking for something. If you tell me what you're after, I'll let you know if it's here."

The Trooper was growing noticeably tense. He said, "Sir, please tell me where you have been."

I hesitated for a minute and said, "I can't imagine why I would do that. I'm not up to anything. Clearly, you are."

The trooper, teeth gritted and face reddening, spun on his heel, got in his car and drove away.

Kathleen was waiting for me when I got home. She was excited when she told me about the clerk placing a telephone call. But she became truly ecstatic when I told her about being stopped by the Trooper.

We relayed our experiences to Ken Stremming then went out to Jasper's for a celebration dinner. In those days the place for celebrations in Kansas City was Jasper's, a white table cloth restaurant in Missouri not far north of I-435, the major beltway around the city.

A week later, Kathleen read in the local Johnson County paper that a joint task force of the Missouri Bureau of Investigation and the Kansas Bureau of Investigation had uncovered a plot that involved the owners of Big Billy's Liquors and Wines in Kansas City, Missouri, and the Johnson County District Attorney and several Kansas State Troopers.

The plot was essentially just as Kathleen had imagined. The store clerks at the liquor store were loading the cars of customers with Kansas license plates then calling the Kansas authorities to tip them off about 'incoming liquor'. The Kansas cops returned the liquor to the store for resale. Johnson County Kansas reaped the rewards of dozens of $500+ fines every month. The store was making a bundle reselling the products and paying off both the employees and the troopers to keep the scheme going smoothly. It seemed likely that the Johnson County District Attorney was also a dupe in the scheme.

An hour after Kathleen read about the fruits of her imagination, we got a call from Stremming. He wanted to stop by and we readily agreed.

When we met Ken Stremming at the door, he was beaming. He entered the front room and took a chair.

Stremming said, "Kathleen. Clark. That was a terrific piece of work on your part. It's exactly the kind of thinking we want. Most people read about the liquor busts at the state line and thought nothing about it. You seemed to see right through the conspiracy.

"Of course, Kansas has every right to nab bootleggers and others who try to import booze into their dry state. But they don't have the right to set up a shake-down deal like the one you found. The guys in the Missouri liquor store broke the law, too.

"I contacted the KBI and the MBI right after you called, Kathleen. At first they refused to accept that Johnson County had anything to do with such a "stupid thing" as they put it. But it took a couple of days of undercover work to blow the scheme wide open. Some folks are headed to jail for a while. I expect Big Billy's will be out of business for some time to come.

"We won this one. I doubt if this one ever would have been discovered if not for your work. Thank you very much."

CHAPTER TEN

In the next year Kathleen and I found a few things of interest to the FBI. Most were minor but one, a scam involving one of the city's leading developer/builders was a big deal. I got on to it when I was going over budgets for a new building at our corporate campus. The bribes and the over-charges were there for anyone to see. The two partners, both formerly leaders in the community, pled guilty and went directly to prison.

We had one direct assignment. Ken Stremming wanted us to observe the comings and goings in two bars in the River Key area.

The River Key section was targeted as a tourist destination. The area abutted the Missouri River where it makes a big loop just north of downtown. Old warehouses and other mostly abandoned business were converted to restaurants, trendy retail stores and bars.

Two blocks from the renewal area a core of old fashioned Italian joints that served whiskey, pasta and women survived.

Tourists seemed to know to stay away from these places just as tourists avoid certain places in New York's Little Italy. And, just as Joey Gallo's murder at Umberto's Clam House in New York had cooled the tourist trade, more than one violent event at the River Key directed tourists and the locals away from the Italian bars, joints and clubs.

I began thinking about changing jobs. A company in California had been making overtures in recent weeks. I dreaded bringing up the move to Kathleen. She was happy in her job and seemed to be at home in Kansas City.

Kansas City is probably the best city with the worst reputation in the nation. Easterners, westerners and southerners are forever demeaning the Midwest, in general, and Kansas City, in particular. But the city has broad avenues, possibly more fountains than any city in the world, huge oaks and gorgeous gardens. The city affords people many varied opportunities for recreation and culture. Kathleen really enjoyed all that Kansas City offers.

But Kathleen is, if she is anything, unpredictable. She surprised me. She told me she had been thinking about a move, too and the idea of living in California appealed to her. "These Midwest winters and humid summers are beginning to get to me," she said.

I called Ken Stremming a couple of weeks later and gave him the news that Kathleen and I would be moving by the end of the summer. There was a moment of silence, I presumed because he was surprised by my announcement. "I'd like to see you two as soon as possible," he said. Since Kathleen and I were at home for the evening, I said, "Why not now?"

We were a little apprehensive that he'd try to interrupt our plans to move. I had accepted a great position in the San

Francisco Bay area. Kathleen was very close to agreeing to head up a new organization in the North Bay area. We had timed our joint resignations for the very next day.

Stremming arrived a short thirty minutes later. He took a seat in the living room and accepted Kathleen's offer of a cup of coffee. He wasted no time in putting his concerns on the table.

"Your call caught me a little off guard. I've been working on a new development in the volunteer program and was counting on you two to play a part in my new plan."

"Sorry. But our careers have run their course here and we hate the winters. California looks good to us."

"Do you mind if I try to influence your decision?"

Stremming and I had become informal friends. I looked for and thought I saw a combination of disappointment and determination. I sighed and said, "Ken, we're going to move. But we've liked knowing you and working with you. So, if you have something to say, now's the time."

Stremming knew he had a chance. He said, "Have you made a decision about where you'll live?"

I said, "Well, my new job will be in Walnut Creek, just east of San Francisco and Oakland. Kathleen is looking at a position in the Napa Valley. We'll most likely try to find something in the middle."

Stremming smiled and relaxed. He said, "I came over here tonight to try to get you interested in living in the Napa area. Looks like no convincing from me is needed. I just can't believe this." This time I saw true relief on Stremming's face.

"Ten years ago, we saw Napa as the perfect command center for a new home for North San Francisco Bay FBI and after 9/11, Homeland Security joined us. Back then it was a sleepy little backwater town where not much went on – we felt we could operate almost out in the open. But in the last ten years, Napa has exploded. Now, a lot is going on, including some things that are of a bit of concern to us."

Kathleen was skeptical. She said, "Really? We get interested in the Napa area and suddenly it's exactly what you had in mind all along? Pardon me if I'm just a tad wary." She looked from Stremming to me and back again. "Wait a minute; this is hinky even for you, Clark. Tell me, did you two have this set up all along? I bet you did. Did you?" I could see her dander getting up at the thought of being manipulated. If there's one thing Kathleen Royal doesn't like it's having things go on behind her back. If she actually decided that Ken and I had cooked this up big trouble would be in store for me and for our marriage.

"Kathleen, I did not. We did not. We would not." Stremming said, holding up his right hand as if in a pledge. He knew he was on very thin ice with Kathleen and he chose his words carefully, "If I had my way, you'd stay put and work with me on my revised version of the volunteer program. I had in mind asking you to move alright, but not California. I wanted you in of those new high rises condo places on the Missouri River, close to downtown Kansas City. We're very interested in some of the things we see in that area. You guys are young so you'd fit right in. If that sounds attractive, that offer is still open."

Kathleen put her head down and after a full minute said, "Ken, we've known each other long enough to be open with each other. I think you were just now, but, you work for the government and for most of these years you haven't always been completely forthright. Sometimes our suggestions seem to simply fall into a black hole. We do all the talking and you do, I don't know, whatever it is you do. Mostly, we never know how things turn out. And, I think sometimes we might have been at risk and I wonder if something happened to one or both of us, what would our families, our friends and the whole world would be told?"

She hesitated, and then continued, "Ken, we're moving to California. If you want us to continue in the program, this is a real good time tell us exactly what is expected of us in Napa. If that sounds like I'm demanding full disclosure, you're hearing me correctly. These past few years have been ok, but honestly, I have to know more about what our roles are in the whole scheme of things."

I saw an opening and interrupted, "Ken, she's right. We've had enough of the "ask no questions" deal. Tell us what you want."

Kathleen said, "Ken, there is one more thing I want to know. Bluntly, do you have our house or our phones tapped? Do you read our mail?"

Stremming said, "Absolutely, 100% not. In spite of what you read and see in the movies, we don't operate that way. Now, to be very clear, if you gave us reason to do those things, we would. But at that point you would be out of the program and we certainly would not be asking to pay your way to California.

"You have to understand that we've done a lot of good work together in the past, even if you didn't always know how it turned out. But there's more changes coming than just your move. I'll be retiring soon – and you'll be working with a new agent if you go to California."

She said, "A new handler, you mean?"

65

Stremming frowned and finally said, "Kathleen, call it what you will. In my office, our term is Volunteer Manager. Your use of that word, handler, puts me off a bit. I prefer to think of you and, myself, as operating at a higher level. I'm not certain why I'm having such a hard time getting you two to accept that you're both important to us. You are.

"Look, law enforcement can't possibly play every role in finding and solving crime. Our nation has become more complicated. Take the Big Billy's case. Neither the Kansas City cops nor the Kansas state cops really had much interest in shutting down the Big Billy's scam. We know now that folks on the Missouri side were sharing in the profits. And it's certain that the Kansas cops and their bosses liked the ten thousand or so in fines they got every week. Who knows how long it would have gone on? But, you forced the issue by bringing us in on what was clearly an interstate crime. We'll simply expect you to continue what you've doing – being observant.

"Unfortunately, politics have forced local law enforcement in big and little cities into the role of tax collectors. They call it fines. The truth is they collect taxes from people who have already paid their real taxes. Highly trained officers spend their days handing out traffic citations for violations that mostly are causing no harm to anyone. City Councils and County governments demand this miscarriage of law enforcement. The day the public catches on to this mess will be an exciting but sad day.

"We know that companies across the nation are working on electronic gadgets that will enable local cops to issue more and more tickets. Cops are fascinated with gadgets. They would welcome a robot that would prowl the streets and hand out tickets for minor speeding violations, yellow light violations and parking violations. Their enthusiastic acceptance of radar for speed patrol proves that what I say is true. When we have some time I'll you how to defeat police radar all the time. The easiest speed gun to defeat is the one using lasers. The cops believe the vendors who tell them that laser speed guns cannot be defeated. The vendors lie. I'm sure it will be just as easy to defeat the new gadgets when they come on line.

"Let me put a fine point on this. Back in the Nixon days the Congress created the Law Enforcement Assistance Administration. The idea, a very good one if I do say so, was to make funds available to local police so they could upgrade their equipment such as radios and cars. But the Congress always forgets that we live in a market-driven society. In no time dozens of entrepreneurs began to develop and sell zillions of items that cops "needed". Everything from tick proof uniform pants to body armor to radar guns to first aid kits went on the market to local police agencies. These things were irresistible to the cops and to the cities. A whole new market was created overnight. Crime statistics fail to show any positive results from all this spending. Traffic revenue went up but issues with gangs, drugs and organized crime soared. Training in traffic patrol became common. Other training, vital training I think, has just about disappeared. I have been to police weapons ranges where only three of ten cops could qualify with their duty weapons. I saw one hapless fellow draw his revolver to fire only to discover that the gun was so filthy from lack of cleaning that it would not fire. He couldn't even pull the trigger. The instructor took the gun back to the bench, cleaned it and handed it back to the officer for another try at qualifying. Unbelievable! In our organization all the non-qualifiers, the dirty gun guy and the instructor would be out of work that day.

"I'll get off my soap box now and get back to where we were.

"Now, when you meet the new agent in California, he might have something different in mind. I can't impact that. If it turns out you don't like it, quit then. You'll still be where you want to be and you'll have given the program a chance. One thing I can say is that you will have a much more hands-on role and you will always know what is happening. That much is certain."

We could see he was trying to be straight with us so we relaxed a little and sat back to listen to what he had to say. Kathleen had done what she rarely does. She had opened herself so Stremming could see the cold steel that she is made of. Kathleen usually used her head and found soft, gentle ways to control what goes on around her. But when the time to be firm came, Kathleen could get anyone to back down. We contrasted in our methods. I'm much more likely to pitch a grenade in first then try to reconcile the leftover pieces.

"First, here's why we're interested in Napa. Everyone knows Napa for wine. No doubt about it, Napa and wine are one in the same. I love to go to Napa for a vacation. Many people do. The entire County has about 135,000 people but more than five million visit annually.

"But Napa has other sides, too. Sides that most people don't know. Some good, some not so good. All carefully sheltered and managed."

He paused and said, "Please pardon me but I have to ask. You recognize that this conversation is confidential, right?"

Both of us nodded and I said, "Sure, we know that."

Kathleen joined in, "Actually, secret or not, we'll not repeat whatever you say because, well, sometimes we wonder what would happen if we did."

Stremming chose to let Kathleen's remark slide by. He said, "Napa has three other sides. You'll get more information on all this when you get there. For now, I'll outline a couple.

"First, when you drive into Napa and cross a huge bridge, the Butler Bridge, over the Napa River, most people notice a huge satellite dish farm beside the bridge. Ask and you'll be told it's a cable TV and communications facility. In fact, it's the largest NRO, National Reconnaissance Office, communications operation on the west coast. Also, it's a very important hub for the Department of Defense's communication system. Those big dishes are sucking down communications from one end of the Pacific Rim to the other. They afford us instant contact with every ship, airplane and every man in the field. Both the DOD and the NRO have chosen to be very low key about all this. One of the side-effects of that decision is that the dishes and the entire facility are not protected as well as some people think they should be. Sure, most forms of attack on the facility would be tough to do because of distances and other complications. Any manned attack would get very well planned responses from local agencies — police, sheriff and so forth. The security staff at the site is among the best in world. One of your goals will be to keep your eyes and ears open in case someone somewhere decides to do something to the site.

"Second, immediately after 911, the FBI, the CIA and other agencies set up emergency facilities in a building at the Napa County airport. All these years later the operation is still going strong."

He smiled and said, "You know how it is. Give the bureaucracy a small office and they'll fill a skyscraper in no time."

"Seriously, it very well could be the best example of cooperation between the FBI, the CIA, DEA and, now, Homeland Security and the private sector. You'll get a full briefing on this when you move to Napa. I think you'll find the inclusion of the private sector to be, well, innovative to say the least.

"Finally, Napa is a worldwide destination. People from all over the world go to Napa to drink wine, eat great food and see the incredible sights in the Napa Valley. More and more of these people arrive in Napa in private jets. That means they don't get the best shot from Homeland Security's Transportation Security Administration. We think Napa is a great place for someone to get on the ground in an area that might afford terrorists a target rich part of the United States.

"I said 'finally' but actually there are a couple more things I want to mention. First, we will compensate you for what will amount to an increased role in our program. We'll pay each of you for your time, a base and more if the work takes more time and, of course, all your expenses. We want you to penetrate very deeply into the society in the Napa Valley so you'll need to pay for dinners, events, clothing and whatever, even a certain amount of philanthropy if it's necessary. Napa is the epicenter of 'silent auctions', in this case side shows at events where people bid up ordinary wines to about three times their real value.

"Second, you'll have credit cards that you can use in this work. The cards will be 100% ordinary credit cards. Even the statements will be sent to your home and you'll pay with your normal payment method – check, Internet banking or whatever. The difference will be that none of this will actually enter your banking accounts and there will be no way for anyone to detect that the FBI is paying your bills.

"Third, we'll be paying your telephone, Internet and cell phone bills the same way. Calls and computer activity on our behalf will simply disappear from your records. This is one thing we do very well. You will appear to live normal lives. The screens that we set up will be totally opaque to anyone who wants to look.

"Finally, and this time I mean it, you'll have a way to contact us instantly if you need to. Personal contact with us will be different that it is now. No one will ever come to your home as I've done. All your contact will be at the airport complex. That kind of direct contact will increase a ton."

Stremming watched for our reaction. We were reeling with the impact of what we had heard. No doubt, if we went along with Stremming's offer, we would become confidential agents for the US government. And, it sounded like more active than we had ever been. Did we want that?

"Questions? If I were in your place I would have tons of questions. No doubt about it, this will change your life. If you're not interested, say it now."

Kathleen stood and began walking around the room. Her hands were behind her back and her head was down. I could see tears forming in her eyes. She walked up behind me and put her hand on my shoulder. I began to speak but she interrupted me.

"Clark, let me say what I have to say. I want to do this. I've felt very good about myself these past few of years, like I'm contributing something worthwhile. I'm good at my job, my profession, and I'll be good at what I do at my new job.

But, honestly, after a while it all becomes the same old thing over and over. This kind of thing keeps me interested. I want to do this, Clark, I want us to do this together."

I was shocked. I had been sure Kathleen was going to bail. I suspected that Stremming felt the same way. I took her hand and turned to Stremming, "Ken, I guess she said it all. I feel the same way. When I started looking for a new job in a new place it took forever because I didn't want to give all this up and lose this commitment. Whatever you need in Napa, or anywhere, we're in."

Kathleen went into the kitchen and returned with three flutes and a bottle of Piper Heidsieck Brut Champagne. She said, "Guys, this calls for a toast. Clark, will you do the honors?"

I opened the bottle of champagne and poured three glasses. We touched glasses, smiling at each other, and sat back to enjoy the champagne.

I said, "This is the French stuff, Ken. From now on I guess we'll be drinking the local champagne, local in Napa, that is."

Stremming joined in, "Well, the first thing you need to do is learn the terminology. Out there it's called 'sparkling wine'. We use that term in this country to keep the French happy. Those frogs got upset when the people in Napa began making champagne as good as or better than the French stuff. All they could think to do was to claim that 'champagne' is their term and Americans can't use it. So the Americans came up with the sparkling wine term and continue to send the French and their hoity toity wines packing. You will find many more such stories when you get settled in Napa."

We drank the wine, Stremming barely sipping any; after all he was an FBI agent on duty. He stood, handed each of us a business card and said, "After you get settled in Napa you'll be contacted by my friend and associate, James Berry, or Jim as he likes to be called. If you have any problems, call the number on this card. The card shows Napa Avionics and Training, a real company, but perhaps not what most people think it is. Jim Berry will fill you in and answer any questions you might have. I've known Jim a long time. He is old school FBI like I am."

He continued, "Your drive out will be enjoyable. Take your time. Use your credit cards for everything. When you get close to Napa, call Jim and tell him where you want to stay. He's expecting your call. Good luck."

After the normal handshakes and hugs, Stremming left. The idea that we were actually leaving our home for an adventure in faraway Napa, California, hit us. We looked at each other and smiled. "This is gonna be fun," I said. Kathleen mentioned we could have some fun right that moment. I'm not sure if it was the champagne or the idea of a bigger role with the FBI, but either way, I wasn't turning the offer down.

CHAPTER ELEVEN

Three weeks later, we were near our destination, Napa, California and the Napa Valley. Just before we left Kansas City, we fund a perfect little dog. When we first saw her on the Internet she was eight weeks old and weighed about a pound and a half. She was a tricolor Coton de Tulear. She was bred in a small town in southern Sweden. We paid the breeder at once and waited for her to arrive from Copenhagen.

She was white with charcoal and apricot ears and an apricot marking on her right hip. She was so tiny and her coloring reminded us of a toasted crouton. So that became her name, Crouton, which evolved to Crute, Miss T and so forth. Dog experts say dogs can remember about twenty-two words. Maybe that is why Crute seems to be so backward at times. Maybe all twenty-two of her word memory is taken up with her many names.

Coton's tend to bond strongly with one family member. When she bounded out of her crate at the Kansas City airport she looked around then headed straight for me. It has been that way ever since.

We had packed up our home and loaded Kathleen's CTS Cadillac with enough things to drive to Napa and enjoy the trip along the way. I sold my Ford truck because I would get a company vehicle in California. I had my eye on a new Honda Ridgeline with all the goodies. I particularly liked the hidden truck feature under the pickup bed. You never know when that might come in handy.

Just before we left the Kansas City area we had taken a three day course in wine. It was taught by an instructor from the FBI in Quantico. The course concentrated on terminology, history and the current wine growers and winemakers. Stremming felt it was necessary to offer this training in Kansas City rather than the Bay Area to make sure we had all the information we needed when we arrived. Stremming seemed to want us to be ready when we hit the ground in Napa.

Much of the class work had to do with the federal and state laws on wine. We learned that growing, producing and selling wine had grown more and more complex in the years since the repeal of prohibition. Many of the states, relying on obscure passages from post-prohibition federal laws, had become particularly difficult.

As we drove across the country, we talked about gasoline prices. It seemed that the farther west we drove, the higher the gasoline prices rose. In the coming months we would learn that almost everything would have higher prices in the west and, especially, in California.

Crouton spent her travel days in the back seat or nestled into Kathleen's lap. She became antsy from time to time. We stopped and let her pee then gave her treats and water. She was so tiny that Kathleen could sneak her into hotel rooms.

It was spring and the snow was long gone. We hoped the highways would be clear. We had plenty of time so we had our choice of which route to take. We had decided to make the first day a long one, almost ten hours. We drove northwest into Nebraska, across a bit of Colorado and just over the Colorado line into Wyoming. Both of us enjoy long drives. The first night found us in Cheyenne at a Hampton Inn. After a drink in our room we took a taxi to a great steak house across town, The Little Bear Inn, a Cheyenne original.

We shared an appetizers selection which included rocky mountain oysters, actually fried beef testicles. I love them. Kathleen was a little squeamish until she had her first bite.

Kathleen always stops reading a menu when she encounters the word 'lobster'. She was very satisfied with the Brazilian Lobster Tails. This dish, which I was surprised to find in Cheyenne, is warm water lobster. They're delicious.

I opted for a buffalo steak. Buffalo is an almost fat free meat with the texture of beef. I like it. The Little Bear Inn did the buffalo justice. If the chef isn't careful, buffalo dries out quickly.

We headed out early the next morning. Wyoming was new to us so we stopped frequently to see roadside monuments and such. We saw huge herds of pronghorn antelope. We learned that the locals call them prairie goats. They're protected by the state so their numbers have exploded in Wyoming and South Dakota. We lost count at 150 antelope in one herd just east of Rawlins. Pronghorns are beautiful creatures. They can sprint away in no time yet reappear a thousand yards away.

We arrived in Salt Lake City in time to get a room at the downtown Hilton and take a short tour of the Mormon Church properties and other buildings. We were in luck. We got there just in time to be seated at a rehearsal of the Mormon Tabernacle Choir. Kathleen's purse was stuffed with Crute. After about an hour, Crute raised her head a let out a high pitched yelp. A very perturbed but very polite usher showed us the door.

We took a horse drawn carriage back to the hotel. We shared a seafood risotto and a New York strip at Fresco, an excellent Italian bistro in downtown. Crute slept through the entire dinner.

Early the third morning, we headed west across the salt flats and into northern Nevada. The landscape changes dramatically at the Nevada state line. Wendover sits squarely on the state line. Historically, Wendover was, in 1944, and is today, the middle of nowhere. Wendover is where a young Ohioan named Paul Tibbets put together the 509th Composite Bomb Group. It was the 509th that dropped the two atomic bombs on Japan in 1945.

Just about daily Col. Tibbets and his team flew from Wendover to the Salton Sea in southern California. In 1944 the Salton Sea claimed title to being the southern California version of the middle of nowhere. They dropped concrete and steel bomb shapes. Every run was photographed and measured. The B-29's returned to Wendover from the Salton Sea where their crew members got the airplanes ready to do it all again the next day or soon thereafter. Those flights were practice runs for real missions to Hiroshima and Nagasaki.

Even the most meticulously documented history books and articles persist in making the mistake of calling the development of the first atomic bomb the Manhattan Project. This is forgivable because the Truman administration set up a war-time project called the Manhattan Engineering District. The code word for cutting through red tape to get funding, materiel and whatever was needed for the project was Silverplate.

Anyone interested in the atomic bomb project will be interested in the small museum at Wendover.

On the western side of Nevada is Reno, one of our planned destinations, we arrived early in the afternoon. Reno is a poor excuse for just about anywhere. Over-the-top tacky hotel casinos line up with the homeless, pawn shops and cheap restaurants. Hordes of retirees have given the place a slow-motion feel.

We got a room at the Reno Hilton, a place that long ago had surrendered to decay and dry rot.

The highway between Reno and Sacramento is one of the most gorgeous drives in the world. Remnants of the old gold mining days line much of the route. Waterfalls, soaring cliffs and enormous evergreens line the highway.

We decided we had plenty of time to cross the Sierras and go all the way to Napa. Both of us were eager to see Napa. This plan would put us in Napa a least two days early so we would have time to explore our new home town. Kathleen had looked at homes a month earlier so we were close to deciding we would purchase a large home on the western side of the City of Napa in an area called Brown's Valley. This afforded us easy commutes, me to Walnut Creek and Kathleen to her job.

CHAPTER TWELVE

Around 4:30 in the afternoon I turned off Interstate 80 onto Highway 12 which is known in the area as Jamison Canyon Road. The signs told me we were 12 miles from Napa. The heavy traffic and endless commercial presence on I-80 quickly gave way to a softer and calmer, rural scene. Within two miles we saw gorgeous horses, fat steers and a small heard of Californian whitetail deer. Soon vineyards lined both sides of the highway. When we turned due west on the road to Napa small clouds, mostly mare's tails, filled the western sky. Entering the Napa Valley was as dramatic to us as entering Shangri-La might have been to the characters in James Hilton's masterpiece, Lost Horizon.

Mare's tails usually signal a change of weather. In the weeks to come we learned that locals would respond, when asked what the weather was going to be, with a standard, "Better." The Napa Valley is one of those places that have great weather most of the time. The local's say, "We actually do not have weather."

I noticed Kathleen totally absorbed by what she was seeing. I turned to her and said, "If you can break away from your sightseeing, any ideas on where we'll stay tonight? You can call this Berry person and get orientated."

She said, "I made a list. I think I'll call to see if he really can get a room."

Kathleen called Jim Berry and introduced herself. Berry welcomed her to the Napa Valley and asked if she had a room choice. He made it pretty clear that most of the hotels were probably full because of the Mustard Festival. Years ago some winegrowers began planting mustard between the rows of grape vines after harvest. The mustard came up bright yellow. Sure enough, local visionaries used the fields of gorgeous yellow mustard as the perfect reason for yet another Napa Valley celebration. Of course, the celebration drew crowds of tourists and the hotel business was booming. However Berry assured Kathleen that he could get a room for us. He asked for her choice.

Kathleen checked her notes and said, "How about the Napa River Inn?"

Jim asked her hold for a minute. He came back on the line and said, "They're expecting you. Have a good evening. I'll check on you tomorrow."

The Napa River Inn is the focal point of the renaissance in Napa and the Napa Valley. There are bigger hotels but nothing comes close to the Napa River Inn for hospitality, location and variety. The building began in 1884 as a grain mill that served the agriculture business in the Napa Valley. The old buildings had been skillfully reconstructed as a luxury hotel. Several restaurants, a bakery and a chocolate shop were tucked in around the buildings.

The place sits on land that was originally a bluff above the Napa River. Warehouses lined the bluff in the nineteenth century. Local products such as tanned leather, cinnabar ore, fresh stone fruits and manufactured products were stored here and then loaded onto ships to take them towards San Pablo Bay and beyond.

The river is Napa's hidden gem. Indeed, in a survey done in 2002 of what tourists like and dislike about the Napa Valley, The Napa River got no mentions – good or bad. Every so often winter and spring rains overcame the river's ability to handle the flow of water and the river flooded much of downtown Napa and several neighborhoods. The citizens voted to tax themselves to widen, deepen and reroute the river. In the early days of the project some experts called the Napa River Flood Control District one of the best projects in America. Yet, the project seems to be one that will continue forever. State and federal money, promised from the beginning, have run into snag after snag. The local Congressperson and the local members of the state Assembly seem to have little, if any, interest in completing the project. The Congressman seems to find all kinds of earmarks for other projects n his district but not a penny for the Napa Flood Control Project. The Republican governor ignores the project out of spite for the local default democrats. He says a default democrat is one who never has really thought about political parties but finds the democrats and their foolish promises release the guilty feelings the democrats have about being reasonably successful.

The locals shudder at the thought of the impact of heavy rains could have on the incomplete project. If there's one issue that has the potential to divide and disrupt Napa, it's the flood control project. Curiously, the local elected officials seem to prefer to not talk about the project. In their silence, a growing din of complaints intrudes on that silence. It's the noise of people who have run out of patience and are beginning to demand answers.

Napa is a small, nearly insignificant part of their Congressional District so the Congressman generally tends to problems in the highly populated parts of his District.

The river has tides that vary the level of the water from five feet to almost nine feet twice each day. The river was at low tide when we arrived in Napa. The water was a flat steel grey color. We could see a very light incoming flow of water from the incoming tide. Tidal shallows were dark grey. The shallows were filled with water birds and several species of raptors. The birds were feeding on shells, small fish that got trapped when the tide went out and the tender shoots of new water plants.

Kathleen and I were escorted to a room with a view of the Napa River. The room was gorgeous. Kathleen noticed a gift basket on a small table by the patio windows. Two half bottles of wine highlighted the basket of fresh fruit, candy and snacks. She said, "My, my. This really is the Napa Valley. We have wine and we're not even unpacked."

I walked over to the basket and replied, "Be a shame to let it sit there. How 'bout a glass right now?"

"You read my mind. Again. Pour the wine while I get rid of these road clothes and get cleaned up. Any ideas for dinner? This is our first night in Napa Valley so let's go for it."

Kathleen could start my launch sequence be simply saying she was going to take off her clothes. The actual sight of her taking off her clothes put the launch sequence into no-recall mode.

I poured the wine. Kathleen disappeared into the bathroom so I opened the patio door and found a chair outside. I scanned through a visitors guide while I sipped my wine. The sun was setting on the other side of the hotel so the view of the river was cloaked in shadows. Water birds – gulls, egret, herons and ducks – walked along the banks of the river. I even saw a pair of sea eagles, Ospreys, observing the area from a tall channel marker in the river. Rush hour traffic was well underway on the street across the river, Soscol Avenue.

Across the way the Wine Train was pulling out from its commissary by the river. The Wine Train offers spectacular views of the wine country on its journey up Valley to St. Helena. Terrific dinners, cocktails and wines are offered during the journey on restored cars that are up to 75 years old.

At St. Helena the train reverses its course to return to Napa. The people of St. Helena, who remind some of inbred hillbillies with money, don't permit the Wine Train passengers to disembark and spend money in St. Helena's many interesting shops. They seem to prefer that tourists arrive in cars, usually two per car, and take all the parking, legal and illegal. Jed Clampett and Mr. Drysdale would have been so proud of the people of St. Helena.

St. Helena is populated by wealthy people, mostly default democrats, who fuss about every little thing, are literally terrified by the thought of fast food stores in their city and latch on to every liberal claptrap notion that comes along. This cloistered, superior attitude will be the downfall of their city when things get tough.

While we watched this fabulous scene, Crute took up residency on the bed, legs pointed straight out and went to sleep. After all those days in the car she was very much ready for a nice bed.

Just as I was running low on wine, Kathleen came out of the bathroom. She was wearing a green silk teddy, for years one of the most erotic items I had ever seen and a sure sign that things were looking good for me. Totally erotic, that is, except for the woman's habit of wearing little sock slippers just about all the time she was at home. Long ago I had learned that my wife's little odd habits were, as I saw it, "Part of her charm."

She came over to my chair, picked up the visitors guide and sailed it through the patio doors onto the floor. "We won't be needing this," she said as she settled into my lap.

I put my arm around her and said, "Want more wine?"

She took my glass out of my hand and set it on the small glass end table next to my chair and said, "We don't need no stinking wine."

I reached up to her and kissed her the way I kissed her when we first began to seriously date. Women like kissing more than men do. Something at the core of men allows a single kiss or even sometimes a touch or a glance to trigger the countdown to launch, to sex. Once the countdown starts it's difficult to abort. If it must be aborted, the same switch that stops the countdown trips a darkening mood and sometimes a disagreement.

Women do not see it that way. That is not to say that women like sex less than men do. That is to say that sometimes women simply want a kiss or a hug or both. I bet it's been that way forever, since Adam and Eve. But there's also a hard wired circuit in men and in women that prevents them from understanding this fundamental, age-old barrier between the sexes. Neither sex can understand it. It is sorta like seeing a roadside sign in Chinese and trying to understand the little wiggles and lines and curves. It will not happen.

She said, "Clark, this has been some life. I always thought I would get a job, raise a family, get old and fade away. But everything we do seems to push all that ahead of us while we have great adventures. Why did this happen? I mean, why do you think it happened?"

In my best John Wayne as Rooster Cogburn voice, I said, "Miss Royal, just being with you pleases me. Always has. Always will."

I watched Kathleen smile and I knew she was thinking about that scene where John Wayne's rough and crude character, Rooster Cogburn, and Katherine Hepburn's prim and proper but tough to the core character, Eula Goodnight, sat on the banks of a river in the classic movie, Rooster Cogburn. I always change the line to fit my mood and to say what I think fits the situation. I could tell she thought I'd hit the bull's eye this time. After a moment, we transferred our groping to the bedroom.

Crouton raised her head and gave us a look of resignation. She jumped off the bed and found a place on the carpet near the balcony door.

Kathleen wanted to make a bigger production of sex. My approach was far simpler. I could see or maybe feel the goal and I saw no problem in going for it. Why on earth would one munch on celery when a steaming prime rib was right there on the table? Early on Kathleen would even put on a wig or a teddy and seduce me. She never understood that I take very little seducing. I tend to stay on orange alert status all the time. The reason is simple.

When Kathleen decides to make love, everything on the planet disappears except the two of us. She can focus 100% of her energy and stamina on me, on us, on making love. It tends to get totally out of balance. I think I receive more than I give.

And, that's reason enough for me to stay on alert all the time. But it still isn't the reason. I remain focused on Kathleen and eager for her because she is the single, most interesting, intelligent and curious woman I have ever known. The fact that she is gorgeous doesn't hurt, either.

Kathleen Royal is just over five feet tall. She is totally in command of herself and, usually, everyone within fifty feet. Most women admire her and most men find her fascinating. Back in Kansas one woman, a socially and politically active woman whose time had come and gone totally despised Kathleen. More than one man had attempted to convince her to step outside our marriage. It never had worked.

Two hours later we sipped the last of the two half bottles of wine and began the best part of our lives together, talk - talk about anything. Kathleen wanted to talk about Napa and our new adventure. I was stretched out on the bed. After almost two hours in bed with Kathleen, I was in a state of paralysis so profound I could barely move my fingers. I didn't try to move for I was certain my spine had liquefied. I wondered if I moved my spine if it would solidify in the wrong position - sorta like when my mother told me that if I crossed my eyes they might stick in that position.

Kathleen said, "What will happen to us in this marvelous place?"

Continuing in my Rooster and Eula dialog I replied, "Watch yourself, sister! Everything in these parts'll either bite ya, stab ya or stick ya!"

"Stop it! Get up and get dressed, I'm starving."

I rolled over and said, "After that much hard work I'll bet you eat like a pack mule."

"Are you calling me a pack mule? Careful how you answer, Bud."

I grinned and ducked a round house pillow thrown by my beautiful wife. I ran for shelter in the bathroom.

Ten minutes later I emerged freshly showered and revived. I began getting dressed. Kathleen went into the bathroom to put on her make-up while I made the evening's dinner plans.

As she came out and began putting on her simple black dress, Kathleen asked, "Did you pick a good restaurant? Did you make a reservation?"

"I called the front desk and they made a reservation for us at one of the places in the hotel."

"A hotel restaurant? Sounds boring."

I said, "Toto, you're not in Kansas anymore. This is Napa. The hotel assured me that the restaurant, Celadon, is one of the finest in the country if not the world. Plus, they welcome Crute to their patio. I think your concerns are not worth the effort. Let's go see."

Celadon is one of the Napa Valley's premier mainstream restaurants. The owner began the influx of great restaurants into Napa with the original Celadon, a tiny little restaurant that left no doubt that the Chef knew what he was doing. Locals and regular visitors to Napa place Celadon high on the list of their favorite places for lunch and dinner. It's located on the ground floor of the Napa River Inn complex, around the corner from the hotel's lobby.

We were greeted by a young woman who checked our reservation and took us to a banquette against the wall. The dinner that unfolded that night was memorable. The service, the food and the small touches that span the chasm between going out to dinner and having a great life-bending experience were all there.

Celadon is the only restaurant we know that offers black napkins to ladies who are wearing black. This simple gesture shows that the management knows the value of the details.

I told the first server that we needed 'emergency' Sapphire martini's, shaken not stirred and served up with two olives, The Queens are the best, and just a little 'dirty'. The server returned in minutes with perfect martini's that were served exactly as I had specified.

I ordered Celadon's Flash Fired Calamari. When it was served Kathleen and I immediately fell in love with Celadon's spicy chipotle and pickled ginger sauce. All this was accompanied by a heavenly Phelps Family Meritage.

We began with an endive and pear salad with blue cheese, candied walnuts and honey mustard vinaigrette. Kathleen chose an entrée of a middle east inspired braised lamb shank with golden raisin and almond couscous while I dug into a delectable grilled Kobe flat iron steak with gratin potatoes, broccoli rabe and a blackberry-cabernet sauce. We skipped desert in favor of Illy coffee and glasses of Jack Daniel's Old No. 7 fine Tennessee whiskey over ice.

We left the restaurant completely satisfied and not just a little tipsy. Starting with a perfect Sapphire martini and wine with every course will do that. Not to mention the Old No. 7.

One of the great attractions of Celadon is the hotel rooms are steps away. As long as we would live in the Napa Valley, we would remember this dinner and come back to Celadon again and again.

The next morning we took a walking tour of downtown Napa. As we stepped off the curb from the hotel, we encountered one of Napa's most unusual characters. Robby, a possibly developmentally challenged man in his forties, came zooming by on his three-wheeled cycle. He waved to us and when I waved back, he made a skidding turn and rode back to us. Robby, we later found out always has a cause of the moment. That evening he was dressed in Santa Claus sweat pants, a T-shirt with a short vest and a Giants cap. His cause of the day was inflation. He wanted to talk about inflation and the collapse of the dollar. Kathleen assured him that the matter was in good hands. He saluted and rode away.

CHAPTER THIRTEEN

We settled into a home in the western edge of Napa. The home was in the area called Brown's Valley. It was located on a quiet neighborhood street. The home was much larger than our old home in Kansas City. It had a good sized back yard with an upper lawn area and a pool. I liked the big kitchen. Kathleen was thrilled with the two-level huge master bedroom. Crute took to the entire place. I installed a doggie door so she could go outside to a fenced in area.

I began my job in Walnut Creek and almost immediately wondered if I would live through the commute. It looked like an easy drive on a map but the reality was far different. Traffic congestion began as soon as I left Napa and got worse as I drove south toward Walnut Creek. What should have been a forty-five minute drive took two hours, at times longer. One day the commute took so long I turned around and got back home nearly six hours after I left home.

Kathleen jumped into volunteer work and, in a couple of months, began thinking about taking a position at one of the Napa non-profits. The pay was not great but she was very interested in the opportunities. The job was challenging and it gave her access into the community.

Two months after we arrived in Napa, I got a call from James Berry, our new FBI contact. Berry had been helpful in getting us settled in Napa. He seemed friendly enough. I accepted an invitation for both of us to have lunch the next day at noon at Jonesy's, a long time Napa steak house that's located at the Napa airport. Jonesy's features good food with large portions and a terrific view of the airplane apron.

I took the day off. Kathleen and I drove out to the airport. We parked in the restaurant parking area. Jonesy's is a large open air restaurant. One side of the place is lined with windows so the diners can watch the airplanes come and go.

James Berry recognized us when we entered the restaurant. He was a large man, the type who tends to dominate any room he enters. Berry had large features. He had big hands and a big, open face. He reminded me of a boxer or an ex-football player.

He directed us to a table away from the windows at the far end of the restaurant. It was not a private room but it provided the feel of privacy. It was clear that Jim Berry is a careful man.

Berry is the very image of an FBI man. He favors dark Brooks Brother's suits, white or blue Oxford button down shirts and black wingtip shoes. He always wears a tie. In fact, he was one of the very few men in Napa that we saw wear a tie.

Berry said, "Thank you so much for taking the time to see me on short notice. I hope you're getting settled into your new home in Napa. I put off calling so you would have an opportunity to get settled into your new home and your jobs."

I said, "We are. Kathleen has a new job. I like my work in Walnut Creek but hate the commute. I might find a way to work from home a day or two a week."

Berry said, "That's interesting. Tell me, Clark, are you thinking of changing jobs this soon? You've not been at the one you have for long."

I knew the correct answer to that question but I also knew what was in my heart. I glanced at Kathleen said, "No, I never have been a job jumper so I'll learn to deal with it. I guess I didn't look into commuting from Napa to Walnut Creek deeply enough. It's less than 40 miles but it takes 90 minutes or more, sometimes way more. Back in Kansas City it would take less than 50 minutes I'll get used to it I suppose."

Kathleen smiled and said, "My commute is about ten minutes and two days a week I work from home so I have a fifteen foot commute. I think Clark is a little jealous."

Berry could see that his two charges appreciated humor and were well grounded. He said, "Clark, hang in there. Things might get better before you know it. For now, let me give you a little background."

I noticed that the servers had not approached the table. I was about to mention this when James Berry said, "If you don't mind, I would like to postpone lunch a little and show you around." He stood and motioned for us to follow him to a side door. Outside the door a GEM was parked. A GEM is a small, golf cart-like vehicle that's common around factories and airports. Kathleen got in the passenger seat. I took the rear seat facing cargo shelf.

The sky was clear from horizon to horizon. The river was close by so water birds gathered around the airport property. We saw dozens of he Canada geese near a slough on the east side of the airport. Gulls and other water birds soared high above us.

We began moving away from the airport office and restaurant toward a group of buildings at the north end of the airport apron. About half way to the cluster of buildings, Berry stopped the cart. We were well away from anyone or any structure.

Berry said, "Folks, there's something that I have to do, I mean I need to make sure you're committed to what lies ahead. Are you?"

Kathleen replied, "Jim, if I may call you that, if the assignment is along the lines of what Ken Stremming told us, I'm in. Clark?"

I said, "No doubt. I think we have a good idea of what you want and we know we can always call if we have problems. Right?" I was a little more cautious that Kathleen.

Berry started the cart and began driving north toward the buildings. I noticed seven or eight small airplanes, mostly red and white twin engine Beech Barons, parked neatly in from of the largest building. Men in mechanics' dress were working on two of the airplanes. Berry explained that the airplanes are used for training by Japan Air Lines. JAL had maintained a training facility at the Napa airport for years.

Berry drove past the airplanes and around on the north side of the buildings. The northernmost building looked like a utility building because there were no doors or windows to be seen. Berry approached a small ramp that looked as if it led to a basement. The ramp was on the side of the building away from the airport buildings and the road. As we approached the heavy roll up door, Berry dialed a number on his cell phone and the door began to open.

Just inside the door stood two heavily armed men in black FBI assault team uniforms. Berry drove into the basement and about a cart length past the two men. He parked the cart in a slot that was marked, SHORT TERM. One of the men said, "Mr. Berry, you are cleared to enter. Please identify the man and woman with you now."

Berry reached into the cart and retrieved a small leather portfolio. I noticed that as he reached inside the cart the second man lowered his HK G38C automatic rifle from the alert rest position to the ready position and intently observed Berry and the two of us.

Berry said, "Gentlemen, you'll find everything in this package and now I think you want me to say, 'Able Eta Victory'. Am I right?"

"Yes Sir, you are cleared to continue to the access marked, SFBay99". The man indicated a door about thirty feet across the basement.

"When you approach the door wait five seconds then open the door in one motion. Step inside. First, however, may I have your guests' cell phones?" I looked at Berry and he nodded. Kathleen fished her phone out of her purse and reluctantly handed it to the guard. I did the same.

"Thank you, and have a good day," He again pointed towards the door.

Berry led the way to the SFBay99 door, waited the specified five seconds and opened the door. We stepped into an elevator cab and let the door close behind us. There was no sensation of movement. Ten seconds later another door opened, this one looking like a standard elevator door. We left the elevator and found ourselves in a corridor lined with several doors. Above each door was a red light. Another armed sentry told us to proceed to the fifth door on the right and to wait outside the door until the red light changed to blue.

Kathleen and I walked side by side. We had no idea what to expect as we walked down that hallway. We took our lead from Berry. We stopped at the SFBay99 door and waited.

When the light above the door changed from red to blue, we stepped across the threshold into a hall way that lead toward a corporate-style conference room with a large table, leather bound chairs for twelve and the usual audio visual equipment.

We knew we were underground but the conference room had lighting and other effects that made us think we were above ground and almost out in the open.

Two men were talking in the hallway just outside the conference room when we walked by. One of the men, the older one, was very emotional when he said, "Joe, this is the most damn fool thing I ever heard of."

We learned later that the speaker was George Brenneman, a Saint Bernard type of guy, about six feet six inches tall, a little paunchy and very jowly. His suit was baggy and badly in need of a trip to the cleaners. I could imagine a briar pipe sticking out of his mouth. We were to learn that he had spent his entire career with the FBI, mostly in second banana roles where he played opposite aggressive and driven leaders such as Jim Berry. Brenneman was the epitome of a government bureaucrat.

Brenneman was speaking to a younger agent, Joe Bruning, a tightly drawn, smaller man who stood and carried himself like an athlete. He hardly ever stood still. He bounced on the balls of his feet as if he was ready to run or fight or whatever. His hair was cut very short so it looked like the hair of a Marine who was a week past haircut time. He wore an Ivy League tan suit, blue shirt and repped tie.

Joe Bruning stood impatiently waiting for the older man to stop talking. When the man finished his tirade he said, "Dammit, George, give this a chance. Kansas City had very good things to say about these people. The bureau's history is very positive on the Volunteer Program. Calm down. Berry's too smart to make a mistake. Let it play itself out. Relax."

The older man leaned toward the younger man and said, "Don't you tell me to calm down. I think Berry is making a big mistake. Too much is at stake to bring civilians into this office. Busting liquor stores and petty mob mutts is one thing. We have the nation's security at stake here."

Bruning said, "All I'm asking is for you to give it a chance." Bruning grinned and gave the older man a playful punch on the shoulder. "I will, too, tell you to calm down if I think you need it." Bruning was smiling when he said that last part. He continued down the hall.

Kathleen and I looked at each other. Obviously, the two men had been discussing us. James Berry cleared his throat uncomfortably to acknowledge the open disagreement between the two men.

We entered the conference room and James Berry directed us to seats one end of the table. Soon a woman entered the room. A moment later, George Brenneman entered the room as well. Berry rose and said, "Clark and Kathleen, this is

George Brenneman and Kerry Blount. George heads the local office of the FBI. Kerry is in charge of Homeland Security for the North Bay area. She's on assignment from the FBI, so we're all family."

We shook hands. Berry said, "Kerry, this is your show so why don't you get us started?"

Kerry Blount is a tallish woman who looked to be in great physical condition. She wore a dark blue pin striped business suit with a white silk blouse. Her arms and face were deeply tanned. She broadcasted confidence and a no nonsense approach to her job.

Everyone in Homeland Security carries a huge burden. No one doubts that terrorism will continue. No one doubts that something like the tragedy of 9/11 can happen again. And no one wants to have whatever happens be on their watch. She rose and made her way to a large white board.

She said, "It really is a pleasure to meet you. We have some friends in common from your days in Kansas City. I understand you were very good there and we're looking forward to good things from you here, too."

Brenneman snorted and said, "Beats the hell out of me why they're even here."

Jim Berry said, "George, everyone at this table is working hard. Except you, that is. If you're not interested, go find something else to do. If you have something to say, now's the time."

Brenneman glanced at me and said, "Alright I will. With all due respect to our guests, we have plenty of national security challenges to deal with. I just don't see why we need a couple of amateurs to be eyes and ears – especially here in Napa Valley. Hell, we're already here."

Berry snapped, "George, we're going to do this. Tell me right now, are you in or out. By the way, 'in' means totally in. Not just sorta in."

Brenneman raised both hands, palms out in surrender and said, "Jim, I'm in. I'm not comfortable with it, but I've had my say. Just remember that when it all goes south."

Berry rose and said, "If anyone else wants to cover your ass in case this doesn't work, now is the time. George, you need to know that I consider what you just said to be reason enough to ask you to leave. We have done good work together and we need you so I am going to overlook it for now."

Berry settled into his chair and Kerry Blunt continued, "As government officials we interact with the local authorities such as police, sheriff, political leaders and so forth. It's simply not possible for us to actually penetrate very deeply into the community. We need you in North Bay and we need you two in other areas.

"Let me draw a line under what I just said. Early in our Napa experience we were drawn to a man in town, a lawyer who had been politically active. He has a record of enthusiastically supporting community events and causes. You know what I mean, the kind of person who helps raise money for every cause and serves on every board of directors for every non-profit within fifty miles.

Anyway, I approached him about some of our challenges. I was circumspect and even a little misleading just to see what would happen. He assured me that he would be discreet. It wasn't a week before we began picking up on his gossip. He did everything but take out ads in the paper. My point is we need your help. You've shown that you're absolutely discrete and that you can innovate when necessary. Welcome to the team."

Jim said, "George, Kerry just described the mission better than I did. We need these people." George nodded silently but his face remained grim.

Kerry continued, "Now, let's get down to it. Following 9/11, the FBI and later Homeland Security set up a temporary operation at the Napa Airport. At first, the location was designated a redundant headquarters in case something happened to our facilities in San Francisco and Oakland. That still is a goal. But we added another element recently. That element is the creation of an anti-terrorism/anti-crime elite unit for the area. When we get this office up and running we'll consider adding similar offices in key locations throughout the nation.

"I want to try to explain something that even the people in this room sometimes don't fully understand. That elusive little booger is this: what is the difference in garden variety crime and terrorism? Sometimes we think the Bureau gets a lot of traction in Congress with terrorism so they talk about it all the time. After all, Congress is generally clueless. They give money anytime someone yells 'terrorism.' Time and time again someone who happens to be an Arab or an Asian or anyone who is not white and has an Anglo-Saxon name commits a crime and because of that person's race, Washington says its terrorism.

"A lot of the work that goes on in these and other field offices is about defining terrorism. Just when we think we're getting close, something happens that throws us back to square one. For now, however, please let us make that decision. The truth is Kathleen and Clark, bout 99.99999 and all the other nines you want to add is not, repeat not, terrorism. Sure, four or five men of Arab descent cook a scheme to extort or steal or destroy something and we are very quick to brand them as terrorists when in fact they are ordinary criminals who could not talk a grandma out of a cookie. The problem is sifting through all the clutter and finding the one thing that is going to be a big problem.

"Back in the days before 9/11 we thought we knew what we were doing. In fact, we did not. We did not see the indications that 9/11 was coming and even rejected some of the most concrete observations. We knew the terrorists were coming, we knew Arabs were taking flying lessons and we knew about money transfers and tons of Internet, radio and telephone chatter. We knew all that but our mind set was such that, I guess, we were looking for something more tangible. Maybe we were looking for hordes of Arabs on gorgeous Arabian horses riding down on us. Who knows at this point?

"So, your roles here are very much, ah, what can I say, experimental? You did great work in Kansas City. But this assignment will be a little different, a little more hands-on and maybe a lot more interesting I am told that you want that. Am I right?"

Kathleen and I smiled at each other. I said, "Possibly. I thought it was all experimental. Am I wrong?"

Kerry continued, "Not really. Let me put it this way, Clark, I'm certain you remember the suicide down by the river in Kansas City? As I recall, the victim was a small time mobster who was mostly involved in ferrying money from Las Vegas to Kansas City. Sometimes he also carried highly concentrated cocaine. Right?"

I nodded to Kerry and she continued, "You were keeping an eye on a place for Ken Stremming. I mean you were just riding by and letting us know what was happening. You parked and walked by the bar and through an alley. You saw a body under some cardboard boxes behind a Dumpster. You stopped to investigate. In no time you came to the conclusion that a) the man had killed himself and b) he had bomb paraphernalia on him. May I ask how you came to those conclusions?"

I moved around in my chair which at that moment seemed to be heating up. The woman had asked me to tell FBI agents what I had been thinking. I decided to be brief, kind of like Joe Friday would be. I said, "Well, the man was shot in the mouth with the gun positioned so the shot went through his palette and exited out the top of his head. Two geysers of blood, one per nostril, had flowed down his lower face and onto his shirt. I figured that would happen with that kind of gunshot wound. I thought there would be little chance of that happening in a murder. I guess I thought most murder victims wouldn't hold still for such a perfect shot. A murderer might shoot directly into the face, on the side of the head or even in the back of the head. Plus, a murderer, particularly if he or she was angry, would probably shoot more than once. Suicide by two shots is just about impossible. Finally, I figured the act took place right where I found it. The heart keeps pumping for a while in a head shot. The victim had a large pool of blood around him but none under him. The blood pool looked to me to be original and not something that could be formed if the body had been moved.

"I noticed the wires sticking out of his pocket. When I pulled the wires out two blasting camps fell out of his pocket.

I grew up in the East Texas oil field. I know what blasting caps look like.

"That's when I called Ken Stremming and told him I was worried about a bomb. He and Kansas City Chief Joe McNamee had the area cleared just before a bomb went off in a Cadillac in a nearby parking lot. The blast was triggered by the Caddy's starter. It killed a petty criminal who people called Pig Iron."

Kerry Blount saw that I had finished. She said, "I think everyone in the room would agree that what Clark did that day is what we wish all law enforcement folks would do all the time. Your quick thinking saved the lives of the people nearby and got local law enforcement on the right tack. My money says that the local cops never would have tied the wires in the suicide's pocket with the bombing down the street.

"Clark, that's another reason why we wanted you on our team right here. And, Kathleen, your elegant deductions on the liquor scam were ideal. Take it from me, very few people, in or out of law enforcement ever show us that kind of thinking. We're very pleased to have both of you with us." He glanced at George Brenneman and said with a big smile, "Even George is happy. He just shows it in a different way.

"We always fret over exactly what the boundaries are with our volunteers. Should we give them more latitude or less? Where should we draw the lines? What is the difference between the logical pursuit of the facts and wide open free lancing? It's our constant challenge in the Volunteer Program. I have said this before but it is very important to keep in mind, "More than 90% of crimes are solved by someone calling the cops. That is where the old saying comes from, 'Cops solve crime when someone drops a dime'. That someone is usually a family member, lover or close friend. The five percent of crimes that remain are the tough ones. They are the ones who demand creative thinking and exhaustive police work.

"Kathleen, I understand that you're thinking about taking a job heading up a local non-profit Coalition group. The Coalition tries to coordinate activities between the NP's, the non-profit organizations, in the Valley. That's a good idea. It's perfect cover and it'll get you involved in almost everything. If it suits you, go for that job. OK?"

Kathleen said, "OK, Thanks. I think I'm their first choice so all I'll have to do is schmooze a couple of board members."

Blount said, "I should tell you that another agency placed someone in that position a few years ago. The placement was just about perfect. The agency wanted to get closer to a couple of the non-profits because all of us had persistently gotten indications that someone in at least one of the NP's was working drugs in a certain segment of the community. Well, the placement went sour when the person got involved outside the marriage so the marriage broke up. What a mess.

"Clark, it's fairly obvious that you're unhappy in Walnut Creek. Well, thanks to a little push from your Uncle Sam, a position as number two person for a company in Napa, Sterile Specialties, Inc. or SSI has come open. I think you know SSI. They're a leader in your industry. What do you think?"

I was absolutely stunned. I hesitated a few seconds and said, "Kerry, I would take a job cleaning up after the circus elephants to get away from driving to Walnut Creak. This sounds great. What do I do?"

She smiled and said, "First, resign your job and offer to pay them back for any costs that are related to hiring you and so forth. If they accept, write a check on the spot. We will cover the check. I'll call in a day or two and let you know."

I interrupted, "I have to say that you guys can get jobs when there are no jobs, get rooms when all the hotels are sold out and you can do all sorts of stuff that seem impossible to me. Are you sure you need us? I mean I know you have said you do but I am just wondering."

Kerry Blount looked at Jim Berry. Berry responded, "Clark. That is a hell of a good point. The reason, I am afraid, is that we are cops and that limits us very much, especially in a small community like Napa. Everyone knows everyone."

Just then a young man opened the door and handed Kerry Blount two small attaché cases. She placed the cases on the conference table and said, "In these cases are cell phones that you can use for personal calls, whatever." She gave us the two cases and continued, "We can use these phones to contact you and you can call us. But I think you'll find that these phones have some interesting features. Please open the cases and remove the cell phones.

"First, notice the background art or wallpaper."

We opened the phones and saw a typical Napa vineyard scene that held for a few seconds then changed to another scene of the Napa Valley. They looked like ordinary cell phones complete with the Verizon label.

Kerry Blount continued, "When we call, the phones will beep once and the wallpaper will change to a shot of the beach."

George took his cell phone and apparently dialed my number. My phone beeped and the scene changed to a beach shot, complete with a pelican on a wharf piling. I held the phone over for Kathleen to see. I touched the answer button and found George waiting on the other end.

I said, "That's amazing."

George said, "The standard cell phone works wherever there's good cell phone coverage. Some places up Valley have spotty service and in the canyons where most phones won't work at all. But these are satellite phones and will work just about anywhere on Earth, even down here in this basement.

"One more thing. Press the 5 key and the 6 key at the same time then press the green call key. The screen will change to a high definition GPS system. The system works all over the world. We can locate you anytime, any place. If you need help for some reason, we'll be able to locate you quickly.

"And, when you're videotaping for us or just talking to us, we get a continuous track of where you are. When you're videoing a picture, you can narrate what you see but you don't need to describe your location. That'll save time and make the system more secure.

"The new phones use your old cell phone numbers and we've recreated your preferences and address files on the new phones. The switchover is completely seamless."

Kerry Blount took charge again and said, "Now for some photos." A screen was lowered from the ceiling and a projector brought a color aerial shot to the screen. "This shot was taken yesterday at noon. We chose noon to reduce the shadows and get more detail. You can see that this shot covers everything from just south of the airport and going north, to the Maxwell Bridge. I want to show this wide shot to give you perspective on the area of interest.

"The next shot reduces the coverage and shows the abandoned Napa Pipe factory and a large satellite farm just to the south of the old factory. You see that the satellite farm is bordered by some local access roads, the factory, a berm that leads up to the Highway 29 Bridge and the Napa River. The satellite farm and its support structure are what we're interested in.

"Most people in the area have some vague idea of the purpose of the satellite farm. The opinions range from a cable TV business to a phone company long distance center. If fact, this installation is a primary reception area for content that originates all over the Pacific Rim – China, Siberia, southeast Asia and more. Through this facility we can suck up just about everything anyone transmits via satellite, shortwave, microwave or anything else. And, this facility is a primary hub for the DOD secure communications system.

"When the facility was built it was in the middle of nowhere and about as close to the coast as we could manage. The location is ideal. If we were closer to the coast we would have more weather and wind to deal with. The temperature in Napa varies very little and any change is gradual. Sensitive electronics like that kind of weather This is extremely valuable to us, the US government.

"We're concerned about two things. First, this is an excellent target for terrorism. None better. Sure, they can blow up buildings and airliners and we can replace them in time. But if they take out the NWCOC, the National West Coast Observation Center, our ability to read hostile communications would go to almost zero for the time it would take to relocated and rebuild. By the way, the locals usually call the satellite farm Intelsat. The public message is that it's a cable TV site.

"Just about everyone who is actually associated with the facility calls it Newcock, which I'm sure you can figure out for yourself.

"But more importantly to us, we have reason to believe that people sometimes try to get into the facility in ways other than the front door. We think they approach from the Napa River and we think someone inside the facility helps them. We have no idea why or even when.

"About 150 people work at NWCOC but there are usually two or three cars in the parking lot. When Napa Pipe was going full blast our folks parked in the Napa Pipe parking lot and entered through a tunnel to the facility. The entrance was very similar to the one that you entered to come to this meeting. When Napa Pipe closed, the cars in the lot were too obvious so we set up a rental storage business on the grounds. That way our people can come and go without being noticed."

I interrupted, "What does this have to do with us? We hardly know our way around."

Kerry answered, "Clark, the fact that you're new and not used to the area is precisely the asset we need."

She continued, "We want you to purchase a small boat and begin taking your boat up and down the Napa River. Get in the habit of stopping often to look around and explore. Stay in the boat but appear as curious as you can. Some of the time you can ride up to Napa to look around. At other times you might explore the marshes and sloughs to the south or even down to Vallejo to Mare Island.

But about every other trip or so, hang around the old pipe factory and see what you can see. We're almost positive that if anyone is making unauthorized visits to NWCOC, it'll be from the pipe factory or the property just to the south of the bridge. A channel runs between the pipe property and NWCOC. My guess is the channel is the point of entry. A grove of trees between the channel and NWCOC affords excellent cover. It could be that the visitors simply go up the channel, tie up a boat and go overland to NWCOC. The walk would be less than 150 yards. Of course, almost anywhere on the river could be good, too. A railroad track borders the river so maybe someone walks along the track. Who knows where the access point would be in that scenario?"

Kathleen asked, "Where do we get this boat and do we even know how to operate a boat?"

I said, "Unless you have in mind the Queen Mary, I can run a small boat."

George said, "When you get home do two things. First go to Google Earth and become familiar with the area. Look closely. You might see something we've missed. I doubt it, but stranger things have happened.

"Next, go on the Internet to Craig's list and search on boats less than 18 feet long in the Bay area. You'll find one in San Mateo, a 14 foot aluminum boat with a 9 and one-half horsepower Johnson motor, a trailer and lots of fishing gear. Call up and buy it. The money's in your mailbox now. Get a hitch installed on your pickup truck and drive down to San Mateo and bring the boat back. You'll find the boat and motor and trailer to be in top condition. When you get to Napa take the boat out to Sea Ranch, a boat and RV storage place on the western side of the Napa River. Rent a space for a year. Money for that's included in the envelope. Can you begin working on this later today? We'd like to have you on the river in three or four days."

I replied, "Of course. But I do have a question. What exactly are we looking for?"

George answered, "The cameras on your cell phones are far from ordinary cell phone cameras. He took my camera while Kerry turned on a flat screen TV monitor that was mounted on a wall."

Kerry said, "Hold the 2 key and the 3 key down at the same time then hit the green call button. Keep all three buttons down until the screen changes to whatever the camera sees. Take a look at this monitor. George, activate the HD camera and show us some art."

George did so and soon extreme close-ups of my face filled the monitor.

George said, "This HD camera takes video or still pictures if you keep the camera steady. The battery will last about six hours. When you activate the HD camera we can zoom in or out and capture what we want. Nothing is stored on the phone, it's transmitted straight to us. We can change the light sensitivity and even go to infrared if the ambient light is very low – even on a moonless night. We'll text message your phone if we want a closer look at something. De-activate the camera by holding the 5 key down for five seconds.

"Oh, and the regular cell phone camera works just fine, too. Unless you have activated the HD camera, you'll have a normal cell phone camera."

Kerry stood and said, "I think that's about enough for today. We'll be in touch shortly. I hope you'll get the boat and get it set up properly today or tomorrow.

"Go by a local store on Imola, Sweeney's, and pick up some Coast Guard and California Fish and Game books on what is required. Both of you'll need California fishing licenses. Be sure to get a salt water stamp, too. Also, get California hunting licenses, too. We think this is necessary because there could be times when you might have your arms in the boat.

"You'll need life preservers, a first aid kit, a fire extinguisher and a few other items. In case you ever go down to the mouth of the river you'll also need a flare gun and a light that can show red or green. Sweeney's has all this stuff. We don't want to get the local law enforcement involved in any way. If they do show up, answer their questions and move away from the location of the encounter. Contact us for what to do next."

Kerry saw Joe Bruning enter the room with the man they had seen arguing with George Brenneman in the hallway. Blount said, "Clark, Kathleen, this is Joe Bruning. He'll become an important resource for you as time goes by. By the way, if you need to contact Joe, he's listed on your cell phone contacts. If you do call, simple let the phone ring three times and hang up. He'll locate you and make contact or meet you shortly."

Bruning said, "It's good to meet you. Thanks for your help. I won't keep you long today. I'll have more to say later. For now, I want to give you the lineup on law enforcement in the Valley. Let's start with the Napa Police Department.

"The Napa cops are, essentially, useless to us. A majority are brand new recruits who will stay around for a year then move to a better department somewhere else closer to where they live. Living in Napa is too expensive, they say. Actually since most of them are paid not far short of $100,000 and most of their wives work, their whining is BS to me. There's another reason. The senior officers are bitter, mean-spirited and can be very hard on the new guys. For these reasons and others they have no real ties to Napa and seem to care very little for Napa and its people. Their equipment is OK but they have deficits in communications and rapid response. Their ability to solve cases is almost non-existence. A couple of years ago two women were brutally murdered and it took them way too long to come up with a solution even though the solution was looking right at them. They also have the habit of trashing crime scenes which is one reason they took so long on the double homicides.

"Much of this dysfunction can be traced to a long time Chief who simply had no idea what he was doing. He hung around because of a very unusual rule in Napa that makes the Chief pretty much immune to discipline or firing. He finally retired. His replacement is a nicer guy but his hands are tied by the BS the previous chief allowed to happen. Some have said that a couple of staff commanders actually run the department. Avoid the Napa PD if at all possible. If you see them coming, contact me before they reach you. Oh, one more thing, the jealousy between the NPD and NSO is obvious even in the smallest thing.

"Most of what the NPD does is revenuing for the City of Napa. They are constantly searching for technology that will produce lots of traffic tickets and lots of revenue for the city. They have laser speed guns, red light cameras and are looking at speed cameras on the freeways.

"The other cities in the Valley have PD's. Some are real departments and some are pay-for-service setups with the Napa County Sheriff's Office. They're good at traffic patrol and worthless for much of anything else.

"The Napa Sheriff has a very professional operation. They have very good lab equipment and mostly good people to run the lab. If you get into real trouble and tell someone from the

SO that you work for us, they'll know what to do. Call me, of course, but you can rely on the SO for professionalism and intelligent processes.

"If you ask me, the local PD's should be shut down and all the work should be given to the SO. It would be cheaper and much more effective. Just about every budget crisis the cities in the Valley have would be eased if the ineffective PD's went away. Politically, this won't happen but it should.

"Next, Napa has a small railroad, the Wine Train. It's a pretty well loved tourist attraction and even the locals take a ride and have lunch or dinner from time to time. The Wine Train, an actual, federally charted railroad, has a small police force. Sometimes they appear out of nowhere and try to assert themselves. They do have jurisdiction along the track right of way so sometimes they try to takeover auto wrecks on the road that runs alongside the tracks. Ignore them and let me know if you see them snooping around.

"The local District Attorney has a sizeable investigation department. It's made up of ex-cops. They're about the best investigators in the Valley. They've pulled the local PD's fat out of the fire more than once.

"The Napa DA sometimes joins in with several other DA's from other counties to, my words, entrap mail order vendors who probably aren't doing much to break the law. But action against a national business can get a much bigger fine or settlement if the perpetrator is caught in four or five counties. Not long ago they did this to a nice guy who happened to show a knife that was sharpened on both sides in his mail order catalog. It is predatory legalism at is absolute worst. But the sometimes big settlements and fines please the County folks so it continues.

"That DA told me, with pride in his voice, that he had stopped someone from selling blow guns. I looked it up. They were toy blowguns. This DA and his associates in other counties are predators with a capital "P".

"Finally, the California Highway Patrol has an office in Napa and a helicopter base at the Napa airport. The CHP is still trying to recover from a bully who ran the service for years. He played favorites, showed his commanders how to cheat on retirement pay and worse. He has been gone several years but his damage persists.

"California has a history of placing bullies in key positions. Even today just such a bully runs one of the state unions. He blusters, brags and struts. He dresses like he tried on clothes at a store and took home the wrong pile. In my opinion everything wrong with the union can be traced directly to that blowhard. I understand the Bureau has a 24/7 on him. He'll step on his on dick one of these days.

"You know the FBI and Homeland Security have public offices at the Napa airport. Now you know both agencies have not-so-public operations, too. This facility is one of those operations."

Bruning made his presentation enthusiastically. He moved around the room all the time maintaining eye contact with Kathleen or me.

He paused to take a short drink of water and continued, "I suppose you already know that the National Security Agency also has a presence here. I think you know about their huge satellite field on the Napa River. That facility is absolutely critical to national defense. They pretty much keep to themselves so I don't think you'll have anything to do with them. The interesting thing is this: The locals, even the people in the County and the cities, accept the lame explanation that the dishes are part of some routine process. They never have wondered about the dish field or even asked questions about why the facility appears to be run by one or two people. Amazing! Anyway, that pretty much gives you a picture of the local yokels. Certainly not Andy & Barney but more like Jackie Gleason's character, Sheriff Buford T. Justice, in Smokey and the Bandit," he finished with a smile.

Jim Berry stood and said, "Thanks Joe. Let me add a couple of things. First, we are not the police. We very rarely make primary arrests or even officially enter local investigations. Federal crimes are another thing. At the local level we do collect information and pass it along to the local law enforcement agencies."

He handed each of us small boxes. "Inside those boxes you will find several small GPS homing devices. They look like half dollar coins but each has a small red pull tab. If you get into trouble and cannot use your phones pull one of the red tabs. This'll notify us that you need help and we'll know exactly where you are. Also, you can pull a tab and toss the device into a car or other vehicle. You can also leave the device on a bumper or jam it anywhere on the car so it won't be found. It'll allow us track the vehicle."

Berry paused, "I should ask, do you have any questions?"

I smiled and asked, "Jim, I'm just wondering why the FBI and Homeland Security have such a strong presence in Napa. After all, Napa is a fairly backwater place in the scheme of things."

George Brenneman groaned and put his head in his hands. Jim Berry smiled at me and said, "Good question. It has two answers. First, federal cops are like everyone else. We like nice things. So when the word came down to set up an operations center in the Bay area but not in San Francisco, we headed for Napa and its airport. Second, the Napa Valley is small, about twenty- five by six miles. You get all that money and all that power in such a small area and it's likely that something can happen. We want to make sure that that something isn't in any way challenging to the security of the United States."

Brenneman added, "...of America."

At that, Bruning stood, glanced at Brenneman, shook everyone's hands and left. The four of us left the room and began walking down the hall toward the elevator. Jim Berry returned to his office.

Kerry said, "Kathleen, you and I will take this door. George and Clark will take the first door down the hall," pointing towards an identical door just a few feet away.

Kerry and Kathleen went through the door. Kerry pointed to a second door and said, "A small rest room is on the other side of this door. Go in, flush the toilet and walk out that other door. The door is locked so there won't be anyone in the restroom. The door will lock behind you as you exit. I'll be out to meet you in a minute or so. We never enter and leave by the same door. Later, I'll show you other access doors."

Before we got to out designated door, I said to Brenneman, "George, we seem to have really upset you. Tell you what, why don't you and I sit down with Jim Berry and decide, up or down, if we will even be involved. I'd like that because knowing that you don't support us makes us uneasy. We wonder if you'd do something to destroy our efforts or at least makes us look bad."

Brenneman was silent.

I continued, "So what about it, George, up or down? I think we have a right to know. Frankly, I'd rather go back in and tell Berry the deal is off than have to continually second guess your intentions."

Brenneman stopped and put his huge hands on my shoulders. He took a deep breath and said, "Please don't take my attitude personally. I would feel the same about anyone who came into this. Hell, I act this way when a new agent comes on board. Tell you what. You do your best and so will I."

It was clear that George Brenneman was not accustomed to such direct language from a subordinate. He took his hands from my shoulders and took a step back. His right came out for a handshake. He said, "Clark, let's try. OK?"

I took his big hand and said, "I am trying, George. Now let's get gong."

When Kathleen left the restroom, she found me waiting in a hallway outside a large restaurant and the public offices of the airport's fixed base operator. Soon Kerry came out as well. We left the building by the front door and found our cart waiting for us.

George drove around to the front of the airport and dropped us off at our car and the two of them began to pull away. Before he left us George sighed and said, "Clark, Kathleen, I'm old school. That makes me very cautious about having you here with us and having you know our strategies and our tactics. I won't get over that anytime soon." He's said what he had to say and then drove away.

Once in the car, we sat for about a half of minute before Kathleen broke into a fit of giggles. She said, "Secret elevators? We can't leave by the same door? I feel like we've just stepped into a Maxwell Smart episode!"

All signs of laughter gone, she continued, "Seriously though, this is different. Very different. But I'm ready for it for two reasons. First, I think it's the right thing to do. Neither of us joined the military and both of us have regretted that. At least I regret it.

"Second, it means I'll get to spend more time with you. You not having to endure that endless commute to Walnut Creek will give you at least two hours a day and whatever we do on this assignment we'll mostly do together. I'm definitely up for it."

"Me, too. Same reasons. For now though, I'm starving. Let's get some lunch and then go home and start working on the boat and the other stuff."

After lunch at Villa Romano, an old time Napa restaurant near the airport, we drove home. Kathleen got the mail and I got busy on my computer. Within twenty minutes I'd purchased the boat and had made arrangements to take ownership of the boat the next day.

When Kathleen had come in with the mail it had included a letter from an "audit" company with an address near the Napa airport. When she opened the enveloped she found a stack of money, mostly in 100's.

I said I would go get a trailer hitch installed on my new truck and then stop by Sweeney's for the accessories and needed items. I made a shopping list and added a grease gun and a couple of tubes of marine grease to the items that Kerry had mentioned. Kathleen said she would spend the rest of the day making the calls to line up support for her new job.

I returned home with all the boat items and the regulations for operating a boat on the Napa River. Because the river connects to a tidal estuary and is brackish, some of the rules for boats on the open seas apply. I took a seat in the family room and began reading the regulations.

Kathleen came in the room and brought me up to date on her job progress. She said, "I'll know for sure tomorrow but it looks as if I have all the support I need to be offered the job at the Coalition. There's a small problem. One of the key board members, a local banker, always has to lead the parade. Because I was not his idea, he might resist. I think I'll ask Jim and Kerry for advice. What's your plan?"

I replied, "I'm going to go through all the regulations. Then we need to go back to Sweeney's and get our fishing licenses."

Kathleen and I drove to the sporting goods store and bought a basic supply of fishing tackle and our fishing licenses. As we walked back to our car, Kathleen said, "Let's go over and get an ice cream cone at the Rite Aid."

I had never known my wife to want ice cream but I agreed. As we approached the store, Kathleen said, "I need to talk about something, Clark. Are they listening to us?"

I said, "Sure they listen to us. At least, I think they do."

"No. I don't mean 'are they paying attention'. I mean, are they bugging our home and cars, you know, *listening?*" she said with emphasis.

I walked several steps and said, "I have thought about it. I suppose it's possible. Actually, if I was in their place, I would. They have shared an awful lot of stuff with us. If we weren't loyal and honest with them, we could do a lot of damage."

"I agree. I guess I just wondered. I don't really want ice cream. I just wanted to get away from the car so I could ask you that."

I smiled and said, "Well, I do. I want butter pecan. Come on. Live a little."

CHAPTER FOURTEEN

Three days later the boat was ready for use. I had driven down to San Mateo to pick it up, then spent a day servicing the motor and the trailer wheels. I installed a small commercial sonar on it. The sonar would let us know the depth of the water and it could even identify fish in the water. As instructed, I rented a storage space at a boat yard at the river.

Saturday morning we made preparations to launched the boat on the Napa River with the intent of heading up stream. A few people were fishing off one of the docks. They seemed to think that my first attempt to back a trailer was hilarious. Kathleen was a big help. When the trailer got off center she would yell at me, "No. No. Turn the other way."

I would yell back, "Which other way?" Crouton barked and did her best to help.

Her response would be something like, "The trailer isn't going straight. Turn it the other way."

Again I'd say, "Which other way?" It went on like this for several nerve racking minutes.

The people on the dock were laughing out loud. I was pleased to make them so happy. Eventually, despite Kathleen's help, I got the trailer lined up and the boat in the water.

The river was at high tide. The dark green water was like glass. Only the bigger reeds stuck out of the water. The top speed of the little boat and motor was about 8 miles per hour. We slowly moved up the river. Our progress was hampered somewhat because the receding tide plus the southerly flow of the river put a strain on the little motor.

Crouton found a place in the boat. Dressed in a bright orange life vest, Crute quickly became a part of the boat ride.

We noticed that every 100 yards or so we could see where fishermen and others had camped on the river banks. As we approached the slew that leads up to NWCOC, the little camps and abandoned lawn chairs grew more common. I could see that anyone could tie up a boat and walk overland to NWCOC.

Kathleen turned her cell phone camera on and began taking video pictures of the south bank of the slew. I slowed the boat and turned to enter the slew that lead to NWCOC. We passed under a small railroad bridge and entered an open water area several hundred yards long. The slew narrowed at the east end. I slowed almost to idle and steered the boat into a waterway that was less than ten feet wide. It was lined with aquatic plants. Here and there we could see where animals or, maybe, people, had crushed the plants. Kathleen said "Any of these places could be signs of entry."

In a few minutes we came to the edge of the overgrown, wooded area that formed the north boundary of NWCOC.

We followed the waterway for another hundred yards then turned back when the water got very shallow.

Kathleen had kept up a running commentary as she swept the river banks with the camera. As the boat reentered the Napa River, she stopped her filming and said, "There's no doubt that boats can, and do, get close to NWCOC. There are signs all up and down the slew of boats having landed. We've no idea why they were there or what the people in the boats were doing. It certainly appeared that they were fishing.

"The interesting thing is that once you're in the slew, you're pretty much invisible from anyone on the river or even on the maze of roads that line the river. You could get to the woods near NWCOC without anyone seeing you. It's a perfect setup for getting close to the installation.

"On Google Earth the slew seems to go all the way up to SSI. But the water gets very shallow and the channel is narrow and overgrown. There's no easy access from that end of the slew. I know a commando or someone like that could make it, but ordinary people would find it very difficult."

I added, "Our time from the launch pier to the slew by NWCOC was about 30 minutes. I think it would take a boat this small or maybe an inflatable like a small Zodiac to get close to NWCOC. The larger boats absolutely cannot make it. I think we should look for boats that have so-called jet drive motors. They would be mostly immune from getting tangled up in weeds and muck. Mercury and others offer those kinds of outboard motors."

Kathleen nodded then said, "That's it for now. Why don't we go on up the river a few miles, maybe all the way to Napa?"

Forty-five minutes later we slowed the boat to take a look at downtown Napa from the river. A construction boom in the downtown area cluttered our view with cranes, bare steel and aluminum construction materials. Geese and ducks clattered after our boat in hopes that we might have some tasty morsels for them.

An hour and a half later we were taking the boat out of the water and getting ready to go home.

CHAPTER FIFTEEN

The Napa Valley has been a beehive of activity for centuries. Long ago Wappo Indians claimed the Valley's rich bounty of fish, game and almost perfect agricultural opportunities. Then came Italian, Asian and middle European settlers who were mostly interested in food crops, stone fruits and ranching. Some began growing grapes for making wine. In the northern reaches of the Valley mining became a big factor in the Valley's economic picture. Gold mining never amounted to much but cinnabar mining was very productive. Mining, processing and shipping cinnabar, the ore that contains quicksilver, known today as mercury, continued until the close of World War II. During the war, mercury was a critical materiel. It was used in electronics and in munitions fuses.

Late in the 19th century the Valley joined the Industrial Age. The Napa River was lined with tanneries, leather goods processing, small factories and food processing plants. Ranching, agriculture and feed mills continued to employ many of the locals. The river was perfect for transporting Napa's bounty to deep water harbors and railroads at San Francisco and Oakland.

Ship building and maintenance facilities in nearby Vallejo and Richmond employed people throughout the Bay area. Many of the ship workers chose to live in Napa because it was close to work, yet it had the feel of being in the country. World War II turned the shipyards into vital centers of national defense. Napa and the surrounding area enjoyed strong growth as more and more people from the ship yards moved to Napa. Some shipbuilding began at Napa. The US Navy moored ships and submarines on the Napa River to prevent sabotage and to protect the ships from bombing by the Japanese.

After the war, Navy retirees and others came to Napa to live. Napa became a city of older blue collar workers and retired military. Those folks influenced the development of Napa all the way into the 1980's, about the time that wine moved into the spotlight in the economy of the Napa Valley.

When the huge Mare Island shipyard in Vallejo closed in 1996, thousands of jobs were lost. This event touched off a negative, skeptical attitude that pervades the minds of long-time citizens of Napa. They trust no one and they especially don't trust the government, any level of government. This negativism has held back progress in Napa and much of the Napa Valley.

Vineyards and wine making had been a part of the Valley's economy for two centuries. In the 1970's, thanks mainly to aggressive families who understood wine making, Napa burst onto the world stage as a center of excellent wines.

In 1976, the so-called Tasting of Paris or sometimes known by the more sinister term, Judgment of Paris, told the world that Napa could produce wines that equaled or even bettered the revered French wines. Two Napa wines, a red and a white, outscored classic French wines. That event forever changed the Napa Valley almost overnight. It's clear today that the event might have been staged for publicity by French commercial interests. Nevertheless, the publicity found traction around the world and Napa became a world wine capital.

People have enjoyed vacationing in Napa for years. Wine tasting, wine drinking and wine buying were the centerpieces of these vacations. But after that incredible wine tasting victory in France in 1976, travel to Napa became a requirement for the emerging class of Americans who doted on great food and even better wine. Julia Child created this class of people with her landmark television show, The French Chef in 1963. In no time, watching Julia Child on public television and buying her cookbooks became a cult-like pastime. Winegrowers and producers throughout California responded to the new interest in wine. Basically, there were two responses from California wine producers. In the central valley and along the coast, winegrowers went for bigger and bigger containers and lower and lower prices. Half gallon jugs then gallon jugs then multi-gallon boxes of wine filled retail wine sections as wine moved from fancy wine shops into grocery stores and even drug stores. Almost overnight restaurants from Denny's to the haute cuisine places in the big cities began to offer red, white and rose wine in single glasses. The public was not aware that the servers drew those wines from five gallon bladder lined cardboard boxes. Many wine drinkers had never purchased a standard sized bottle of wine.

During the anti-war era in the 1960's and into the 1970's, young people at colleges all over American could be seen with the distinctive jugs of Almaden wine and the various Gallo and Franzia packages of wine. These winemakers and their customers thought of three basic types of wine, red, white and pink. They weren't interested in grape varietals and the other arcana of wine. In fact, much of the wine in those big bottles and boxes were made from table grapes such as the Thompson Seedless grapes. Production was done in central valley factories in Modesto and other central valley cities. The wine almost never came from the smaller, classic wineries.

On the other hand, the growers in the North Bay area, including Sonoma, Mendocino and Napa focused on higher quality, standard sized wine bottles as well as higher and higher prices. They built small wineries and set up standards and testing for their products. Mimicking the French and Italian winemakers, they focused on specific varietals and even convinced the State of California to legally recognize "appellations" or areas, sometimes tiny areas, where grapes were grown and transformed into wine.

In short, the central valley wineries tapped into America's youth and those who had yet to develop a taste for real liquor. Wine was a step up from soft drinks and beer in terms of sophistication and alcohol content. At the same time the Bay area wineries, particularly those in Napa, latched onto Julia Child's coattails and began selling better and better wine at higher and higher prices.

The Napa Valley never let the wine people down. It provided unequaled vistas, breathtaking settings with small, hospitable wineries and wine tasting and, before long, world class restaurants.

If one is in the Napa Valley, it is by choice. No freeways or Interstate highways travel through or even very close to the Napa Valley. The closest Interstate highway is twelve miles from the south end of the Valley and a good thirty from the center of the wine area. If there ever was a destination, especially a destination for people with money, it's the Napa Valley. Nearby Sonoma and even Mendocino also work hard to build wine tourism but it's the Napa Valley that is the talisman, the true reward for food and wine lovers. The central coast wineries from Santa Barbara to Gilroy also offer wine and wine tasting, but those areas do business because they're closer to Los Angeles or San Jose or other big population places. Plus, Interstate highways flow right beside the wineries in those areas.

Robert Mondavi, the man whom some say got the whole commercial wine thing started and got Napa moving in the direction of becoming America's favorite wine destination, was quoted in a book about his family, The House of Mondavi, The Rise and Fall of an American Wine Dynasty, as saying, "One bad wine hurts everyone in the Valley. One good wine helps us all." Whether he actually said that or not, winemakers in the Napa Valley worked long and hard to produce better and better wine.

To some, the Napa Valley is like a stack of three discs that share one spindle. The bottom disc, by far the largest, turns slowly with the easy lassitude of family life, retirement and ordinary living. These people built Napa and nothing anyone does can remove the signatures that they left on the City and the Valley.

The middle disc is smaller and turns faster. It turns with the energy of change and the dynamism of innovation and the certainty of people who know what they want and how to get it. The hotels, great restaurants and the shopping were plopped down in the middle of the gorgeous Valley by the people on the middle disc. Theirs is a world of deals and development and making money, big money.

The conflict lies with the people who ride on the bottom two discs. The big disc people blame the middle disc people for the traffic, the loss of a feel of community, the constant changes – good and bad – and they despise the people on the uppermost disc.

The disc on top of the stack turns the fastest. It is the smallest disc. It's the tourists, the wine lovers and the foodies. They come into the Napa Valley and leave the same day or maybe two or three days later. They leave their money in the Valley and they go home, already planning another trip to this Mecca of food and wine. The fact that the Napa Valley sits just above San Francisco, one of the world's premium tourist destinations, is the icing on the cake that makes the Valley so attractive.

Kathleen and I began to become more and more acquainted with all three levels of these discs as we settled in to our work routines. Kathleen dug in at the Non-Profit Coalition and me at Sterile Systems, which turned out to be owned by a French company. She found her job at the Coalition to be very frustrating. Just about every NP in the Valley could use help – financially, administratively, with purchasing and simple management. Most took their problems to Kathleen, expecting sympathy, but none would make any substantive changes.

I found many of the same problems at SSI. The French owners swept in from time to time and ordered changes in this and that. When they went back to France, things settled down to the same old status quo.

Still, we were happy in the Napa Valley. The climate was close to perfect. Terrific views were around every corner. The people were friendly, if somewhat closed to new thinking. We thrived.

The Napa Valley makes thriving easy. The Valley offers an overdose of God's eye candy. Every season surpasses the last. First, in the late winter, brown and stark vines on the rain fed fields of green grass interspersed with the inevitable yellow mustard. In spring, everything is green and the vines begin to slowly come to life with buds filled with the expectation of another growing season. The summer is dominated by miles and miles of vines heavy with pale yellow and deep purple grapes. Summer gives way to fall and its coppery reds, brilliant blacks, oranges and every other color the creator has in mind. In the fall Napa rivals anything Vermont or Colorado has to offer. All year long the vineyards seem to change hourly as the sun passes overhead. Shadows, bright sunlit areas and the symmetry of the plantings engage everyone who takes the time to drink in the sights.

Most weekends we spent at least a few hours on the boat. We saw that people fishing and enjoying rides on the river are very common on the weekends. Kathleen concluded that it was unlikely that anyone would try unauthorized visits to NWCOC on a Saturday or Sunday. The area just had too much activity then. That left weekdays and nights for any intruders to be discovered.

Curiosity finally gave way to pure fun. We took the boat up and down the river. One Saturday we went all the way north to the famous Napa River Ox-Bow, an ancient cut-off that wraps around the once designated center piece of Napa, Copia, and the American Center for Wine Food and the Arts.

Copia seemed to be doomed from the start. Powerful donors demanded that Copia feature art, mostly the kinds of art that they preferred. They ignored Napa's fame as a wine and food center and turned Copia into an art museum. In the midst of the incredible popularity of the Food Channel, recipe book and magazines and celebrity chefs, they wanted art. They ignored the fact that no one had ever come to Napa to see art. They simply wanted art. Copia died a slow, lingering death that drug out so long that every last cent was spent and recovery was impossible. In the end well-meaning but not so qualified people tried to work out a solution with the debtors and, finally, the bankruptcy court. Their efforts were wasted. The County and the City sat by and let it happen.

Copia never did draw crowds but it did draw attention. It made the papers and the magazines and drew people to Napa. When they got to Napa it took about twenty minutes to see that Copia was a bust. But they stayed and bought wine, rented high-priced hotel rooms and ate in the Valley's restaurants. So, the loss of Copia is a huge deficit to Napa. As the lawyer in the Broadway play, Chicago, said, "You can't bring him back."

Copia might be resurrected but it will not be the same and it never will have the charismatic ability to draw people to Napa. Several groups were vying to buy Copia out of bankruptcy. Unfortunately, the best funded groups were simply trying to get the Copia property and develop or sell off the pieces to profit from the property.

I anchored the boat just off the small amphitheater at Copia. We had beer and chips and talked about the greatness that Copia never attained.

One of the things that I liked the most about my wife was her continuing surprises. I was especially surprised when she said she wanted to run the boat.

I said, "Do you know how? I mean, do you want a quick lesson?"

Kathleen smiled and said, "When will you learn? Of course I can run a little boat like this."

We changed places. I took the forward seat, opened another beer and relaxed while Kathleen steered the little boat back down the river.

After twenty minutes I turned my chair around and began my favorite pastime, looking at Kathleen. She was intent on running the boat when suddenly, her eyes opened wide and she seemed to be trying to speak but failing. Finally, pointing at something up ahead of us she spit out, "Big. Big! Big THING!" Crouton began barking and howling.

I turned and saw an enormous barge about 50 yards ahead of us. The barge was being pushed by a tugboat. It was bearing down us and common sense said that the barge was not very nimble. Before I could react, Kathleen skillfully slowed the boat and steered over close to the river bank. The barge passed. Kathleen winked at me and accelerated back toward the landing. I was always amazed at the range of my wife's skills and particularly her coolness in any kind of emergency.

I've always thought that a person's reaction to surprise was either good or not good and in any case, telling. Some people handled surprise very well and nearly always reacted calmly and correctly. These people usually steer their cars away from trouble and tend to maintain control when things get difficult. Others shriek, throw up their hands and generally lose control for a second or two. These people freeze at the wheel and drive right into traffic crashes. They also tend to be victims. They even marry consecutive jerks. They provide muggers and other attackers the time they need to act. Kathleen, I thought, was definitely one of the survivors who always came out on top.

CHAPTER SIXTEEN

I began taking the boat out, with a friend from work, several times during the week. He was originally from Germany. Like many Germans he was an avid hunter and fisherman. He taught me a lot about fishing in the brackish Napa River.

My friend fished and I pretended to be interested in fishing but kept a close eye on the stretch of the river along the slew that ran beside Napa Pipe. I saw very obvious indications that someone had pulled a small boat up to the shore directly across from the wooded area that ran up to NWCOC. I kept this observation to myself but under the pretense of stretching my legs, stood to see if there was anything out of the ordinary on the shore. Sure enough, I saw a fresh trail of broken grasses running from the slew toward the wooded area. Feigning a sudden need to get back home, we took the boat back to the storage yard and parted ways. The fishing had been slow so my friend seemed to be OK with cutting the trip short.

As soon as my friend drove away, I used my cell phone to contact George Brenneman. I got a familiar message and waited a minute for a callback.

George called within a minute, "Clark, hope you're doing well. What's up?"

"I was fishing around the slew a little while ago. I saw very clear signs that someone had pulled a boat up close to the woods and walked toward the woods. No doubt about it. It must have happened during the night or early this morning because the path wasn't there yesterday afternoon."

George sounded exasperated, "Why didn't you send us photos?"

"I was with a friend, so I couldn't. Anything else I should do?"

"Well, the pictures would have been nice, Clark. Since we didn't get a photo, can you draw a map and show us precisely as possible where you saw the path? With that, I think we can get some good sensors and night optics on the area in a day or two."

"I'll get right on it," The line clicked and George was gone. I drove back home and went to work on the map. I took a photo of it with my cell phone, knowing it would transmit directly to the center and George.

Two days later I read in the San Francisco Chronicle that Homeland Security had arrested three men after a short gunfight on a bank of the Napa River in southern Napa County. According to the article, the men were approaching an access road to the Napa County Airport sometime after midnight when they were discovered and arrested. One of the men was wounded in a brief but conclusive gun battle with federal officers.

The article made no mention of NWCOC, the satellite field or how the federal agents knew where and when to intercept the intruders.

George Brenneman never mentioned NWCOC or the river assignment again. His attitude toward us and our assignment grew more bizarre every time we spoke. We considered discussing it with Jim Berry but decided that Jim was probably very well aware of George's thinking.

Jim Berry took the time to call us and to let us know that the intrusion problem at Newcock had been solved. It was an inside job that was created to bring drugs up the river and place them in secure storage on the Newcock grounds. Dogs were ineffective because the inside people were the dog handlers.

Kathleen and I expanded our lives in Napa. We were encouraged by Jim Berry to continue to work hard to get involved in local issues and, especially the wine industry.

There's an old law enforcement axiom that says: The more regulations the government puts on an industry or an activity, the more likely one will find laws being broken, by intent or by accident.

The maze of federal, state and even local laws that governed the wine business had grown steadily over the years. Basically, the federal government wanted the money that the taxes on alcohol generated. They used 'morality' and pandering to hard core anti-drinking groups to create laws that satisfied two key purposes: more and more tax money and more and more loopholes. The State of California enjoyed the tax money from the wine business but they also wanted control.

One effect of the increase in regulations on the wine business was an evolutionary change in the people at the top of the wine industry. The merchants and farmers who started the business were giving way to lawyers and accountants, most of whom had no idea about growing grapes and making wine. They did know something about making money.

Ordinary people are different from lawyers, especially good lawyers. They think and arrive at conclusions in different ways. If ordinary people are watching a high line for a short time and see blackbirds on the wires, those people will most likely conclude that the birds in the area are blackbirds. Interestingly, most lawyers will say that they see the blackbirds, but will suggest that blue birds or red birds might show up at any time. Most people think in terms of absolutes. Lawyers never do. Science governs much of the thinking and the actions of ordinary people. A foot is always twelve inches, never eleven or thirteen. But a new law is greeted by lawyers as just the starting point for a conclusion. They think that a law is never fixed and it'll eventually depend on 'case law' and not necessarily what the legislature intended.

This fundamental difference in how people think is even more obvious in the difference between farmers and lawyers. That key difference, more than anything else that happened, took the wine business into more and more complex territory. These differences produced turmoil within the industry but it was mostly invisible to the people who purchase and drink the wine.

An interesting article from the space industry recounts the story of a Congressman and a NASA manger discussing NASA's growing difficulties in innovation and project management. The NASA manager, an engineer by trade took the congressman to a huge building south of Houston. One floor of the center area was packed with desks in small cubicles.

Large, windowed offices lined all three sides of the floor. The NASA man pointed to the cubicles and said, "These are the engineers. It's their job to innovate and contribute to project successes." He then pointed to the large offices and said, "Those large offices are for the lawyers who tell the engineers why something won't work. In effect, they cancel each other out.

"I wonder if you know, Sir, that in all the great launches and missions that NASA has done, there was not a single lawyer in Mission Control. When the folks at Grumman designed the Lunar Lander, not a single lawyer was on the team or anywhere near the project. Today, I understand the LDAC-1, the project that will give us a new lunar lander, has more than 125 lawyers on or near the engineering team. Sir, is it any wonder that the project began to slip within days of the start of the project?"

Another factor that changed the wine business was an acceleration of corporate acquisition of high profile wineries. While there had always been corporate investment in wine growing and wineries, beginning the mid-1990's, corporations of all sizes and in many industries decided to get into the wine business. The products of some of the greatest and most innovative wineries in the business became nothing more than brands after corporate takeovers.

There came a time when there were three kinds of wineries in the Napa Valley. Many of the most recognizable brands belonged to corporations that had headquarters in New York or Montreal or even in other countries. Next were the so-called dot com wineries. This group was made up of mostly smaller wineries that had been bought or started by some of the people who made fortunes in the Internet stock era.

These wineries rarely got headlines and their sales were usually small compared to the better known wineries. In most of these wineries the owners really didn't care about sales and profits. After all, they had lots of money. Some would say they had more money than sense.

The Valley's old time wine growers and winemakers comprised the third group. Increasingly they felt the pressure of competing with the corporate wine companies. They were out marketed, out distributed and outsmarted. They existed because they made excellent wine and that wine had the word 'Napa' prominently on the bottle. When they glanced over their shoulders they saw sons and daughters who had no interest in farming and wine. The young people had gone to universities and returned as doctors, lawyers and researchers.

In many ways these old wine folks, mostly men in their sixties and seventies, felt lonely. They had their backs to the wall. Solutions were elusive. Then came a day when these old men got telephone calls about a meeting, a meeting that could change their Valley forever.

CHAPTER SEVENTEEN

Wine production is pretty much a singular effort. Farmers grow grapes and turn the grapes into wine. To our surprise there are countless associations and groups and clubs for grape growers and wine makers. Sometimes it is difficult to tell them apart.

For almost forty years, a group of winegrowers and vintners in the Napa Valley had met from time to time to share information and to seek solutions to problems. From the outside this group might seem to be treading on antitrust boundaries. In fact, that was not the case. The men who were part of the group, they called themselves the "Founders," never shared proprietary information. That sort of thing was jealously guarded sometimes even within families.

The purpose of the Founders was to maintain an edge by constantly improving the farming, the grapes and the wine – that and influencing legislation at every level in Napa County. A couple of the elected supervisors owed their positions to huge campaign contributions from the Founders. It is no surprise that those supervisors do just about anything the Founders want them to do. The original group was seven men. Over time, the size of the group varied from four to as many as twelve. On this day there were five Founders who were free to meet.

These five had been very successful. Still, none of the five had ever reached the peak of individual winemaking. None had produced a real Icon wine or even an ultra-premium. In fact, every man in the room was jealous and maybe even a little bitter. It would be this jealousy that would change their lives forever.

Sid Zaccaria, now 76 years old and one of the original Founders, always called the meetings. And, he always chose the meeting site. More often than not, Zaccaria chose the Meadowood Country Club, perhaps the Napa Valley's premier social and cultural hotel.

Zaccaria had called this meeting on two day's notice. Usually, he gave the men at least two to three weeks advance notice for each meeting.

One by one the Founders passed the security house at Meadowood, surrender their cars to the valet, entered the lobby and made their way to The Grill, Meadowood's all day dining room and bar. The first one to arrive asked for a table for four. It was customary to have a light lunch prior to the meeting. Sometimes Zaccaria joined them, sometimes not. One of the men motioned the server over to the table. He took their orders for Cobb salads and glasses of wine, three Sauvignon Blanc and one Viogner.

If the others noticed Zaccaria, wearing his trademark Greek Fisherman's cap, sitting on the other side of the room at a table for two with a huge, robust man who looked vaguely middle-European, no one mentioned it.

Younger Russian men, particularly the ones who had embraced capitalism, were far different from their older counterparts from the USSR days. For one thing, they had learned to dress and to appreciate expensive haircuts. The days when Soviet leaders were significantly outweighed by their wives were long gone. The man with Zaccaria was easily six feet six inches tall and weighed around 300 pounds. He carried that weight easily and gracefully.

Seated by a window, having lunch and enjoying a perfect day in paradise, Kathleen and I noted the men as they came into the restaurant and again when they left.

I turned to Kathleen and said, "Take a look at those two across the room, the big guy with the little guy."

Kathleen turned to see Sid Zaccaria and the huge Russian. She smiled and said very softly, "They don't look like the same species. The older man is almost tiny. I think that's mostly because he must be a hundred years old. The big guy is, well, big, real big. He looks foreign, maybe Russian or middle European."

"I'll say. He is enormous. I pick Russia as his home. Unlikely looking pair, aren't they?"

About forty-five minutes after the Founders began having lunch; Sid Zaccaria rose and shook hands with his guest. He left the room and walked down a path to the meeting room. The meeting was to be held in a private room that was known as the Courtyard.

The Courtyard Room is in a small building that's snug against a wooded hillside. There are no other rooms in the building. While doors open out to a private patio, the indoors affords almost total privacy. Zaccaria had chosen the Courtyard for exactly that reason. While there never had been much notice paid by others to the Founders meetings, he always wondered what would happen if the wrong person got wind of the open, free-flowing talks that were typical when the Founders met. The men who attended Founders meeting had great respect for each other and almost as little respect for the countless other winemakers up and down the Valley. No doubt about it, these men despised the newcomers, particularly the ones who turned out the super premium wines that continually attracted the best prices and the most exclusive buyers and wine drinkers. They felt that it was unfair and generally wrong that some dot com zillionaire could buy his way into the levels of super wines.

Soon the other four found their way to the meeting room. As the men took their chairs, Sid Zaccaria rose. This meeting was called for a specific reason, a reason that Zaccaria had not shared with anyone in the group. It was obvious from the start that this meeting would be different from others. For one thing, the table was literally covered with wine glasses. There were eight wine glasses at each chair. Normally, one glass per person was all they ever needed.

Zaccaria waited a few seconds for the small talk to die down. He said, "Gentlemen, thank you for taking the time to be here. I apologize for the short notice but considering all that I'll say, I think you'll understand.

"I'll get to the point. I see two problems or maybe I should say two problems that create one huge opportunity. One could be critical and the other is, well, perhaps a little more practical."

The men shifted in their chairs and look at each other to see if anyone had any idea what Zaccaria had in mind.

He continued, "I'll mention the critical problem first. Believe me friends, what I'm about to say is real. You know that we have all worked hard for forty years to create and protect the excellence of our wine and our Valley. The result has been world-wide acceptance of the wine and of the Valley as one of the world's most outstanding places for wine grapes."

Zaccaria bent and retrieved a folder from his brief case. He said, "I apologize for not handing out copies of what I'm about to read but I think you'll agree that the subject must be carefully controlled."

He slipped on reading glasses and began, "Ten days ago one of my most trusted people came to me in private with startling news. I was totally unprepared for what he told me and you will be, too.

"This paper came to me containing the results of a chemical test. It was sent by someone who wanted me to know these results. I think the testing was conducted in another state under the strictest security. When my man came to me I ordered more testing immediately.

"Everyone in this room knows that in the Napa Valley's distant past, mining was a source of commerce. I suppose that's true of just about any valley in northern California."

One of the men said, "So what's the big deal. Mining and California go together and always have. Are you telling us there's gold in them thar vineyards?"

Laughter filled the room but Zaccaria remained serious. He said, "No. This isn't about gold. It's about mercury."

Tom Fletcher, a winegrower and winemaker in his 50th year in the Valley said, "Sid, this is old news. Why, I read about the mercury content of the old mines around the James Creek and Lake Berryessa in the last couple of years in the Napa Valley Register. Everyone knows about the mercury and one of the ores that contain mercury. What is it? Not silicon, but something like that. I can't recall."

Zaccaria responded, "Cinnabar, Tom. Let me continue. I know the history of mercury mining in the area and have known it for years. The US Geological Survey has talked about it on and off as long as I can remember.

"Let me get back to this paper. Listen closely. Most researchers say the upper limits of methyl mercury, a chemical that's abundant in some of those old mines, is from 0.5 mcg to 0.1 micrograms of mercury per kilogram, per day, of body weight in humans. In case you're wondering, a microgram is real tiny. But mercury is a bad actor. It's a heavy metal poison like lead. It attacks and destroys the central nervous system. There's nothing good about mercury. Many countries have outright banned it.

"I don't want to drag this out any more than I have to. This paper, based on a first class analysis of a dozen wines from the upper part of the Napa Valley, and all the wines were made by the people in this room, out of that dozen tested, seven of them have a high enough content of various forms of mercury to provide a dose of from 0.3 to 0.18 micrograms to a healthy adult person. That's based on consumption of about 8 ounces a day."

The men were dumbstruck but a couple began to argue. Zaccaria said, "Hold on. Let me finish. The really devastating information is from this paper." He pulled out a second sheet of paper and continued, "I ordered testing of soils from sixteen vineyards. Five tested positive, to one degree or another.

The vineyards themselves are contaminated and I'm told the contamination probably goes down way past where remediation is possible. In fact, it's likely that rain runoff continues to bring mercury down the hills and into the vineyards. Even if we could fix it, the crap would return every year."

Zaccaria sat down. Suddenly he looked like a tired old man. He stared around the room at the other men. They were speechless.

Finally, he said, "I have a little more to say before I get to that opportunity that I mentioned.

"First, this cannot leave this room. If one hint of this gets out all of us and every other winemaker in the Valley will be destroyed.

"Second, please don't leave here and begin doing mercury assays. That will only attract attention and lead to our problem becoming public.

"Third, we can ignore this and hope that no one else stumbles onto it. I think we all know that if we know this someone else will, too, sooner or later. Or, we can try to come up with a strategy to deal with it. But remember, no one knew that Perrier water contained benzene once upon a time. No matter that the company did when the cat was out of the bag, the brand of water was a goner. When the benzene was discovered, Perrier was the leading brand of water in the country. It almost disappeared from the market when news of the benzene contaminant got out.

"Finally, I do have a solution but before I talk about it, I need to know that we're united in secrecy. If anyone cannot accept that, please leave now."

Zaccaria looked at each man in turn then said, "OK. We're together on this. Before I show you the light at the end of the tunnel, let me touch on the other problem that I mentioned. Compared to the first problem this one is annoying but not fatal.

"Almost from the beginning of what I'll call the modern era, about the past forty years, a lot of winemakers have attempted to take the step of going public with their companies. We all know that this has been almost uniformly unsuccessful. And, we all know the reasons. Variations in rainfall, sun days, ground moisture and a zillion other things that we cannot control impact the quality, taste and so on of our wines. One year we have a great wine and the next it's not so great. We understand that this is how the business works. But the lenders and the investors, the "wall-streeters" who should understand it but don't, want constantly improving wines. That's not possible and we know it. They should know it but they're not investing, they're speculating. They want the impossible and we're caught in the middle because we want and need their money."

He paused to add a little drama and said, "Gentlemen, what if we could have truly premium, no, super premium wines all the time, every year, forever? What if all the risks were gone? Gone forever!"

The men in the room looked at Sid Zaccaria as if he had grown a second head. Finally, one of them, Larry Arbuzzio, head of three of the Valley's most successful wineries said, "Sid, I think you've flipped. I think you're up to something. I don't know what, but something. First you tell us that some of our wine might be poisonous. Really? If that was true, wouldn't there be people falling off bar stools all over the world? Our wines are consumed nearly worldwide, so wouldn't we have single handedly solved the overpopulation issue?

"I tell you what, Sid, whatever you have up your sleeve must be really good or I'm walking out of here and never coming back."

One of the men, Paul Mortine, agreed. He said, "Sid, I am willing to listen but I'm not promising anything." Mortine was one of two sons of one of the original founders of premium wine in the Napa Valley. Most people thought his brother, James, was the smarter of the two. There was every indication that that consensus was correct. But Paul had always gotten the support of his parents. People in the Valley were fond of quoting Dr. Laura Schlessinger: "Parents always support the slower of two children. Why? I suppose because they think the smart one can make it on his own. Or, maybe mothers feel guilty about bringing a dud into the world."

Two others expressed similar sarcastic opinions. It was clear that Zaccaria was at the point of putting up or shutting up.

He got to his feet and said, "Larry, I understand. Now, come up here and help me pour wine." On a table behind Zaccaria's chair were several aluminum cases. Sid Zaccaria opened one case and began removing bottles. He placed four bottles on the table. The bottles were what the industry knows as 'shiners'. They had no labels. He removed the corks and asked Arbuzzio to help him serve the wine to the others.

He said, "Please, keep an open mind before you taste this wine. There's no need to swirl it. It's ready to drink. Now please sample the wine and see if you can identify it."

The men cautiously sipped the wine. After the first small taste, all the men took bigger sips and smiled as they brought their best wine tasting skills to bear on the wine.

Zaccaria said, "Fine. Now, who can identify that wine?

151

One by one, the men smiled and gave confident looks toward Zaccaria. John Thompson, a winemaker who was heavily invested in modern winemaking methods said, "Sid, remember who we are. This is one of Warren Winiarski's finest cabs. Did you think you could fool us?"

Zaccaria smiled and said, "Before I answer that, John, let's taste more wine." One by one Sid and Larry poured five more wines. Bottle shape gave some clues but beyond that and the color of the wine, the men were on their own.

One by one the men tasted the wines and easily identified them, even the one that almost certainly was one of Mouton-Rothschild's most spectacular wines.

When the tasting was done, Zaccaria took the floor again and said, "Thank you for going along with me. You know, I really do appreciate it. You could have walked out of here and marked this whole thing up to Alzheimer's or some such. I think you didn't do that for three reasons. First, you're my friends. Second, the tasting was kinda fun. Third, you know I'm right about the poor investment mess and what it has done to us. And, maybe there's a fourth reason on this list. Maybe you think I might actually have a solution to the mercury problem. Whatever.

"Am I correct that you all believe you have been privileged to taste six of the best wines in the world? Am I correct?" The men nodded in general agreement then turned to hear more of what Sid Zaccaria had to say.

"And, are you certain that each of the wines was handmade carefully and with love and blended to perfection then aged to perfection for years and years?" Again, the men nodded in general agreement.

Zaccaria leaned across the table and said with an excitement that reminded the men of a Sid Zaccaria of thirty years ago, "My friends, none of those wines existed ten days ago. None of those wines were made from fruit and none of them ever came in contact with a grape or a winemaker until today. None of those wines is a real wine. Those wines were made in a laboratory by an associate of mine who can make those exact wines over and over and over in no time and for pennies. He can make one of those wines, or any other wine, in a day or two and sell it for whatever super premiums go for. If sold at the winery, one of these wines would go for $75.00 to $125.00 a bottle yet the base cost would be, including the federal excise tax, about $4.00. My friend can eliminate the mercury problem from our brands, and maybe even leave the upstart winemakers to deal with it on their land, while we finally make some money. My friend can show us how to produce wine that's so consistent and so steadily improving that we can easily satisfy lenders, investors and wine drinkers.

"Let's take a few minutes now. Enjoy the wines, talk it over and decide if you want to meet the man who made these wines. I'm prepared to drop the whole thing if that's your judgment. But before you make up your minds, remember this: The technology exists and wines like these will be produced by someone. My thought is it should be us. We have the most to lose and the most to gain. In my thinking, I think we're the ones who have the right, the absolute right, to bring this great wine product to the market. Are we in the wine business or the wine making business? Be careful how you answer, because each one leads down a different road."

Sid Zaccaria placed more wine on the table, poured himself a glass and began his classic "working the room" method of getting his way.

CHAPTER EIGHTEEN

Thirty minutes later, Zaccaria again took the floor and asked the others to be seated. He said, "I know you have questions. Before we get to your questions I need to know something. Do you wish to continue?"

The men raised their hands or indicated in other ways that they were interested.

Zaccaria said, "Thank you very much. I know you are trusting me and I deeply appreciate it. Now, I want to introduce someone."

He walked to the door and said to someone outside, "Anapa, come in please. I want you to meet my friends."

The huge Russian from the lunch room entered the room and began shaking hands with the others.

Zaccaria said, "Friends, this Anapa Krasnodar, another of my friends. Anapa is from the Black Sea. His family has been in the wine business for many years. Anapa, I guess that is centuries, am I correct?"

Krasnodar replied in almost perfect English but with a slight accent that most Americans associated with Bela Lugosi, "You are correct, my friend. My family has made wine almost three hundred years. Yes, we have vineyards and facilities in the Black Sea area but also in Austria. I am honored to be with you today. We have made wine for many years. You have made great wine for a few years. Thank you for seeing me today. I am honored."

Zaccaria said, "Now, for your questions, please."

Paul Mortine stood and faced Krasnodar and said, "Well, Sir, I think the real question is three questions. First, did you really make these wines? Second, can you do it again, that is, can you do it consistently? Finally, what does it cost to get started and what is the unit cost, in the bottle?"

Zaccaria smiled at Krasnodar and motioned for him to respond to Mortine's questions.

Every man in the room stared at the huge Russian. He put his head down for a few seconds as if he was thinking about the questions.

He said, "I know you do not mean to insult me when you ask if I truly created these wines. Yes. I made these wines and I made them in a way, how do you say, in a process, that I developed over a period of ten years.

"Of course I can do it again. And, again. I can make these wines or any wine. I can do it over and over and it'll be the very same every time. Give me a bottle of wine and I will make that wine.

"If we work together we will be partners. I would be honored to be your partner. I think Sid has told you that the base cost, bulk as you say, is about $4.00 per bottle equivalent. I mean a 750 milliliter bottle. I'll charge you an additional

$5.00 per bottle and you can sell the wine for whatever you want. Since most of the wines you have before you sell for $50.00 to $250.00 a bottle, you can see that you'll make more money from the partnership. I think you can also see that you can charge those prices year after year."

Larry Arbuzzio took the floor and asked, "I might be skipping ahead but please tell me if, in the partnership, will you produce the wine or will we produce it?"

Arbuzzio sat back down and Krasnodar responded, "I do not think you want the apparatus of my process to be around for all to see. So, I will produce the wine in a facility that I will build close enough to the Valley for convenience, but not so close as to be suspicious. The facility will look like a soft drink plant. The finished wine will enter the current system via truck from my facility to your storage facilities of your choice in Napa County. You will pay for the transportation and, of course, for your own storage. What you do with the wines when they enter your facility is up to you."

Arbuzzio said, "I have a million questions. The more I think about this, the more questions come to mind. Some are just details but some of this just scares the hell out of me.

"You know Sid, if we get caught doing this we'll have destroyed the Napa Valley and ourselves. We'll be criminals. We'll destroy our wealth and we'll destroy our families and friendships.

"Yet, I stand here saying these things but I also think that if we do it, almost all our problems will simply go away."

Krasnodar interrupted, "Gentlemen, please. Let me tell you more about my offer to you today. First, if you say 'No' to me today you will never hear from me again. This offer will not be repeated, ever.

"Second, I will offer each of you two wines, both reds. You can purchase the equivalent of 5,000 cases of one and 9,000 cases of the other. Let's say you price the first at $75.00 out of your warehouse and the other at $60.00. This will give you about $11 million in sales. Your cost will be about $1.6 million, an attractive net gain. None of you have ever done anything that even approaches this large of a margin.

"Also, we will work out delivery schedules. You are to pay my representative the amount due with cash for the $4.00 a bottle-equivalent charge and cash for the $5.00 fee. Payment must be made on the spot with no delays of any kinds. I will ship a two percent overage to make up for breakage and so forth.

"Third, I must have, from each of you, in exchange for not approaching other winemakers anywhere in the world, $2 million in cash within five days of when I ask for it. Cash, gentlemen, no checks, no paper payments of any kind.

"If any of you decides to drop out or if one of you dies, the survivors can select another winemaker who can take the vacant place."

Krasnodar smiled and looked at each man in turn. The he added, "Gentlemen that is my offer to you. You have five days to decide. Mr. Zaccaria knows how to get your initial payments to me." He turned and left the room.

Sid Zaccaria stood and called the meeting back to order. He said, "So, my friends, that's it. Anapa did not cover the obvious. Each of us knows that if we have one or two fabulous super premium wines that we can afford to sell in the mid-range, all our wines will respond. Sales will outpace anything that any of us have ever seen. If we take care to market our new wines properly, we will finally have the money and the prestige that we all want and deserve."

Zaccaria began putting his papers in his briefcase. He looked around the room and said, "I'll see you here in four days. Let's meet earlier, say, ten o'clock. We should be done by noon."

The men filed out of the room. Once they had all left the building, Anapa Krasnodar came back into the room. He and Zaccaria took seats by the fireplace and began to talk. They knew they had two of the men on their side. But John Thompson worried them. Zaccaria shrugged and said, "We'll know in four days."

Anapa Krasnodar was not so sure. He reached for his cell phone and placed a call. Zaccaria watched the big man say something in Russian, then hang up the phone. He smiled at Zaccaria and said, "My friend, we must not take chances. We must be sure. You are correct, my friend, we will know for sure in a few days. I look forward to meeting you and your friends and to getting started when that day comes. You were right to select the meeting for earlier in the day. I think we will have much to discuss."

CHAPTER NINETEEN

Meadowood is located on the Silverado Trail, a narrow, winding country road that offers great views of the Napa Valley. Many wineries are located on The Trail, as locals call it. All those wineries and vineyards have unmarked and uncontrolled entrances onto the Silverado Trail. The Trail can be dangerous if drivers are not paying strict attention. It's an unfortunate fact that many of the drivers along The Trail have enjoyed one or two wine tastings too many.

Twenty minutes after the meeting broke up, John Thompson pulled out of the Meadowood driveway and turned north on the Silverado Trail. Four miles north of Meadowood the road goes through a series of sharp turns. Thompson had driven this route hundreds, maybe thousands of times and he usually punched his Boxster up way over the fifty five miles per hour speed limit.

As Thompson entered the final turn at seventy his mind was on Sid Zaccaria and Anapa Krasnodar. He saw the garbage truck about a half second before he hit the truck's huge garbage bin which was loaded almost to the maximum. In another half second his brain stopped working as the deceleration ripped it to pieces. John Thompson died at the wheel of his car. No one saw two men place a lifeless body in the driver's seat of the garbage truck or set the truck on fire. No one saw them get into the back seat of a BMW seven series and no one saw the BMW head south on The Trail.

Three hours later Sid Zaccaria reached for his ringing office phone and found Arthur Benson, the mayor of St. Helena, on the phone.

"Sid? Art. John Thompson was killed in a wreck on The Trail this afternoon. He slammed into a garbage truck just north of Meadowood. He was by himself in the car. The truck driver was killed, too. It must have been a pretty spectacular wreck; the fire closed the Trail for quite awhile. I know you two were friends and wanted to let you know. John always did drive too fast on The Trail."

Zaccaria hung up the phone and sat staring out the window for a long ten minutes. Eventually, he dialed Anapa Krasnodar's cell phone. The Russian answered on the first ring.

"Anapa, we have a problem. John Thompson died in a car wreck today. It must have happened soon after our meeting broke up."

The Russian replied, "So we do. I think you know you must get a replacement in the next day or two. I do not envy you that job, my friend." The line went dead.

Sid Zaccaria sat at his desk well into the evening. He went over his options and worked on a plan to recruit a new member to their group. He finally narrowed his choices down to two men who sometimes attended Founder's meetings.

Robert Manitoba was the fist to come to mind. Manitoba was a long time Valley winemaker. He and his family had been innovative in the wine business. They had always been more interested in the wine business than in wine growing or wine making. They produced huge volumes of average quality wine from large vineyards throughout northern California. If there was any reason that Manitoba wouldn't be a good choice it would be his age. He was nearing 90 years old. Some saw a failing memory and a failing body. Still, Zaccaria made a note to call Manitoba the next morning.

The second was Kurt Johansen, a giant of a man whose family had been in the wine business for more than 50 years. Johansen was the second in his line to head the business. He made good wines but the truly great cabernet sauvignon had always been elusive. Zaccaria knew that the Johansen family had been struggling financially in recent years. One of Kurt's three sons was pressing for the family to divide its holdings so he could go out on his own. Zaccaria was fairly confident that Kurt Jchansen would see the Russian's offer as a solution to his problems. He might even see that he could give much of the business to his sons and do very well on his own, with the help of Anapa Krasnodar.

CHAPTER TWENTY

The next day's telephone call to Robert Manitoba was not encouraging. Manitoba constantly went back to his early days. He wanted to talk about the way things were in the old days. Zaccaria listened to the old man for a while then politely got off the line.

Kurt Johansen was next. Zaccaria took a different tactic with Johansen. He called to make a lunch appointment, packed his brief case with two bottles of unlabeled wine and drove to Bistro Don Giovanni, a restaurant that was frequented by the Valley's Italian winemakers and was a destination for tourists.

In the Napa Valley wine industry, unlabeled bottles are called 'shiners'. Shiners can be used in pre-marketing tasting and blending and can be common wines that are bottled then labeled for specific customers or even for private labeling programs. It's common to see shiners on the lunch and dinner tables of the Valley's winemakers.

Zaccaria reached the restaurant early and asked for a table somewhat away from the other guests. He removed the two bottles of wine and asked the server to open them and to bring two sets of cabernet sauvignon glasses. Kurt Johansen paused at the door to exchange compliments with the restaurant's owner, then made his way slowly across the restaurant, stopping at almost every table to speak to someone.

Finally, Johansen took his seat at Zaccaria's table and said, "So, Sid, good to see you. It's been a while. What's up?" He eyed Zaccaria with a combination of humor and suspicion.

Zaccaria saw the mixed reaction and said, "All is well, Kurt, I just wanted to see you after, what has it been, a couple of years? But of course I also have something for you.

"But first, let's have a glass of wine." He reached for one of the unlabeled bottles and poured a glass for each of them.

Johansen studied the wine and picked up his glass. Using the technique that has long been mastered by the winemakers in the Valley, he swirled his glass quickly and with enough force that the wine clung to the sides of the glass and exposed itself to the air. He sat the glass on the table and let it stop swirling. Then he picked up the glass and held it so his nose went deep into it. He took a deep breath and held it for several seconds.

Veterans in the wine business chuckle when they see an amateur insist that by opening a bottle of wine a couple of hours before tasting it, the wine will 'breathe'. This, like so much of the wine lore, is considered to be nonsense by the people who truly understand wine.

"Why, Sid, if I didn't know you so well I would swear this is a late 90's Margaux. You haven't been up all night soaking labels off that stuff have you?"

He took a sip and let the wine caress his tongue and spread to the corners of his mouth. "You can get into big trouble doing that, you know." A smile spread across the man's face and he said, "Sid this is real fine wine. I never have made a wine this great and I thought you hadn't either. Congratulations." He extended his hand for a handshake.

Zaccaria was beaming. He said, "Before you give me too much credit, give this one a try." He poured small amounts of the second wine into the second set of glasses.

Johansen repeated his time-tested tasting ritual. When he sat the second wine glass on the table, a troubled look crossed his face.

"My friend, what are you up to? We're in a very popular place and you have quite obviously taken someone's excellent wine and removed the label. This second wine is a Winter NV cab, probably the '05. I'm sure of it. Why are you presenting these as shiners?"

"Now Kurt, you know me better than that. But, you know, your reaction says it all. Are you sure you want to know what I have in mind?"

"Of course I do! You can't drag me out here and play games with me."

"I have no games in mind, Kurt. I'm very serious. But before I let you in on all this, I must insist that you will not speak of this to another human and you will not make judgments about me or what I have to say until you have thought about it. If you cannot do that, especially the secrecy part, let's enjoy lunch and some great wine."

Johansen stared at Zaccaria for a long moment. He took a sip of the second wine and said, "OK. I'll agree to it. Let's get on with it."

Sid Zaccaria leaned forward and in a low voice, almost a whisper, he said, "Kurt, neither of these is wine."

"What? What did you say?"

"I said, neither of these ever got anywhere near a grape or a winery. Someone made them. That someone does not have a vineyard or a winery or even any relationship to the wine business."

Johansen's face turned pale. He stared first at the wines then at Zaccaria. Finally, he scanned the room. Satisfied that no one was eavesdropping, he said, "Sid, what have you gone and done? Have you lost your mind?"

"No, actually I think I found my mind." Over the next twenty minutes he outlined Anapa Krasnodar's proposal. With every detail, Johansen showed deeper interest. He began to ask questions and Zaccaria knew Kurt Johansen was in.

The meeting continued another hour. As they left the restaurant, Sid Zaccaria said, "Kurt, I need to know if you're in no later than tomorrow morning. And, I need to know that if you decide this is not for you, you will honor our secrecy agreement." Zaccaria's demeanor was totally serious.

Kurt Johansen stopped and turned slowly to Sid Zaccaria. He paused then said, "What's to think about? I'm in or I'm out? Most decisions in life are not that simple. If I'm out. I guess you and others will dominate the super premiums completely. Guys trying to do it the hard way, with grapes and all the work won't make it. You will. I want to make it. Of course I'm in." With that he turned and walked away to his fifteen year old F-250 pickup truck. The old truck hesitated then started. Johansen drove down the driveway and back toward his winery. Zaccaria stared after the truck and then into the western sky. Was this the beginning or the end? He had never done anything that he though might hurt the Napa Valley. This Russian's plan had that potential. But oh, what could be accomplished!

He walked to his own car and muttered to the wind, "It is started."

CHAPTER TWENTY-ONE

Sid Zaccaria called Anapa Krasnodar soon after the meeting with Kurt Johansen. The Russian took the news calmly. He told Zaccaria that he was pleased. He proposed a meeting the next day to "sort out the details."

Sid Zaccaria placed the cell phone on his desk and walked out to his stone deck. The deck overlooked almost all of the Napa Valley. The old man searched for familiar landmarks. His body was trembling at the thought of what he had just done. The reality was beginning to dawn on him.

But Zaccaria was tough as well as realistic. As he gazed across the Valley a justification began forming in his head. He thought about how Robert Mondavi had joined ranks with Olympia brewing to accomplish the break away from his brother, Peter. He considered how many of the Valley's top wineries had been bought in recent years. The purchasers were huge corporations that were located back east or, worse in Canada.

He ruminated that the big corporations were run by people from distilled spirits backgrounds or even from packaged food companies. To them, everything was a "brand". Even a top quality wine like Mondavi's Opus was, to its current owner, was just a brand. Rather than try to make better wine, those guys simply sat around analyzing sales and "repositioning" wines and wineries. One even bought a quality winery then, a year later, sold the winery and the vineyards but kept the "brand."

The corporate people persisted in thinking in terms of brands, not hand made wines. They considered wines the same way they thought of cereal or shampoo or any other grocery store product. A box of corn flakes was the same no matter who produced it. So a bottle of wine was a bottle of wine, whether it was Screaming Eagle or Two Buck Chuck. The heavy lifting, they reasoned, was in the advertising, marketing and distribution. It was clear that most of these people had no personal appreciation for the wines. They were eastern raised so a Canadian Club and Seven-Up was their beverage of choice.

They quickly stripped the romance out of every brand. Winery tours and tasting facilities were scaled back or even eliminated. The Valley's long established tradition of no cost "sip of wine" tasting was morphed into $5.00 to $25.00 tastings where the wineries poured quarter or half glass portions. Way too many visitors were totally wiped out after they visited two or three wineries. The specter of DUI arrests, car wrecks and fatalities soared. Tastings became drinking-a-thons.

The corporate managers preferred to let the Valley's farmers take the risk on growing wine grapes. They let others take the very expensive risks on wineries. They simply bought wine and sold it as their "brand."

All that began in earnest with Heublein, a liquor company, bought a large quality winery, Inglenook, only to abandon the winery and put out factory made wine under the winery's product brand names. Inglenook became a brand of jug wine and cheap jug wine at that.

Those corporations would wring every last dollar out of a wine brand then abandon it or sell to some unsuspecting dot com zillionaire who never would know the difference – or care.

Worse, in Zaccaria's thoughts, was the explosion of "wine tasting" retail outlets in Napa. Napa's many empty store fronts reopened as multi-winery tasting rooms. This very clever strategic move took visitors away from the wineries where the corporate thinking did not want visitors in the first place. He believed the wine tasting stores to be the ultimate trashing of his beloved wine Valley.

With these thoughts in his head, Sid Zaccaria set about making arrangements to get this project on the road. His final thought was that he was no worse than the large corporations.

CHAPTER TWENTY-TWO

Zaccaria returned to his office, opened a bottle of one of his top cabs and began to make notes on his next steps. He filled two pages of a pad with notes, questions and ideas.

He was sipping his wine, deep in thought, when his cell phone rang. It was the Russian. Sid said, "Good to hear from you again, Anapa."

The Russian replied, "Cut the bull shit, Sid. This is about business. Do you plan to get your guys together and move this along or have you chickened out?"

Sid answered, "Anapa, we just got the group together yesterday. I need a little time."

"Time is money as I think you Americans say."

Sid was exasperated. He said, "Well, I've been working on it. I have a list of things we need to know."

The Russian exploded, "You dumb shit, tell me you have not written anything down about this project?"

"Well, that's how I work. I've always..."

"Forget always. This is now. Destroy those pages and the pad under them. Then call me back and I will tell you what you need to know." The Russian slammed the phone down and called his Russian bodyguard.

"Anoly, get over to that man's home tonight and do something that will get his undivided attention. He's an old man. He and his wife are usually in bed by eight. Don't touch them and for God's sake don't be seen by anyone. Kill a dog or burn a nice car. Whatever. I want to impress on him that we're not fooling around. I want him to find out what you did tomorrow morning. Leave no other signs. Call me when it is done."

CHAPTER TWENTY-THREE

Sid Zaccaria called the Russian less than an hour later and said, with an edge in his voice, "OK. I am ready to hear what you have to say."

"Listen to me, my friend. Do not take an attitude with me. Not now, not ever. I am going to make you rich. All you have to do is sit there and behave yourself."

Sid said nothing. He was seething. No one talked to him this way. The Russian needed him, too.

"Sid, you Wop, speak to me!"

Zaccaria had never heard that word aimed at him. He gripped his cell phone so hard it broke in half.

Minutes later his desk phone rang. He picked it up to hear, "Never hang up on me. Never."

"I didn't. The phone broke. Please, let's be calm." Sid was pleading for some kind of order. He could feel the sweat on his palms and he was unfamiliar with the anxiety he was feeling as he waited for the Russian to respond.

Krasnodar smiled to himself. He knew he had Sid Zaccaria where he wanted him. Zaccaria was pleading with Krasnodar for peace. The Russian knew that people who plead for calm are terrified. In this case, terror was excellent.

Krasnodar was silent. He let Zaccaria stew and finally Sid spoke, "Look, Anapa, we got off the wrong foot today. I accept the blame for that. Please tell me what I can do."

Anapa softened his voice and said, "Sid, my friend, we have a difficult time ahead. We need to be together. I came to you with this idea. Please, let me lead the way."

Sid Zaccaria was only too eager to comply and said so. He wanted the project to be successful. He was eager to sacrifice his own integrity and to silence all those warning bells in his head for, well, money, a lot of money.

Krasnodar continued calmly, "Sid, please get your men together for a meeting at the Hilton Garden Inn in Fairfield tomorrow at ten in the morning. Room 328. Tell your friends to arrive singularly, not as a group. I have reserved a large room with a conference table. Our meeting will take three to four hours. After the meeting they should have much free time for this project. They should clear their calendars."

He hesitated for effect and said, "And, Sid, remember that you and I must be together on this. We are united on this cause. Understand?" His final tone was a little more ominous.

Sid responded, "Count on it, Anapa. I want this as much as you do."

Anapa hung up the phone and thought about Zaccaria's last statement. It was a perfect example of subservience. This was going better that Anapa Krasnodar had expected.

Sid Zaccaria spent the rest of the day locating and getting his friends up to speed on the next day's meeting. True to his word, he was enthusiastic and almost like a cheerleader for Krasnodar. He did not reveal his fears.

CHAPTER TWENTY-FOUR

Sid Zaccaria's home on the Silverado Trail north of Napa was quiet. The old man and his wife had been in bed two hours when Anoly softly walked up the driveway at ten o'clock. Anoly preferred to do his work in the early evening hours because it was easier to explain his presence at, say, ten than after midnight.

Fortunately for Anoly, the night had a new moon. The property was dark. Anoly knew there might be motion sensitive lighting around the residence. He also knew how to defeat such lighting. Basically, people always set up such lighting to monitor the pathways that they used. That is, they set it up to shine light on themselves, not prowlers and burglars. Anoly had learned that lesson years ago when he prepared to escape from a Russian prison. He knew to approach a home by walking toward a side of the home that had no outside doors. People protected doorways, not walls. But when one got to a wall, it was easy to sidle in behind the motion sensors. He would use this secret tonight at the Zaccaria home.

Every few steps he paused to listen for a sound that some-one else was on the property. As he neared the residence he noticed a small stable and corral off to the left. His instincts told him that the stable was so close to the residence because someone kept much loved animals nearby. He also knew it would be unlikely that the stable would be protected by electronic security. He changed his direction and slowly approached the stable.

No lights went on near the stable or the adjacent corral. He listened careful and could hear the gentle breathing of a large animal. As his night vision improved he saw that the little facility was home to a horse.

Anoly eased his way into the corral and moved toward the stable. The stable was actually a pole shed with some cabinets and storage shelves along the back wall. A feed trough lined one side wall. An automatic watering basin stood next to the trough.

He entered the shed and found a magnificent black horse standing beside the cabinets. The horse was calm and readily accepted Anoly's nuzzling and rubbing.

Anoly put his hand into his jacket pocket. The horse murmured as if to anticipate a handout of carrots or apples or maybe even sugar cubes. The horse had no idea what Anoly retrieved from his jacket. The horse had no idea why the thing smelled like a car or a tool. The horse had no idea when Anoly held the thing to the horse's ear and he had no idea why his world went away when Anoly pulled the trig-ger on the suppressed Ruger Mark II twenty-two caliber pistol.

The horse fell on his knees then rolled over very dead. Anoly took a small flashlight, a SureFire, from his other jacket pocket and checked himself for blood and then checked to see that the horse was indeed dead.

Anoly took a Ken Onion Whirlwind knife out of his jacket. The knife was made by Kershaw a brand of fine cutlery that the company sourced in the ancient Japanese cutlery center, Seki City. The Whirlwind was basically a California street legal switchblade. Ken Onion made his mark on the knife market by invented a fast opening device that circumvented the knife laws in most states, including California.

Anoly opened the knife and in one smooth move, sliced an ear off the dead horse. He put the knife away and wrapped the ear in a cloth he found in the barn. He reached over and cut the phone line connection to the barn telephone.

Anoly retraced his steps out of the corral and down the long driveway. He had a sour taste in his mouth. His chewing gum had lost its flavor. He opened a stick of chewing gum and from years of habit, wrapped the old gum in the wrapper and tossed the whole thing to the ground. He had left his car in a small grove a mile down the Silverado Trail.

Twenty minutes after the horse fell, Anoly was driving back toward Napa with the intent to go to his home in nearby Solana County. Driving through Napa he decided to stop for a drink and maybe a bite of food.

He called Krasnodar and reported his success. Then he told his boss that he was hungry and planned to stop for a burger. Anapa Krasnodar told him to hurry along. He was sure the man would stop at a McDonald's.

As Anoly crossed the Napa River on Trancas Street, he slowed to toss the Ruger into the river. He waited until he heard a satisfying splash. He accelerated and drove down Soscol to downtown Napa. He knew little about Napa but did remember a steak house somewhere downtown. He turned right onto First Street, then, seeing familiar land-marks, turned right on Main Street. A couple of blocks away he saw Cole's Chop House, one of the Valley's top restaurants.

Anoly found a parking place along Main and walked into the restaurant. The night was winding down so there were few people in the dining room. He did notice a youngish couple seated at a table for two along the back wall.

The bar was a different story. Only one seat was vacant. It was the last seat at the end of "L" section of the bar. He claimed the seat only to be challenged by a young man who had gone way past his limit on martinis.

"Excuse me," the man said. "My friend is sitting there."

Anoly saw the man was small and effeminate. He was about one half Anoly's size. Anoly knew the man was not threaten-ing in any way but he could not resist mocking when he said, "Excuse me. You and your friend can eat shit. I am here now."

The bartender saw what looked like trouble but didn't hear what was said. He moved closer to Anoly and the man and said, "Jay, is there a problem?"

The bartender didn't see the incredibly evil look Anoly directed toward the young man. Quickly sensing that this was not a battle he wanted to engage in, the man backed down and said, "No. Not at all. We were just leaving."

To close the matter, Anoly said, "Please, sir, be my guest." Anoly reached for the man's bar tab and put it into his shirt pocket. He turned to the bartender and said, "Stoli on the rocks. Save yourself a trip and make it a double. And bring along something for dinner. A burger or whatever."

The bartender poured the drink then told Anoly, "We've got burgers on the bar menu, It'll take a few minutes."

Anoly ignored the man and drank about half his drink. He said, "Bartender, your doubles are light. I will have another and this time don't be so shy on the pouring." He knocked back the rest of his drink.

Across the room, Kathleen and I were having dinner. I said to Kathleen. "Take a look at that big guy at the bar. I think he's alone. Looks Russian or something close. I've been watching him since he parked across the street. He just about threw two men out of the bar and now he is sparring with the bartender. There's something about him that is very much out of sync with Napa and with this place. Plus, this is the second huge Russian we've seen in four days."

I continued, "Tell you what, do you remember how to use that camera?"

"Of course I do," she said with a little excitement in her voice. Kathleen was always ready to use our new found skills and technology.

"OK, go to the opposite end of the bar, ask for something like a bottled water or whatever. While the bartender goes to get you the water, take a picture of the man. Use the feature that goes straight to the office. I'll go to the server station and stand beside the man and ask for a dessert menu. That'll distract the Russian from you and your camera."

After a minute Kathleen strolled over to the end of the bar. She told the bartender that it was her husband's birthday and she wondered if he could arrange for a little cake or other dessert. He moved from behind the bar, giving Kathleen a clear view of the Russian. Meanwhile, at the opposite end of the bar, I asked the man next to the Russian for a dessert menu, distracting them both from looking toward Kathleen.

She and I had practiced this kind of surreptitious picture taking. She placed the camera in her palm and raised her hand so it looked as if she was exploring her makeup. The camera lens worked fine between her fingers. In ten seconds she has three pretty good pictures of Anoly, one full face and two profiles of the left side of his face. She returned to the table and smiled when I showed up twenty seconds later, dessert menu in hand. She looked toward the bar and saw that the Russian, if that's what he was, was not looking at them. He had missed the entire thing.

Kathleen knew that people with certain skills, say, criminals, rarely think that other people might also have those skills. She knew it was why professionals always said the easiest people to surveil or track were cops. Cops thought that no one would dare follow them.

I was ready to leave the restaurant. Kathleen told me that we had to stay a few minutes. Just then the waiter arrived with my birthday cake. I caught on quickly. We enjoyed the cake then headed for the car. The Russian was still at the bar. When we left the restaurant, I gave Kathleen the keys and told her to go to the car, start it and wait for me. I told here that if I did not get there in four or five minutes she should use her phone to call Joe Bruning.

I walked over to the shadows by the building and waited. I could see the Russian at the bar. After a couple of minutes I decided the Russian was oblivious to any activities around him. Based on the empty glasses around his place at the bar, he was well into at least his fifth double Stoli.

I returned to the car, got in, and Kathleen drove away. I said, "Just for safety, drive around a little and let's see if we have grown a tail."

Kathleen turned in a direction away from a straight route to our home. Just as she did, my cell phone rang. It was Jim Berry.

Berry said, "We got your images. Can you tell me how this happened? Be specific."

Kathleen quickly brought Jim Berry up to date on the dinner at Cole's Chop House, my decision to photograph the Russian and our general feel of unease about him.

Berry asked, "What drew your attention to the man?"

I said, "Well, he was just very much out of place in the restaurant and he was pushing people around. He really enjoyed making the two guys leave. There was nothing gentle about it. I guess I just though he was the most un-Napa person I had seen in Napa."

Berry said, "Anything else?"

Kathleen, thinking for a moment added, "Well. He's the second huge Russian we've seen in a few days." She told him about seeing the huge Russian at Meadowood.

Berry asked several questions about the Meadowood lunch. He seemed to pass it off as a random event.

He said, "Kathleen, Clark, once again, your instincts are excellent. The man is Anolstinsky Baranovich, a Russian national who is in the country illegally. He goes by Anoly. He's extremely dangerous. We know he's been hired to kill people throughout Europe and Asia and now he's here. We've been looking for him for months. You guys did a great job. This is exactly what we wanted."

He continued, "I don't suppose you saw how he arrived there, do you?"

Kathleen told me she had seen him drive up in a silver Lexus.

He continued, "Great! Now, can you head back to the restaurant? We want you to place a GPS coin in his car. Now guys, this is no time to be heroes. Be careful. Just get the device on his car and get away from there."

Kathleen looped back to Cole's. The car that Jim Berry described was parked on Main Street. Kathleen pulled in behind it. Clark got out and tossed the GPS device through an open back window. It landed on the floor and rolled under the front seat.

CHAPTER TWENTY-FIVE

Jim Berry's staff located Anoly's car and tracked it south out of Napa then east across the connector road that leads to I-80 about twelve miles away. Berry called the CHP and the Napa Sheriff. He asked for their cooperation in permitting the Lexus to pass. He mentioned that the driver was probably under the influence.

The CHP, who had practically no delegated decision making authority, had to check with their leaders in Sacramento before they could commit. Berry knew the answer from Sacramento would be to stop the car. Berry shook his head at the way the management of "California's Finest" turned almost any small incident into a self-aggrandizing, self-promoting drama-fest. Berry felt that had it not been for the glorification of the CHP on television in the 1970's and 80's, some progressive governor would have reined the prima donnas in long ago. It was probably too late now.

Finding it difficult to leave the subject, Jim Berry thought about the mentality of a police agency that would spend millions training and equipping CHP officers and then send them out to check on cell phone law compliance.

He knew that the single biggest impediment to security – personal, local and national – is the utter failure of police agencies to cooperate with each other. Invariably when one agency asked for assistance, the other agency opened its own file on the case. Before long the two agencies were stepping each other's dicks while the miscreants skipped away.

Another huge issue is the almost pathological need for publicity and the spotlight. One new sheriff in southern California spent more time designing new uniforms and car paint schemes than he did on actually being a sheriff. The local police departments in that county got frustrated and refused to cooperate with him at all. They wouldn't share information. They stopped inviting him and his staff to local meetings. He retaliated by leaking stories about the inept local cops. It goes on to this day.

Berry tracked the Russian's car into Solana County then east on I-80 a couple of miles until it left the Interstate and headed into the hills to the north. The car stopped at a large estate and stayed there.

In minutes Jim Berry knew the property was registered to a long time Solana County resident who had rented it to some people from out of the area. He scheduled satellite photography for the next day and assigned two teams to watch the property and keep a casual eye on the Lexus, but not necessarily follow it since it contained the GPS apparatus. He leaned back in his desk chair to try to get some sleep. It would be long night.

CHAPTER TWENTY-SIX

The next morning Anapa Krasnodar arose early and went downstairs to his kitchen. Anoly was sitting at the table drinking coffee.

Krasnodar said, "You look like hell. What happened last night?"

Anoly turned and said, "It went well, Anapa. No one saw anything. I stopped in Napa and had a couple of drinks and a burger. Nothing more."

Krasnodar said, "For your sake, I hope that's all."

Krasnodar poured a cup of coffee and sat down to read the newspaper. In a few minutes he turned to Anoly and said, "Where is your car, Anoly? Is it outside? Let's go take a look."

The two men stood and walked outside. Anoly was terrified. He had no idea why but he was very concerned that Anapa suddenly wanted to see his car.

When they reached the car, Anapa opened each door and looked inside. He stooped to looked under the seats. On the passenger side he went through the glove compartment. Finally, he opened the hood and the trunk and searched each compartment carefully. While Krasnodar was going through the car, Anoly reached inside his jacket and touched his Walther PPK. He had no idea what his boss was looking for but he knew that if anyone had placed anything in the car, Anapa would surely kill him on the spot.

As Anoly tightened his grip on the Walther, he couldn't see that Anapa Krasnodar had brought along a Sig 226 in forty-five caliber. The gun was tucked inside Krasnodar's front waistband so it was very handy. Neither of the men knew how close they came to a gun fight at only three feet apart.

Krasnodar turned to his bodyguard and said, "The car is fine, my friend, but you must lose some weight. Coins fall from your pockets. There is enough change in that car to buy a nice lunch." He turned and walked back into the house.

Anoly looked under the seat behind the driver. There were three coins, a quarter, a dime and a half-dollar. He examined the half-dollar carefully. At first glance the coin looked genuine. But it felt somewhat heavy so he took a closer look. He could see a seam that ran around the edge of the coin. He put the coin between his palms and twisted. It easily parted and came into two pieces. The inside of the coin was filled with miniature electronics. His stomach felt like he had just dropped 30 floors in a fast moving elevator.

Anoly looked toward the house to see if Anapa was watching. He was not. Anoly carefully twisted the coin halves back together and put the coin into his pocket. He closed the car doors and walked back to the house as calmly as he could.

Inside he called to Anapa, "I am going for cigarettes. Do you need anything Anapa?"

His boss yelled back that he needed six double A batteries and a box of Equal, the kind in the little packets.

Anoly went back to the car, he drove four miles to a supermarket. Inside he collected his purchases and went to the counter. He checked out and paid with one dollar bills and some change. The coin was included in the change. The clerk glanced at it and dropped in the cash drawer. If she noticed that Anoly was wearing driving gloves she didn't react to it. Since there were no other shoppers in the store at that early hour, no one noticed what he had done. At least that is what Anoly thought.

Twenty-two miles away Jim Berry tracked the coin as it traveled down the hill to the shopping center. When there was no further movement, Berry knew the coin was not longer in the Russian's car. He contacted one of the agents who had been tailing Anoly. They quickly surmised what had happened. Berry told the agent to retrieve the coin and the store's surveillance camera tapes.

An hour later, Jim Berry and his staff were watching the store videos. They had three clear views of Anoly entering the store, shopping and checking out. They could see that he was armed by the bulge on his hip. He seemed to be nervous, glancing around often to see if anyone was watching him.

On closer inspection of the GPS device they saw that the seal on the coin had been broken. Berry speculated, "I think we're watching a man who actually is very frightened of someone. He doesn't know about us, but he has his antenna all the way up now. He was on to the tracking device for sure. If the seal hadn't been broken we could believe he just used the coin as a normal half dollar. He disposed of the coin the best way he knew. And, judging from the way he did it, he wanted to keep someone from knowing that he had the coin. Who is that someone? Is he or she in that house? And why are they residing in Fairfield, a place so close to Napa? Right now none of us can answer those questions. But I have an idea that we have a very short time to find the answers.

"Because the Russian is now hypersensitive to his surroundings, we have to be very careful."

One of the men said, "We have tight coverage on that house. Sooner or later that someone has to come out. Right?"

Berry responded, "Maybe, but what if he or she has no need to come out? Maybe they're doing whatever they're up to just fine from within the place. Besides, if a person is in the back seat of a car that has heavily tinted windows we lose most of our surveillance effectiveness. That car can drive right past us and unless we stop it, which we can't without cause, Jimmy Hoffa could be in it. We'd never know."

He paused then said, "We need to find out who's in that house. Run trailers from Anolstinsky Baranovich to wherever they lead. Call Customs and see if we can find when he entered the country. Send them our photos and tapes for comparison. If they hesitate one second hang up let me know. This is no time for their bull shit. Am I clear? File a case with NSA and make sure they know how critical this is. Redundancy is OK as long as you know they'll come back to us with results.

"What I'm saying is this needs to be taken to every effective agency right now for immediate consideration. Correction, every agency except the local ones. Don't go to any of the Napa county cops."

The men left the room. Berry sat back. He was literally exhausted but he felt that he was making progress. One of the worst actors in international crime and espionage had been seen right in the middle of Napa. The man was comfortable enough to have dinner out in the open in a busy restaurant. By the grace of God, Berry thought, his two stringers had not only seen the man but had possessed the good sense to take pictures and send them to their contact. He was pleased but a little worried that they had taken their roles of helping out to far past anything in their original job descriptions. Berry knew that he was out on a limb because of that. If anything happened to those enthusiastic young people, he'd surely be on point for 100% of the blame. Intuitively, he knew he'd set it up that to go just that way. He picked up the desk phone and gave someone very specific instructions.

CHAPTER TWENTY-SEVEN

About the time Anoly was returning to the house, Sid and Annette Zaccaria awoke. Their morning routine had been set for decades. He went down the driveway to get the papers. He would read the front page of the Napa Register as he walked back to the house where Annette would have set out his morning coffee and a delicious pastry from The Model Bakery in St. Helena. She'd then make the trek out to the stable to take a different kind of treat to her prized horse.

As he walked down the driveway he noticed a bit of paper on the lawn beside the driveway. He stopped to retrieve the paper and saw that it was a Juicy Fruit wrapper. "Strange", he thought. "How did this get here? And who on earth in this day chews a sugar bomb like Juicy Fruit?" He was surprised the stuff was even on the market. Then he noticed that the wrapper contained used chewing gum.

"Gross." He put the gum wrapper in his shirt pocket.

Suddenly, he heard Annette scream again and again. Zaccaria ran from the driveway toward Annette's screams. He knew she was in the horse barn. He tossed the newspaper aside and picked up speed as the driveway leveled and the running was easier. The old man was out of breathe but he struggled to get to his wife.

Zaccaria rounded the corner and ran inside the barn. Annette was on her knees with the horse's head against her thigh. She was sobbing hysterically. He saw dried blood where the horse's ear had been and a dried pool of blood on the floor of the barn.

Annette began to shake and quiver. She was gasping for breath and going into shock, maybe worse. Her heart wasn't all that strong. He grabbed for the telephone on the wall of the barn. The line was dead. He dug his cell phone out of his pocket and dialed 9-1-1. He called for an ambulance then went back to his wife. He knew the ambulance would take at least fifteen minutes.

Using what little knowledge of first aid that he had, he tried to make his wife comfortable. He covered her with a horse blanket. He got a bottle of water from the barn's small refrigerator next to the horse's stall and tried offering her a drink. She sipped carefully but her body was shaking all over and the water dripped down her chin and onto her blouse. Sid held her close, stroking her hair and trying to calm her down. "Shhh, shhh," he crooned as he rocked her slowly.

He thought about the horse. She called it Bella even though its original name was Texas Tutor, a horse that became injured in the Preakness after she won the Kentucky Derby by seven lengths. The horse's owner was furious at the trainer, the jockey and the horse. He vowed to send the horse to Mexico where it would end up as food.

Annette paid whatever the owner would take and had the horse shipped back to Napa. For a full year she and a local veterinarian worked hundreds of hours nursing the horse back to health. It could never run a horse race again but it could be the best companion horse that a lady ever had.

Sid had the stable and corral constructed while the horse was in transit to Napa. The day the horse arrived Sid and Annette hosted a small party to welcome Bella to health in her new home in Napa. From that day forward, Annette and Bella had been forged together in friendship. Celebrating Bella's return to health became an annual event in the Valley. The celebration grew every year. Sid and Annette evolved the event into a fund raiser, Bella's Back. A year ago it had raised over $3 million for local charities.

Now, several years later, Sid was faced with a scene of unimaginable horror. He knew Annette might not recover from the loss. He wondered if would recover from the loss of Annette.

CHAPTER TWENTY-EIGHT

Kathleen and I got text messages to meet Jim Berry soon after our work day ended. The location of the meeting was new to us. Berry had given us instructions to a private gun club range in the northeast part of Napa. We were told very specifically to be at the gate just off Monticello Road at 7:00 pm that night.

We had just enough time to stop in at Bay Leaf for a quick dinner. Bay Leaf was located on Monticello Road, too, just over a mile from our destination. We took seats in the bar area, ordered iced tea and burgers, agreeing that since we were meeting Jim, it might be best to skip our usual pre-dinner drink.

We met the very impressive owner who went by the name of Monier. He stopped by to greet us and to offer a small appetizer to share. Bay Leaf and Monier are what passes as "counter culture" in Napa. Monier offered wedding dinners and receptions, parties and other family-type attractions. The food was classic. Where else on the west coast could one find real Beef Wellington? The bar menu featured classic drinks such as Manhattans, Rob Roy's and Gimlets. It was that kind of place. The restaurant would be very much at home out in the country side in New Jersey or Connecticut.

After dinner we headed north to the turnoff that Berry had specified. The turnoff was almost hidden from the road. The driveway dove down at a steep angle to a gate. Just as we approached the gate, it opened automatically.

The driveway continued down for one hundred and twenty-five yards and leveled out to a large flat parking area. The parking area was shrouded with huge oaks. I thought this would be one place where a helicopter or even a satellite might be blocked out by the dense foliage. I hadn't noticed any other men at the gate or in the parking lot. It seemed as if we might be pretty much alone, with the exception of Berry.

Jim Berry was standing in the open door of a neat but old-fashioned low-slung wooden building that had the look of a club house of some sort. He welcomed us inside and shut the door.

We all took seats at a worn wooden table. The room was loosely decorated with gun pictures, hunting pictures and sporting scenes. A large bulletin board was filled with notices of various items for sale. The room had obviously seen years of service. It had a masculine but homey feel.

Berry told us that he had called the meeting for an extraordinary purpose. He said, "After what happened last night I found myself worrying about you. I don't particularly like that sensation. So, I want to offer both of you the opportunity to have access to handguns. If you agree, we'll set up a training course in this facility. The local PD and the CHP have a training facility across and up the road a ways. I like this place because a couple of local men conduct classes for the California Concealed Carry Weapon program. So, if someone sees us here they would think we're simply part of the regular activities of the club."

Berry let his comments sink in, then continued, "You guys OK with going through a weapons course and with having access to weapons of deadly force?"

Kathleen spoke first, "Well, Jim, we certainly are moving right along. We've gone from being 'eyes and ears' to a far different role. But, I'm OK with it. Frankly, I would have felt a little better if I'd had a gun when we saw that Russian last night."

I said, "Me, too, Jim. Let's get going."

Berry placed a large case on the table and said, "Have either of you had any experience with guns, especially handguns?"

I smiled and said, "We're not without a little experience, Jim. I've been around handguns and long guns all my life. I've been through a couple of training courses, most notably Gunstite in New Mexico back when Col. Jeff Cooper was still around. Seven years ago I talked Kathleen into going to a range with me. I was shooting a full sized Glock 21 in .45 caliber. I had owned the gun about six months. I thought the gun was too big for her and maybe even not a good idea. After all, full sized forty-five is a lively round. I relented and she took a position that Weaver or Jordan wouldn't recognize but she put eight rounds into an inch and a half at seven and a half yards. We moved out to 25 yards and her groups opened up to about three inches.

"After shooting several mags she turned to me and said, 'What will your gun be?' I lost custody of the Glock that day. That's OK. I shoot a Les Baer custom 1911 type. I'm fairly good with it but not as good as she is with her Glock."

I couldn't resist adding, "Of course, her fingernails make it tough for her to load mags. I guess I can be her ammo caddy."

Kathleen grinned and kicked me under the table and said, "Ignore him. Better yet, humor him. He'll mature one of these days. I'm counting on it."

Berry smiled and said, "Well, this training course might be shorter than I had planned."

He opened the case and said, "Take a look at these handguns and let me know what strikes your fancy. I have to make a call. I'll be right back."

I stood and looked through the guns in the case, extracting a Glock 37 in .40 caliber. After checking to see that it was not loaded, I handed it to Kathleen and said, "This is cute. It's a forty. The bullets are not as big as the forty-five's but they go a lot faster so the end result on a bad guy is about the same. It holds nine rounds plus one in the barrel, a real advantage. Plus, it's smaller and might fit your hand better. I know it'll fit in your purse or you jacket pocket better.

Kathleen took the gun and said, "You might be right. I have to shoot it to know."

I took another Glock out of the case. This was also in forty caliber, the pistol that tons of cops use, a full sized Glock Model 22. It holds fifteen in the mag and another in the barrel for a total of sixteen. I also like the idea of both of us using the same ammunition.

Kathleen, said, "I thought you would never leave your favorite forty-five. But your idea seems good to me. I'm fine with it."

Berry reentered to room as we were talking. He said, "See anything you like?"

I replied, "We've made our choices. She wants the Model 37 and I'll take the Model 22."

Berry said, "Good choices. I use a Model 22. And, the Model 37 should be perfect for Kathleen." Berry led the way to a door on the west wall. We went through the door and found ourselves in a well-equipped, if austere, indoor shooting range. There were six positions each with automatic target retrieval systems.

Another man seemed to be waiting on us. Berry said, "Clark, Kathleen, this is Jim Riley. He's a master FBI instructor. Normally he hangs out in Virginia at the Quantico FBI center. He came out here today to help us. Jim?"

Riley took control of the meeting and said, "Thank you. My goal is to evaluate what you know and correct your mistakes. I'm not particularly interested in whether or not you like what I have to say. But if you learn from me you will have a much better opportunity to stay alive. I can't make that guarantee if you get pissed and fail to learn.

"By the way, this is serious. Deadly serious. You'll find that I do not have a sense of humor in this room.

"Jim Berry tells me that you chose .40 caliber Glocks. Good choice. But let me give you your first lesson. The choice of caliber, up to a point, does not matter. I have seen many dead people who died from be shot with a gun. Whether the gun was a .38 Special or a .50 caliber Smith & Wesson, all were dead to the same degree. Kathleen and Clark, there are two important considerations. First, shoot first. If you delay you might be dead. This is so important.

"Second, put the bullet in the right place. If you shoot someone in the forehead or in the temple your gun can be a .22 or whatever. You will have won and you will be alive. That is you will have won if you got your shot off first.

"Clark, Kathleen, these weapons have been thoroughly fine tuned at Quantico. We have ballistics data as well as very detailed data on the firing pins, the extractors and so forth. If one of these weapons is fired, we'll know it and we'll know it was you. Law Enforcement is given a special privilege, the privilege of carrying weapons. But in a shooting, you must do it correctly. You have no special dispensation that lets you break the rules or the law.

"Does that sound iron-assed and unfair? Maybe so. But the FBI takes weapons very seriously. Any questions?"

Kathleen said, "When will we learn the laws on using our weapons?"

Riley said, "You'll get most of it here and some in Jim Berry's office in a few days. Actually, that kind of learning never really stops.

"Now, most of what is taught in so-called combat or self-defense courses is not only bull shit but it's downright dangerous. Forget about learning to roll around on the ground and run sideways. It won't ever be needed. That stuff is for show. Clark, I bet Col. Cooper never made you roll around on the ground or run sideways.

"I think it's pathetic for a bunch of grown men to pay a lot of money so some jackass can abuse them as if he was a marine sergeant. Those old men will attempt to learn how to shoot prone, standing up, running and in just about every pose the human body can assume. What nonsense.

"Have either of you had any formal training at all?"

Jim Berry said "Clark has been to Gunsite and he's trained Kathleen."

"Good for you, Clark. Gunsite is one of the best training centers in the nation. It might be right up there with Quantico. I know you learned something and I'll bet it was not about rolling around on the ground. Am I correct?"

I responded to Riley's question, "I think I did learn something. Most of what I learned was how to make a weapon part of my thinking and part of me. We did a lot of listening and lot of responding to threats that were rarely more than seven or eight feet from us."

Riley continued, "Thank you. Now, if you get in a gun fight it'll almost certainly be at less than ten feet distance, probably in the dark and you'll fire from one to four rounds. If you're much farther away than that, get the hell out of there. Everyone gets hurt in a real gun fight. An old police joke goes like this, 'Cops carry handguns so they can make enough noise to allow them to get back to their car and get the shotgun.' It's not just funny, it's accurate.

"So forget about what you've read or heard. Listen closely to me and years from now we'll meet and you can buy me a drink because you're alive. That's what I'm giving you. Life. Your roles are so unusual I'm not certain I agree with the concept and I am very uneasy with the execution. I will do my part. It is up to you to learn."

Riley was a wiry man about six feet tall. He was dressed in military-like khakis and black jump boots. He wore a plan black baseball hat. No doubt about it, Riley was the real deal.

Riley questioned us and lectured us for two hours. Abruptly, he said, "I'll be back in three minutes. Stay seated. When he opened the door to return we could hear a toilet flushing. He brought in three cans of Diet Coke and three bottles of water. He said, "Odd, this a gun club that's touting its affiliation with the NRA. Yet, they have a Pepsi machine out there. Are they so stupid they don't know that Pepsi, along with ConocoPhillips and Levis are the gun owner's worst enemies? They fund more anti-gun campaigns and legislation that you can shake a stick at." He shook his head. "America's a nutty place!"

While we opened our drinks, Riley continued, "Now for some shooting. Who wants to go first?"

A short live fire session followed. The time seemed to pass quickly but a glance at the clock showed it was one in the morning when we were done.

Kathleen said, "I'm surprised that the neighbors put up with this noise. We must have shot a couple of hundred rounds."

Berry responded, "Actually, Kathleen, they don't even know we're here. A couple of years ago we funneled a lot of money through an NRA grant program to completely sound proof this building. The club doesn't know about our involvement and they never will. We needed an indoor range and our choices were to either build one or improve this one. The cost analysis was all the way from about $1 million for the new range to around $30,000 for soundproofing this facility, so it was an easy choice."

Jim Riley said, "Well, I expect to see you folks tomorrow night at seven. Same drill. I think we need another couple of sessions and then you'll be set." He replaced the pistols in the case and left the building. We all left right behind him. Kathleen and I went straight to bed when we got home. I don't know about her, but I had dreams all night about shooting targets.

A couple more nights turned into four. By the end of the sessions we were even more exhausted. We'd practiced five nights in a row, about six hours each night. We'd shot more than 800 rounds of high powered ammunition. We had learned to maintain our weapons and what do to if something broke. Jim Riley gave us little bags of gun parts. He said, "If anything breaks on a Glock, it'll be one of these." He showed us how to know what had broken and how to replace each part in the dark, standing and sitting. Jim Berry gave us two sessions on California and US firearms laws.

Finally, Riley produced what appeared to be a standard Glock. When he took his position at the range, we were shocked to see and hear that the pistol was fully automatic. Riley let each of us become familiar with the weapon. It was a surreal experience. Kathleen controlled the weapon very well. I was somewhat less than enthusiastic. My rounds flew all over the target. After several attempts my accuracy finally improved. Kathleen's teasing did not help the situation.

Jim Riley also gave us a short rifle with open sights. He said, "From what you have told me, both of you're comfortable with long arms. This is a Ruger Mini 14 Rifle in .223. It's an excellent close to medium range rifle. The round, the .223, is standard issue for the US armed forces and many other countries around the world. To keep it legal in California, we've produced very reliable ten round magazines. California has a stupid law that limits the capacity of magazines to ten rounds. They seem to think that crooks will not know how to switch mags. My observation is that crook's never consider the laws they are breaking as impediments to their work. I suggest you keep this in the boat with you when you're on the water. It's stainless steel so you shouldn't worry about getting it wet. You have hunting licenses so there should be no problem. Just keep it out of sight. Oh, one more thing. This version has a selector for semi-automatic or three auto-rounds. Let's go over to the shooting table and get you familiar with that feature."

At the end of the last session, Berry congratulated us and presented each of us with unique concealed carry permits. The permits were signed by the Attorney General herself. People who saw the card were asked to call a toll free number to verify the permit.

Jim Riley had left to catch a Bureau plane back to Quantico, leaving Berry to bring us up to date on the Russian.

He said, "We have Anoly under surveillance. We know he works as a bodyguard from time to time and that he usually appears when something big is about to happen. There's still no confirmation on who he is guarding.

"That's about all we know. Well, there is one other thing and we have no idea if it relates to the Russian. It's really more of a local incident. The night you saw the Russian in the bar, a prized horse in a private stable up Valley was killed. The killer used a suppressed Ruger 22. We know it was suppressed because of the debris that was in the wound channel. The killer knew what he was doing. He shot the horse in the head and then severed its ear. The horse died immediately."

Berry referred to notes in a black notebook and continued, "The horse was owned and kept as a personal pet by

Annette Zaccaria, the wife of Sid Zaccaria, one of the Valley's long time wine gurus. Neither one of them heard or saw anything. They're older people who go to bed early. The killer must have known that because the horse was killed about ten that night.

"The timing certainly doesn't rule out the Russian as the killer. He easily could have done his sorry work and gotten down to Napa in time for you to see him in the bar. His manner in the bar was somewhat hyper, bullying, a normal thing for someone who had just completed such a heartless task.

"The Napa Sheriff's Office responded to a call from the ambulance company," he said, referring to his notes, "Piner's is the ambulance company. The first officer, a Deputy Sheriff, reached the scene about ten minutes after the ambulance had gotten there. Piner's and the SO work well together so the scene was pretty much intact. Apparently that lasted about another ten minutes when three more SO cars and one from the Napa PD arrived.

"There was literally nothing left to analyze. One of the other of cops did retrieve the bullet. That probably won't be of much help because the Ruger is one of the most common handguns in the country and twenty-two bullets are so soft that they deform and even break apart. I pulled some strings and got the bullet expressed back to the FBI lab. So far they have nothing. Actually, I'd be surprised if anything comes of this. I plan to speak with Mr. Zaccaria when he is available. Tomorrow or the next day at the latest. I'll keep you posted.

"Recent observations show the Russian is carrying a handgun under his jacket. He leaves it in the car when he goes places where the bulge of the gun might draw attention.

Large people find it pretty difficult to conceal a handgun. It always stands out no matter what they do.

"That's about it. I think you two deserve some R&R right now. Why not take a few days off and maybe enjoy your boat?"

We shook hands and left the gun club.

CHAPTER TWENTY-NINE

The next day Sid Zaccaria and his associates arrived at the hotel in Fairfield. Anapa Krasnodar and Anoly were seated in the room. Anapa had the seat at the head of the table. Anoly was sitting on a sofa off to one side.

It was clear the Zaccaria was not himself. He slowly entered the room and took a seat.

When all the men were present, Krasnodar stood and said, "Welcome, gentlemen, I am so pleased that we are together.

"Now for business. I am notifying you now of the deadline for your first payment. Five days. Cash. No exceptions and no delays.

"Second, each of you will receive two lots of the wines of your choice. I need to know within one day what your choice for the 5,000 case and the 9,000 case lots will be. You will text message two lines to Mr. Zaccaria. Each line should be a choice. For example you can send the words: Screaming Eagle 88 5000 and that will be your choice for the 5,000 case lot.

"Also, I will need cash for the wine. The price is $4.00 per bottle equivalent so I require $240,000 for the 5,000 case lot and $432,000 for the 9,000 case lot.

"Finally, within twenty days from right now, I need labels for each lot. The labels should be on roll stock, pressure sensitive and other standard specifications. You will order the labels very soon from the label maker, Trag. Email art and other specifications to Trag and specify which label is for which lot. Also, on these labels you can specify the alcohol content, between 9.9% and 14.5%. The other details are up to you.

"Now, you must wonder how do you work this wine into your inventory, eh? You can destroy this quantity of your own wine, a bad idea I think, or you can complete a purchase agreement with a company I own. The agreement will show that you bought so much wine from us. I recommend that you attach this agreement to wine that you already own so it'll appear that the lots are from your grapes.

"Within twenty days of the deadline, that's five days from now, I will notify each of you when the wine is ready and where you want it delivered."

Krasnodar looked around the room and continued, "You must have questions. This is not the time for questions because both of us know that you already know the answers. No, my friends, this is the time for action. I bid you goodbye for now. I will be in touch."

Slowly, the winemakers stood and walked out of the room. Sid Zaccaria noticed that Anoly left the room, too.

When he and Anapa were alone, Anapa said, "Sid, my friend, you do not look so good. Is there anything I can do?"

Sid studied the man, then said, "Anapa, a very unfortunate and unexpected thing has happened. I hope you'll forgive me, but I must ask if you or your men had anything to do with it."

Anapa replied, "Sid, I am offended with your question. But I will let it pass. Listen to me. In life, there are lessons that we must all learn. In this case, you have learned that I mean what I say. Am I clear?"

Sid sank back into his chair, a withered and tired old man, unsure of exactly what Anapa meant, but knowing it was a veiled threat. He said, "Sure, Anapa. Sure."

When Sid looked up Anapa Krasnodar had left the room. Sid Zaccaria stood slowly and walked out. He rode the elevator down and left the hotel. He had no choice but to move on. Or did he? What if he simply told Krasnodar and the others that he had lost interest in the project? Surely they would understand about Annette's health and Sid's need to be with her.

He walked out to his car and started to get in for the drive back to Napa. He noticed a rag in the front seat. The rag looked familiar. It looked like the rags that Annette used when she bathed Bella. Annette must have tossed in into the car. "Strange," he thought, "I don't recall seeing this when I drove here earlier."

He reached in the car to get the rag. When his hand touched the rag he felt something hard inside. He opened the rag and saw Bella's ear clotted with blood.

Sid turned away and vomited right there in the parking lot. He threw the rag down. He stood up, feeling sick, frightened and so, so alone. What had he gotten them all into? What could he do? How could he keep his family and friends safe now?

Sid's drive back to Napa was the longest drive of his life. He tried not to think about the rag and the gruesome message it held. Instead he thought of what he had to do immediately. He must go to St. Helena Hospital to see Annette. Then, he had to begin assembling the cash, almost $2,750,000, probably all the cash he and Annette and his company had.

CHAPTER THIRTY

Jim Berry drove up Sid Zacharias' long driveway unannounced. He pulled into the large turnaround in the front of the house, got out of the car, walked up to the front door and rang the bell. He waited twenty seconds then rang again. Two seconds after the second ring the door opened. Sid Zaccaria, looking exhausted said, "I'm sorry. We're not having visitors right now. Can you come back?"

Berry handed Zaccaria a card and said, "Mr. Zaccaria? I'm Jim Berry from the local office of the FBI. We heard about the misfortune with your horse. May I have a few minutes?"

Zaccaria heard alarm bells go off in his head, but calmly said, "I suppose. Please come in. And, it was my wife's horse. I think she cared for that horse more than anything in the world, probably even more than me."

Zaccaria led Jim Berry into a small sitting room. He said, "Well, here we are. What do you want to know?"

Berry replied, "Well, I think I got many of the details from the Sheriff. I suppose my questions center around any possible perpetrators that come to mind. Any ideas?"

The old man knew exactly who did it but he also knew he was helpless and couldn't give that information to anybody.

"No. I have no ideas. None at all."

"Did you notice anything, anything at all that night or the next morning that might point to someone or something?

Zaccaria thought for a minute. It came to him that if he could implicate the Russian without actually involving himself, it might end the wine deal before it got going and before any money changed hands.

He said, "Well, there was one thing. I got up early as usual and went to get the papers. Annette, my wife Annette, would get the coffee poured, set out some breakfast pastries. Then she would take her coffee and some apples or carrots out to her horse, Bella.

"Anyway, on my way down the driveway, actually right at the top of the driveway, I saw a piece of paper on the lawn. It annoyed me that trash was on the property so I picked it up and saw that it was a gum wrapper, Juicy Fruit."

"Do you still have that gum wrapper? Did you put it in the trash?"

"Let's see, I think I put it in my shirt pocket. With all the excitement that followed, I'd quite forgotten it. If you don't mind I'll check in the clothes hamper to see." He stood.

Berry said, "Mr. Zaccaria, please let me go with you. If the wrapper is there, we'll need to protect it for analysis."

"Sure, come on."

They went through the house and upstairs to the master bathroom. Zaccaria opened a wicker clothes hamper and found a shirt that might be the one. The pockets were empty. He dug around in the hamper and found another shirt, a denim work shirt with western stitching. Sure enough, in the left front pocket they could see a small wad of paper.

Berry said, "May I take the shirt?"

"Sure. It's an old shirt. I won't miss it."

Berry took out a wallet notebook and wrote a receipt for the shirt. He wrote two copies and each of the men signed each copy. He gave one copy to Sid Zaccaria and kept the other.

He said, "Thank you very much. If you can't think of anything else I should know, I'll go. You have my card. If you think of anything else, please give me a call. "

They shook hands and Berry drove away south toward the Napa airport. He used his secure car phone to call his office and alert them to have a courier bag ready to go to Washington ASAP. He was certain the gum wrapper would tell him who killed the horse and he was beginning to be certain it would be the Russian, Anolstinsky Baranovich. The uncertainty was why the horse? Why the Russian? Why the house in Fairfield? How they all were connected and what were they missing?

Berry called his office again and scheduled an "all hands" meeting for eight that evening. He asked that we also be on hand. Then he asked his assistant to bring in food and beverages. It could be a long night.

CHAPTER THIRTY-ONE

Anapa Krasnodar sat at his kitchen table with Anoly Baranovich. It was almost dark but the house was already in darkness because it was on the east side of the hill.

Krasnodar said, "Anoly, my friend, I do not run your life. You do what you wish. I do not keep tabs on you. I never ask you where you have been. I know a young man, especially a young man who is so pretty to the women, has his needs.

"Sure, you should enjoy the nice women in the Napa Valley. I want you to do that. Go tonight and have your fun. But Anoly, tomorrow I need you to do a special job. I need your total attention and your intelligence. What you do will bring rewards to us. It'll have nothing to do with the wine business.

"So go. While you're in Napa, I want you to do two things. First, stop by the boat store on Soscol. That's the main street that runs up to downtown Napa. The boat store is on the right. Do this first because the store closes around six.

You will see the boats parked by the street. Anyway, go in the store and buy these things. Second, go out to the satellite dish installation and observe how one might gain access to the facility. And this last, you should do this before you come home. And Anoly, be home early. We have a very busy day tomorrow." He handed Anoly a typed list of the items he wanted from the boat store. "Anoly, the flashlights must be the SureFire models that I've indicated. No substitutes, please. If the boat store does not have them ask them if they know where to buy SureFires."

He handed Anoly a small backpack and said, "Stash this somewhere out of sight around the facility. It's water proof so you might tie a rope to it and sink it in the river. Just remember where you stash it.

"And, Anoly, please be back here ready to go in the morning. We have lots of big things to do."

Anoly, having prepared for his night out, was looking forward to another evening in Napa. He draped his suit jacket over the passenger seat, and whistled softly as he drove.

Anoly's first stop in Napa was the boat store. He bought all the items on Anapa's list, mostly rope and a medium anchor. The boat store did not stock SureFire lights but the clerk thought that a local gun store might have them in stock. The clerk was very helpful and called The Last Gun Shop to verify that they had them in stock.

Anoly drove about a mile across the Maxwell Bridge over the Napa River to the gun store. They had the SureFire flashlights and the extra batteries. When he left the store, the owner, Jake Jackson, went to the front window and copied down Anoly's license plate number.

Jackson returned to the store and called the Napa police department. He asked for a friend, Archie Landis. Landis came on the line. They chatted briefly for a couple of minutes then Jackson said, "Arch, a guy just came in the store. He was big, real big. From his accent I'd guess he's Russian or close to it. He's wearing a dark suit jacket. He purchased about $900 worth of top of the line SureFire flashlights and extra batteries for each. He leaned over the front counter to look at some pistols and when he did, I noticed that he was packing. He had a holster in the small of his back. But this guy was so big the jacket couldn't conceal the gun. My guess is a standard sized semi auto. Thought you would want to know."

Landis was taking notes. He asked, "Anything else you noticed?"

Smiling to himself, Jackson said, "Oh, I almost forgot. I got his tag number."

Landis said, "Sure, you almost forgot. I can see how you would forget a little insignificant detail like that." He jotted down the tag number and said, "If anything else slips your mind, please call."

Landis hung up and fed the license number into his computer. He was more than surprised when his screen lit up red and the blinking message told him to contact the local Homeland Security office at once and to avoid stopping or detaining the driver of the car.

Kerry Blount answered the phone call from Landis. It was after six and she was the only one in the office. Landis relayed the information from Jake Jackson. She replied, "Thanks, Archie. We appreciate your help. I can tell you we're on this guy. We're trying to come up with the reason he's here. Ask your guys to stay clear if at all possible. We know the big

Russian piece of crap is a heavy drinker and represents a very easy DUI. That, plus the concealed weapon would make him an easy but possibly very dangerous target for patrol officers. If the gun is that easy to spot, you can expect to get more calls. If you can, let Dispatch and Patrol know to stay clear of this guy. And, please call me if you have any contact with him. Thank you so much for your help."

CHAPTER THIRTY-TWO

After the shopping stop at the gun store, Anoly headed straight for Celadon. He'd seen it advertised and knew it had a full bar. He slid his gun into the outer pocket of his suit jacket. Once inside, he hung his jacket on a coat rack just inside and to the left of the front door. His gun would be less obvious hanging on the rack than bulging out as it tended to do when he wore the coat. He took a seat at the far end of the bar.

As Anoly was coming into the restaurant, Kathleen nudged Clark and said, "Hey. It's the same guy we saw that night at Cole's." We'd chosen Celadon, a favorite since that first night in Napa when we stayed at the Napa River Inn. We were here for a quick dinner before the meeting with Jim Berry. Our seats were against the wall in the middle part of the restaurant. Anoly was about fifteen feet from us.

We'd just finished sharing Celadon's terrific calamari and a salad and had about thirty minutes to get to the airport for Berry's meeting.

I leaned over and whispered in Kathleen's ear, "I think I'll drop another one of the GPS coins in his pocket. I saw him hang his jacket on that coat rack."

I reached into my pocket and pulled one of the GPS coins. I held the coin low in my lap and pulled the activating strip off the coin. We left a tip then walked casually towards the door. Anoly was nursing his second vodka and had paid no attention to us. As I reached the coat rack, I paused and looked around the restaurant. No one was watching. I slipped the coin into one of the inside breast pockets. Kathleen and I hurried out of the restaurant.

CHAPTER THIRTY-THREE

We met Jim Berry outside Jonesy's at the Napa airport. One by one we went into the restrooms and retraced our steps from the last visit to the underground federal law enforcement complex. We emerged from the complex of tunnels and doors into the same conference room that had been used in our first meeting.

Jim Berry took control of the meeting. He opened with, "I want to let you know where we are and then we'll see what each of you may have found out. Kathleen, Clark, this will be a good update for you. Join in if you feel the need."

Jim Berry did the classic 'how a leader establishes who is in charge' by standing and removing his suit jacket. He said, "This might take a while so feel free to get comfortable."

I said, "Jim, we do having something to contribute. A half hour ago we were in a restaurant, Celadon, and the big Russian, Baranovich, came in. He sat at the bar. We noticed that he had left his suit jacket on a coat rack by the front door. As we were leaving, I dropped a GPS coin in one of the pockets. I hope that's OK?"

The room grew silent. Berry had his head down. Finally he said, "It's fine. Thank you. I want to talk about that a little later."

The meeting continued. Jim Berry pulled all the pieces together and got all his staff on the same page. The staff had little to contribute. Joe Bruning was the exception.

Bruning said, "Just before the meeting I got a fax from Quantico. Jim, the gum wrapper that you picked up at Zaccaria's home had one clear partial finger print and plenty of DNA on the used wad of gum. We couldn't go to court with one partial but I can tell you the wrapper was touched by our friend, Anolstinsky Baranovich. Chances are the gum was chewed by Baranovich, too. I suppose this is all interesting but it really doesn't go far enough. We can place Baranovich at Zaccaria's home and we can infer that he was there the night the horse was killed. But that's about it. We need to get close enough to this guy to see where he goes and what he does. Something tells me we've got a limited time to get a handle on this thing. Any suggestions?"

Kathleen glanced at Jim Berry. She spoke up, "Jim, Joe, I think we took a risk we shouldn't have taken but I also think we solved that where and when problem for you."

Bruning said, "Kathleen, when you mentioned that earlier I didn't know what to say. You're right. It was risky and it way oversteps your defined role. But if it works, you'll be the hero of the day. We certainly weren't getting it done."

Jim Berry interrupted, "Easy, Joe. Kathleen, I love it when a staff member provides his own reprimand. Let's move on."

Berry turned to Gorge Brenneman and Joe Bruning and said, "George, Joe, can you step out and see if that GPS coin is working? Let us know."

I spoke to Jim Berry when the two men had left the room. I said, "Jim, I know it was risky but the coast was clear and he couldn't see me. Maybe I shouldn't have done it but I did get away with it. The coin is inside his breast pocket. There's very little chance that he'll accidentally find it. OK?"

Jim Berry said, "Clark. Let it go. It's done." He smiled at his two rookies.

Joe Bruning came in and said, "Jim, the tracer is working perfectly. George is printing out the history right now. He'll be here in a minute. This is great!"

Just then Brenneman came back into the room. He said, "The GPS coin has worked from the time Clark activated it and is still very strong. It should work at least four or five days."

He tacked a schematic of Celadon on the wall. "You can see here that Clark was in the middle of the restaurant when he walked over and dropped the coin. Clark never was in danger. All the sight lines are blocked. Thirty minutes later Baranovich retrieved his jacket and walked out to the parking lot. He got into his car and drove out to the Silverado Resort. He apparently valet parked and went into the main building and to the bar. That's where he is now. I've got agents waiting outside Silverado. The tail will be loose. After all, he can't go anywhere without leaving a very clear trail on our GPS set up."

Berry turned to us and said, "We have our best resources in place. Let's keep at it. OK. Folks, that's it. We'll keep each other informed."

Jim Berry used one of the most effective investigative methods ever devised. Jim's method has long been sanctioned by the FBI. It requires a unified team, total trust up and down the organization and long hours.

Most police agencies investigate crimes with the 'meeting' method. Once or twice a day the investigative team meets to share information. This method tends to let hot information cool off for several hours. It also pits individual team members against each other as the others vie for who has the most information. And, unfortunately, it gives the team leaders the opportunity to focus on what they think will get them on the front page of the local papers.

Berry's method called for the constant, real time flow of information from the field to the command center where it could be processed and fed back out to the field. Berry could do this because he had a very strong, trusting team in the field. Most police departments cannot do this for exactly the opposite reason.

CHAPTER THIRTY-FOUR

Joe Bruning and George Brenneman stayed behind to follow Baranovichi's route on the GPS system. Kerry Blount had called to relay the information on Baranovich's purchases at the gun store.

Baranovich had mentioned to Jake Jackson that a tip from the boat store led him to Jackson's store. Bruning sent an agent to the boat store for a field interview. The store was closed so the agent contacted the owner by telephone. He learned that Baranovich had purchased other items including an anchor and several lengths of rope The agent reported this to Bruning.

Bruning and Brenneman watched the Russian's progress as he left Silverado Resort, crossed town on Trancas and headed north to Yountville on Highway 29. He parked on the street not far from Hurley's, a popular restaurant that featured hearty meals and, from time to time, wild game.

Anoly entered the restaurant and took a seat at the bar. He studied the others in the bar, especially the women. All the women were in small groups or with dates or husbands. The men looked ordinary. None of them fit the Russian's vision of what an American cop looked like. In the midst of his review of the people in the restaurant, a man and a woman walked in. They, too, didn't fit the part of cops, but in fact, they were FBI agents who were in the restaurant to watch Anoly.

The big Russian ordered a double Stoli and asked for a menu. His manner was gruff and almost threatening. The couple sitting closest to him paid their bill and left the restaurant. Anoly didn't notice. He ordered another double Stoli. The bartender apparently wasn't moving fast enough to suit Anoly. He yelled at the bartender, "Hey, are you ignoring me? I told you to get me a drink. Get going!"

Everyone in the restaurant sat back and looked to see what would happen. Anoly continued to scream at the bartender, "Do you want me to come over this bar and teach you how to make a drink?"

The restaurant's manager hurried to the bar. He saw the big, heavily accented man screaming and yelling at the bartender. He also saw his customers leaving half-eaten dinners in a rush to avoid the scene. He saw that the situation was rapidly escalating.

He said to his bartender, "Henry, take a walk. I'll handle this." The bartender hurriedly left the bar and went to the outdoor patio.

Anoly turned his attention to the manager. He growled, "And what will you do about it. Do you need a lesson, too?"

Calmly, the manager said, "I've already called the police. I think they'll be here in a couple of minutes. You can leave now or you can deal with the police. Your choice."

"I ought to break your scrawny neck." The Russian was trembling with anger.

"Do what you want to do. It's only going to add to your discussion with the police." The manager glanced out the front window and continued, "I was wrong, the cops are already just up the street. You have about twenty seconds to get out and save yourself a ride in a police car."

The Russian looked around. He stood and said, "You Americans are so soft. You can bet I will be back." He ran out of the restaurant and drove away in his car.

One of the FBI agents walked outside to call Joe Bruning.

Bruning took the call and said, "What's up? Are you at Hurley's?"

The agent responded, "We're at Hurley's. The target came in and in no time he was in a screaming fight with the bartender. The manager called the cops. They got here about a minute after the big guy left. I can tell you this could have been worse, much worse. The target was carrying. I think everyone in the restaurant saw the bulge of the gun under his coat. He is gone now but he did make a threat to come back. Joe, this guy is scary. He is huge, very agile and his temper is just right there. Someone is going to get hurt."

Bruning said, "Back off. We want to track him on the GPS as long as we can. Another agent will set up behind him now. We show him going to 29 now. He turned north on 29 and, wait a second, reentered Yountville at the north end. Stay where you are. If you see him return to Hurley's, do what you have to do to protect the people. His trace shows him approaching the restaurant about now. Do you see him?"

"I see the car. He is stopping now. I think he sees the police car. He does. He is driving past. You should have him about even with the French Laundry."

Bruning said, "We do have him. This time it looks he really is leaving. Tell you what, we're on him. Stay around the restaurant, have dinner and be prepared to deal with him if he returns. OK?"

'Got it, boss. Dinner on the Bureau. Whoopee!"

Bruning went back to following the GPS trace. Baranovich did return to southbound 29. He drove south towards Napa. Eventually he stopped in downtown Napa. He was going back to Cole's Chop House on Main.

Bruning notified his agents that Baranovich was back in Cole's. The two who were closest, a woman and a man, went into Cole's and took a table so they could see Anoly.

There were no further incidents. Anoly sat at the bar and drank his Stoli doubles. Around ten he returned to his car and drove slowly down Soscol. He left Soscol and entered an industrial park south of downtown. Eventually, he drove down the street that leads to the satellite dish installation. He parked in a vacant parking lot just down the street from SSI, a pharmaceutical company, got out of the car and leaned on the hood of the car. He smoked a cigarette and studied the huge facility.

After almost an hour, seeing no activity, he retrieved a small backpack and a length of rope from the car. He walked closer and noticed a ditch that widened and led to the Napa River. The ditch ran under the railroad tracks that border the river. He saw that the ditch was a drainage feature that helped move excess rainwater away from the facility and nearby buildings and into the river. He walked to the river. Before he crossed the railroad bridge he tied one end of the rope to the backpack and the other end to a crosstie on the road bed. He tossed the backpack into the river. Then he crossed the ditch by walking on the railroad tracks and then continued along the opposite side of the ditch. He found himself on the property of the satellite facility and within easy reach of the nearest of the dishes. In the moonlight he could see five or six huge dishes facing due west as well as ten smaller dishes that faced southeast. A large building plus several small buildings completed the facility.

Anoly walked up to the chain link fence that surrounded the facility. He sneered and thought that the Americans know nothing about security. In the first place why would they locate a sensitive operation in the middle of a tourist town? Anyone could figure out what it was and how to get close to the facility. A small sack full of hand grenades could take the facility out. How stupid!

He walked along the fence for fifty yards. He could find no security devices on the fence. He thought that a pair of bolt cutters could have him through the fence in minutes.

Anoly retraced his steps and went back to his car, smoking a cigarette as he walked. He tossed the cigarette butt aside when he got to the car. It landed within five feet of the butts he had tossed away earlier.

He was pulling out of the parking lot when a police car crept along the street. He wondered if it was just a cop car out on regular patrol or if they were looking for him. Maybe there were devices along the fence. He removed his pistol from its holster and placed it on the seat beside him. He could take no chances.

The police car continued past the parking lot and up the hill to the famous "Crusher" statue that signals the beginning of the Napa Valley and its wine businesses. Anoly relaxed. There were no problems. He waited until the police car drove down the hill and disappeared down the street.

On a whim, Anoly drove to the Crusher monument. He noticed several people with telescopes. They were using the elevated park for star gazing. As he suspected, the small park afforded an excellent view of the satellite installation as well as the surrounding area.

Anoly returned to his car and drove back to Fairfield. He had a partly successful, mostly frustrating evening. He had completed all of Anapa's assignments but not had any luck with any women. At least he would get home early enough to please his boss.

CHAPTER THIRTY-FIVE

When Anoly left Hurley's, Joe Bruning and George Brenneman followed his GPS track to Cole's and then down to the parking lot beside SSI. They noticed that he paused for almost an hour when he reached the parking lot.

Kerry Blount had joined them. She transferred her Homeland Security communications into the FBI suite. In a rare moment of planning, the feds had essentially created a full-service communications desk for everyone in the building. So she had all her resources at her fingertips. She logged onto the Homeland Security network system. She reduced the Homeland Security window on her computer screen and brought the FBI window up.

They asked Blount to contact the security office at NWCOC, the satellite facility and ask for cooperation. NWCOC security committed an open line to Bruning. They also agreed to point an observation camera on the man who was standing outside their facility and to patch the observation camera to Bruning's office.

Over the next hour they watched Anoly lean against the front of the car. He chain smoked. They watched as he walked down to the railroad tracks and then as he crossed the tracks on the bridge. Midway across the bridge he paused for thirty seconds and seemed to be tying his shoe. NWCOC security notified Bruning they were getting perimeter excursion signals. Bruning asked them to engage the automatic response system.

NWCOC had an automatic response system that brought other observation devices online. It displayed a large real time video map with the intruder's location highlighted. Dog handlers in a linear building at the point of a "V" that was formed by the west facing and southeast facing dishes were put on alert. The dog handlers also had a video map of the perimeter of the building and the location of the intrusion potential.

By the time all this had been done, the FBI, Homeland Security and NWCOC security watched Anoly from every angle. They watched him walk along the fence. They watched him return to his car and toss away his final cigarette. When he left the parking lot they followed him to the Crusher monument and finally as he drove away. Their attention switched back to the GPS tracking system. In forty-five minutes they saw him park his car at the house in Fairfield.

Bruning called a meeting and arranged to have Jim Berry connected to the meeting via his secure cell phone.

Bruning said, "It's late, so let's get this done. First, we know our Russian friend has more than one interest. He has something going up Valley that might have to do with

Zaccaria and the wine business. Now we know he is also interested in Newcock. What he did tonight was very stupid. It shows his contempt for us and the US. Maybe he just doesn't know that a sensitive facility would have state-of-the-art security systems. If they had let the dogs out we'd be out there picking up pieces of him. Either that or a sniper would have sent him to big Russian heaven. Everyone there has orders and top level clearance to use deadly force – no warnings and no foolin' around.

"Tonight we need those cigarette butts. Take them to the airport and dispatch them to Quantico. Someone stay on it and let me know what they yield. Tomorrow morning we need to have a discussion with Newcock to see if they have anything they need to share. I'll do that and, Kerry, will you go with me?"

Kerry Blount replied, "I'll be here at six. Let me know when you're ready."

"Great. And let's have Clark and his wife out here around ten. By the way, I am relaxing about those two. Especially Kathleen. She's a smart lady. Did you see her scores with Jim Riley? I bet she can outshoot nearly all the female agents we have and 95% of the men. Her scores on the double-tap were almost unbelievable. Time after time she put two forty caliber rounds within an inch of each other. Her double tab is so great it almost sounds like one shot."

A double tap is a military tactic in which the shooter pulls the trigger on a double action handgun then quickly but precisely releases the trigger just to the point where the sear reengages. Then the shooter pulls the trigger a second time. When the double tap is done properly, the shots appear to be almost simultaneous. The one who receives the shots gets a double load of trouble. A double tap almost always results in quick death.

Jim Berry said, "Everyone up to date? Then let's go home."

CHAPTER THIRTY-SIX

Kathleen called Jim Berry early the next morning. She and I had thought of something that might or might not be important in this project. Berry took her call on the second ring and said, "Kathleen. How are you this morning?"

"Oh, I'm fine. But there's one thing we wanted you to know. When we first got to town, Clark and I had lunch at Meadowood one day. While we were there a huge Russian – not the one from Cole's – was having lunch with a much older man. Unless we were imagining it, four others had lunch at another table. They got up and left the table. A few minutes later the Russian and the older man left, too. We could see none of them drove away or left the place right then. Our guess is they were going to a meeting somewhere else on site at Meadowood."

Berry said "Kathleen, hang up and wait for your cell phone to ring. When it does, take a look at the picture on the screen and then call me back."

In two minutes Kathleen's cell phone rang. She picked it up and saw a picture of the older man she had seen at Meadowood. She called Jim Berry. When he answered, she said, "Jim. That's the man who was having lunch with the Russian. Does this mean anything?"

"I'm not sure, Kathleen. The man is Sid Zaccaria, one of the Valley's most respected wine growers and vintners. His wines are known all over the world.

"We need to find a way to connect our Russian, Anoly, to this new one you saw at Meadowood. Now let's try this phone/picture thing again. I'm going to send you another picture – tell me if you might have seen him at the other table." Berry sent the picture to Kathleen's cell phone.

Kathleen recognized the man immediately and called Berry back. "He was at the other table, Jim, who is he?"

"I just had a hunch, but I don't have enough to put it all together yet. Until I do, I'd rather not share that with you, Kathleen. But this additional information is really helping to tie some things together I think. Thanks and keep it up. I'll get back to you."

In five minutes Berry called Kathleen back. He said, "Sorry, I forgot about one thing. We have confirmed that Baranovich has an interest in Newcock, the satellite facility on the Napa River. Based on a surveillance that he did last night and the equipment we know he has, we think something will happen soon.

"So, we want you and Clark to stay away from the facility. That means by boat, too. It could be dangerous and it certainly could blow whatever they're doing. So please do stay away. If things change, we'll bring you back in. OK?"

"Um, OK, I guess."

"Kathleen, this isn't a suggestion. It's a direct order."

"Jim, it seems odd to me. I don't know about Clark. He isn't here. But it seems that we've been providing information that seems to be important and relevant to you. If that's true, why hold us back? I mean, I'm not arguing, I'm just asking."

Berry's voice expressed his caution, "Kathleen we're the FBI. We're delighted to have your services. Your "heads up" style has probably saved Newcock from damage of some kind or worse. You've been very valuable to us. But Newcock is now listed as one of the most highly endangered Homeland Security sites in the nation. They, and we, think somebody will try something at Newcock in a day or two. We don't want you and Clark in the line of fire so to speak."

"OK. We're fine. Thank you, Jim."

They broke the connection. Kathleen felt hyper-charged with all the things going on around her. She understood what Jim Berry had told her but she was not happy about it.

CHAPTER THIRTY-SEVEN

Anapa Krasnodar sat in the breakfast area of his home. He softly called for Anoly. Soon enough Anoly came down the hall and joined his boss. He looked tired but alert.

Anapa said, "Anoly, my friend, you look a little tired this morning. Are you ready to go to work? You know we have a couple of things to do. Am I right? Did you get all the things on my list?"

"I did, Anapa. I have them in my room. Do you want them now?

"No, no. Later is fine. Tell me. How did the visit to the satellite dish area go?"

Anoly paused for a few seconds to get his thoughts in order and said, "Anapa. Americans are stupid, greedy people. That facility has almost no security. It only has a fence. I walked down the creek that you mentioned. At the end of the creek is a railroad bridge. Just a little one. Maybe five meters. I crossed the bridge and walked back up the creek but on the other side. I walked over to the fence, shook it and then walked maybe sixty meters along side it. No alarms. No dogs. No guards. I am not sure anyone was even there."

"Did you leave anything?"

"Only the backpack, as you instructed. I walked back to the car and drove away. Oh, one other thing. I saw a monument up on a hill. I drove up the hill and found a small parking lot. I could see the entire facility from up there. Good thing to know."

"You did well, my friend. How was your visit to Napa?"

"Napa sucks. Yountville sucks even more. They're not for me. I will not go again."

"Good for you. Now, we have a meeting with our winemakers. This is money day. I want you by my side start to finish. This is the day something might happen. I want to be ready and I want you ready. If I point to someone with my right hand, that man will need a lesson. If I point with my left hand, we do not need that person in our group any longer. Understand?"

"I do. In front of the others?"

"As you see fit. Discrete is better. Get dressed and ready to go."

CHAPTER THIRTY-EIGHT

I said to Kathleen, "It looks as if we're being put on ice for the duration of this project. Why not come home a little early and lets put the boat in the river? I can be ready around three. We can be on the river by four thirty, maybe earlier. I checked the tide chart and we should be able to launch just before the high tide."

"Good idea. I could use a little change of scenery." I could hear her working with her Blackberry. "I'm open all afternoon I can leave any time."

"Great. I'll get home as soon as possible. If you have the time can you pick up some snacks and a six pack of beer?"

"I can do that. See you later."

At three that afternoon we were towing the boat to Moore's Landing, a public access launching ramp south of Napa on the Napa River. Kathleen had packed a cooler with sandwiches, chips and Corona. The trip down to the launch ramp took about twenty minutes.

The little boat was easy to launch. In no time we were cruising down the river at nine miles an hour. The Napa River is lined with marshlands. Birds and other water loving critters teemed on the river bank. After thirty minutes I turned the boat and headed up river toward Napa.

After an hour we anchored and had a sandwich and Coronas. Kathleen took over operating the motor. We slowly made progress up river until we found themselves alongside the abandoned Napa Pipe and Newcock.

Kathleen steered the boat south and within ten feet of the dock at the abandoned plant. It was fascinating to see the old dock fittings, the huge machinery and other industrial items. Kathleen told me the plant looked like something out of a Stallone movie. She thought it was a little creepy.

Shortly after we passed the plant we found the small railroad bridge. We could see Newcock to the east of the bridge. The satellite dishes were huge. They were much larger that commercial dishes.

I was trying to see if the boat could pass under the bridge when I noticed a bright black ski rope tied to a crosstie. I motioned to Kathleen to stop the engine. I paddled the boat over to the bridge and grabbed the rope. A small backpack was tied to the other end of the rope.

Kathleen said, "Clark. Put it back. I think we should call Jim Berry."

I said, "I agree but we ought to take a picture and send it Jim and wait to hear what he says."

I held the backpack out of the water while Kathleen took a picture and transmitted it. I dropped the backpack back in the river. In less than three minutes Kathleen's phone rang.

Jim Berry came on the line, "I assume you're on the river and near Newcock, am I right?"

Kathleen said, "Yes, we're drifting by the little railroad bridge."

Berry's voice was tense, "Kathleen. I directed you to stay away from this. What the hell are you guys doing?"

"Not a damn thing, Jim. We took the afternoon off to take the boat out. Remember, you told us to get familiar with the river. We were exploring the old abandoned pipe plant. When we drifted south a little Clark saw the brand new black rope tied to the bridge. He pulled it up. We figure it's probably someone's drug stash but we wanted to let you know."

Berry calmed down and said, "That's fine. I jumped to a conclusion. Tell you what, put the bag back in the river and move away. Later today I'll have someone examine the bag and then we'll decide what to do. Enjoy the river."

Kathleen said to me, "He was pissed but he got control over it and tried to make it sound like nothing. Let's get out of here."

We headed north again and went back toward Napa. We passed the community college and gorgeous residential areas. The river had been terraced in the huge flood control project. The terraces were perfect for water birds. The saw flocks of Canada geese. The females were watching over and training little goslings. The boat glided to within six feet of the geese. We knew we were seeing these birds in a way that most people never can, up close and almost a part of their routines.

A pair of Ospreys watched over the scene from perches high in the trees that lined this part of the river. The female was huge. Her wing span was close to six feet. The male was a little smaller and leaner looking. His breast was a soft brown.

Her breast had a distinctive darker breast band. Ospreys are very much the equal of bald eagles. Their size shows that but it's their total dominance of their habitat that confirms their status among birds.

The Osprey pair ignored the boat. They seemed to take turns doing sentry duty and looking for small fish that were feeding near the surface.

Kathleen continued north and shortly rounded a bend in downtown Napa. The view of the little city was very impressive. It was a mix of old, maybe turn-of-the-century buildings and conforming new structures. In Napa and in most cities, stark, gray buildings told one instantly of the presence of government. A jail, a huge county building and an old courthouse dominated one view from the river.

I said to Kathleen, "I think we can learn something here. If the government, in this case the county, is so clueless on the buildings they design, why do we think that have any sense on any other issue? These buildings would pull down any town in America. What drove them to put their buildings smack in the middle of town and make no attempt to design them to reflect this little town's heritage?"

Kathleen said, "Clark, they are clueless. Get over it. The last thing government thinks about is the people, especially the individuals and their tastes. They probably went with the lowest bidder."

We followed the river past downtown Napa under two bridges and around Napa's famous Ox Bow curve in the river.

Just past the old Copia site, Kathleen turned the little boat south and headed back down river. She kept the speed slow so we could watch the animals. We opened fresh Coronas and talked.

Kathleen said, "Do you have any idea at all what is happening at Newcock?"

I responded, "Not a clue. Something is shaping up down there. Who knows what? Jim Berry sure is sensitive about it."

She nodded, "Do you think the underground FBI offices are connected to Newcock? You know, maybe with a tunnel or something."

"Could be. I know this sounds odd, but that facility somehow feels much bigger than what we have seen. I mean if it had just a few offices why would the underground restrooms have so many toilets. The men's had eight toilets plus six urinals. What about yours?"

"I hadn't even thought about that but you're right. There were a dozen stalls in the women's room. Wow! There must be lots of people down there. What are they doing?"

"Good question. You know, I bet when we communicate with Jim Berry and Joe Bruning I bet our phones go through Newcock. I bet it handles a lot of communications."

Kathleen's phone rang. It was Jim Berry, "Where are you now?"

"We're still on the river. Let's see. We went to Napa and Copia and are now coming up on the Maxwell Bridge."

Berry said, "Can you speed it up and come back to the railroad bridge? Someone will meet you there and take the boat. He'll give you instructions on what to do."

Kathleen said, "Are we in trouble?"

"Kathleen, I'll explain everything when you get here. Please hurry."

Twenty minutes later we approached the railroad bridge. Two men in state game warden uniforms met us at the railroad bridge and helped us out of the boat and onto the land. One asked for my truck keys then got in the boat and headed south. The other motioned for us to follow him.

We walked along the grass beside the little drainage ditch and eventually along the Newcock fence to a small grove of trees. The grove was due north of Newcock. Hidden among the trees was a gate built into the other fence. At this point along the fence there were actually two fences. So when we went through the first gate we were between the two fences. Our guide motioned for us to walk about fifty feet along the fence to another gate. We went through the gate and found a large steel door before us. The guide entered several code numbers into a keypad and the gate opened. We went inside a small room. An elevator door was the only feature in the room. The guide entered more numbers into a second keypad. The elevator doors opened. We stepped inside and after the doors closed we had the sensation of going down. After twenty seconds the doors opened. The three of us were standing beside a small tram or shuttle. The guide motioned for us to take seats.

A ride of about ten minutes followed. I began to feel claustrophobic because the ceiling of the tunnel was just inches above my head. The tram came to a stop in another room. I knew we had made the trip to the FBI airport facility. Sure enough, Jim Berry was standing there to greet us.

We followed Berry to the same conference room. George Brenneman, Joe Bruning and Kerry Blount were all seated at the table. We took seats and Jim Berry walked to the head of the table. George was grinning from ear to ear.

"First, let me take a second to assure you that you are not in trouble." A smile crossed his face. He continued, "I understand that you were taking a day off and found the backpack by accident. Or maybe I should say you found it because you're alert and curious, a perfect combination.

"Now, here's what we know. The backpack contained a small but very powerful signal generator. If someone had set it off around Newcock the facility would be out of service until someone found the signal generator and destroyed it. That would have been very unfortunate because the backpack also contained four kilos of D-Nex, a very powerful explosive that would have taken out anyone within one hundred feet. Depending on where the backpack was placed the explosion might have done severe physical damage to Newcock.

"We have removed the generator parts and the bomb and placed the backpack back in the water. We have every resource aimed at that location.

"So, that's one problem. On another front, we also know that someone is setting up something with several of the Valley's winemakers. We know a couple of names. We feel that whatever is happening will get underway soon. We don't know when, where or what. It could be simple extortion or something more sinister. I think somehow John Thompson's death and the death of the horse play into it, too. We suspect, but don't know for sure, that both problems are being run by the same people.

"So, we have two big problems on our plates. They could be simple or complex or anywhere in between. My bosses in Washington want us to raid the house in Fairfield, triple the security around Newcock and get some answers now. I talked them into waiting a little. But seven trucks full of FBI raiders are in place about five miles from that Fairfield house at Travis

Air Force Base. I hope they don't go in yet, but they can be activated from Quantico and then it's out of our hands."

George, still grinning, broke in, "Jim, please, a bomb by a key facility and you still want to run this operation like a grammar school play, don't you? I think it's time to thank these people and send them home. They could have gotten their asses blown off. How would that have looked? You and probably the rest of us would be spending our days on the DEW Line tracking polar bears."

Kerry Blount spoke up, "Jim, I can appreciate your stance on this but Newcock is extremely important to our intelligence around the Pacific Rim and down through Mexico. You know as well as I do that Napa was not the ideal place to put Newcock and we both know it should have far better security. In my view, it should have a minimum of one mile perimeter with at least four antiaircraft missile batteries. But it's here, without that security, and we simply cannot afford to lose it now. I'm beginning to think George might be right."

Berry responded, "Kerry, I don't know if that was a lecture or not. I think I agree with you but I'm also sitting in the middle of all this and I know at least two big deals are going to go down sooner or later. I see tantalizing clues to what they might be but I need time. I just don't want a bunch of heavy-handed, federal, take no prisoners, types jumping in here with me. That time might come. Until it does, I want to play this out a little more. Are we on the same page, Kerry?"

Kerry Blount threw up her hands and said with a little edge of sarcasm, "Always, Jim, always."

Berry turned to George and said, "George, you're pushing me. Think before you say something like that again."

He went back to the meeting's subject, "No one is going near that backpack. Anyone who tries will be picked up on the spot. I've gotten notice that the men in the Fairfield house are now in the Fairfield Hilton Garden Inn in a meeting. Someone specified a different meeting room at the last minute. We have no equipment in the meeting room but we do have some fairly thin assets in the hotel. I wish we had more. If it looks like we need more I can get a team from Travis Air Force Base. They've been briefed and are ready to go. They can be on the scene in fifteen minutes or less. That is, assuming the scene remains the Hilton.

"We know who's in the meeting. Joe Bruning has been receiving and ID'ing photos of the men all morning. The strange thing is, there are five men from the Napa Valley and all five are beyond reproach. They're model citizens, financially successful and known throughout the wine industry.

"In addition to the five I mentioned we know Baranovich and his boss are there. Bruning is trying to ID the boss right now. We got a lot of pictures in the hotel parking lot and in the hotel. But he wears a hat that droops down and covers most of his face. He also wears sunglasses. Bruning thinks he has a 60% chance of getting an ID from the lips and nose.

"One more thing. Another man, much smaller than the other two Russians, seems to be loitering around the perimeter of the hotel parking lot. He seems to be very observant. We don't know if he is involved. More on him later.

"We very nearly had the car pulled over by the CHP before it got to the hotel on the probable cause that the windows are illegally tinted. I pulled the plug on that though because I couldn't think of a sane reason why the CHP would interview the back seat passenger on that probable cause. The

Highway Patrol in Sacramento said it was possible that the officer might develop more during the stop – a weapon, drugs, invalid driver license, no insurance, whatever. But all I could see was a colossal screw up and our targets disappearing.

"We have someone going through the car looking for fingerprints, cigarette butts or other sources of DNA right now. We noticed the back seat guy was wearing thin leather gloves when he got out of the car at the hotel. So I don't hold out much hope.

"A team is observing the house now. If they can be sure no one is at home, they'll go in and look for whatever they can find. We should know in a few minutes.

"George, what do you have for us?"

Brenneman stood and passed around a three page file. He said, "We know the bomb is from just about anywhere in the old Soviet Union. It's called D-Nex. There are no legitimate sources for it in North America. It's a hell of an explosive. I understand DuPont and the CIA have been working to learn more about it for several months. It's never shown up in the Middle East or in Africa as far as we know. The stuff is very safe to transport. You can drop it, stomp it, light it with a match, whatever and it remains inert. But a certain radio signal to the blasting cap sets it off. The blasting cap can be smaller than a paper match. It can receive the signal even if the cap is buried in the D-Nex.

"The Russians produce it and they keep very tight control on it. We know it's the kind of thing that a one ounce charge could take out an airplane and leave very little trace, if any. The stuff creates unbelievable heat with a long time signature so it tends to remove its own traces. I can tell you just between us that he TWA 747 flight 800 that broke up and went into the ocean off Long Island in 1996 did so because of less than three ounces of D-Nex. We finally found less than one milligram of the stuff in the wreckage. Back then the only source of the stuff was the Russian military. So they either placed the charge or had someone else do it. Bill Clinton refused to believe either version and insisted that it was done by Arabs. Even in the face of evidence to the contrary, that's what he believes.

"George Bush had the same kind of ideas. We urged him to face Putin with what we know and he refused. Deep in his heart, I think Bush knows that the Russian government blew up the airplane."

He smirked and rolled his eyes a little as he said, "'Course Bush also knows that at least three times on his watch, someone sprayed crops, mostly spinach, lettuce and tomatoes with e-coli and salmonella. He knows that some of the tainting has happened on trucks coming out of Mexico and he knows that the California crops were contaminated by Mexican nationals. He's afraid that it'll make things worse, not better, to tell what we know.

"I suppose we could have leaked it and we did think about it. But the FBI guy who took over the investigation screwed it up so thoroughly we figured that, once again, we had no credibility.

"At any rate, the presence here of D-Nex tends to confirm the Russian involvement in whatever this is."

A buzzing cell phone interrupted the meeting. Joe Bruning listened for a minute, hung up the phone and said "No go on the house. Our guys found heat signatures of two women and two kids, probably little ones, in the house plus two large security guys. There's no way to get inside. And, if I may say so, I don't think the FBI teams should be there either. For all we really know, Jim, this could be a family vacation and a rich guy meeting with wine guys. We need to be careful, boss."

Berry said, "I hear what you're saying. So maybe we need a plan somewhere between walking away and watching something nuclear destroy this city. Let me know what you think. You, too, George and Kerry. We're not quite back to the starting point but unfortunately we might be in sight. We need to solve these two problems. If we don't I feel strongly that we'll end up regretting it. I hope to get this done without a bunch of shooting and raids. But make no mistake about it, if it does come down to that, I'll say the word.

"Clark, one of our guys took your boat back to the launch ramp. In a few minutes your truck and the boat will be parked in the airport parking lot. It might be there now. The key will be on the left front tire. Again, you guys very well might have saved us on this bomb and signal generator thing. That rope would be tough to see at night. We owe you!

"The thought of the bomb being set off makes me sick. Why not go over to Jonesy's and have a drink before you take off for home? And, please stay in touch. If you think of something, call me or Joe."

We were escorted out of the facility. We went to Jonesy's and ordered drinks. I had a Guinness. Kathleen asked for the house Zinfandel. We talked about the private aircraft that lined the airport's apron. It was getting late so we ordered and split a cheeseburger and fries. I had another beer. We were both really thinking about what we'd heard this afternoon but we couldn't talk about it.

CHAPTER THIRTY-NINE

While the FBI meeting was in progress, another meeting was taking place in the Hilton Garden Inn in Fairfield. Anapa Krasnodar was standing at one end of a conference table.

Tom Fletcher and Larry Arbuzzio sat together on one side of the table. Kurt Johansen and Paul Martine were on the other side of the table. Sid Zaccaria sat at the end of the table opposite Krasnodar. Anoly Baranovich, glowering, sat by himself on a sofa to one side of the room.

Krasnodar said, "I notice you have brought large brief cases. I assume you are prepared to make your entry payments now."

Martine interrupted, "Entry payments? I thought this amount also got us some wine, two lots of it. What is going on?"

Anoly stood and watched the men. Krasnodar said, "Now, now. Of course it does. It was an unfortunate slip of my tongue as you say."

He continued, "And, I assume that each of you has described the wine for the two lots. One red lot and one white lot. Am I correct this time, Mr. Martine?"

Paul Martine said, "Sorry, Anapa. I'm a little jumpy I guess. There's a lot of money in this case. I don't mean to question you. I just wanted to make sure."

"No problem, Paul. Now, have each of you brought the money, the lot choices and the delivery address?"

The men nodded to indicate they had met the terms. Krasnodar looked at each man in turn. His gaze was both intimidating and demanding. There was no doubt about who was running the meeting.

Krasnodar continued, "Fine. Now, please leave your lot choices and delivery locations on the table. You will have your wine within three weeks. The label guy, Trag knows where to deliver the labels. If there are no more questions, you may go."

Sid Zaccaria spoke up, "I think I speak for everyone, Anapa. Can you please tell me what happens if we receive the wine and find it's not what we expected?"

Krasnodar glanced at Anoly and said, "It'll exceed your expectations. If you do your part, I will make you rich. If not, well, we will see." He made sure the men saw him glance at Anoly a second time. The men left the room and made their ways to cars in the hotel's parking lot.

They did not notice a small, compact man on the edge of the parking lot. The man slowly bounced on the balls of his feet. He wore huge sunglasses that were very much too big for his size. He was dressed in an Ivy League outfit with gray slacks, a blue shirt and dark blue tie. He wore Ox blood loafers shined to a mirror finish. A hop sack cloth blue jacket gave him an almost invisible look. When the last of the men had driven off he got into a ten year old Ford F-150 pickup and left the area.

CHAPTER FORTY

George Brenneman walked into Jim Berry's office. He had a stack of paper in his hands. He said, "Jim, sorry to intrude but this is important. We got a hit from Mentor a few minutes ago."

Mentor was the FBI's highly experimental facial and body type data miner. Brenneman continued, "We have one bad dude here, Jim, we have Anapa Krasnodar operating right where we don't want him.

"I'm very concerned about his sniffing around Newcock. I did some checking and learned that we're about three or four months away from an alternative to Newcock. A combination of satellite and ground based equipment should come on line by then. Newcock will become a back up. DOD will continue to maintain it and operate but we will have a safer location in the Sierras. Also, Newcock and the new installation will be able to triangulate on some signals and pin down the source very accurately. Right now that's done with satellites but a satellite's location changes at more than 18,000 miles and hour. Until the new place comes on line, Newcock is it.

"Now comes the scary part. If Newcock went off line the United States and Canada could be blinded to just about anything that anyone decides to lob at us. If that isn't bad enough, during that time a hell of a lot of communications would go by with no one on our side listening. NASA is working to get a piecemeal solution, a listening satellite, up within a couple of weeks. But we know that the Chinese and maybe the North Koreans, Pakistanis and Indians might be tempted to knock down any satellite that's obviously a flying ear for the US.

"I want your support in getting some help. I'm thinking about bringing in some Rangers or Seals. What do you think?"

Berry said, "George, how sure are you of this?"

Brenneman placed the stack of paper on Berry's desk and said in a tense, curt voice, "Read it for yourself. I'm very concerned."

Berry said, "I'm not challenging you. I just want to be sure before I do something like this. Have you shared this with Kerry Blount and her Homeland Security group?"

"I gave her a copy of this file," he said as he pointed to the stack of paper he had placed on Jim Berry's' desk. She's had just about enough time to have read it."

At that moment Kerry Blount rapped at Berry's office door and said, "Jim, I think we need to sit down and talk about this." She held up her copy of Brenneman's file.

Berry said, "Come in." He walked over to his small conference table and took a seat. The others followed.

He said, "Do you agree with George that we have a very bad guy among us and it seems to be clear that his target is Newcock?"

She replied, "I do. But George looks fairly calm. I'm very concerned."

Berry said, "You both used the same sentence, 'I'm very concerned.' That's enough for me. Let's get to work on this. Now, tell me more about this guy. Who is he, which rock did he crawl out from under and where did he first come on line with our agencies? Who wants to go first?"

Brenneman jumped in first, "Jim, Anapa Krasnodar is a Russian. He grew up all over the place and until about a year ago, he was usually seen hanging around Vladimir Putin's brother, Anatoly. We have always suspected that Putin used his brother for all sorts of dirty work, including wet work.

"Anapa dropped off our scopes eleven months ago. The French think they spotted him in Calais four months ago. The Canadians had him in customs but got into an argument with themselves over whether or not they would interview him in French or English and he simply walked out of the room, down the hall and disappeared into thin air. It makes sense that he entered the US shortly thereafter.

"The man is huge so he doesn't melt into the scenery. He would have to have help moving around in Canada and here. We should be embarrassed that he has moved in practically next door and has at least two projects going. Anoly Baranovich is with him. He is just as bad and just as scary.

"The odd thing is, Krasnodar seems to have brought his family, including some kids. This is so strange that it blows my mind. I've never heard of a bad guy traveling with his family."

Kerry Blount said, "Well, guys, it is strange. I have an idea. I'll share it with you but it's pretty rough. OK?"

Berry said, "Anything you say will be saner than a master bad guy bringing along his family. Let's hear it."

She said, "Well, we, my staff and I, brainstormed this for a few minutes before I came to you. Here goes.

"There might be two completely unrelated projects. One, Newcock, could be a 'for hire' deal which Krasnodar accepted because the Russians offered him a way to enter the US and set up housekeeping in the Napa Valley. I'm thinking it might be a 'spy who came in from the cold' type of thing. He'd do one last project for them and they'd let him retire to do whatever it is he wants to do here in the Valley."

Brenneman, said, "That certainly does put everything into a neat bundle. It explains the family. He has no intention of ever going back to Russia. Did you guys get a handle on his other project?"

Blount said, "Not really. We know this very day he had another fairly short meeting with some wine growers and vintners. This tells me he wants to do something with wine. Skulking around might just be how he works, you know, the only way he know."

Berry said, "I agree. Maybe he wants to become legit and somehow get involved in the wine business. My reports from Fairfield show that five well known winemakers met with him and Baranovich this morning at the Hilton Garden Inn in Fairfield. All the men entered the hotel with large briefcases, almost large enough to be small suitcases. They left empty handed. Let's assume there was money in those cases. That would suggest that they paid him. That's rather odd. I would have thought that if he wanted to become a winemaker he would be paying them for whatever he wanted. A winery, grape vines, technical guidance, whatever."

Kerry Blount said, "Agreed. It is odd. Very."

Jim Berry said, "It all seems to be above board but there is that horse killing at the home of one of the men, Sid Zaccaria. To me, that smacks of intimidation. And I'm still not convinced that Thompson's death was an accident, no matter what the local yokels may say.

"But I do think we're correct about the other. I do think Newcock is his target and that it probably was ordered by the Kremlin. And, I think it's so important to them that they offered him an out. They might not even know anything about his private venture. They might think he's retiring to become a winemaker."

Blount said, "Maybe he's extorting winemaking secrets from the men."

Berry added, "Could be. For me, Kerry, whatever wine scam he has going could be damaging but the real prize is Newcock. I think we focus on Newcock but keep an eye on the wine thing."

Kerry said, "I can use the Patriot Act to get taps on his line and all the lines the five men have, personal and business. I'll use the Newcock threat as a back door to get the taps authorized."

Jim Berry said, "Great. Do it. George, keep at this line of research and let us know what else you find. Folks, this is accelerating. I think the three of us plus Joe Bruning should keep in contact with each other in real time to make sure something doesn't slip by. Sooner or later we need to bring the Californians on line with this. I want to think about that for a little while more. It could blow the whole thing sky high.

Keep in mind California law enforcement is obsessed with traffic, red light runners and people talking on cell phones. If the people in California thought about it for single minute they'd be outraged that so much law enforcement money is going to pure D trivia and not crime.

"If you have any thoughts on that, let's all discuss it. I plan to stick close to the office so if something comes up don't knock, come in.

"For now, let's get to work."

CHAPTER FORTY-ONE

Kerry Blount walked into Berry's office two hours later. She said, "Jim, this is very strange."

Berry looked up and raised his eyebrows to question his counterpart.

She continued, "I got the taps approved almost at once. We've been on the Fairfield house lines for more than an hour. About once every fifteen minutes we get a short incoming burst, maybe one-eighth to one-quarter of a second. Fifteen seconds later we get an outgoing burst that's so short we cannot easily measure it.

"Clearly, this is some form of communication. But it's strange because conversations don't run that way. Conversations run on with intermittent strings that vary in length. This is more like some data feed. We think there are fifteen minutes breaks because it takes that long to unbundle each burst and prepare for the next.

"My question is who's doing this in the house? There must be more people in that house than just Krasnodar's wife and kids. It just baffles me, Jim. By the way, we've recorded the bursts. They don't yield to our routine decrypt programs. I've forward a couple to the NSA and the Navy. So far, they're stumped too."

Berry said, "Are the bursts all the same length and size?"

"Pretty much. Occasionally one will be shorter or longer. We have not found a real pattern. Of course we only have a handful as of now."

Berry continued, "Any luck on the origin of the bursts?"

"Yes, I have should have said that we do. Their origin isn't terrestrial. Maybe they're coming from a satellite or satellites. Come to think of it, Jim, the frequency would suggest several orbital communications satellites or one geostationary satellite. Can you get Newcock to take a look at the frequency of the bursts?"

Berry reached for his phone, dialed a number and said, "This is Jim Berry. Please connect me to Dave Monez. Thank you." Berry held the phone for ten seconds and then said, "Dave. Jim Berry. I need a favor. I wonder if you can watch a particular frequency for a day or so and let us know what you get. We're interested in the origin and whatever you can tell us. Yes, I'll be in all day." Berry relayed several radio frequencies to Dave Monez and hung up.

He turned back to Kerry and raised his shoulders in a "who knows" gesture. Kerry nodded her head. "I know, it seems like we've got bits and pieces, but nothing is adding up to something we can get our arms around," she said dejectedly.

As Jim began to reply his phone rang. He picked up the phone, "Jim Berry."

He listened for a minute, then said, "Thanks, Dave."

"It looks as if you've taken the lid off something strange. That was Dave Monez calling me back. He said he found out that the Newcock security system had detected the same bursts. He said they increased in frequency and length a few hours before the so-called attempted security breach a couple of nights ago. His people think they're coming from two orbital surveillance satellites. Both are Russian."

Blount said, "Monez and his people are good. If they're 100% on this I bet they know more. Why not call him back and see?"

Berry redialed Dave Monez and said, "Dave, do you guys have any idea at all about the content or the purpose of these radio signals?" He pressed the conference button on his phone. "Dave, I have Kerry Blount with me."

Monez said, "Hi, Kerry. Well, we're not certain. That's for sure. But one of my guys thinks the signals could be Go-No-Go for some kind of device. His best guess is they could be working up toward turning something important On or Off."

Blount said, "That something could be Newcock. You think?"

Dave Monez said, "We've talked about that possibility, Kerry. We have one theory that the intrusion was a practice run. Maybe someone wants to get close enough to install a device that will shut down or confuse Newcock for a short time.

"I suppose I don't have to say that we have been on our highest threat level since that theory was hatched. We're at a point where we can't lose Newcock for even a few minutes."

Berry said, "Well, maybe we can tell when they're about to go after us. I mean, we can look for increased activity from the satellites.

"Let's stay on this and please keep everyone in the loop. Dave, what do you have in place around your perimeter?"

Monez responded, "We have a high definition camera on the condo office buildings where the Russian parked last time. We also have one on a utility pole. It's trained on the railroad crossing but is also maneuverable. We have a tug and barge coming up to the old Napa Pipe property tonight. The tug will deploy eighteen specialists around the Napa Pipe area. There are a couple of thousand pallets of construction materials on the south side of the property. The specs will be out in that area. Finally, we have very good listening equipment all around out perimeter and up to one hundred yards from the fence.

"If you plan to add to that, please let me know. We don't want to shoot each other."

Kerry Blount said, "This seems to cover the north and west sides of Newcock. What about the east and south sides, Dave?"

Dave Monez replied, "We're working on that and will have something in place in a couple of hours. It occurred to us that the run a few nights ago might have been done to fool us into loading our resources on that side of the facility."

Blount continued, "Dave, any thoughts on what they might try?"

He replied, "Not really. I think we initially made a mistake and heavied up too close to Newcock. Anyone could do a hell of a lot of damage with a rocket grenade. They could do it from the river, from Napa Pipe or even from a chopper. Beyond that, it gets insane. A really good guy could use a Barrett fifty caliber rifle and play hell with us from a mile away. Hell, a shooter in a van on the Butler Bridge on Highway 29 could place a dozen shots in here and drive smoothly away in two or three minutes. If the shooter took up a position on the "Crusher" statue park it would be even easier.

"I guess this leads to a plea for more bodies. I need a couple of guys on the statue area, one or two small boats along the river, a couple of cars orbiting around the bridge and, well, I guess that would be a start. Just keep in mid that if you can help, everyone you bring on board must have the appropriate communicators and enough sense to stay out of the way of the specialists. We need eyes and ears, not muscle."

Jim Berry thought for a few seconds and said, "Dave, I'm thinking about speaking with the Napa County Sheriff. That talk might lead to the resources we need, especially out on the long perimeter and on the river. I won't make a decision to bring them in unless the Sheriff can convince me they can be discrete. I know they're capable of hot dogging and that's the last thing we need. Are you OK with that?"

"I am, Jim, just let me know where and when and who. By the way, I have about two dozen communicators and battery sets. I can spare maybe a dozen. Just let me know."

"Thanks, Dave." Jim Berry hung up the phone and turned to Kerry Blount. "Kerry, more and more I think whatever is happening is going to happen soon. I'm going to call everyone in, including Kathleen and Clark. Can you stay?"

"Sure. I'll be in my office." She left the room as Berry turned back to his telephone.

CHAPTER FORTY-TWO

We left work early and met at the airport. Ten minutes later we were in Jim Berry's conference room. Joe Bruning and George Brenneman were there. We took our seats just as Kerry Blount and Jim Berry walked in.

Jim Berry took the next forty-five minutes to very meticulously bring everyone in the room up to date. He then turned to a blow up map of the area and marked the position of the Newcock specialists and the others who were deploying around the satellite listening facility. He covered the locations and purposes of the in-place electronics equipment. When he had finished, he asked for questions.

Joe Bruning said, "Man, I would hate to be a hummingbird that accidentally flew near Newcock."

George Brenneman replied, "Yeah, well, they won't be sending hummingbirds. My money is on a single person who knows what he is doing. We have to be careful that we don't walk all over ourselves and leave an opening as big as a barn door. There is such a thing as having too much cover, you know."

The comment made Jim Berry a little anxious. He said, "I hear you George. And, I guess I think the real problem might be too many spoons in the soup. I guess that's why I rejected the idea of bringing in the Sheriff's Office. The local SO is pretty competent as far as it goes with small town stuff. But I guarantee you they don't have a person who has ever trained for something like this."

He looked over the people in the conference room. Finally he said, "We're going to go with what we have. Stay out of the way of Dave Monez's specialists. Keep your communicators on. Use your earpieces. We don't need to add to ambient noise." He pointed to a stack of black plastic boxes that everyone in the room recognized as Glock pistol cartons.

Berry said, "These are Glock Model 17's. They differ from the standard Model 17's in three ways. First, you'll notice the compensator cuts on the top of the slide. This feature will greatly reduce the recoil and, therefore, improve your accuracy. Second, notice that the barrel isn't flush with the end of the slide. The barrel sticks out a little and is threaded. You can screw on a small sound suppressor. There's a suppressor in each of the boxes. Just remember. If you use the sound suppressor, you must block the compensator cuts. Again, there's a snap-on device to do this in each box. If you've not used a suppressor before, keep in mind this is not the movies. The movie folks seem to think a three inch piece of metal tubing will reduce the sound of the shot to almost nothing. In reality, there are three components of noise when a handgun is shot.

"First, there's the mechanical noise." H picked up one of the Glock pistols, checked to make sure it was not loaded, then racked the slide back and pulled the trigger. He said, "The noise as the slide being cycled to reload the chamber makes plenty of noise. And, that noise cannot be suppressed.

"Second, there's the noise of the cartridge going off. The suppressor contains some of that noise and it greatly reduces the flash from the barrel.

"Finally, the bullet starts out supersonic. Like a supersonic jet airplane, it makes a long, continuous sonic noise or boom. We can use subsonic rounds. They're a little quieter. But subsonic rounds are not as accurate as our issue rounds. The trade off for being quiet is poor accuracy.

"The real contribution of a suppressor is the reduction of the muzzle flash and toning down the initial noise of the cartridge going off. For my money, the suppressor is great for close up work at night. Otherwise, forget it.

"You'll also notice a control on the left side of the slide. In the up position the Glock is a standard single action semi-auto. Put the control down and it becomes a fully automatic weapon with a rate of fire of about 300 rounds per minute. The magazines have 18 rounds so you can empty the magazine in a little less than four seconds. You'll have six full mags each with 18 rounds. Use them wisely.

"I think everyone here has test fired a weapon similar to this one. Clark, Kathleen, Jim Riley brought you up to date on this, didn't he?"

Kathleen spoke up, "He sure did, Jim. I think Clark has nearly recovered from that experience." She grinned at me with a wink. Everyone in the room laughed.

Berry brought the meeting back to order. He said, "Joe, George, I want you here monitoring the area. You can always reach me on my communicator. Kerry, you have your own jobs to do. Keep in touch."

Motioning to us, he said, "And, here's what I want you two to do."

He outlined a plan that would put us in our small boat anchored about a few hundred yards south of the railroad bridge. We were to tie up to a bridge support structure and observe and wait. He gave us the Glock boxes and two back-packs with food and other supplies. He said, "We installed a second fuel tank with about fifteen gallons capacity on your boat. Remember to switch tanks well before the first tank runs dry. A switch to change tanks is mounted on the tran-som beside the motor on the right side of the boat. If you don't, you'll have to restart the engine.

"We also added stocks of water and a couple of jackets and caps. We replaced your unit with a depth finder of sonar that also has a GPS feature so you can see where you are. The unit we installed has a light shield but if someone is directly behind you, they could see the light from the screen. There's a cover for the screen. Use it unless you must see the screen and then use your body to shield the screen's light."

Indicating two packages about the size of shoe boxes, he said, "These contain night vision eyewear. If you use them the night will turn into day. They're very efficient. But your field of vision will narrow and you'll lose some of your natural ability to sense things happening around you. And, if the bad guy has the same equipment, he'll be able to see your beam. Like everything else in life, nothing is free. Gain something, lose something.

"Oh, one more thing. Your boat motor has had a major upgrade. You now have a 25 horse jet model engine. It has no propeller so you can easily navigate very shallow water.

"I suggest you launch just before the launch ramp closes at ten tonight. Someone will be there to drive your truck and trailer away. If you leave it at the ramp some enterprising local patrol cop might have it towed. When you return to the ramp the truck and trailer will be there. We'll take it back around six the next morning or sooner if you need it. If I need to give you more information for tomorrow, it'll be locked in your truck.

"Now, get ready for an important assignment. Let me know when you're in place at the bridge. We want to keep the communicators very quiet. We think they're secure but one never knows. Good luck."

CHAPTER FORTY-THREE

The last light was leaving the Napa River when we launched our boat. Kathleen wore black jeans and a black long-sleeved T-shirt. She had black hunting boots. I wore similar clothing.

The Napa River was flowing toward the bay. The water was flat and shiny like painted steel. It reflected every light from distant homes and from airplanes on approach into the Napa airport.

We sat in the boat and got our bearings. I checked the supplies and got familiar with the controls on the new outboard. I saw that I could switch from the main six-gallon tank to the larger second tank by simply moving a control that was mounted on the transom beside the outboard. I calculated that the new outboard motor could run flat out for at least six hours on the twenty-one gallons. We had more than enough fuel for the mission. I started the engine and was amazed how quiet it was. At idle I could barely hear the motor.

We had placed our Glock pistols, with the suppressors in place, in the backpacks. We retrieved the pistols and placed them on the seats beside us. I also laid the Ruger rifle alongside my seat in the boat. I wondered why I needed a weapon like the Ruger. It was compact in size but I could not imagine why I would need that much firepower. Hadn't Jim Riley said that most gun fights happened at less than ten feet between the two people who were involved? The idea of a gunfight of any kind did not sit well with me.

Kathleen pulled the jackets out of the backpacks. Even this early in the night there was a chill in the air, the kind of chill that always comes along when one is on the water at night. She opened two bottles of water and handed one to me.

I rigged the fishing rods and placed one in the rod holder up toward the front of the boat and one in my rod holder. I said, "Berry said if we get busted by the locals we have two actions. First, get rid of the pistols. Second, start fishing and make it look real."

Kathleen took her seat. I eased the boat out into the river and began making my way south for a few minutes then turned back north toward the bridge. I kept the speed about half of what I figured the rig would do. I had no intention of drawing attention to us.

I continued past the bridge and about two hundred yards past the abandoned Napa Pipe factory. At one point I thought I saw a shadowy figure move between the storage pallets. Thousands of pallets were stacked on the apron of the pipe factory. I decided it was a bird. To think otherwise was not acceptable. If those so-called specialists over there were moving around in plain sight when their orders were to be invisible, this would be a long night. I hunched down in the boat and continued past the old pipe factory. I turned back south and pulled up to the bridge piling. It was even darker under the bridge. Kathleen put the anchor on the ledge of the bridge piling. It held fast. By the time she secured the boat it was eleven-twenty. There was not a sound except for the occasional sound of a vehicle crossing the bridge.

I noticed that Kathleen's Glock was nowhere in sight. I decided she had put the gun inside her jacket. I thought about it for a minute and reached for my gun.

Things started to come unraveled when a heavily accented middle European voice behind me said, "My friend, please do not touch the gun. Now, please pull yourself up on the ledge. Missy, you just sit and look pretty. We will talk later. And, if either of you turn around I will have to shoot out your eyes. We do not want that, do we?"

I eased myself over to the side of the boat and hoisted myself up to the large ledge that was the top of the bridge support. I sat on the ledge with my feet hanging over the side. I could just make out the man's shape in the dark. He was enormous.

His voice continued, "Now, my friend, please tell me why you are here with your big pistol and your little lady? And, please, do not fuck with me. I think I know the answer and if I think you are lying I will kill you and then her. I have a suppressor, too."

I stared into the blackness and said, "We work for the government. We're out here looking for illegal immigrants." He paused.

Kathleen knew that I was lying and it terrified her that the man might know the same. She thought about where I was and where the man was. She was sitting with her arms folded to keep her hands warm.

"I thought you were too smart to try that with me, my friend. Tell me, please, what is your name?"

I answered, "Clark Davis."

"Thank you, Sir. You are lying. I like to know the names of the people I kill. Now is your time for killing."

I turned to see that the man was less than five feet from me. The man was raising his gun.

Blinding flashes and the metallic clanks of a pistol cycling filled the air at the same time that the top of the man's head exploded. Kathleen had fired five rounds and it seemed that each of them found a home in the man's head, neck and chest. The force of the bullets literally pushed the man backward.

I turned to Kathleen to see her holding her Glock on the man. Her hands were steady and she was ready for another shot. She said, "Fucking Berry forgot the part about the explosive bullets."

Kathleen put her Surefire light on me and stifled a scream, "Clark! Are you OK?"

The side of my head and my body down to my waist was covered in blood. Kathleen was sure she had also shot me.

I looked at my side and said, "I'm fine. I think this is what they call 'splatter' on Court TV." I eased myself back into the boat and retrieved my pistol. I wiped my face and hand with a shop rag that I kept in the boat and said, "Get down. Sit in the bottom of the boat. Put on your night glasses. There could be others."

We knelt down behind the gunwales and searched the river bank. We couldn't see anyone else around.

284

At that moment we felt more than heard a shot from the direction of the old pipe factory. We crouched down behind the bridge ledge. Another shot then two more clanked around us. The bullets were hitting the bridge piling and the water. One glanced off the seat where Kathleen had been sitting one minute earlier.

Kathleen said, "Someone's shooting at us. Start the motor and let's get the hell outa here." She grabbed the anchor rope and hauled it in hand over hand.

I started the outboard and tried to push the boat off so the bridge piling would be between us and the pipe factory. Another shot splashed about a foot from the boat. The flash from the shot reflected off the pallets of construction materials on the apron at the pipe factory. I could see a man standing about seventy-five yards away. He was moving slowly in our direction. He would stop and crouch at a storage pallet, then move forward to another pallet.

I got the Ruger rifle from the boat seat and put the motor in idle. The man fired one more shot. I heard it zing over my head. I could see Kathleen and knew she was OK. I brought my rifle up and fired the three three-round bursts. I ejected the magazine and retrieved another from my jacket pocket. The flash from the muzzle of my rifle was very bright. I moved the throttle on the outboard to full power and steered the boat away from the bridge piling. There were no more shots. I continued to steer the boat south toward the launch ramp.

After a few minutes, I pressed the Call button my communicator. Jim Berry came back immediately, "What the hell is going on, Clark?"

"Jim, I think it might be over. We're at the bridge. Send someone right now."

"Are you and Kathleen OK?"

"We're fine. Just get over here. I'm going to need a change of clothes. Kathleen shot the big Russian. Another man started firing on us from all those pallets on the pipe factory lot. I put a full mag in his direction. I either hit him or he left. He isn't shooting at us now."

Less than five minutes later a helicopter flooded the area with a very bright light. Ten minutes after the helicopter arrived, others began pouring in. I turned the boat and went back toward the light. I pulled the boat up to the bridge piling. Kathleen tied the boat to the piling.

Jim Berry was among the first to arrive. He handed me a shirt and jacket and a plastic bag. He said, "Holy shit, Clark what happened? Are you OK? There's blood all over you."

I said, "I'm fine. The blood's not mine. I think it belongs to that big guy on the piling. When Kathleen shot him he sorta exploded."

Less than an hour later all the key players were in Jim Berry's conference room. He stood at the head of the table. Joe Bruning was absent, as was Dave Monez.

Berry said, "Clark, Kathleen, one of you please tell us exactly what happened out there on the river tonight. Take your time."

I had changed clothes but still had blood in my hair. I began, "Well, we launched the boat and rode up to the pipe plant and turned around back toward the bridge. Just after we tied up, this guy, this Baranovich, got the drop on us and told me to get up on the bridge piling. It was dark as hell and I had no idea where he was.

"I got up on the bridge and sat there. He told me to tell him what we were up to. He said he was pretty sure of the

answer but he wanted to hear it from me. He said he would
kill me if he thought I was lying. I started telling him we
were look for illegals. He stopped me and asked my name. I
told him my name. He said I was lying and he always liked
to know the names of those he killed. I turned to see him
and I think that distracted him for a second. Just as I saw
him standing there about to shoot me, his head blew up. He
wasn't paying much attention to Kathleen and he sure didn't
know she had her gun in her hand and she damn well knew
how to use it. I wish it hadn't happened that way. Mainly I
wish those bullets hadn't been about six inches from my head.
Kathleen saved my life, our lives. I hope we didn't screw up
our assignment." My hands were clasped on the top of the
table. I dropped my head and began trembling, the adrenalin
was wearing off and I was coming to grips with how close a
call we'd had.

Jim Berry turned to Kathleen and said, "Kathleen, can
you add anything to that?

Kathleen replied, "Not much. In another second Clark
would have been dead. I would have found myself in a gun
fight with a guy who probably was better at it than me. I did
what I did." She sat up proudly and seemed to dare Jim Berry
to say something.

I said, "Oh, another thing, Jim. Just as we were calming
down we started getting shot at from the pipe factory. At
first I decided to try to get the boat going south and away
from the shooter. I think he had a long gun and the shots
kept coming and kept getting closer. So, I killed the engine
and shot three three-round bursts at the shooter. He stopped
shooting. I either hit him or he ran. I don't know which,
honestly."

Joe Bruning entered the room with a large backpack. He looked at Jim Berry and said, "Sorry I'm late. We found another backpack on the bridge piling. It has an electronic device that Dave Monez's guys say could have put Newcock out of action for weeks or months. This bomb is quite a lot more powerful that the first one. It also had a small dirty bomb – D-Nex and some radioactive lead particles. That would have made repairing Newcock all the more difficult. Obviously, the bomb isn't still in the backpack.

"I'm not sure what happened out there at the bridge but whoever did it saved Newcock and very well might have saved much, much more. So who did it?"

Berry said, "Kathleen and Clark engaged Anoly Baranovich. Clark was about to be shot by Baranovich when Kathleen used her full auto Glock to remove the man's head. When that happened, they thought it was over. It wasn't. They began receiving incoming shots from over at the pipe factory. The guy probably shot five or six times. Clark returned fire. Joe, will you get the chopper up and see what you can see from the pipe factory. Look next to the river next to those pallets. Get back to me.

"We had specialists and operatives surrounding Newcock and it took our volunteers to save the day. Kathleen, Clark, thank you."

Berry stood and said, "Folks, tonight is off the scope. The mess has been cleaned up. We expect you to keep the lid on. No exceptions. Don't discuss it on cell phones and don't discuss it among yourselves. Starting right now, tonight did not happen. You were trying night fishing on the Napa River and spent most of your time up around the Maxwell Bridge. When you get home you'll find two large stripers cleaned and packaged in your refrigerator. The bones and heads will be in sealed plastic bags in your garbage container. Your boat will have been cleaned up and restored to its original condition."

Ten minutes later Joe Bruning called on Berry's conference line and said, "Jim, there's a man lying dead beside the pallets. We found a firearm, a Wilson AR-15 type rifle, on the ground beside him. A team is a minute away. Tell Clark I can see three hits. Good shooting!"

Berry said to the group, "Well, this has been some night. Again, Clark, Kathleen, thank you and sorry to be so blunt, but keep your mouths shut. The rest of you work here and here is where you were all night. Now, everyone go home and get some rest. We know Krasnodar is still capable of something and we need to get moving on it."

CHAPTER FORTY-FOUR

Anapa Krasnodar did not sleep the night of the raid on Newcock. He repeatedly attempted to contact his agent, Anoly Baranovich. Every attempt failed. Finally, around three in the morning, he reasoned that if there had been a big problem at the satellite dish facility, it would be on the television news. He rotated between local and national news programs until after nine in the morning. The programs didn't cover any such problem. He searched the Internet news feeds and came up with nothing.

Surely, he wondered, the Americans would have any big problem on the news in no time. He tried Anoly's cell phone again and then decided to drive over to Napa to see what he could see around the dish facility.

Joe Bruning called Jim Berry to tell him that Baranovich's cell phone was being called every few minutes. The calls began around midnight and continued through the morning. Routine call tracing had been unsuccessful but they had traced the caller to a cell antenna in Fairfield. The signal strength indicated the caller was about a mile from the antenna. Bruning said it was highly likely that the caller was in the Krasnodar home in Fairfield.

Berry ordered a 100% shadow for Krasnodar. He wanted four men watching the home and three cars trailing Krasnodar's car if it left the home. The cars would be discrete but they also wouldn't let Krasnodar escape their observation. He also stationed five 'trade off' cars along the road from Fairfield to Napa. The trade off's could fall in behind Krasnodar and let the original tailing car drop back. This would reduce the opportunity for Krasnodar to detect the tails.

Krasnodar drove the short distance from his home in Fairfield to the Butler Bridge across the Napa River. He slowed and studied the area north of the Bridge. There were no police vehicles and no other signs that anything had happened.

He turned around for another pass along the bridge. This time he noticed a pull off area on the east side of the bridge. He carefully eased his car over to the pull off area and got out of the car. Again, he saw nothing unusual. He was too far south to see the dish facility. He returned to his car and drove to the end of the bridge and turned right onto the road that led to the Crusher statue. As he approached the parking lot near the statue, he noticed a dark blue Suburban truck in the parking lot.

Krasnodar saw four men standing on the area's highest spot. They were looking toward the dish facility and talking. They had not seen him approach the parking lot. He quietly stopped and backed down the hill. He immediately drove back to Fairfield. He had no doubt that something had happened in that area and he also had no doubt that the men had not seen him.

When he returned home he assembled some radio equipment and sent a one second burst. He set the equipment to repeat the burst five more times to make sure at least one of the satellites had received his coded message.

Then Krasnodar took the equipment apart and hid the components. Later he would destroy it and distribute it around the area in dumpsters and other disposal areas. It had been a close call. Too close. He concluded that Anoly had been killed or, perhaps, captured. He doubted that Anoly would permit himself to be captured though.

Krasnodar went into his office and began to carefully analyze his situation. He had set up the raid on the secret facility in exchange for money and a promise that he could stay in the United States and would never again be contacted by his former bosses in Russia. He thought that he had given it his best and told himself that he could not be responsible for Baranovich, an agent who was not picked by Krasnodar but by his Russian boss, Anatoly Putin.

From the beginning he had thought that Baranovich was dense. The man took orders well but he always introduced his own elements into his missions. He spent time at bars when he should have remained out of sight. He womanized when the truth was his size and mannerisms gave him no chance with women. Even whores were wary of him. The man exaggerated his role in everything.

Now, he concluded that Baranovich was dead. That was an important thing to Krasnodar because Baranovich would never be able to contradict his side of the story. He concluded that he had given it his best and it had failed, mostly due to the thick Russian's clumsiness. So he was free of Russia and he was free of Anatoly Putin. He had told the Russians as much in his communications burst. There was nothing he could do to change whatever had happened the night before.

Krasnodar shifted his thinking to the wine program. He had the money from the five winery operators. He could simply take the money and go into hiding. The money would last a long time if he was careful. When the money ran out, he reasoned, he could think of another way to make money. After all, he was in the United States, a place where people had too much money and were very gullible and greedy.

He decided to bring the wine program to a conclusion quickly. If the Russians did something, he would deal with it when it happened.

CHAPTER FORTY-FIVE

By the end of the day Jim Berry and the others had wrapped up the raid on Newcock. They concluded that the big Russian had been on assignment to destroy or disable the facility. As the Russians usually did, they had totally miscalculated the security. The attempt had been clumsy, poorly planned and even amateurish. While the Newcock security manager enthusiastically praised what we did, he said it was very likely that his staff would have shot the attempt down. After all, they did monitor Anoly when he conducted his reconnaissance mission.

Jim Berry would leave it to the National Security Agency to figure out who and why. For now, he wanted more information on Anapa Krasnodar. He called a meeting for six that evening to begin to find answers to his questions about Krasnodar.

Kathleen and I joined the others in Jim Berry's conference room. When we sat down, several of the others gave us thumbs up signs. George Brenneman turned to Kathleen and said, "You are something else, lady. Ninety-nine percent of the cops in the country wouldn't have taken that shot. Clark was too close. It was very dark. I could go on and on. Wow!"

Kathleen smiled and said, "George, thank you. I did what I had to do. In another second he would have killed Clark. There was no time to think about it."

Brenneman responded, "I'm just saying what you did and what you just said reminds me of one of John Wayne's great movies, The Shootist. Wayne's character, John Bernard Books, was teaching a young Ron Howard to shoot. Howard's character was asking endless questions about the number of men Books had killed. The kid wanted to know how Books had not been killed himself.

"Books said, 'Most men will hesitate or take a breath and think about it. I won't.' That surely describes you, Kathleen. It's a pleasure to work with you."

Kathleen said, "George, I'm not very pleased to have killed a man no matter how bad he was. But I'm very pleased to still have my best friend and husband. If I had any thoughts at all last night it probably had to do with keeping Clark alive. Before any of you ask how I feel about killing a man, well, so far, I have no bad things in my head. I slept very well last night, ate a chicken fried steak breakfast at Gillwood's and am ready to do whatever comes up. And, to tell the truth, I enjoyed being on the river at night and plan to get back out there as soon as I can."

I pushed my chair back and said, "As the person who failed to take a good look around the bridge piling before anchoring, I know I'm damn lucky to be here. Strike that.

I'm damn lucky to have Kathleen, a person who can put five automatic forty caliber rounds on target."

Kathleen interrupted, "Oh yeah, Jim, it seems you left out the exploding bullets part. The results were very impressive."

Berry smiled and said, "Kathleen. There was nothing 'explosive" about those bullets. I know it must have looked like they exploded. I think the fact that you really did put five – not seven – .40 caliber rounds in a persons head in less than two seconds – that caused some impressive damage. I am told that the first shot did the work. The others simply put a lid on it. Kathleen, you have joined the ranks of Bureau people who have ended a problem and saved other lives. Everyone in the Bureau is totally in awe and in your debt.

"Now let's talk about Krasnodar. Here's what we know. First, Krasnodar has met with five winery owners at least three times in the past few weeks. Joe Bruning took a look at the bank accounts of all five men and noticed very large cash withdrawals in the past week. Each of them rounded up about $2.8 million. My guess is the money was in the suitcases they took to their last meeting with Krasnodar in Fairfield. This means Krasnodar has somewhere around $14 million in cash.

"Second, I believe one or more of the winery owners balked and Krasnodar had Baranovich kill a very much loved horse that belonged to one of the men's wife. Just to get his attention and send a pretty direct message.

"Third, Krasnodar is now operating alone unless he has others in deep cover. I don't think he has. I think he is freelancing on his own and looking for an even bigger payday.

"Fourth, maybe Krasnodar is simply running a scam. Maybe he has something on those five men. Whatever it is, it's very powerful and I want to know what it is.

"There you have it. Any comments?"

Kerry Blount said, "Jim, why don't we grab one of them and see what we get?"

"Let's think about that. Somehow it might tip off Krasnodar. Or, the men might be just as guilty and if they talk to us there's the self-incrimination issue. I'm going to hold off on that, Kerry, but I have to tell you it's certainly a viable option.

"Anyone else?"

I spoke up, "Well, we could single one of them out and make friends. I'm sure Kathleen can find an excuse to approach someone on the fund raising side. Maybe by the time we get close you'll have enough information to tell us what to look for."

Joe Bruning said, "I like that approach, Jim. We could just get close to one of them and see what happens. Of course, that won't be all we do, but it's a strong starting place. I like it."

Berry said, "I like it too. There's no downside. If it doesn't work, nothing is lost or risked. If it does work we'll look like we know what we're doing." He smiled at the group and continued, "Any suggestions on which one of the men to target?"

Kathleen spoke, "What about the man whose wife lost her horse? Seems like he might be spooked but he also might be a little bit angry. Angry people tend to act before thinking it through. He might be vulnerable."

Berry said, "Good idea. Let's go after Sid Zaccaria. I'll get back to you on the best place to contact him."

The group continued to discuss Krasnodar for almost an hour. When the meet concluded, Kathleen and I drove home.

CHAPTER FORTY-SIX

Anapa Krasnodar called Sid Zaccaria's number. When Zaccaria answered, Krasnodar said, "Sid, my friend, I have good news. I want to meet with you very soon. I have some wine for you. And I have a plan to get this wine going. Can we meet today?"

Zaccaria replied, "Sure. Tell me where." His voice was cold and detached. He had lost his nerve for the wine program and he detested Krasnodar.

"I would like to meet you in the parking area of Cindy's Back Street Kitchen, in St. Helena around one this afternoon. Please park in the lot. I will find you. Drive your Escalade EXT, the one that looks like a truck but is really a car."

Two hours later Zaccaria parked where Krasnodar had indicated. He sat in the car, waiting and worrying. Finally, he saw Krasnodar leave the restaurant and walk down the steps. He was picking his teeth with a toothpick.

The Russian walked to his car, retrieved a case of wine and walked over the Zaccaria's car. He said, "Thank you for coming, Sid. You will be very glad you did."

The Russian opened the back seat car door on the driver's side and placed the case of wine on the seat. He walked around the car and took a seat beside Zaccaria.

He said, "In that case of wine you will find two reds and two white wines. Three bottles of each wine. I want you to take the wine with you and taste each of the wines. Take your time. I want you to be convinced that this is the real thing. Will you do that?"

Zaccaria nodded to indicate that he would.

"Then, my friend, I want you to take a bottle of each wine to the American Wine office in Napa. Do you know the place? It is a restored Victorian home. I think it is almost in the middle of town."

Zaccaria said, "I know the place. I've been there. What then?"

Krasnodar said, "Before you go call and make an appointment with Jonathan Beale. Do you know him?"

"I do. I also know he doesn't meet with winemakers."

"Tell him you have something very interesting to share with him and that you will give him exclusive rights to it. I trust you to make it happen, Sid. Now go to it. You can make the appointment on your car phone. Here is the number."

Krasnodar handed Zaccaria a small piece of paper with a telephone number. He left the car and walked away. Sid watched the Russian walk away, looked down at the paper in his hand and took a deep breath. This was spinning out of control and he knew it. What next? Was the Russian going to control every part of his life? He gave an involuntary shudder at the thought. Slowly he started his car and rolled out of the parking lot.

CHAPTER FORTY-SEVEN

One of Jim Berry's agents called and reported the details of the meeting, "Zaccaria drove about a block then made a telephone call. Are you on that call?" he asked.

Berry said, "Thanks. We're on it, keep me informed."

Three minutes later an agent handed Berry a transcript of the call.

Voice: "American Wine. May I direct your call?"

Zaccaria: "Jonathan Beale, please. This is Sid Zaccaria. He knows who I am." There was a mechanical click of being put on hold and a pause.

Voice: "Mr. Beale would like to know the nature of your call, sir."

Zaccaria: "Tell him I have something that he wants and tell him it'll be exclusive to him if he takes the call."

Voice: "Yes, sir. One moment please."

Beale: "Mr. Zaccaria. This is Jonathan Beale. I'm on deadline so please get to the point." Beale was his usual arrogant, pompous ass. He had made his reputation being an ass and he got better at it as time passed. If one compares Beale with other wine writers, it is clear that he is not comfortable with his level of power. He compensates by being an ass.

Zaccaria: "Jonathan, I'm willing to let you sample my four new wines. No one knows about these wines. If you agree, I'll drop off the wines at your reception desk within the hour. No meeting is necessary. Please, Jonathan, I think you'll be glad you did."

Beale: An audible sigh, and then, "Fine." The connection was broken.

Berry told the agent to stay on the phone. He read and reread the cell phone transcript. He knew the answer was in that conversation.

He called Kathleen, "Kathleen? Jim Berry. If you and Clark have the time, I have something for you. I'm afraid it's not as exciting as your trip on the river. Are you free?"

"Sure Jim, we're both here. What's up?"

"I want you to go over to the American Wine office on First Street. Do you know where it is?"

"Yes, we've noticed it, but we've not been in."

"Great. Put on something scholarly looking and go to the office. They keep back issues and a reference system. Ask for the November issues for 2000, 2001 and 2004. Take the copies into the reading room and start reading. Make notes now and then. I need you in there the rest of the afternoon. Let me know what goes on inside. We'll have agents watching the outside."

Kathleen said, "That sounds easy. We'll be there in fifteen minutes or less."

Kathleen and I threw on the appropriate clothes and took off for the short two mile drive from our home to American Wine. Maybe five minutes after we began reading the magazines, Sid Zaccaria walked in and approached the receptionist. He placed a wine case on the desk and spoke quietly to her.

I was struck with an idea. I rose, walked toward Zaccaria and said, "Mr. Zaccaria. I hope I'm not intruding, but do you have a second? I've always wanted to meet you and ask some questions."

Zaccaria eyed me for a moment, looked around himself as if to see if he were being observed and said, "Well, how nice of you. Sure, I have a few minutes."

I shook his hand and guided him back into the reading room. Out of the corner of my eye I noticed that the receptionist took the wine case upstairs.

I said, "This is a real pleasure Mr. Zaccaria, this is my wife, Kathleen Royal. I'm Clark Davis. We're pretty new to Napa."

Zaccaria said, "Please. Call me Sid. Welcome to God's country. Now, what would you like to know?"

Now that I had him in front of us, I was momentarily at a loss for what to ask him. Just as I was about to speak, Kathleen broke in and said, "Well, I think the main thing is this. I know your time is valuable so I'll get to the point. You've been very successful in the wine business. One of your hallmarks has always been consistency. I think your wines are close to perfect," she smiled at him warmly. Then she said "So, what's your reaction to the newer winemakers who go for high alcohol, more fruit and rangier tastes?"

Zaccaria stared at Kathleen and considered her question for a minute, then said, "Are you saying my wines are obsolete or are you saying the newer wines are fads?" His attitude was clearly challenging. Yet he was open and friendly. I thought he was a little on edge. His voice was just a little strained. I could tell that Kathleen thought so to, and knowing her well, I could tell her mind was racing and trying to deal with all the mixed signals she was getting from Zaccaria.

She said, "Oh, I hope I didn't offend you! I admire your wines more than ever. If you don't mind me saying so, I know what to expect from Zaccaria wines. The consistency is amazing. But year to year I find subtle differences of the kind that tell me that while I enjoyed your wines in the past, the latest ones fill in notes that I didn't even know were missing."

Zaccaria seemed surprised by her remarks, but he accepted the compliment with a big smile. He said, "Thank you. I can't talk about it right now but I have some very different wines that I plan to bring out soon. I brought some by for Jonathan Beale to try. That's why I'm here today. Any more questions?"

Kathleen said, "Not really. But you didn't answer my question."

Zaccaria smiled and said, "So I didn't." He glanced at his watch and said, "Answering your question will take time. I don't think you're a reporter or writer but since you obviously know a little something about wine, I want to make sure you understand my answer. Tell me, can the two of you meet me for drinks in an hour or so? Wait, no, that won't work. My wife is cooking tonight and I need to be there. She's an excellent cook. Why don't you two come to our home for dinner tonight? I'll call my wife and let her know. She always way over cooks so there will be plenty. Will you?" He seemed surprised at himself for the spontaneous offer, but pleased at the same time.

I said, "We'd be honored, Mr. Zaccaria."

Zaccaria took a piece of paper from his shirt pocket and jotted down the directions to his home. Kathleen noticed the man's hands were shaking as he wrote the note. He offered it to me and said "Please, call me Sid. I'll see you at seven. Maybe I'll give you a sneak peek at my new wines." He smiled briefly, turned and walked out of the building.

When we were alone, I said to Kathleen, "You're amazing. Berry suggests something and a day later you've wangled an invitation to the man's home for dinner." I sat back and thought, "No doubt about it, she's more into this than I am."

She replied, "You're the one who got us introduced to him! But, Clark, that man is very troubled. He seemed so grateful for a little attention and a compliment on his wines. I don't know why, but I sense that he's carrying a big burden of some kind." She collected the magazines and said, "Let's turn these in and get home to change. And, we need to call Jim Berry."

When they were in the car, Kathleen called Jim Berry. Before she could say anything we heard Berry say, "I can't believe what I was just told – Zaccaria telling his wife he's invited you two to dinner! You're actually going to the man's home tonight?" Obviously they were listening in on Sid's cell phone.

"We are. Any special things we should know?"

"Well let me bring you up to date. First, my agent at American Wine said the box Zaccaria took to American Wine looked like the same one Krasnodar placed in Zaccaria's car.

He said it looked 'lighter' which I guess means it contained less than it did in St. Helena. Second, when Zaccaria left you he drove over to a local law firm on Coombs Street in downtown Napa. He's still there.

"Kathleen, how did you read Zaccaria?"

"He was cordial but I think he is distracted. I flattered him and he bit but still had an edge in his voice and maybe a little suspicion, too. I never met the man but in the time we talked I saw two sides of him."

Berry thought for a few seconds and said, "OK. We know Krasnodar gave a case of wine to Sid Zaccaria when they met in St. Helena. We know Zaccaria took some of the wine out of the case and delivered the rest to American Wine in Napa. Let's hope that you'll get to taste some of the same wine tonight.

"OK, guys, I would really like you to get a sample of that wine and bring it to me tonight. If all else fails, spill some on your shirt. I need some of that wine for the lab. Drive straight to this office. Use the outside door. I'll have a JetStar waiting at the Napa Airport to get the sample to the laboratory at Quantico tonight. And, I'll have the others here for a debriefing. Call me when you leave Zaccaria's home." He broke the connection.

Kathleen said, "When does Jim sleep? He seems to have meetings all day and all night."

"Who knows? Got any ideas on how we play tonight? I think we should continue with our "we're just curious" act that worked so well this afternoon. Let him come to us. Let's just relax and let it play out."

Kathleen nodded, "I agree. We don't know enough to make up a plan. But it is exciting. We're having dinner with one of the most famous winemakers of all time. I can hardly wait."

CHAPTER FORTY-EIGHT

The home in Fairfield was quiet. Anapa Krasnodar sat in his office and reviewed web sites for news and blogs that attracted cops and other law enforcement people. He wondered about Anoly. He saw the man's faults but in some strange way he felt an obligation to take Anoly from Russia and to give him assignments. His feelings were mixed. He should have left the oaf in Russia. Almost anyone could have done a better job. Yet, Anoly was loyal and he had the skills that Krasnodar needed. His work with the horse was perfect.

Meanwhile, Jim Berry thought about how Anoly Baranovich had left a trail of clues as he worked and as he went through life. Berry and his staff knew Baranovich had killed the horse. They knew he had surveiled the NWCOC area and they knew enough to correctly guess when he would return so that they could put in place an overwhelming reception committee. Plus, they knew where he lived and many facts about the occupants of the home. They knew enough about

Krasnodar's plans to begin looking at the five winemakers. The Davis' invitation to dinner at Sid Zaccaria's home was proof that they could penetrate the group.

Jim Berry went back and forth from thinking of the winemakers as criminals to a more sympathetic view of the men. Clearly, if they were involved with Krasnodar, they were either criminals or extortion victims. Time would tell which they were. Would he be arresting them or saving them?

CHAPTER FORTY-NINE

Jonathan Beale called Sid Zaccaria. Beale seemed confused and maybe a little angry. When Zaccaria answered the call Beale said, "Zaccaria, what the hell is this? These wines aren't your wines. What the hell are they? Is this your idea of a sick joke? Are you trying to trick me into making a mistake? Let's hear some answers now."

Zaccaria was stunned. He had no idea what Beale meant. He tried to calm down before he responded. In time he said, "Jonathan. Please tell me more. You know the criticism of my wines, that they're consistent but never changing or evolving. You know. You said it yourself. What's the problem?"

"The problem is, Sid, you're trying to pass off European wines as Napa wines. It's as plain as can be. The wines are good, very good but they are not from around here."

"Jonathan, I assure you they are. The fruit is from my vineyards and no other. Look, it's late. Let me come to your office tomorrow and explain it all."

Beale said, "I guess I owe you that. Make it ten in the morning. I'll be waiting. Just keep in mind that you may very well be on the verge of destroying everything you've worked for all your life."

Sid Zaccaria pressed the END button and dialed Anapa Krasnodar's number. Krasnodar answered on the second ring. He said, "Sid. So good to hear from you. How can I serve you?"

Zaccaria said as calmly as he could, "Anapa. Jonathan Beale at American Wine called me a few minutes ago. He tasted the wines that you gave me in St. Helena. He openly accused me of switching European wines for Napa wines. He said it was very clear."

Krasnodar responded, "Who is this man? Is he so important that you are losing trust in me, your friend?"

"He is very important. If he writes what he said it could put too much light on these wines. Maybe even the cops will wonder about the wines, too."

"Let me think about this for a while. I'll call you in the morning." The Russian broke the connection. He sat at his desk for almost an hour. Eventually, he changed into jeans, a sweater and a black wool cap. He stuffed a Sig 250 into his waistband. The Sig held 16 rounds of 357 Sig ammunition. The gun was finished in a camouflage style. He put two extra full magazines in his back pocket.

He also put an L4 LumaMax Surefire flashlight in his shirt pocket. The last item was one of the world's most powerful flashlights. It was powerful enough to stun a person for a few seconds. Yet the L4 was only five inches long and could easily be concealed in the palm of a man's hand.

Anapa was considering a desperate move. His natural instinct was to remove obstacles to his success. Jonathan

Beale was, clearly, an obstacle. Anapa could easily drive over to Napa and remove Jonathan Beale.

He thought about Beale for a few minutes. Maybe he should let Zaccaria try to convince the man in the morning. Maybe Zaccaria could pull it off. After all, Zaccaria knew what to say and how to say it. His outrage at being accused of chicanery would appear to be real. Maybe Beale would back down. Maybe things would be OK after all. Maybe he should be patient. He could always remove Beale. He decided to wait.

Anapa put the pistol and the magazines and the flashlight away. He walked into the kitchen and opened an Amstel Light. He downed the beer in two big swallows and opened another. He went outside to his patio and took a chair by the pool. He watched his children and their mother play in the water. He was so close to putting his past behind him. He needed one more round of wine sales and he could take his family away for good. He sipped his beer from the bottle and considered all that was happening.

He still had no word from Anoly. His analytical mind told him Anoly had been killed or captured. Capturing Anoly Baranovich would be almost impossible unless he was badly wounded. Anoly would die or accept any amount of pain and would not talk.

Anoly had shown his resolve and his strength in Chechnya. The rebels had trapped him and put more than thirty nine millimeter bullets in him. He was held in a former jail that was in the center of the small city just outside Grozny. When they stabilized him they tortured him for weeks. Anoly did not talk. He conserved his energy and concentrated on waiting until his wounds healed. By the time he was ready, the rebels had grown used to him and hardly gave thought to a possible escape.

One evening they returned to his cell with more torture in mind. There were three guards to escort him to the torture room. They made him stand and pointed to the door. He walked slowly to the door. It was a narrow door so the guards lined up with him, one in front and two behind. At precisely the right time, Anoly slammed the door against the two men behind him. The one closest to him was killed instantly when the steel door struck his head. The last guard fell, stunned. Anoly kicked the guard on the bridge of his nose. Sharp shattered bones serrated the man's brain and he died. The lead guard turned just in time to see Anoly's fist inches from his face. With two incredible blows, the man was dead.

Anoly retrieved the guards' keys and weapons, including two large folding knives. In less than a minute he was out of the cellblock and into the prison yard. A roving guard had the misfortune to round a corner and walk right into Anoly. Anoly grabbed the man's throat and lifted him off his feet. Slowly the man's throat ripped free and the body fell to the ground.

Now Anoly had an AK-47 and more than 100 rounds. It was the military model with a full automatic selector switch. Anoly put weapon on full auto and headed toward a sally port. The sally port was locked and guarded on the outside. Anoly opened one of the knives and screamed to the guard, "Open. Now. This is your commandant. "

The guard, in reality a sixteen year old kid, hastily opened the door. Anoly burst through the sally port and cut the man's throat with one lightning fast motion.

A guard on the wall peered over and yelled at Anoly to stop. The guard's chest exploded as Anoly fired a burst of six shots. Anoly disappeared into the city and was not seen in Chechnya again.

Anapa knew he would not see his friend again. He sat for a long time reminiscing the days when he and Anoly had been in action in their homeland.

Late into the night his equipment received several more communications bursts. Krasnodar knew the Russians would be demanding confirmation or at least information on the NWCOC raid. Perhaps he should give them something that would buy a little more time. Time. Without more time Anapa's dreams would fade to nothing. His family would be alone in this strange place with no one to guide them. He could not hold that terrifying thought. He must formulate a plan that would give him a little more time.

He read the communications and composed a reply. The reply would be sent five times that night so one of the orbiting satellites would be certain to receive it.

His message informed the Russians that there would be a delay. He said the raid got under way but Anoly observed many men in place around the facility. Anoly had learned that they had the misfortune to plan the raid for the night of a routine training exercise. He told them that to be sure it worked the second time, they would wait two days. He added that Americans have sort attention spans and would forget all about the aborted raid in a couple of days.

Anapa went through the process of setting the message up to send. Then he went to bed and tried to find sleep amid the anxieties and the problems that he faced.

CHAPTER FIFTY

Joe Bruning called Jim Berry and said, "Jim, the satellites are bombarding highly directional bursts toward the area of the home in Fairfield. Some of the bursts are unusually long, up to five seconds. NSA told me that longer encoded messages are a little easier to decode. They said something about the more comparisons they can make the more likely it is that they can find a handle. Up to now about three seconds has been the longest burst. Now we have almost twice that. Keep your fingers crossed. If we're able to read one of these bursts we might be able to read all of them. NSA is very excited to have the challenge. My contact told me most Russian communications are micro-bursts that are as short as one one-hundredths of a second. The Russians did use a longer burst system in Afghanistan and in Chechnya. They said they wonder if our group is a break-away from the Kremlin, a rogue operation that uses very good but not state-of-the-art communications equipment and processes.

"To me, that makes sense. I can't imagine the Kremlin getting behind an operation on US soil. No way!"

Berry responded, "Keep at it Joe. This is very good work and…"

Bruning interrupted, "Sorry Jim, someone just put a note in front of me that tells us five outbound bursts just left the home in Fairfield. The bursts appear to be identical. My staffer tells me it's common to send three to five bursts to ensure that one is received by an orbiting bird. We know they have two birds up there so five is a reasonable number."

Berry broke in, "Great, Joe. Just great. Let me know the second you have more."

Just as Jim Berry was disconnecting from Joe Bruning, we were getting ready to drive to our dinner date in St. Helena. Kathleen finally decided on black pants and a grey silk shirt. She usually wore western boots and this night she chose a pair of custom pointed toe Tony Lama Vaquera's in black with soft Roma leather uppers in denim blue. She chose rings, a bracelet and ear rings of lapis set in sterling silver.

I took one look and was reminded that I have a very beautiful woman in my life. I had been worried about her after the shooting. I know she had internalized the entire episode and I also know that one of these days she would let it surface. For now, she was totally secure with herself and assured, even excited.

The dinner with the Zaccaria's was exciting. Word around the Valley had it that dinner with any of the top winemakers would be memorable. Most of them had full commercial kitchens in their homes and some had private chefs.

The drive to the Zaccaria home would take us about thirty minutes. I set our GPS to the address Sid Zaccaria had provided. Jim Berry had reminded them to take it easy on the Silverado Trail. He said it was a favorite hunting ground for the Highway Patrol and the Napa Sheriff's patrols. He was concerned that a simple traffic stop might blow our cover.

As a precaution, I stored our weapons in the truck bed trunk of our Honda Ridgeline. Several months ago I created an equipment bag that I keep in the trunk. The bag contains flashlights, ammunition, two knives and other items that might come in handy. Just in case, I also put in a supply of bottled water and a professional first aid kit.

As we were leaving our house Kathleen said, "Clark, how should we play this? Jim seems to think something is going on with Mr. Zaccaria. I mean, what if he blurts something out or something?"

"I know nothing that you don't know, Kathleen. We'll take it a step at a time. If we see an opening, we might go in. But remember, neither of us are experts and this kind of thing. We certainly don't want to have Zaccaria get scared and run. Or something worse. Let's just be careful."

The drive out of Napa up the gorgeous Silverado Trail was always a treat. Every time we take a drive through the Valley, Kathleen says that it's her favorite time of the year. She says that if the vines are bright green in the spring, darker green and laden with fruit in the summer, or when the leaves with earth tones of every imaginable color in the fall and stark and stripped naked of foliage in the winter. The colors and shapes and shadows varied constantly through the daylight hours. She told me she thought the Napa Valley had all the light magic of Taos, New Mexico but set in a softer, calmer setting.

We easily found the Zaccaria driveway. We drove up to a turn around close to the front of the house. As I opened my car door, the front door to the house opened and a small, striking woman walked out and down the front stairs. She had a serious and concerned look on her face. She walked directly up to me.

She said, "Mr. Davis. I'm Annette Zaccaria. I just hope it's OK that I tell you and your wife something."

I said, "By all means. And, this is my wife, Kathleen Royal."

Annette said, "Pleased to meet you both. But before we go in let me just explain something. My husband Sid isn't feeling his best right now. He might seem a bit preoccupied. Please just let it go. He's actually just fine.

"Now, let's go in. I'm so happy that you had the time to come to our home. You know, Sid brought a new chardonnay home today and I'm dying to try it. Tell me, Kathleen, do you enjoy a nice cold, crisp chardonnay?" She took Kathleen's arm and walked into the house with her.

Kathleen said, "Oh, yes. I do. Years ago when Clark and I first met, an ice cold, flinty chardonnay was our drink of choice. I think we settled on Clos du Bois as our favorite. Oh my! That one is from Sonoma, isn't it? Will I be branded a traitor?" she joked.

Annette responded with a laugh, "Oh yes. We usually shoot folks who drink Sonoma wine but just this time we'll let it go. Besides, I think this new wine will convince you without a shot being fired."

When we walked into the front room of the house, joking and laughing, Sid Zaccaria met us. It was clear that his mood contrasted ours. He shook hands and withdrew to get the wine and nibbles.

Five minutes later he made a big entrance with a tray of four glasses of white wine. The glasses sparkled with condensation from what must have been ice cold wine. He had added an assortment of cheeses and thin breads to the tray.

He said, "My new friends, you are about to be among the very first to taste our new wines. This one," he said, "is very special.

"Let me tell you about it. The most popular white wine in the world is chardonnay. The classic Napa chardonnay is a soft, some say buttery, wine with an oak finish. When we introduced our chardonnays from the Valley, the world accepted them with open arms. Yet, in the past few years chardonnay sales have sagged a little. My theory is that new wine drinkers prefer a sharper edged – note I did not say sharp or acidic, I said sharper edged, flinty and fruity white wine. Years ago, Robert Mondavi tried a pinot grigio with poor success. He changed the name to Fume Blanc and couldn't keep up with the demand. Since then white pinot Gris and pinot grigio and pinot whatever are everywhere. And, they've just exploded in the marketplace. They're cheap and easy to make and, just between us, the standards and the laws are somewhat confused. Some say anyone can make a sharp edged white wine and call it pinot grigio.

"The wine in these glasses will change all that. At least it'll change it for the high end of the white wine market, for the people who will pay for what they want.

"I think you'll agree that this wine is unlike any you've tasted. You'll find the sharp, flinty edge that I mentioned. But it also has a clear fruit base, prime white grapes grown by people who know what they're doing. You'll find it's best ice cold. If you taste that ice cold edge and let the wine warm to your mouth that little journey will take you from a very sharp, flinty edge through pears and apples and into a finish that's all earth. There's no oak. No butter. No softness. The alcohol is in the European tradition for whites, about 9% plus or minus a little.

"Will you be my guests and taste my new wine?" He passed the silver tray to each of us and took the final glass for himself. The glasses were standard Riedel Vinum Red & White. Each glass held about an inch of a shimmering amber liquid.

Kathleen looked at the wine then put her nose into the glass. Sid interrupted, "Kathleen, my sweet, this wine is very cold so your nose has nothing to do until the wine warms in your mouth. I hope I've not offended you. I only want to make sure you get all this wine has to offer."

She said, "Oh no. Not at all." She tilted the glass and took a small sip.

Sid said, "Now keep your mouth closed for a few seconds then draw warm air over the wine. I think your tongue should be coming awake about now. Am I right?"

Kathleen followed his advice then swallowed the sip of wine. She put her hand to her mouth and said, "Oh my. That's..., oh my! I don't know what to say. I've never had anything like that. Clark, you've got to try this wine."

I did, and I had a similar reaction. I said, "Mr. Zaccaria. This is amazing. I'm no wine expert but I'm sure I don't need to continue my search for my favorite wine. This is it. Wow!"

Sid Zaccaria smiled. It was fun for the old man to see these two young people enjoy his new wine. A thought ran through his head, 'What would they say if they knew the wine was produced in a warehouse in Fairfield by people who had no idea how real wine was made?'

Annette beamed at her husband. She could see his mood lifting. Maybe it was nothing after all. Maybe he would be OK tonight. She escorted their guests into her spacious kitchen and dining room.

Like many California homes, the kitchen and dining rooms had given way to huge cooking dining centers all in one room. One wall of Annette's kitchen displayed every appliance that one would find in a first class restaurant kitchen. She had a five place induction cooktop as well as a six burner Wolfe gas range. A large center island that was topped with maple hardwood had two small freezers under the countertop. Racks of shiny cooking utensils hung from the ten foot ceiling.

A semicircular table had ten padded swivel chairs. One side of the table was curved and the other side was straight. The chairs were arranged around the curved side of the table. Guests could sit at the table and watch their meals being prepared. The chef could easily serve tastes and full plates.

The dinner was marvelous. Annette did all the cooking. Sid kept up banter about this and that, mostly about the wine business and how it had changed. He reminisced about the 'old days' that he said were gone forever.

CHAPTER FIFTY-ONE

After dinner Kathleen insisted on helping Annette clean up the kitchen. Sid and I walked out to a huge patio on the side of the house. The view was spectacular.

Sid pointed out homes in the area. He identified Wappo Hill in the distance and told about how Robert Mondavi had built his huge one-level home on the property and guest houses down the hill. Sid loved to talk about the Valley's history and did so for half and hour.

At that point, Sid Zaccaria began a long story about the Valley and the wine business. He said, "In recent years there have been many corporate acquisitions. Long time winemakers have sold their businesses to huge corporations. Many in the Valley have acted like Chicken Little. They have cried that the Valley will be changed forever. Some say we're at the mercy of those big owners back east or in Canada. I must admit I see what they mean when I see family businesses like

Robert Mondavi and others no long controlled by people the Valley.

"But, Clark, you know it's always been that way. Even Robert Mondavi had to have a big corporate sponsor when he spilt away from his brother and Charles Krug. Coca-Cola, several whiskey companies and other corporations have had long time presences in the Valley. Frankly, I've always been surprised that Anheuser-Busch and the other big beer companies have not come in. They have the hard part sewed up, the distribution in every conceivable outlet. The same is true for Coke and Pepsi. The answer is elusive. Maybe they're just not good at expanding, the New Coke kind of thing.

"But sometimes the problem with the big corporations is that they think of everything as a 'brand'. They're utterly incapable of seeing the human appeal and the tradition.

"I'll tell you a story. Years ago one of the great wineries in the Valley was Inglenook. They did good work and they had good wine. The sold out to Heublein, a big eastern company. They were the ones that pioneered the mixed drinks in little cans. So a guy could walk into a store and walk out with a pretty good martini or rum and coke or whatever. It was a genius stroke at the time. It fell off the cliff when the states started getting serious about open containers and driving and drinking.

"Anyway, those smart Connecticut folks at Heublein were watching Gallo and all their bulk wines. So they converted the Inglenook product to non-vintage reds and whites. They completely bastardized the company. And, they couldn't get used to having a factory in a priceless replica of a French manor house. They abandoned the place. Had it not have been for Francis Coppola who bought the winery and the vineyards, it would have gone to ruin. If you ask me, if we had a dozen more winemakers like Francis we would be in good shape. As it stands today, the corporations are not willing to pay what a great winemaker or vineyard manager can get. So good people are leaving some of those corporate wineries. The quality of their products, their brands if you will, will be heading out the same door pretty soon.

"So the corporations think the Robert Mondavi winery is a brand, not a history bedecked part of Americana. They do have me worried, Clark."

I listened and hung on every word. When Sid paused his history lesson, I said, "Sid, it's a real pleasure to learn about the Valley from someone who helped make it happen. You have so much to proud of. You've always done the right thing."

Sid's face seemed to change when I said that to him. He suddenly looked sad and old. He walked away a few feet, turned and said, "I've tried to do that. I have not always been successful.

I sensed an opening and said, "Sid, is there something I can do? You do seem distracted. Are there problems?"

The old man placed one hand on the patio railing. He seemed to need the support. He said, "Clark who are you? You and your wife. Who are you?"

Clark considered his reply very carefully and finally said, "Kathleen works in Napa for a non-profit group. I work in for SSI, the pharmaceutical company."

Sid pressed his question, "I mean who are you, really? What makes you think you might help me? Do you know something you've not shared?"

In every conversation there comes a time when one must continue or retreat. Either choice can be a huge mistake or sometimes both choices can bring the whole world down on the participants. Clark sensed that they had reached that point. He looked across the Valley and took his time in answering.

"Sid, we never know all there is to know about others and sometimes even ourselves. If there's a problem, I can help. You must know that it's never too late to correct our mistakes. Never.

"I think it has something to do with the wine we had tonight. Maybe you've over extended yourself or maybe you've made promises you can't keep. The excellent chardonnay that you served is so reminiscent of the French burgundies I had in New York and France thirty years ago that I found myself wondering how you could produce a classic French wine in Napa. Not only that, I wondered why? I can tell you this, if you market that wine lots of people will also wonder. Sid, for heavens sake, if I can see it, others will, too. The wine is terrific. The provenance is another story. You're a good man. If we can help, say so, please."

At that moment, Kathleen and Annette joined them on the patio. Annette said, "You two seem to be way too serious. What's up?"

I looked at Sid with what I hoped was an encouraging expression and said, "Sid has been giving me a first hand account of the history of winemaking in the Valley. I guess I'm mesmerized by his stories and his charm."

Sid said nothing. I felt that the women had showed up just as Sid was considering sharing something. I gently put a hand on Kathleen's shoulder and said, "This has been a wonderful evening. But all things must end. We need to get going."

Kathleen said, "Oh darn! I left my bag inside. I'll just run inside and get it."

I thanked Annette for the great dinner and she gave me a hug. "I love cooking for people who enjoy food," she said, smiling. With that she returned to the house. Sid walked me around the house to the truck. He said, "I think I might call you tomorrow. Will that be OK?" I nodded just as Kathleen came out and walked to the passenger side of the truck. I went around and opened her door, closed it and turned to Sid. I shook his hand and climbed in the cab. Before I closed the door, I quietly said to Sid "Remember, it's never too late." We drove into the night.

As we made out way out of the driveway and onto the Trail, Kathleen said, "What on earth were you and Sid talking about? He had a look of shock on his face when we came out to the patio."

"I think Sid was about to tell me about whatever it is that he is doing with the Russian."

"Did you tell him about our connections?"

"No. Not a word or a hint. The conversation just lead to the fact that he is very distracted. I offered to help the way any friend would help."

"Clark, we're not really friends, you know. We just met them. Did you go too far?"

"Nope. I just offered to help the man. He told me he would call tomorrow. Now, call Berry and tell him we're on the way. It'll be about forty minutes."

Kathleen made the call and confirmed to Jim Berry that we were on the way. Berry told her the meeting was nearly over and if they hadn't gotten the sample we could go home. She told him we did have more information and would be there soon.

We walked into Jim Berry's conference room. Kathleen said, "Sorry we're late. We had a great dinner with Sid and Annette Zaccaria. It was terrific. I think Clark has something to add."

I said, "Sid served two of his new wines. The first was a chardonnay. It was excellent but I'm afraid it might be too close to a classic Burgundy white wine. It had all the characteristics – color, low alcohol, fruity. The second was a cab. Again, it made me think of very good French reds."

Kathleen interrupted, "I got the samples you wanted. They're soaked into this linen napkin."

Jim Berry said, "You mean you swiped a napkin?" Berry took the napkin, placed it in a plastic bag and gave it to an agent. The agent left the room to deliver the bag to a waiting government jet.

"Not at all. It was one I took with me in my purse. When Clark and the Zaccaria's were on the patio I went back inside and dipped my napkin in the two wines."

Clark continued, "The bottles weren't labeled. I never saw the corks or the capsules so I can't say if the wines were sealed or not. But let me say one thing more, whatever Sid is doing, Annette isn't aware of it. It's about wine. Somehow the Russian has gotten five of the Valley's leading citizens involved in something strange."

Berry said, "Do you guys think the Russian is bringing in bulk French wine and bottling it as Napa Valley wine?"

I shrugged and said, "Who knows. That occurred to me and I even suggested it to Sid in a roundabout sort of way. I told him the wines reminded me of French wines from years ago."

Bruning broke in, "What was his reaction to that?"

"He got very quiet and about that time the ladies joined us so the conversation stopped. By the way, he told me he might call me tomorrow sometime. I encouraged it."

Jim Berry stood and said, "Well then, when he calls, use the feature on your cell phone that gives me a connection. Let me ask you, Clark, do you think Sid Zaccaria may have gotten involved in something wrong and is thinking about finding a way out?"

"Could be, Jim. It's something like that for sure."

Berry said, "Fine, let's go home and keep in touch."

CHAPTER FIFTY-TWO

A ringing phone brought Sid Zaccaria out of his sleep. He reached across the bed and picked up the telephone, "Sid, Jon Beale. I completed my tasting of your wines last night. Sid, these are very good wines but they are not Napa Valley wines. You haven't labeled the bottles you gave me. How will they be labeled? Whose wines are they?"

"Jonathan, they are my wines. I grew that fruit right on the Valley floor. What are you saying?"

"I'm saying that I think you have given me some ringers. Do you take me for some kind of fool? If these wines came to me from France I'd rate them nearly off the chart. The chardonnay might be the first wine ever to get a '100'. I love it.

"You made them? No way. I'll stake my reputation on it. I admire you, Sid, but you're up to something. I don't want to hurt you but if you put these wines on the market without a believable explanation, I'm going to challenge you in print. I mean it."

Sid replied, "Fine, I stand by what I said. I did you a favor. You returned the favor with rudeness and arrogance. I should have known better." He hung up the phone and stretched out beside his sleeping wife.

Sid Zaccaria thought his world was coming to an end. He was afraid to tell Krasnodar about Beale's threat and he was terrified to tell his partners. He had no idea what to do. Maybe he should simply come clean and walk away from the Russians. He could afford the money he had spent. Kimball Johansen had worried about getting some kind of guarantee. The Russians had rejected that question and chastised the men for their lack of faith. How he wished he would have pushed for some sort of escape clause.

Knowing he wouldn't be getting any more sleep this night, he quietly slid out of his bed, tiptoeing out of the room and into his home office. The room was dark, shadows playing on the wall until he turned on the small banker's lamp on his desk. He sighed as he sat heavily in the worn, oversized leather chair. Slowly he picked up the receiver and punched in Anapa's number, dreading the conversation he knew he had to have. When the Russian answered the call, Sid said, "Anapa, Beale has given me what amounts to an ultimatum. He wants to know where the wines came from. He's absolutely convinced that the wines are not from this Valley."

There was a slight pause. Sid heard Anapa curse slightly, under his breath and in his native tongue. "What will it take to shut him up?"

"Anapa, listen, let's think about this. He won't do anything if we don't release the wine. If we do, he'll murder us in the press."

"My question was, 'What will it take to shut him up?'"

Sitting up straighter, with a lump of fear growing steadily larger in his chest, Sid's voice began to rise, "Anapa, Beale has nowhere near the influence of Parker and others. If we shut him up we've only delayed the problem for a few days or weeks. Please, if Beale saw through this, so will the others."

Krasnodar said in a menacing tone, "What are you saying, Sid?"

Zaccaria paused, took a deep breath to bolster his courage and said, "I'm saying I want out of this deal, Anapa. And, I know the others will want out, too. I want out and I want my money back now."

Anapa's voice came across the phone line like a steel snake coiling and ready to strike, "My friend, it is too late for that. You and your friends paid me to do a job. I have done that job. The wines are almost ready to deliver to your warehouses. It is too late to back out now. Why can't you see that, Sid?"

Sid replied, "You presented a deal. You didn't deliver. The wines are very good but they're not Napa wines. You sound like you're threatening me, Anapa. Don't forget that I have my resources, too. Now, let's undo this thing and get on with our lives.

"And, don't forget about Beale. Right now he is very dangerous to us."

Anapa Krasnodar said, "My friend, let me convince this Beale fellow." He hung up the phone.

Krasnodar had no intention of any 'undo'. His back was to the wall. As soon and Anatoly Putin discovered what happened at the satellite dish facility he would come for Anapa.

He needed to make the wine thing work long enough to get the money he needed to disappear. He knew he had to remove Beale from the equation. And, he knew that the time was coming to put his fist on Zaccaria.

CHAPTER FIFTY-THREE

Anapa Krasnodar got a weapon from his small 'armory' at the Fairfield home. It was a Spyderco Civilian G-10, a version of the knife that the legendary Spyderco Company had developed for undercover federal law enforcement agents in the 1990's. The knife had a thick, full deeply serrated blade that tapered to a curved point that resembled an animal's claw or a raptor's beak. The knife featured a quick-opening four inch blade.

Anoly knew from experience that a strong swipe with the knife's four inch blade at a man's groin or neck would bring about almost instant unconsciousness from the collapse of the circulatory system. Death would follow in less than fifteen seconds. The victim would likely remain quiet because of the searing pain and the confusion that led into unconsciousness and death.

He dressed in a khaki colored Haspel poplin suit from Frank Stella in New York. The suit was perfect for the

California weather and though inexpensive, looked perfect on Krasnodar's huge body. He wore Allan Edmonds loafers. In the style of California, he wore an open collar Ike Behar shirt with French cuffs. His cuff links were solid gold from Tiffany.

Anapa knew he had failed at his first mission. He knew the wine project was beginning to come apart. Reluctantly and stubbornly he knew it was time for him to disappear. He had one or two loose ends to tie up and then he would change his identity and fly south to a proven haven in Venezuela.

He sat for long minutes and tried to find another way, a way out of what he had to do.

After kissing his wife and children he walked out to his Escalade and loaded everything into the car. His demeanor was calm. He showed no hint of his mission. He returned to the home and brought out several large suitcases and loaded them into the Escalade.

Finally, he returned to the home one last time. As he entered the home he held his Sig at his side. The FBI agents did not see the pistol. Anapa Krasnodar met his wife in the hallway. She looked surprised and seemed not to notice the Sig as it came up to the level of her head. She was trying to bring her hands up and to form a scream when the forty caliber bullet entered through her open mouth and continued through her head and into the wall behind her. A gush of bright red blood erupted from her mouth. Her body seemed to loose its bones. She fell straight down in a heap.

Anapa stepped over his wife's body and turned right into a playroom where his kids looked up to see their father come into the room. They were assembling a Lego castle on a rug on the floor. Before they could greet their father he quickly shot both of them one time in the head. The children fell where they sat.

He had placed one shot each in the children and in his wife. He stood over them, cold, calm and purposeful in the way that some men might spray dandelions on a lawn.

Tears filled Anapa's eyes. He had done what he had to do. He could not chance the Russians finding his children. He knew his wife was weak and would tell anyone, Russians or Americans, what they wanted to know to save her life and her children's lives. He took one last look around the house and then returned to the Escalade.

One of Jim Berry's agents saw Krasnodar drive away from the home. The agent called Berry to report. Berry told the agent to follow discretely and to report the Escalade's route and progress. This was not totally necessary because the same agent had placed a microscopic signal generator behind the rubber window seal on the car's back window. The transmitter was less than an inch long and about as big around as a medium-sized nail. In Jim Berry's office the Escalade was a bright blue dot on a computer generated map of the area. The FBI sometimes referred to this combination of human eyes on the target plus state-of-the-art technology as a 'two-fer". It was especially useful when there was a possibility of a target being aware of the potential for a GPS device and might do something to neutralize it or destroy the transmitter. In the early 2000's federal law enforcement scientists had discovered that certain signals from XM Radio could interfere with GPS tracking devices and render them useless. That's why Krasnodar rated a two-fer.

CHAPTER FIFTY-FOUR

About fifteen minutes after Anapa Krasnodar left his home in Fairfield, Jim Berry called me on my cell phone. He wasted no time on pleasantries, "Clark, where are you?"

"Kathleen, Crouton and I just had lunch in Napa. We're taking a walk through town. What's up?"

"Krasnodar's on the move. He left home a little while ago and is on Highway 12 through Jamison Canyon. I think he must be headed to Napa. Tell you what, stay downtown until you hear from me. OK?"

"Sure. It's a great day for a walk."

We walked north on Main from the restaurant, Celadon, in the Napa River Inn. In all the time we have been together Kathleen and I have rarely gone to the same restaurant again and again. Celadon and its owner, Chef Greg Cole, had changed that. It's our favorite restaurant, favorite bar and favorite meeting spot. The place is that good.

On this visit to Celadon Kathleen had chosen an heirloom tomato salad with fresh mozzarella cheese and a light dusting of smoked sea salt. Her go-with dish was one of Greg's perfect crab cakes. She usually orders like that, a salad and an appetizer delivered to the table together. She says she does not like to draw things out and prefers to get everything at once.

Chef de Cuisine Marcos Uribe saw us come in and made sure I knew that he had chili on the menu today. Chef Uribe's chili is absolutely the best. It has large chunks of melt in your mouth beef, a long simmered sauce that hits every flavor note known to man. All that wonderful creation is served with a grating of just the right amount of sharp cheddar cheese. I can't resist it and once had Marcos' chili three lunches in a row.

The server brought Crute a dish of cold water. She is so spoiled that she insists on cold water and likes it even better if the water dish has a couple of ice cubes.

We enjoyed a glass of Peripoli Sauvignon Blanc with lunch and excellent, rich Illy coffee after our meal. We had left the restaurant and walked along Main Street toward the heart of Napa. Crouton was sporting a new pink halter and matching leash.

We turned west on First to take a look at some of the newly restored buildings and shops along Napa's central street. Napa is in the midst of one of a progressive metamorphosis from a tired little labor town to a vibrant, interesting small city that ranks with many of the top tourist destinations in the nation.

People have traveled to Napa for forty years to taste the wine and see the winemaking process. They always drove past Napa to get to up Valley wineries and inns. This trend came to a halt around 2002 when Napa began building world class hotels, innovative restaurants and upscale shopping. Not long after, the city found itself with more than twenty wine-tasting storefronts where visitors can sample wines, buy wines and learn about wines. Tourists began to come to Napa and never go anywhere else in the Napa Valley. Napa has savvy new leadership who saw the new trend developing and opened the city to even more hotels and attractions.

Along First Street we saw interesting new stores, several hotels near completion and gorgeous mid-rise residential projects. We decided to walk farther west on First to see some of Napa's Victorian-style homes. As we were about a block from the Noyes Mansion, the home of American Wine, Robby rode toward us on his three wheeler. When he reached us he pointed to a man who was standing in front of the Noyes Mansion. Robby said, "Bad man! Bad man!" and rode away.

Kathleen touched my arm and said, "Clark, look at the man who just got out of the Escalade. Isn't that the Russian we saw in Jim Berry's photographs?"

Crouton was beginning a very soft grumble. She put her ears back and her tail down.

I stopped and said, "It is. Hold on while I call Jim."

Berry came on the line with his usual, "Clark, what's up?"

"Jim, we're about a block from American Wine. The big Russian just drove up and got out of this car, an Escalade SUV."

"We're tracking him, Clark. What can you tell me about him?"

"He's dressed in a very nice suit. When he got out of the car and leaned back in for something, I think we saw that he's armed. I mean, I think we saw the bulge of a handgun under the back of his suit jacket. He's just standing on the sidewalk reading from notes or a piece of paper."

Berry said, "Stay with him, Clark. We have two agents on the way about three minutes away. Don't let him see you. Don't stand there and look at him. Keep walking and go past him. We want him to think you're a harmless part of the scenery."

"Okay. Should I keep this line open?"

"No. He might hear something when you walk past. This guy is good at what he does and can be very dangerous, Clark. If you need to talk with me, find a place and call back. When you see my two agents, leave the area."

"Okay. Here goes."

I put my phone away and we walked toward the Russian. I was surprised when the Russian turned to me and said, "Pardon me, Sir. Are you from Napa?"

"Yes we are. Can we help you?"

"I hope so. Are you familiar with this building? I mean have you ever been inside?"

I paused then said, "Well, yes. They have a library on the first floor. We've stopped in."

"Are the offices on the first floor or up on the second floor?"

It dawned on me that I might be providing information on the place to a criminal so I said, "I really don't know. We never went to the offices. Just the library."

He glanced at the building and said, "Thank you very much. I will find out." He turned and walked toward the front door.

We walked past the building down to the corner. Kathleen said, "Clark, we can't just stand here. Something is about to happen. That man is scary to me. I think we should do something. Jim's men are not here. Call Jim and tell him."

Crouton was tugging on her leash. She pulled and barked and howled.

I pressed Jim Berry's speed dial button. He came on the line and said, "I know. My men aren't there yet. They got caught in one of the almost daily tie-ups on Jamison Canyon Road. I'm trying to get backups in place."

"Jim, the Russian went into the building. He stopped and asked us about the layout of the place. We're worried."

"Okay, Clark, do something to draw his attention and, if possible, get him out of the building."

I hung up and, Crouton in the lead, we headed for the front door of the building. I went through the door first. The receptionist we had met a few days ago was sprawled over her desk. Blood was dripping down her shirt and onto the floor. Her throat had been cut. I stepped back to avoid the flow of blood.

Kathleen glanced up the stairs in time to see the Russian top the stairs and turn left and out of sight.

Kathleen said, "Clark, he's on the second floor. There's a fire alarm signal by the front door. Hit the alarm." I ran to the front door and activated the alarm. Instantly a screeching fire alarm filled the building. I knew the Napa Number One fire station was only a couple of blocks down the street. We'd have manpower on the scene in minutes.

Just then Jonathan Beale appeared at the top of the stairs. He was heading in the same direction the Russian took.

Kathleen said, "Clark, a man I think it Jonathan Beale just walked by the top of the stairs. I remember seeing his picture in the magazines. I think he is heading toward the Russian."

I said, "I'm going up. Stay here until the others arrive."

I reached for my Glock and checked to see that it was loaded and ready to go. I dropped Crute's leash. She broke for the stairs. I started up the stairs and immediately knew that Kathleen was right behind me. We were half way up the stairs when we heard a scream and someone saying, "Get the hell out of my office!" The voice was full of panic.

We heard the Russian say, "Stop it you little shit. Don't try to get away from me. I promise not to hurt you. Sit down."

We cleared the stairs and ran toward the voices. I could see the Russian standing over Beale. The Russian was holding a very strange knife with a curved, jagged blade. He was holding Beale by the hair. It was obvious that he was about to hurt Beale and possibly kill him.

Crouton was barking and howling. The tiny dog seemed to be bent on attacking the Russian. The Russian hesitated a minute to look at the dog. That was my chance to do what I had to do.

I dropped down on one knee and brought my pistol up. I was squeezing the trigger when I heard two quick shots from behind me. The Russian fell backward. In the movies people who are shot in the head turn to look at the shooter with a questioning look on what is left of their faces. In reality, they drop like stones and spew blood all over the place. The lower part of Anapa Krasnodar's face, from the eyes down, was splattered against the far wall. The window took most of the blood. It had the curious look of a holiday window in a department store. Blood gushed from where his lower jaw had been. Bright red blood was pumping from a second wound on his rib cage. It was clear in an instant that the Russian was very dead. His body collapsed in a heap. His Spyderco knife thudded on the polished hardwood floor.

I turned to Kathleen who was standing behind me. Her Glock was still pointing toward where the Russian had been. She moved past me and into the office where Jonathan Beale sat stunned and shaking. She kept her Glock in the ready position as she approached the Russian. She put her arm around Beale and tired in some way to soothe and calm the man. His face and the front of his shirt were covered with blood. From where I stood Jonathan Beale looked like he'd been shot. He was sobbing uncontrollably.

Kathleen turned to me and said, "The blood's not his. He's OK. The Russian isn't."

Just then we heard firemen enter the building. Heavy boots thudded on the stairway. I yelled, "It's all over. Come on up."

The first fireman reached the top of the stairs. He was dressed in a heavy coat, boots and a hard helmet. He was carrying a large satchel that probably contained his tools and first aid supplies. He told me to get out of the way. I said, "I said, it's over. We set off the alarm to stop a murder. There's no fire."

The fireman looked at Beale and then saw the Russian's legs. He said, "It looks like you failed. Is that a dead guy in the end office?"

I replied, "It is. He was the attacker. He was shot as he tried to cut that man's throat. I think you probably saw the other dead person in the reception area downstairs."

The fireman was confused and not sure what to say. While he was deciding who to believe, two of Jim Berry's FBI agents came up the stairs. They saw me and the fireman and one of the agents said, "FBI." Pointing to the fireman he continued, "Sir, please go downstairs and wait for us, Sir." The fireman went back downstairs. We could hear the firemen downstairs yelling and talking to each other.

The FBI agent said to me, "Mr. Davis, what happened?"

I walked toward Kathleen. She was kneeling beside Jonathan Beale. The man was sobbing and shaking. He knew he had been saved by seconds.

Sometimes a person who isn't on a first name basis with violence will sense that his or her end is at hand. When that happens they begin accepting the fate of death. They scream but the screams are about the coming pain and not about living. If something intervenes and they live through the ordeal they almost never come all the way back from their near death. It haunts them and challenges them and terrorizes them for the rest of their life. Jonathan Beale had been very close to death. He knew it. Maybe he even accepted it. He had a tough time ahead of him.

The FBI agents came into Beale's office and saw the mess that used to be Anapa Krasnodar. One of the agents contacted Jim Berry. Berry answered the phone, "Tell me exactly what you see."

The agent replied, "When we got here Clark Davis and a fireman were at the top of the stairs. Oh, yeah, downstairs at the reception desk we saw a woman, dead, from a knife wound at her throat. Someone had damn near decapitated her.

"We went upstairs to find Mr. Davis and a fireman. I think the fireman was trying to make a decision about what he should do. Down the hall in a large office we saw Ms.

Royal comforting a man who was very upset. Apparently the man was about to be killed by Anapa Krasnodar. I think Ms. Royal came along just in time and shot Krasnodar twice. The first shot blew away part of his head. The second shot struck him in the right side ribs and probably took out his heart and lungs and God knows what else. He's dead."

Berry said, "Have you checked to confirm Krasnodar's death? Is the building secure? What have you done?"

"If you could see Krasnodar you would have no doubt that he is dead. Ms. Royal's' shots were perfectly placed, a double-tap that would have taken the man out with either shot. The double tap was very effective. The timing of the shots was perfect. Either shot would have done it. The double tap closed the deal.

"Mr. Davis set off the fire alarm and the fire response got here just ahead of us. The fire station is just down the street. My partner, Keith, told the firemen downstairs to seal the building and that that were to stay in the building until released. I'm on the second floor with Davis and his wife. The building is secure."

Berry said, "Keep it that way, Roger. I'll be there in fifteen minutes. Preserve the crime scene. If a Napa PD or sheriff shows up, tap dance them until I get there. Kerry Blount and I are on the way. George Brenneman and Joe Bruning are getting the cleanup in motion. Whatever you do, let no one in that building. I mean no one. Use whatever resources you need but this cannot go public. Put Clark on the phone and tell him to find a secure place to talk – another office or whatever."

I took the phone from the agent. He said, "Jim, this is Clark."

"Clark, first tell me how you and Kathleen are, and then tell me what happened."

"We're fine. Well, Kathleen's very upset. She's pretty much anti-violence but she's killed two men in the last few days. Here's what happened.

"We saw Krasnodar outside the building and were watching him from up the street. That goofy guy, Robby, with the three wheeled bicycle began pointing to the Russian and saying, "Bad Guy!" over and over. Just about then the Russian went into the building. We knew your guys were on the way. But we made a decision to go inside the building to see what was happening. We found the receptionist dead and saw Krasnodar at the top of the stairs. I ran up the stairs first with Kathleen just behind me. I saw the Russian getting ready to cut Jonathan Beale's throat. I knew he meant it because the lady downstairs had had her throat cut. I knelt to shoot the Russian but Kathleen was faster. She shot the Russian twice and killed him. I had set off the fire alarm so the firemen began arriving about that time."

Berry said, "Take care of Kathleen. We're half way there."

Jim Berry made another call. He told an agent that the home in Fairfield should be secured and that all the people in the home should be taken into federal custody and taken to an FBI safe house just off 4th Street in the downtown area of Napa. He ordered that this be done immediately. Berry told the agent to seal every room and closet and to seal all computers and other electronic equipment with tape.

The FBI agent downstairs assembled the fireman in the foyer. He told them this was a Homeland Security issue and they should stay in the building. They agreed. One asked if they could contact their station. The agent told them to please hold off until more people arrived from Homeland Security and the FBI. Then he carefully searched the downstairs of the building.

In five minutes, a Napa PD officer drove up and walked to the front door. He banged on the door and was greeted by an FBI agent. They talked for a few minutes. The officer demanded access to the building. The agent refused. Finally, the officer stepped away from the building and called his Commander for instructions. The agent contacted Jim Berry who immediately called the Napa Chief of Police and asked for cooperation. The Chief agreed. Apparently the officer on the lawn got the message and returned to his car.

Ten minutes after the officer arrived, Kerry Blount and Jim Berry arrived. They went directly to the second floor of the building. Berry pulled Kathleen and me aside. He said, "Okay, what happened?"

Once more I outlined what we saw beginning when we first saw the Russian and ending with Kathleen killing Anapa Krasnodar. "All this happened in a minute or two. We saw the dead woman downstairs and knew this was no simple thing. When I got to the top of the stairs I dropped to my knee and took aim at the Russian. There's no doubt he was about to kill that man in there. Kathleen did the shooting, however. The second my knee hit the carpet, I heard two quick shots from behind me. I turned to see Kathleen deciding if a third shot was necessary. It wasn't."

Berry turned to Kathleen and said, "Anything you want to add?"

She said, "Not much. I guess I went up those stairs knowing that I might have to shoot someone. When Clark went down it ran through my mind that he might have been shot.

I didn't hear a shot but then I didn't hear the two that I fired at the Russian. The fire alarm was too loud to hear anything. Anyway, I shot him and killed him. I think Mr. Beale might have been killed if I'd hesitated even a couple of seconds. The Russian's knife was on its way to Mr. Beale's neck.

"I've killed two people within a few days. Clark killed a man at the old pipe factory. Jim, I'm just not prepared for this. I know we did the right thing but still, we've killed three people. And we did it like we knew how and like it's something we do it every day." Her voice was getting tighter and closer to hysteria.

Crouton went over to Kathleen and put her front paws on Kathleen's legs. Kathleen kneeled and pick up the dog.

Berry put his hand on her shoulder. He said, "Kathleen, from where I stand you were right. You prevented two murders – Clark's and Beale's. Clark was right, too. He may very well have saved your life and his. The man was very well armed and could have kept shooting until he hit you.

"Now, I want you two to go into one of the other offices and wait for me. Don't talk to anyone except me. No interviews, no comments to the cops and certainly nothing to anyone from the local law enforcement. Leave it to me. I can handle it. Not a word. Got it?"

We both nodded towards Jim Berry. We found an empty office next door to the crime scene. Kathleen concentrated on staying calm but found that to be more and more difficult. I put my head in my hands. I sat very still and felt pretty calm.

Finally, Kathleen took a big deep breath and said a low, quiet voice, "Clark. I'm done with this. You could've been killed. I could've been killed. Both of us could've been killed. No more. I'm out."

"As usual, you beat me to the draw. Me, too. Having an interesting and exciting other life is one thing. Getting into gun fights on a regular basis is something else entirely."

She said, "So, how do we tell Jim Berry?"

I snapped, "The minute I see him I'll put it on the table. Actually, you just told him. I don't know how much clearer you could have been."

Kathleen slumped in her chair. I began to pace. This was not going to be easy. I thought of how to convince Berry that we're done with playing FBI.

Half and hour later Jim Berry and Kerry Blount entered the office and closed the door. Berry said, "Sorry to make you wait. This is a little touchy and we want to be careful. How are you?"

I said, "Jim, we're done with all this. It's way more than we thought it would be. I hope you understand."

Berry said, "Listen you guys, I can imagine how you feel. We're very grateful and I know Jonathan Beale will be grateful. By the way, Beale gave us some information that might open this thing up a little. And guys you can relax. By the time this is over your cover will be totally and utterly blown anyway. If you want out, fine. But for now, I need you to sit tight. We still have some sort of scam going on and I don't want to tip our hand. I can promise you that the gun work is done in this case. The others are fairly sane and good citizens who don't use guns. Will the two of you stay around till we wrap this up completely?"

Kathleen and I looked at each other. She said to me, "Hell no, Jim, what part of that do you not get? In a few days I've nearly lost my husband and had to kill a human being to prevent Clark's death. Today, I had to kill another person.

You know, Jim, I wonder what our life would be like if we just reminded you of our true agreement every time you try to send us out to kill people. We're supposed to be 'eyes and ears' not hired killers. No, Jim, no."

I jumped in, "Jim, she is right. We've had enough. You guys knew this Russian was a bad guy and you asked us to delay him until you could get your shit together. We did that and we damn near got ourselves killed. Maybe you and your kind can take this. We can't.

"Let me ask you, Jim, how many people have you killed? More importantly, how many people have you killed to prevent someone close to you from being killed? Forget it, Jim. Where in hell do we go from here? I mean two gunfights a week can only get worse."

Jim Berry motioned for the other agents to leave the room. He took a chair and folded his arms. He looked from Kathleen to me and back to Kathleen. Finally, he said, "Okay. I do get it. No one ever thought this would come to this kind of thing.

"You don't owe me a thing. But I am going to suggest that you still owe your country something. Maybe I think you even owe Napa something. We know there's some sort of crime going on or about to happen as a result of all this. We want you to stay put and help us shut the crime down. I'm asking you to do this. You might walk out of here." He paused and then looked directly at my wife. "Kathleen, don't you worry about the shootings. I'm pretty sure we can keep you in the clear. I mean, you did what you did and we'll just do our best to make it OK."

Kathleen erupted. She jumped up from her chair and flew at Jim Berry. When she stopped, her face was four inches from his, "So that's it. You're holding us hostage with a promise to 'take care' of the shootings? Well, Jim, kiss my ass. Call the cops or the D.A., call the damn White House if you want. Go ahead and file the charges. We can deal with it. Frankly, I don't care what you do."

She took a step back and said, "You can take your fucking magic phone and your fucking pistol and shove 'em up your ass."

She reached into her pants pocket and said, "Oh, yeah, Jim, take your little signal gizmos, too. It's for damn sure that I won't need them again. I'm out of here."

She reached for my arm and said, "Clark, let's go before I say something I might really regret. The nerve of this bastard to try to force us to keep up this stupid charade."

I stood to follow her out of the room. Jim Berry stood up and blocked the door. He said, "Kathleen, settle down, please." He ran his hand through his hair and a look of desperation mixed with frustration was on his face. "Of course you can go. But right now there are cops all over the place and if they see you they might start asking questions. Please, just stay in this room until they leave or lose interest. We told them an agent did the shooting. So far, They've gone along with that. I think we'll be fine if we're careful. Please. I honestly don't want you to get involved in this and the local law."

I put my hands on Kathleen's shoulders. I said, "I think he's right. Let's wait."

I turned to Jim and said, "Please, leave us alone and just let us know when we can leave."

Berry left the room. Kathleen sat down and stared out the window. She said, "I think every law enforcement car and fire truck in Napa must be here. We're going to be lucky to have this go away. We, I really, have killed two men in a few days. Can Jim really make this just go away?"

"I don't know. But I have to believe him."

We waited four hours. An agent brought us water and coffee and later on a bag of burgers from McDonald's. The time crawled by. Around seven o'clock Jim Berry came in and said, "Most of the cops are gone. The firemen went back to work hours ago. I still have the Chief and one of his commanders. I think they'll leave in a few minutes. Want to meet them?"

I said, "How would that work? Wouldn't they get curious about us being in this room for all these hours?"

Berry replied, "No. They think you're undercover feds. The shooting has gone down as being done by one of my agents, Andrew Olds. You were in the building and got involved on the fringes. You're OK."

We walked out of the room to meet Richard Marin and his commander, Thad Cornet. We shook hands and chatted. Marin said, "That was incredible shooting, wasn't it. Did you see it Ms. Royal? Mr. Davis, I understand you were still downstairs trying to help the receptionist. Right?"

Kathleen took the lead, "Yes, I think he was on the stairs. He and I heard the Beale fellow scream and went up the stairs. I saw what was happening. The big man was about to cut the other man's throat. Andy, the FBI agent, shot two times and it was over. The big man fell backward. The other man slumped in his chair. I think he's OK."

Marin said, "That about does it for us. We'll get back to work or go home or whatever. You ready go Thad?"

Cornet answered, "I am if you are."

358

An agent downstairs overheard Cornet say to Marin as they left the building, "Chief, you know damn well there's more to it that that. I think we ought to shut down the whole thing and find out what."

Marin replied, "Well, Thad, you go to it. My position's that the minute the Feds walked in the deal was theirs. I plan to leave it that way."

I saw Kathleen go back into the office room and retrieve her Glock and other things. She stuffed all the items into a combination purse/brief case and joined me in going downstairs.

Minutes after the last of the local cops left, Kathleen and I climbed into an FBI SUV and were taken to our car. We were totally exhausted when we got home. Kathleen grabbed her mail and sat in a chair in our family room. She got through one envelope before she was sleeping. I woke her and helped her get upstairs and into bed. She was already asleep when I pulled her covers up.

CHAPTER FIFTY-FIVE

I was getting ready to get in bed myself when my cell phone rang. There was no call identification on the panel. I thought about letting it go but eventually picked it and said, "This is Clark Davis."

A weak voice responded, "Mr. Davis, this is Sid Zaccaria. Do you have a moment for me?"

I took a deep breath and said, "Of course I do. How can I help?"

"I want to see you now, Mr. Davis. I can be at your home in thirty minutes or you can come here or we could meet somewhere. Will you do that? I know this is an imposition, but I need to see you."

I thought about going back cut. I was tired but I had basically been sitting in an office for hours. Mine was the kind of tired one gets after a college examination or a BAR examination. I was not physically tired. I was emotionally exhausted. I sensed that Sid's call might somehow wrap this up and get us out of it. He sounded worried or maybe even desperate.

"I'll be at your home as soon as possible."

"Thank you. Have you eaten? I can fix something if you like."

"No, thank you. I'm fine."

The truth was I was hungry. It had been far too long since we'd had lunch at Celadon and the burgers hadn't appealed to either of us.

I thought about calling Jim Berry from my cell phone. Of course he'd want to know. But how did I know if Sid Zaccaria's call was personal or somehow had to do with the scam or crime or whatever? I decided to take this a step at a time. I knew Kathleen would be furious when she found out. We had agreed to put this FBI mess behind us. I suppose not calling Berry was my way of building a story to convince my wife that I was not getting back in with Berry. I knew it would be interesting whether it was personal or not.

I left a note for Kathleen. I knew she would check her bedside clock. The note was placed in front of the clock. I went downstairs and out the door. I locked the door on my way out. While I was tired, it was still only eight o'clock and the streets of Napa had lots of traffic. I headed north and up the Silverado Trail. In about twenty minutes I was turning in Sid's driveway. As I drove slowly toward the home I could see Zaccaria standing on the front steps. He waved to me. I parked and met him at the top of the stairs.

He said, "Clark, I hope it's OK to use your first name, the last time we were together, you said something that made me curious. You told me, your dinner host, that I could contact you if I needed help. Why did you say that, Clark?"

"It was nothing. Just a kindness, I suppose."

"Are you sure that's the truth, Clark? Are you sure you didn't have something else on your mind? Can you tell me what it was, please?"

I shrugged my shoulders and kept silent. It was clear the man had something to say. I wanted to hear it.

A curious thing happens to ordinary men and women when they start working in law enforcement, even peripherally in law enforcement. For one thing, that person suddenly finds that every non-law enforcement person in the world shows jealousy, envy, hostility, anger and combativeness toward him or her. Shortly after that a feeling of omnipotence washes over the nascent law enforcement person. This is a feeling that he or she knows a little or a lot more about what is happening in town, in the nation and even in the world. Ordinary people are mired in mystery, mystical thoughts and imprecise thinking. This is the essence of the division between cops and citizens. It would be easy to end this conflict through training and the introduction of simple concepts. But older officers are difficult to change. They pass their emotions and thoughts down to rookies. The cycle never ends.

Kathleen and I had felt a little distant from others. We made friends but we looked at them differently. We found ourselves looking at each other while others talked. It was especially trying to hear our friends and others speculate about Homeland Security and other agencies.

I followed Zaccaria through the home and into the kitchen. He had seen through my refusal and had set out a feast for ten people. The sight of the food made me even hungrier. I circled the table and began filling a plate. The food was the kind of thing I always thought rich people had on hand all the time. His spread included three salads, shrimp, sliced roast beef, fresh vegetables, cheeses and a tray that probably had every edible nut on the planet. On the side board Sid had open bottles of five wines plus the makings for martinis.

I took my plate and a glass of a remarkable zinfandel to the table and sat down. After a couple of bites and a sip of wine I looked at Sid with an expression of 'what now'.

Sid Zaccaria sat down across from me and after a few minutes he said, "Clark, I'm going to tell you a story. It's a sorry but true story. I'm not certain why I'm telling you this story. But I have to tell someone. I told my wife and she took off for her sister's home in Santa Barbara. Are you ready for this, Clark?"

I took another bite to give me time to think. Finally, I said, "I'm ready and happy to listen. I can't promise that I can make your problem go away. But I'll listen."

The old man told me a story of the struggles in the wine business, of the possibility that up Valley wine might have too much mercury from the soil and of his being threatened by a huge Russian. He said he was afraid of the Russian more than anything. He told me he suspected the Russian or one of his associates killed his wife's beloved horse. Finally, he told me about the wine scam. It was the information I wanted and needed.

I thought about this, some of which I knew or suspected, and let him continue.

"Clark, I don't know what to do. The wines are very good but they're not Napa wines. Napa wines are different from French and Italian wines. For all I know their wines are better. Who knows? But our wines much more clearly define the fruit and reflect the miracle of the fruit, its complexity and its simplicity.

"When our wines won the tasting in Paris in 1976 it was because our wines are true to the grape. Clark, I cannot try to pass off these wines as Napa wines. It cannot happen and will not. I'll try to control the others. But cannot promise. I know I've committed crimes. So be it. '

I took a sip of the zinfandel, wiped my mouth with a linen napkin and said, "I don't mean to diminish your problem in any way. I can't imagine how you feel because I've never done anything like this or even heard of it. But let me say that the first step in putting anything behind you is recognizing that the problem exists and facing it head on. You've done that.

"I want to set your mind at ease on a couple of points. First, take it from me that the Russians are out of the picture. They're gone. They won't harm or threaten you, or anyone, in any way. There were two Russians and a Cuban. All of them are out of the picture now.

"Second, Sid, you've planned a crime and brought others into the planning and the implementation. That might rise to the level of a conspiracy. But you and your friends did not actually do the wine scam. You walked right up to the edge and are standing there now. But you might not have done anything so far that will attract the interest of a prosecutor.

"I think you should let me call some friends of mine and have them come here right now. OK?"

Sid put his head down and began to sob. "Will I be arrested?"

"I don't know. I'll try to prevent it. After all you're not going to run off or try something foolish."

"No, I'm not. Let's do it. Call your friends."

My cell phone was in my shirt pocket. I though about walking outside to place the call but didn't. Sid Zaccaria had been straight with me. I would be straight with him.

Jim Berry answered on the third ring. He said, "Clark, I would have thought you'd be in bed. What's up?"

I briefed Jim Berry on what I had learned and concluded the call with, "Jim, I think this is the thing you were worried about. Can you come now? You won't need an army. And, Jim, I told Sid that I didn't think he would be taken into custody. I hope you won't make me out to be a liar."

Sid and I talked for the half hour it took for Jim Berry to get to the Zaccaria home. When Jim's headlight beams announced his arrival, Sid grew tense and nervous. I said, "Sid, we'll all get through this. The man who's coming up your front steps is a good solid man. He'll do the best he can."

CHAPTER FIFTY-SIX

Jim Berry joined us in Sid Zaccaria's home. He passed on the food and wine. He got directly to the point, "Mr. Zaccaria, Mr. Davis has told me a little of what you're doing. It's very disturbing. I can tell you that you and your group have had us chasing our tails for a long time."

Berry paused for that to sink in then continued, "But, Mr. Zaccaria, I think it's likely that while we know you went into this with your eyes wide open, it's possible that you haven't actually committed a serious crime. Yet, you're close and maybe you have crossed the line. That's what I want to know and I need to know it now.

"First, let's talk about the Russians. I can tell you that two of the Russians are dead. We caught both of them just as they were about to commit even worse crimes. Mr. Zaccaria, tell me, how many Russians were involved with you?"

"I met one. Anapa Krasnodar. Only one. Another man sometimes accompanied him. I don't remember his name. I don't even know if I ever heard his name."

"Did this Krasnodar come to you or did you contact him?"

"He contacted me."

"Tell me about it, Mr. Zaccaria."

Zaccaria stared into space. It was as if he knew that he was describing his crime to an FBI agent and that he might very well leave his home in handcuffs. Finally, he said, "He asked me to get some other winemakers and meet him at Meadowood. We did. He talked for a while then invited us to taste some of the most interesting and perfectly made wines we ever tasted. Those wines were absolutely perfect. Then he told us he made the wines. Made. Not grew grapes and produced wine. He said he made it in a laboratory. Mr. Barry, we didn't even know if making wine in a lab was illegal. We started out just in awe of the quality of the wine.

"I can tell you, Sir, that we were astonished. We've worked hard to produce excellent wines for forty years or more. Yet we've never even come close to the quality and the shear perfection of the wines we tasted at Meadowood that day. We were, I'm afraid, literally mesmerized by the Russian, his wines and his story of how easy it is to make such perfect wines in a laboratory."

Berry commented, "Scams like this, Mr. Zaccaria, always are mesmerizing. That's why good people like you and your friends find it so easy to break the law. Please continue."

Zaccaria said, "Well, we did agree. Each of us would buy some reds and whites. We put up a hell of a lot of money. At one point, I saw where this was going and I told the Russian

I wanted out." Zaccaria's voice got stronger. Some of the old world pride showed through in his tone and his physical appearance.

"I called and told him I wanted out. He was calm but firm. I guess I knew I should be careful. That night, my wife's horse was killed while we slept. I think the Russian did it to warn me."

Zaccaria seemed to run out of gas. He slumped in his chair and hung his head.

Berry waited a while then said, "Mr. Zaccaria, we know pretty much all of that. We weren't with you at Meadowood but not long after that meeting we began monitoring the Russians' telephone calls and, eventually, yours and your friends. All this was done with legal wire taps. Now, I have a list of questions for you. Before I begin, I am required to tell you that you are a suspect in a crime. Whatever you say can and will be used against you in a court of law. You have a right to remain silent and you have the right to legal representation. That means you can stop now and call your attorney. If you do, you'll be using your Constitutional rights and doing so won't place you in more jeopardy. Do you understand?"

Sid Zaccaria nodded to indicate that he understood his rights.

Berry said, "Mr. Zaccaria, I need a verbal acceptance."

"Yes, I understand."

"Do you wish to continue?"

"I do. Yes, I do. I'm ready to get this behind me."

"Thank you. Your government and I appreciate your willingness to cooperate with us."

Berry referred to a notebook he had been carrying in his suit jacket pocket.

"Did everyone in your group participate equally?"

"Yes, they did. Well, in the beginning we had a member who was killed. He indicated his rejection of the plan at Meadowood. He was killed in a car wreck later that day. Wait, I hadn't thought about it but do you think the Russians killed John?"

"It is possible. We'll probably never know. How much did each of you pay the Russian and how did you pay it?"

"We each gave the Russian two million dollars in cash. He was very clear about that. No checks, no credit cards. Only cash. We brought it to a meeting in Fairfield at the Hilton. We had suitcases. The other Russian took the suitcases. We also paid $4.00 a bottle for about 14,000 cases of wine. He guaranteed that price per bottle for a set period of time. I recall very well that we bought wine for about $1.6 million that we could sell for more than ten million. It seemed so simple, Mr. Berry. I think some of my friends even convinced themselves that it was OK. I mean they told themselves that this was just like making wine the real way."

"Did you ever sell any of the wine?"

"No, not a bottle."

"Did any other person taste or accept any of the wine?"

"I gave a couple of bottles to Jonathan Beale at American Wine."

"Where is the wine now, Mr. Zaccaria?"

"All of use put our wine deliveries in a warehouse out on Green Island, south of the airport. It's there now under lock and key."

"What happened that convinced you to contact us?"

"Two things. First, Jonathan Beale apparently tasted the wine and called me to say that it was not Napa Valley wine.

He thought it was very good but not from here. He thought it was French wine being passed off as Napa Valley wine. Because of the quality of the wines, I know that doesn't make any sense. Why would anyone take very high quality French wine and try to pass it off as California wine?

"Anyway, I knew Beale was onto us. I believed it would a matter of time until somehow he or someone found out the truth. That would destroy me and it could destroy the Napa Valley. I'm an old man. I can deal with anything. The Napa Valley is precious. It would never recover.

"Mr. Berry, do you remember when Perrier was the top brand of bottled water in the nation? And if you do, do you remember when someone discovered a tiny amount of benzene in Perrier? The amount of benzene was so minor it was harmless but if you follow all this you know that the brand, Perrier, is gone for all practical purposes. Rumors persist to this day that the sales of Perrier overwhelmed the company's ability to bottle and produce the water in France then ship it to America, so they began producing the water in a factory in New Jersey. Who knows if that's true? We'll never know, I suppose. But the damage was done, wasn't it?"

Berry asked, "And what was the second thing?"

"I was frantic. For some reason Clark here seemed to be a solid guy who would understand. I called him, admitted everything and he convinced me to let him call you."

Berry said, "Mr. Zaccaria, will you excuse me. I need to place some telephone calls. I'll go to my car to do the calling. I might be gone thirty minutes or more."

Jim Berry left the home. Sid and I sat together and said nothing for almost half an hour.

371

Finally, Sid said, "I wonder what Mr. Berry is doing. Should I expect reinforcements to arrive? Am I going to jail tonight?"

"I truly don't know, Sid. He should be here soon. Can I get you something? Coffee? Wine?"

"I'm fine. Just a little nervous."

Ten minutes later Jim Berry came back to the kitchen. A trace of a smile foretold what he would say.

Berry said, "Alright, Mr. Zaccaria, here's what I can offer you. Listen carefully and make sure you can accept what I'll say.

"First, we're certain that the Russians are gone. You can relax. The Russians and all they represent are completely out of this. Anapa Krasnodar and his associate Anoly Baranovich are dead. There's no doubt about that, Mr. Zaccaria.

"Second, The US Attorney in San Francisco agrees with me that while we might prosecute you and your group, it could be difficult and you would probably go free. You and the others won't be arrested and won't be prosecuted."

Sid Zaccaria slumped in his chair and began sobbing again. He said, "Thank you, sir."

Berry said, "Don't thank me. Mr. Zaccaria, if I could, I would put you under the jail. You and your friends took part in a shitty deal that left two men dead. The Napa Valley is still in jeopardy because of your greed.

"Now, there are three conditions. First, you'll authorize us to destroy the wine. Second, you won't get your money back. Third, you and your pals will all put your wineries up for sale within the next 90 days and continue to sell vineyards you own until you are completely out of the wine business. In no case may you own vineyards or wineries one year from today. If you fail to do exactly as I've said, we will begin prosecution proceedings immediately. You can take a day to decide if your freedom is worth that.

"Don't leave this house. Call your friends and have them meet you here tomorrow morning at ten."

Berry was interrupted by car headlights coming up the driveway. He said, "That'll be some of my associates. By the time they leave tonight, this room and this house will be totally wired. We'll be able to hear something as small as a mouse fart. And that includes everything you and the others say tomorrow. Do I have your permission to do that?"

"You do."

Berry said, "In this case a verbal will not suffice. One of my associates is coming in the house now with a document for you to sign. I strongly urge you to sign it."

CHAPTER FIFTY-SEVEN

Fifteen minutes later I left Sid's house and drove home. It was well after midnight so the traffic was light. Napa is like most small towns in America. After ten o'clock at night it's just about impossible to drive through the city without being observed by at least one law enforcement officer.

I saw a Napa sheriff when I made the turn from the Silverado Trail onto Trancas Street going west. A Napa PD car was in the Safeway parking lot at Trancas and Jefferson. Another officer observed me as I drove along Redwood toward our home.

When I parked my car and went inside, Kathleen was sitting at the kitchen table drinking coffee. She was dressed in a robe that I had given her for Christmas years ago. She wore her little black slippers that looked like they might have been designed for dancing.

I was about to speak when she waved her had as if to make me stop talking. She said, "Clark, I can only imagine where you have been and why. After we promised each other to get out of this I was shocked to know that your commitment lasted less than two hours.

"Clark, I'm not happy. If I can't trust you, who can I trust?" This is one of the things that women say when they've had it with a boy friend or husband. Any time a woman tells a man that trust is gone, the end is near. That also applies to, "Fine, do what you want to do," and the equally deadly, "Whatever."

I walked over to the kitchen table and pulled out a chair. I was careful to give her space. I took a chair opposite hers. I said, "OK. Here goes. When we got home last night you were a zombie. I put you in bed. When you woke up you might have noticed that you had your shirt and socks on. Just as I was undressing my cell phone ran. It was Sid Zaccaria. The man was terrified. He wanted to see me. I didn't know why. He said he would come here or meet me at his home up on the Trail. I chose to go there.

"Honey, Sid confessed to me. He and a group of his friends were in a plan with the Russians to produce fake wine. The Russians would produce the wine in a soft drink factory in Fairfield.

"I heard him out and then talked him into letting me call Jim Berry. I did. Jim came out and took a complete confession. For a variety of reasons, the feds agreed to not charge or prosecute the group. By this time tomorrow, the fake wine, about seventy thousand cases of it, will be destroyed. The group will be out almost twenty million dollars in cash. Jim got that agreement signed by Sid. I left Sid's and came home. Here I am. If you would have done differently, I'm listening."

She sat for long minutes and looked first at me then at nothing. Kathleen isn't a big person. At this moment she seemed even smaller. She had both hands on her coffee cup. She drew her right hand to her face to wipe away a fallen strand of hair. I saw her hand was shaking. She put her hand in her lap so neither of us could see it shaking. Tears filled the corners of her eyes. I could see that stronger tears had ruined her makeup. Kathleen has strong shoulders. Those shoulders sagged and one side of her robe had drooped down to reveal her shoulder and collar bone. Her skin was always perfect but tonight I could see blotches on her skin.

Kathleen straightened in her chair as if she was reading my mind. She pulled her robe up to her chin and clutched it tightly. I could see that she was shaking, her whole body was shaking. After a while she said, without looking at me, "Clark. I'm so tired, so worn, so confused and so ready for help. I cannot handle this.

"I know I sound like a broken record but I've killed two people, two men in a few days. Now you tell me that men I should admire have fallen prey to pure D greed. Greed.

"My world is falling apart. When I thought you had lied to me or broken your word to me, I just lost it. Clark, I need you and I need us. Can you understand that?"

She was crying and I could tell it would get worse before it got better. I stood and walked over and took her in my arms. She was racked with sobs. I held her for minutes.

I said, "Babe, this'll pass. You and I have to be in lock step." I pulled her up to me and then gently walked her over to the family room. I put a little pressure on her shoulders and she sat down on the carpet. I joined her there, brought her down to a prone position and held her tightly. Slowly the crying quieted. I could feel her body relaxing and, bad timing or not, I could feel myself hardening.

She said, "Shouldn't we take this upstairs to bed?"

I grinned and said in my best imitation of Manuele Donde who played El Jefe, the Mexican bandit in The Treasure of Sierra Madre, "We don't need no stinking bed."

Later, as we lay on our backs on the floor of our family room, Kathleen said, "Clark, what are you thinking? I mean right now."

"Honest, you really want to know?"

"I do."

"Well, I saw what the big Russian was going to do. I guess seeing the dead receptionist told me he really was going to kill Beale. I dropped to one knee to take the shot but before I could get into position you shot twice and hit him twice. How did you do that?"

She said, "Stop it, Clark. I just did what I had to do. I love you."

"I see. Well, that is good to know. The next time things get tense between us though, I'll keep in mind that you can outdraw me."

"You might want to keep that in mind all the time," she said with a grin. My girl was back.

I rolled over and took her in my arms and before she could object, was deep inside her. This time it was hurried and full of energy. She got into the rhythm and joined me in a bone breaking orgasm.

She collapsed me on top of me and said, "I think you outdrew me that time, podna."

When the sun came up we were asleep on the family room floor. I woke to a family of crows stomping on our roof. The nutty lady next door put out food for crows, possums and coons. Why is this a total mystery to us? I think I mentioned that she is nutty.

Kathleen poked her finger onto the tip of my nose to wake me up. I opened my eyes and found her face six inches from mine. She said, "Your choice. Are we still in this?"

I tried to move and let out a groan. After a night on the floor, I could feel every bone in my body and none of them felt particularly great. I grinned at her and said, "Are you saying I screwed some sense into your hard, but pretty little head, my dear?"

"Don't push your luck, bud. Get your ass up and get me some coffee."

I kissed her and tried to stand. She had dissolved most of my bones and turned my muscles to pasta. After a few tries, I made it up and walked into the kitchen to get the coffee started. She followed in a few minutes. Her robe was sorta on. Her feet were bare and her hair was a mess.

I thought about what she had done. Anyone can get a gun and anyone can learn to shoot a gun. And, I suppose anyone can learn to hit a target. But I bet it's very unusual for anyone to get to the level where Kathleen is. The Glock is as much an extension of her body and mind as a golf club is to a golf professional. Jack Nicklaus said that he started playing golf when he was five. He said all those years made him good at golf but he also said he kinda started good. Kathleen was good from the start, too.

She came into the kitchen grabbed her coffee and said, "I'm heading upstairs to shower and get dressed. No work for me today. Join me? Oh, yeah, I would like to go to Gillwood's for breakfast. Their lox and bagels breakfast is calling my name."

"I'm on it. Get going."

CHAPTER FIFTY-EIGHT

On our way to breakfast I told Kathleen more about last night at Sid Zaccaria's home. And, I told her that all the participants would meet with Jim Berry this morning. We wondered if we would hear the results of that meeting.

As we were walking to the restaurant, Jonathan Beale came along. He seemed to recognize us. As he drew near, I could see it was Kathleen he recognized.

Beale put out his hand to Kathleen and said, "Excuse me. I don't know your name but I know what you did. You saved my life. I'm under orders not to talk about this. I guess it's OK to talk to you, though. We're sort of insiders, I guess. Thank you."

He started to walk past us when Kathleen said, "Mr. Beale. Thank you, too."

Breakfast at Gillwood's is always a treat. Gillwood's is a Napa institution. Open for breakfast and lunch only, Gillwood's offers an almost endless selection of fresh food and great service. New York has the Stage Deli; Napa has Gillwood's.

Kathleen ordered her standard, lox and bagels with extra capers and sliced tomatoes. My standard, which is also her standard when a restaurant does not have her main standard, is two soft poached eggs on wheat toast with crisp bacon and, if the place knows how to do it, hash brown potatoes. Gillwood's knows how to do it.

After breakfast we took a walk through downtown Napa. We were standing front of the Opera House when my cell phone buzzed. Jim Berry had given us tiny little Blue Tooth devices that fit inside the ear canal. A light touch on the device activated it.

I touched the device in my ear and said, "This is Clark Davis."

Jim Berry came on the line and said, "Good morning Clark. Are you somewhere where you can talk?"

"Jim, you know very well where I am. What's up?"

"You got me on that one, Clark. When can you and Kathleen come out to my office?"

I glanced at Kathleen. She shrugged her shoulders to let me know that she was in. I said, "Any time, Jim. We can drive out now."

Berry said, "Give me thirty minutes. I'm driving in from St. Helena." He broke the connection.

I turned to Kathleen and said, "Jim wants us to come out. He had a meeting with the wine group this morning. I expect he wants to bring us up to date and close this thing."

She frowned and said, "Clark, I mean it. I still have huge reservations about all this. I will go out to see Jim if you want me to but that's all. A recap and then we're going home. I want to get my desk in order tomorrow and then go somewhere that's calm with you for three or four days."

I said, "Wow! That sounds great. Would that somewhere have a beach by any chance? If so, let's go over to Williamson's and let me get some beach shirts, you know, Nat Nast and Tommy Bahama, that kind of thing."

"Deal. I'll be at the Mustard Seed looking for just that kind of thing, too. It's close to Williamson's."

An hour later we drove out to the airport. I could see smoke and even flames a couple of miles south of the airport. The county dump was in that area so we didn't think much about it. After we got to the airport, we went though the rigmarole to get to Jim Berry's office. Berry was waiting for us. Kerry Blount entered the office right behind us. Berry stood and motioned us to his conference table.

Berry dispensed with the niceties. He said, "Kathleen, Clark, I want to begin by expressing your government's most sincere appreciation for what you've done here in Napa. I'll add my personal appreciation and, even though they'll never know about it, the appreciation of every person in Napa County and the entire California wine industry. Thank you."

We nodded that we understood. Berry continued, "To say this operation went way beyond what anyone ever intended is an understatement of the first degree. You ended a well-planned attack on an important, no critical, US security installation. You discovered a complex plot that could have destroyed the wine industry in Napa and maybe even the whole shebang in the California wine industry. Kathleen, your amazing focus saved Clark's life and the life of another, totally innocent man, Jonathan Beale. Clark, your contact with Sid Zaccaria turned out to be critical. Your quick decision on the man at the pipe factory probably saved your lives and pre-vented what could have been a very difficult shootout with the people we had in the air.

"It turns out that the man you shot is a Cuban national. He entered the US illegally from Mexico sometime in December of last year. He connected with the Russians about two months ago

"He was carrying excellent identification. In fact, his ID was so good he was able to buy the rifle and several rounds of ammunition at a local store in downtown Napa. The rifle is a Wilson AR-15 type rifle with a Leupold long eye relief scope. Long eye relief means the scope can be mounted for-ward on the rifle so the shooter does not have to get the scope up close to his eye. This gives the shooter and advantage on small targets and moving targets. He can use both eyes wide open to find the target the focus on the scope for the shot. It's an excellent weapon for the kind of work that man was doing. Incidentally, his name was Arturo Vena. As I said, he was Cuban.

"Now, I want you to hear it from me that before Krasnodar left for Napa he murdered his two children and his wife. It was murder, plain and simple. All three were shot at close range.

"We're grateful to both of you.

"Kerry and I met with the five men who were involved in the attempted wine fraud. Kerry and I as well as key people in Washington, worked hard to find a solution that would a) not destroy the wine industry in California and b) hold these men accountable.

"This morning we think we accomplished that. First the men acknowledged what they had done in writing. This amounts to a permanent probation for the men. One mistake and they're done.

"Second, they agreed to let us destroy the fraudulent wine. You might have noticed a fire just south of here. The warehouse is burning and destroying all the wine. The men agreed that they wouldn't file insurance claims. We know the owner of the warehouse is insured. She'll get her money from the US government but will believe it came from her insurance company. By the way, Uncle Sam has no problem with this because we found all the money the men paid to the Russian in Krasnodar's Escalade. Our agents saw him move the money from the house to the car just before he drove to Napa.

Third, the men will sell their wine businesses and their vineyards within one year from today. If they default on this agreement they'll see what we can do with the signed documents that amount to guilty pleas. We will not hesitate to use what we have. By the way, Sid Zaccaria thinks you're a god, Clark. I expect he'll try to contact you to thank you in some way. My advice is to not take a call from Sid Zaccaria.

Joe Bruning came into the office. Jim Berry said, "If you're ready Joe, there's someone on the phone for Kathleen and Clark."

Bruning said, "Here we go." He pushed a button on the speaker phone on the conference table. A very recognizable voice came into the room.

"Kathleen and Clark, this is the President. Jim Berry was kind enough to let me call and personally thank you for what you have done. The loss of the security facility in Napa could have harmed this nation in a way that might have taken years to overcome. Your intervention with the wine scam certainly did save the California wine industry. On behalf of your country, Kathleen and Clark, please accept our extreme appreciation. I know that you're aware that all these events must remain confidential, probably forever. I fondly wish I could tell that this nation of our two heroes in the Napa Valley. Now, Jim Berry has more to tell you. Goodbye for now."

Kathleen and I were stunned. Was that really the President? Had we really done those things?

Kerry Blunt said, "Let me add that Homeland Security appreciates what you did, too. We were caught flatfooted. You pulled our fat out of the fire and, literally, saved the day. Clark, you were magnificent. Your calm decision to go, on your own, to see Sid Zaccaria and convince him to come clean was the stuff of training cases for the FBI, Homeland Security and law enforcement everywhere.

"Kathleen, I've been in law enforcement and investigations for thirty years. I've never met anyone, anywhere who is as calm and effective as you are in very serious, very dangerous situations. If you had hesitated a half second, Clark might be dead. If you had hesitated a tenth of a second, Jonathan Beale would be dead and you would have had a 250 pound highly trained Russian warrior coming at you from ten feet away. In our training we stress that the outcome of that kind of confrontation almost always ends with the agent dead and the charging thug still alive. I doubt that you know that. I never will doubt that you are, singularly, the most impressive person I've known. It's a pure pleasure to know you and to have worked with you. I, for one, am sorry that won't continue."

Jim Berry filled the silence in the room when he said, "Guys, I second what the President and Kerry said. I have a suggestion and I have a request. First, I would be derelict if I did not try to talk you into continuing to work with us. Your appreciative government wants you to take a vacation. We'll make it OK with your employers. You can go anywhere you choose and everything is on us."

Jim Berry raised his hand and said, "One more thing. I think everyone will appreciate this. The report about mercury in the up Valley wines was bogus. Krasnodar had the report created to bring the others into the scam. There's no mercury in Napa Valley wines. Even so, if that story had gotten out, this Valley and maybe the rest of the California wine industry would have been damaged severely."

Berry placed two credit cards on the conference table. "Use these credit cards to pay for everything – hotels, cars, meals, drinks, sightseeing and even whatever extra clothing you want. No limits. And, my suggestion is this: wait until you return in a week or so to tell us what you want to do. I would be lying if I failed to say that I want you on my team."

Kerry Blount said, "Take it easy there, Jim. I want them on my team!" A big smile crossed her face.

Berry ended the meeting by saying, "Now, go home, pack some bags and call this number and let the person who answers know where you want to go. Come back to the airport and you'll find a government Gulfstream waiting for you on the apron right outside Jonesy's. OK?"

I said, "Well, Jim, I don't think we need to go home. After all, we have these credit cards for anything we need." I scooped the cards off the table, glanced at the names on the cards and handed Kathleen the one with her name on it. I turned to Kathleen and said, "Key West and South Beach?"

She smiled and said, "You got it, bud."

I turned to Jim Berry. I said, "Is that Gulfstream ready to go?"

Kathleen, always the mother and always practical said, "What about the house and Crouton?"

He laughed and said, "We will close your home and an agent is on the way with Crouton. Time is wasting. Get to it, bud."

EPILOGUE

I don't care who you are, a Gulfstream jet airplane is delightful. It's a machine that can, in the words of Larry the Cable Guy, "Git 'er done.' Twenty minutes after we boarded the airplane, we were at 41,000 feet. Napa was far behind. A crew member announced that we would be flying from Napa airport direct to Key West. He invited us to relax and enjoy the hospitality of the United States government.

Minutes before we boarded the airplane and FBI SUV drove up. An agent brought Crute up the ramp and handed her to Kathleen. In no time Crute had inspected the passenger cabin and was pawing at the door to the cockpit.

We had to remind ourselves that it was a government airplane. The walls were done in soft grey leather with custom inlays of an American Flag and the logo, "United States of America". The flooring was deep pile carpeting laid over even thinker soft foam. The windows had shutters that not only cut off sight lines into the plane but also electronically damped the vibrations from speech so when the plane was on the ground no outside listening devices could pick up conversations inside the airplane. Seating groups of two and four opposing groups of seats filled about half the cabin. A door to the back of the cabin blocked the aisle. We had no idea where the door lead but imagined that it was something we could not see.

A uniformed Marine entered the cabin and stopped by our seats. He said, "Madam, Sir, we'll be in Key West, Florida in about five to six hours. Our route will take us over the southwest, over southern Nevada and northern Arizona, across New Mexico and Texas between Dallas and Houston and out over the Gulf of Mexico and then into Key West.

"I'll have a snack for you soon. A full dinner is ready when you want it. Today we have cold southern fried chicken and potato salad or a filet mignon. Sir, we also have a full bar on board. Please let me know how I can make your journey enjoyable Thank you, sir."

I nodded to Kathleen. She said, "Thank you. I think the snacks sound fine and maybe a Bloody Mary. How about you, Clark?"

"Sounds fine to me. Make mine spicy – horseradish and Tabasco."

We flew on in silence for ten minutes. The Marine brought a scrumptious snack tray and tall Bloody Marys. Mine was exactly as ordered. He said, "Sir, Ma'am, if you want, ah, privacy, you can use the compartment at the rear of the airplane. The compartment is configured as a bedroom." The marine's face turned bright red. "You'll also find a fully stocked bathroom with a shower." He backed away. So, we learned that the room that we imagined to be a den of spies turned out to be an ordinary bedroom.

In a little while Kathleen said, "I feel 100% better, Clark. Are you OK, too?"

"I am. I can't help but believe that Jim is doing all this to try to convince us to stay with the plan. I mean he could have simply let us walk away."

She replied, "Well, my mind is reeling. I've gone from 'no way, Jose', to thinking maybe I really do like this and all the way back again. I have to admit, I never had a call from the President. It impressed me, Clark, it really did. When I used to see those kinds of calls on television, you know, to astronauts and such I always thought it was contrived or BS at the minimum. But being on the receiving end of it sure changed my mind. It rung my bell. We really did make a contribution and we really are a part of the history of the nation. Course, no one but us will ever know, but it's true. This is going to take some thinking."

I said, "I'm so happy to hear that. I'm going through the same thing. Tell you what. Let's have a fine time in Key West for a few days then lets spend a couple of days in South Beach and try to work in a couple of big orders at Joe's Stone Crabs. I only hope they have a couple of orders for us." We both laughed at the inside joke.

We went to Joe's a few years back. The waiter came over and told us that if we came for the crab claws, we should get our order in right away. He said, "I was just in the kitchen and they have a couple of the big orders left. They won't last long." Of course we told him to reserve those two orders for us. We were feeling special until we over heard him tell a group of eight people the same tale, "We just have eight orders left tonight."

"Sounds good." She put her chair back and was asleep in no time.

The Marine came back and kneeled beside my seat. He said, "Sir, Will you need hotel reservations and a rent car?"

"Yes, we want to see if we can get in at the Sunset Key Resort or, if that isn't available, the Westin. We'll be there four nights. Then we'll need a car. We plan to drive up to South Beach. We would like the Setai if possible. We'll be there three nights and we want to keep the car."

"Sir, I can assure you both hotels will be delighted to see you." He glanced around the leather lined passenger cabin and said with a huge grin, "In this company reservations are not necessary. Your employer can get reservations anywhere, anytime."

He stood to go back to wherever he stayed then turned and said, "Most of our guests prefer suites. In this case ocean front suites or maybe your own house at Sunset Key. Will that be acceptable?"

I smiled and nodded. He walked away. Kathleen stirred and said, "I heard that. You can pass yourself off as a big shot with the greatest of ease. Maybe we ought to become grifters."

"Maybe we are grifters, posing as FBI agents. Ever think of it that way?"

Just then the marine returned with a blue leather bound portfolio. The seal of the United States of America was embossed in gold on the cover. He said, "Sir, I have confirmed your itinerary." He handed the portfolio to me and continued, "When we land at Key West – we'll be using the civilian airport, about two hours from now, you'll be met at the gate by a car and driver. The driver will escort you to the pier where a launch to Sunset Key will be waiting. Please take this card. If you need anything, please call this number. We would appreciate a 24 hour notice for scheduling your return trip to Napa. Oh yes, one more thing, I took the liberty of reserving a Corvette convertible and hope you enjoy it. If you won't needing anything now, please enjoy the remainder of your journey, Sir."

It was night when we landed at Key West airport. The pilot eased the big jet down so there was no sensation when we touched down and began the rollout. We could see the lights of the town and on fishing boats in the waters around the island. A huge cruise ship was pulling in at the pier. Kathleen and I have taken two cruises. To my surprise, I really enjoyed both. I thought that maybe we should take another cruise soon.

When the Gulfstream rolled to a stop the Marine opened the door and activated a stairway. We walked out into humid, hot air. A black Tahoe waited at the bottom of the stairs. The back door was open. I helped Kathleen into the car and went around to the other side where another Marine held the door for me. Our brief cases stayed with us. After all, we still had our Glocks and some other FBI gizmos.

The car pulled out for the short drive to the pier where the launch would be waiting. The driver greeted us and said, "Welcome to Key West. This will be a short trip. Sunset Key is accessible by launch. The launch runs on demand and will be waiting for us. Is there anything you need before we get to your launch?"

I said, "I can't think of anything."

Kathleen looked pointedly at me and said, 'Well, I can. I need a drug store and maybe we should stop so we can get casual shirts and shorts and stuff. And shoes. I can't enjoy a Florida vacation in heels."

The driver said, "I know just the places. First stop, Walgreen's. There's a Ross on the same block. I will park. Take your time." The driver occupied Crouton while we shopped.

We loaded up on all the stuff we should have brought from home at both stores. The driver opened the back of the car to hold all our bags. Ten minutes later he was helping us load the shopping bags onto the launch. In another ten minutes the launch pulled up to the Sunset Key pier. We were surprised to be met by two golf carts, one for us and one for our stuff. I'm afraid we looked a little like the Beverly Hillbillies with our shopping bags full of cheap outfits and flip flops.

Sunset Key Resort is located on a twenty-seven acre island about 500 yards off the coast of the island of Key West. The resort features cottages of from one to three bedrooms. Perfect, flawless service, including food and beverage service, is available 24 hours a day. It's one of the premier ocean front resorts in the world.

We were taken to an enormous three bedroom cottage. A candle lit setting for two was in place in the dining room. The porter took our Walgreen's and Ross shopping bags to the master bedroom. He returned shortly and showed us around the cottage.

When the porter had completed his rounds, he said, "Sir, if you please, we have arranged to serve a private dinner in your dining room in about an hour. I was told that you and

Mrs. Davis prefer martinis made with Sapphire gin, dirty, up and very cold with olives. You'll find a pitcher waiting for you on the sideboard in the front room. If your taste is for another beverage you'll find a full bar on the other wall in that same room." He winked and said, "I think you and Ms. Davis will appreciate that we have put in a good stock of Old No. 7, the original and to my taste the only, Jack Daniel's fine Tennessee whiskey.

"One more thing, Sir, Our café, Latitudes Beach Café is open from seven in the morning until ten in the evening every day. Our guests at Sunset Key Guest Cottages enjoy special privileges from Latitudes Beach Cafe. Cottage guests receive a complimentary Breakfast Basket delivered to their cottage porch each morning consisting of freshly baked muffins, other bakery specialties, orange juice and newspaper. Cottage guests may also choose to have one of our chefs cook for them in their cottage by requesting the Private Chef Service. Normally, this service requires advance notice but you're approved to request it at any time. Cottage dining service is also available. Just touch the number seven on any telephone in the cottage.

"We have a variety of activities at your disposal, Sir. Just touch the number three on your telephone. Each evening in Latitudes the Chef offers what we would call in Texas a Blue Plate Special. Tomorrow night he is fixin' southern fried wild quail, pan fried catfish, black eyed peas, mashed potatoes and gravy, corn bread and fresh strawberry shortcake or a slice of his pecan pie. You can find the nightly specials on your daily bulletin which we place on your door early each morning.

"Sir, may I be of further service?"

I said, "No, thank you." I put my hand in my pocket to get money for a tip.

The porter said, "Sir, your gratuities have been taken care of and very generously if I may say so. Good night, sir.

"Oh, we have a complete selection of food and treats for your puppy. Just call if she needs anything."

I turned to Kathleen. The last thing on my mind was intrigue and FBI stuff. Kathleen was standing there looking small and vulnerable much as she appeared when I first met her. I said, "Babe, this has been some ride. The fact that we are standing here and that we have learned to trust each other totally, even more than most married couples, means that we are a team as well as lovers. I like that idea and want to continue this way.

"But now, I sure wish you had that green teddy of yours. I've got the wine," I raised my eyebrows and tried looking both expectant and hopeful.

She said with a big grin, "You know, Clark, you do not have a romantic bone in your body. Sometimes I could just shoot you. But that will have to wait. I have something else in mind for you right now." She turned and went into the bedroom. It didn't take me long to follow.

The End

THE AUTHORS...

Kate King lives in the Piney Woods of East Texas where she feeds the birds, nurtures her catfish and blue gill and tends to three game feeders and five game cameras. Deer, foxes, dove, turkey and birds – every kind of bird that can live in the area – cardinals, hummingbirds, woodpeckers, blue birds, jays, mockingbirds, buntings, nuthatches, sparrows, crows, owls and heaven only knows what kinds of birds eat her feed and frolic in her bird baths.

Kate has two dogs: Amazing Grace, a huge black lab who wandered and fought for her life for four years in southern Louisiana after hurricane Katrina. Today, Amy defends her spot on the hearth. Crouton is a Coton de Tulear who is the most loveable critter ever but, alas, not real smart. On the scale of dog intelligence Coton's rank about 198 out of 200 or, two levels above grass.

Kate's career included development for a hospital and a couple of theaters, management of Chambers of Commerce in San Marcos and Napa, California and co-chair of the California Small Business Board for then Governor Arnold Schwarzenegger. She retired after more than 25 years in the non-profit world.

Both Joe and Kate are Certified Lay Ministers in the United Methodist Church. They are Partners in Ministry and co-pastor a beautiful country church in Harleton, Texas.

Joe Turner was in top management in the pharmaceutical industry in New York, New Jersey, Kansas City and Los Angeles. For the last 30 years he has owned a consulting firm specializing in quality and Customer Service in the new home building industry. He also wrote extensively on that industry and was sought after for speaking.

He retired to east Texas where he helps Kate maintain and develop her farm. Joe is a lifelong hunter and has enjoyed fishing and boating. He is involved in a project to reestablish quail in east Texas.

Joe claims Crouton for his own. Crute tends to agree. Kate tolerates both of them.

Both Joe and Kate are Benefactor members in the National Rifle Association.

Email is welcome at jmturner@joeturner.com

Additional and future books can be ordered at www.pineywoodspress.com

COMING IN 2012...

NAPA WHITE
WHITE IS FOR INNOCENCE

CHAPTER ONE

The Napa Valley is just about the most perfect place on earth when the spring rains turn the Valley from grayish brown to Irish green. Late in the afternoon the greens darken as shadows come over the Valley. The sharply defined neat rows of grapevines in the vineyards soften in the fading light.

This is the perfect time of day to pull away from the day's work. For the old man who owns the vineyards and the adjacent winery it is the time for relaxing and enjoying his very own wine. Sandford Lucianno, known as Sandy by his friends, was a successful man. He has been growing grapes and making wine in the Napa Valley for decades. He began with seven acres of vineyards in the wrong place to make the great wines of his dreams. Gradually, by one way or another, he acquired more vineyards. Today he has almost a thousand acres of wine grapes. Some of those acres produce the finest grapes the Valley has to offer. One way or another he accumulated his acreage with methods that run the range from outright purchases to some other ways that might not be OK to observers.

As the old man sipped his wine he began to think about those other ways. It is possible that people who engineer great frauds and schemes can feel some regret later on. The old man was tinged by regret over his scheme twenty years ago to steal another man's vineyards. The scheme had worked and the old man added perhaps the most prized vineyards of them all, the legendary hopo'ka met'ai or in the language of the Wappo Indians, Three Woman Vineyard, just south of St. Helena against the mountains that line the western edge of the Valley.

He thought about the young lady, fresh out of the University of California at Davis, who stopped by that afternoon to talk about an internship at his winery. She was intense and hard looking for someone so young. He thought she should be more open. After all, she had a master's degree from the top wine school in the world. He wondered why she even bothered coming by. Anyone could see that she could be trouble. Yet, he wanted to help. Maybe he could teach her something. He asked her to come back in a week and gave her his private cell phone number.

He took another sip of wine and set his glass down. He wiped his forehead on his sleeve. He thought, "Must be hotter than I thought. I sure am sweating. He took another sip of the cool red wine."

His mind went back to the Three Woman Vineyard and his plan to loan the owner, a wine grape grower named Charlie Pagash, ten thousand dollars to get Pagash through the crush season. The loan was informal but there was an agreement written on a page from a Big Chief tablet, the kind of paper a school kid would have. The agreement was almost a joke between the two men. They shared a laugh with each other then they shared a glass of wine and the deal was done. There never was any doubt that Charlie could and would return the money when his wines shipped in five or six months.

But wine making is farming. Farming is risky because the weather, the markets and the timing can vary all over the place. When the time came, Charlie Pagash could not repay the loan. Almost like a lion pouncing on a bunny rabbit, Sandford Lucianno seized the prized vineyard and began his grape growing in the place where the Valley's finest wines had been raised. No one seemed to care that the vineyard was worth many times the $10,000 value of the contract. Other farms clucked and tsk'd but none stepped up to help poor Charlie Pagash.

The old man noticed the light fading even faster. He continued to sweat. In the back of his mind he felt dizziness. Taking a breath, even simple breathing became more and more difficult. He stood to try to catch his breath. But standing seemed to make it worse, not better. In an instant he was out of breath. Whatever systems had made him breathe all his life stopped working. Slowly he began to settle to the bench beside the table. He continued to slide down and by the time he was on his knees on the ground he was dead.

A person witnessing this scene would see an old man having a heart attack. A fatal heart attack. An hour later when the old man did not appear to wash up for dinner, his wife, a much younger woman who once worked as a nurse at Napa's Queen of the Valley Hospital, immediately concluded that her husband had suffered a fatal heart attack. An hour later the Napa County Coroner concluded the same thing.

In California the state code requires that the County Sherriff's office handles the duties of a Coroner. Big counties do this better than small counties. Napa's Coroner setup is sort of on the line between being effective and being incompetent. For a small county is progressive. But they are not seers. They take a look at what they see, discuss the person's health with family members and, if it seems like a good idea, they call the person's doctor.

In the case of Sandy Lucianno, all the responses to the Coroner's questions pointed toward a heart attack. After all, Mr. Lucianno had suffered a couple of mild heart attacks a few years back. Sandford Lucianno's death certificate listed the man's age, poor cardiac history and, finally, that death came from a heart attack after a long day's work in the California sun.

When the cops and the Coroner left the scene of Sandy's death, a housekeeper cleared away the wine glass and the half empty bottle of wine. She washed the glass and poured the remaining wine down the sink and rinsed the bottle before she put the bottle in the recycle bin out by the back door to the home.

Two days later Sandy was buried in a small plot in Napa's Tulocay Cemetery. More than five hundred people attended the funeral in St. John's Catholic Church. Another 500 stood outside in a very light rain. Mrs. Lucianno, Rosemary, invited a small group of family and friends to her home. About a hundred friends and family made the drive back up Valley to the Lucianno home.

One of the invited guests was Kathleen Royal. She brought along me, her husband, Clark Davis. We parked down the hill from the huge home and walked about 200 yards up the hill to the home.

Kathleen said, "I feel almost like an interloper. After all we got to Napa less than a year ago."

I replied, "She invited you, personally, at the service."

"I know but it feels strange."

"Don't let it go to your head. You are important in her life. Your work with non-profits is important. She probably gives more to the non-profits than anyone. Relax. Let's pretend we're rich, too."

I took her hand and we continued to walk.

At the front door a tall thin man in a formal jacket showed us in and took my Stetson. The fit man fit the expansive Mediterranean style home perfectly. When he spoke his thick accent was just right for the place.

We walked through the entry way into an enormous great room. I guessed the room was at least sixty by eighty feet. I could see the glimmer of a large pool at the end of the room. "How Napa," I thought, "Tudor on the outside and nouveau riche modern on the inside."

The north half of the room was crowded with the other guests. They stood in groups of four to six and talked softly with each other. Uniformed servers offered glasses of wine, hors d'oeuvres and plates for filling at the buffet table on the west wall. Kathleen and I took glasses of a perfect sauvignon blanc, the wine that some in the Valley call a "breakfast wine" because of its distinct citrusy, grapefruity taste and aroma. The wine was served ice cold.

Mrs. Lucianno came over to welcome us. She said, "Thank you so much for stopping by. I appreciate it very much. Kathleen, I know we had planned to meet later this week. I hope you understand why I must postpone that a few days. There is so much to do. I don't even know where to start."

Kathleen responded, "Of course I understand. Mrs. Lucianno, is there anything I can do to help? I am not sure what to do either but I can be with you if you wish."

A tear escaped the eye of the woman. She wiped back the tear and said, "Oh, Kathleen. Would you?" More tears followed the first one and she continued, "I know others are lining up to help, but it would be so comforting to have you here. Somehow having someone who I haven't known forever seems a comfort. I know you won't be here to pick the bones as they say."

Kathleen said, "When you are ready, call me. If I don't hear from you I will call."

The two women hugged and stood holding hands for a long minute. Finally. Mrs. Lucianno seemed to compose herself and pulled away to see her other guests.

I said, "I have never seen anyone who can penetrate into other peoples' lives like you can. That was really something."

Kathleen smiled and began to work the room. I tagged along with no particular agenda. I love to watch my wife interact with people. After an hour of chatting and nibbling excellent little bites of food, my email receiver vibrated silently. I excused myself and walked across the room to the huge swimming pool.

When I was by myself, I looked at the email. Jim Berry was asking when we could come out to his office at the Napa airport. I replied that the reception should wind down in an hour and a half or so. In seconds I received a response from Berry. The meeting was set for two hours from then.

I managed to get my wife's attention. I told her of Berry's request for the meeting. She said she would begin looking for an opportunity to leave.

Ten minutes later we were saying our goodbyes. Kathleen reminded Mrs. Lucianno to call when she was ready to get together. I retrieved my hat. We walked down the hill to Kathleen's CTS Cadillac.

Kathleen said, "What's up with Jim?"

I shrugged and opened the car door for Kathleen. "Beats me. He did want us there as soon as possible. It sounded routine but with a little dose of urgency."